THE SMELL OF SUGARCANE

Beverly Ann Menke

Hamilton Books
A member of
Rowman & Littlefield
Lanham • Boulder • New York • Toronto • Plymouth, UK

Copyright © 2014 by Hamilton Books
4501 Forbes Boulevard, Suite 200, Lanham, Maryland 20706
Hamilton Books Aquisitions Department (301) 459-3366

10 Thornbury Road, Plymouth PL6 7PP, United Kingdom

All rights reserved
Printed in the United States of America
British Library Cataloguing in Publication Information Available

Library of Congress Control Number: 2013953999
ISBN: 978-0-7618-6286-4 (cloth : alk. paper)—ISBN: 978-0-7618-6287-1 (electronic)

Cover artwork: *Ladies in White* by Beverly Ann Menke. Oil on canvas. 4' x 6'.

∞™ The paper used in this publication meets the minimum requirements of American National Standard for Information Sciences Permanence of Paper for Printed Library Materials, ANSI/NISO Z39.48-1992.

For Nadine,
Wishing you the best always!

Love,
BEVERLY

For,
my siblings, my children and
the men that mattered,

Steven Caldwell Menke

and

Anthony Ferguson Jones

CONTENTS

Acknowledgments — vii
This is a true story — ix
Sugarcane — xi
Prologue — xiii

1	The Painting	1
2	Medicine	5
3	The Essence: The Core	15
4	Rural Life, Smoke and Ashes	25
5	Venezuela in Turmoil	41
6	Puerto Rico, Another World	47
7	Mask of Deception	73
8	Music	113
9	Fruits of Deceit	129
10	The Face of Evil	145
11	Silent Heroes	163
12	Mali, Singapore, Madagascar	173
13	Everyday Staple, Traditions and Sugarcane	179
14	Poetry and a Kiss	201
15	A Sparkle in the Rough	219
16	Maryland	227

17 The Crossroads	235
18 The Dream: University	243
19 The Face of Love	261
20 Travel, Suitors and True Love	267
Epilogue	285
Sugarcane Mills of Puerto Rico's Past	287

ACKNOWLEDGMENTS

The true story of The Smell of Sugarcane waited many long years to be told. As I put my pen to paper the folds and dust of time were lifted to let me see and remember its details. I am forever grateful to Hamilton Books for discerning in this story a message of consequence. With great detail and professionalism the team worked in harmony to place this book before you. I am honored to have worked with people of such integrity and dedication. Wholeheartedly I thank each of you:

Julie E. Kirsch, Vice President/Publisher, graciously gave her nod of approval enabling the book's publication.

Nicolette Amstutz, Assistant Editor, University Press of America/Hamilton Books, a newcomer that jumped right into the thick of things, polishing and producing excellent work.

Beverly Shellem, Senior Production Editor, University Press of America/Hamilton Books, like extracting a butterfly from its cocoon, she carefully laid out each page, transforming them into the book it awaited to be.

Chloe Batch, Designer, Rowman & Littlefield Publishers, Inc., gave us the attractive covers.

A special thanks:

Laura Espinoza, Assistant Acquisitions Editor, University Press of America/Hamilton Books. There is always a liaison, a person that works intimately with the author patiently listening, so as to understand the author's dream and move it along. Laura was that person. A beautiful young lady, dedicated and capable, whom I have had the pleasure of meeting and will never forget.

THIS IS A TRUE STORY

The names of certain characters have been changed in order to protect their privacy.

The first page of each chapter contains verses from one of the author's published songs. These songs originally written in Spanish appear with their English translation. The song *The Night* is the exception, originally written in English, it appears in its entirety.

SUGARCANE

The scent of sugarcane is a pungent odor, a mixture of sweet and rancid, if one can imagine that. The unique, dour sweetness of this odor is unforgettable. It can linger in one's memory a lifetime, transporting anyone, in the blink of an eye, to that past where the smell lies.

Stalks of sugarcane grow tall—over ten feet. At every eight inches or so of the long stalk, there is a thick, protruding ring that goes around it like a badly healed, stiff joint. The skin that wraps around the meat of the stalk is real tough. A skilled person can wield a large machete and make it sail into the tough cover of the stalk in a continuous stroke that slides down from joint to joint, uncovering the sweet fibrous body within. To sink ones teeth into it could be, for some, a daunting task, which would undoubtedly make one wonder if it were going to be worthwhile. As teeth reluctantly settle into what might feel like wood, one's heightened sense of alert and awareness are surprisingly rewarded by a glorious sweetness that floods gums and makes a person hang on and suck the fibrous, uninviting cane.

PROLOGUE

It was in the golden fields of barley of California where the foundation of her character was laid, but it was in the green waves of Puerto Rico's sugarcane where that foundation was tested. For Sophia James, the testing of her inner core revealed that we are who we are, no matter where we are…and we had better be strong.

The island of Puerto Rico is beautiful. The saying "Good things come in small packages," suits it. One hundred miles long by thirty-five miles wide, it boasts a central mountain range that dramatically rises to a peak 4,390 ft. above sea level. Its mountainous, orchid-filled, rain forests tower above green, flat lands that extend to a skirt of sandy beaches. On the north of the island is the Atlantic Ocean and to its south are the warm waters of the Caribbean Sea.

Rich with subsurface water Puerto Rico is strategically placed in the Atlantic—cause for the lust of many. For centuries its rich history speaks of invasions and desires to conquest *La Isla del Encanto*, the Charming Isle. Spaniards, English, Africans, North Americans, and of course the Taino Indian, indigenous to the island, left their trails resulting in a population rich in diversity. White skin with dark eyes or dark skin with light eyes, all embrace traditions that span centuries and make the place exotic.

The island moves at a sluggish pace and its culture feels foreign and alluring. English is heard but the dramatic intonations of the Spanish language, is what echoes throughout. Vibrant and colorful are the people of Puerto Rico, where music rides every wave length and juicy gossip is the prelude to laughter.

However, no matter how beautiful, interesting and desirable a place, it will always be people's circumstances that allow them to see these things. Those circumstances will dictate the size of their window and the limits of their vantage point. The children of this story, in their struggle to survive, were limited to a very small window and the beauty of Puerto Rico was mostly lost to them.

I

THE PAINTING

"DIMELO ESCULTOR" ~ "TELL ME SCULPTOR"
"Escultor que esculpes con las manos ~ Sculptor that sculpts with his hands,
"Viendo promesa desde lo crudo, ~ Seeing promise within the rough.
" Escultor que imaginas belleza, ~ Sculptor you who imagines beauty,
" Y lo logras con suave pulso. ~ And attains it with a soft pulse.
"Dime tu, quien busca perfección, ~ Tell me, you who seeks perfection,
"Y la encuentras desde la nada, ~ And finds it amongst the rubble,
"Dime tú como ver más allá, ~ Tell me how to see beyond,
" Sin la vista empañada. ~ Without clouded vision.
" Dime tu, escultor, ~ Tell me, sculptor,
"Donde encontrar amor. ~ Where to find love.
" Si como en tu escultura, ~ As in your sculptures,
"Algunos vemos y no vemos. ~ Some of us see, and yet do not.

PUERTO RICO, JANUARY 6, 2013

The woman was running alongside the parade of horses and riders that were celebrating Three Kings Day. She was trying to take a shot with her camera. A specific shot, one that showed off the ladies that were dressed in white. With the sun at their backs they were striking. Each tall and proud in her saddle, with a large red flower in her hair and flowing long white dresses that covered them, as much as their horses.

CHAPTER I

Their mounts were beautiful Pure Puerto Rican Paso Finos that with each small step made their graceful gait appear seamless. They were fascinating and the music created by the sound of their hooves on the asphalt, was comparable to the castanets of a flamenco dancer. The clickety-clack, clickety-clack moment was a vision that spoke of gentility and of traditions long gone. Sophia James was taken by it and the decision was clear: she would capture the scene in oils and paint a large canvas, in bold striking colors. She would take that blue sky moment on the island of Puerto Rico, and trap it forever.

Run carefully, she thought, *you don't want to twist an ankle, you're almost sixty, girl. Behave yourself!* Besides that thought, she was mindless of what she looked like, probably quite silly as she stretched high and bent low, snapping away, seeking the perfect instant for the perfect shot. She continued running alongside the horses; she knew she didn't have the shot yet.

"¡Sophia, Sophia, pero muchacha móntate! Come on, get in," called out the beautiful blond, blue-eyed Tensi, urging her to get into the golf cart driven by her husband Antonio. There had to be a stream of a hundred other golf carts all following and wanting to be a part of the parade. It was a fun, carefree time, with music dancing in the air provided by a well-equipped pickup truck, harnessed by loudspeakers, faithfully blasting traditional music. Everyone was excited and feeding off what had become a patriotic moment.

"You are going to wear yourself out!" said Tensi, shaking her head and smiling. Laughing and glad to be rescued, Sophia jumped into the golf cart and quickly, as island tradition would have it, stretched forward and gave them each a kiss on the cheek.

"I'm trying to get my hands on a specific picture for a large canvas," she said, out of breath and excited. "I'm going to paint a wonderful painting of this event!" Not realizing that her words might sound boastful, something quite uncharacteristic of her, she was obviously off guard with Antonio and Tensi. "Look, I'll ride with you for a while, unless you can maneuver this thing, Antonio, and get me up close. This is my chance and I don't want to miss getting that shot."

Immediately he gunned the cart and Sophia, sitting precariously on the back seat blindly, hung on as her long hair whipped across her eyes and she struggled to regain composure. In moments they were up front and soon after, Sophia had the shot she'd been looking for. It was the one that showed what for decades she had longed to see.

The painting would be much more than a painting for her. It would embody love and refinement, beauty and good breeding; it would symbolize what she had found out about Puerto Rico, late in life. The juxtaposition of cultures—of past with present—would help cleanse her from the remnants of the debauchery she once knew. The scene of the ladies in a white so pure was the island's olive branch; and the painting was the reconciliation.

A week later, the large, six-by-four-foot canvas was in place, propped up on two chairs against a wall in her living room. The oceanfront property was comfortable, quaint and inviting. It was an escape, a place where Sophia would get away from the cold, drab outdoors of winter in Maryland, her home the rest of the year. Back home she would be guarding herself against slipping on ice. Instead, she was in the warm, colorful tropics wearing a light sundress while joyfully prepping the canvas.

A nice large squirt of cadmium yellow light onto her palette would take care of the first ground layer her canvas would hold. She patiently began working the paint onto the surface with a rag and smiled at how ingeniously she had maneuvered to support her huge canvas without an easel. It was at the right height and she wouldn't hurt her back.

With the first layer down, she quickly began a loose sketch and soon the image on the horizontal surface began to take shape. The light-skinned, dark-haired woman gently picked up her palette knife and began to work. She knew exactly what she wanted. She wanted the painting to be filled with light—a light so bright that the warmth of the tropics would emanate from it. That was her goal.

There was history between Sophia James, the girl from California, and the island of Puerto Rico. In many ways, it had been the engine that powered her desire to succeed in life. However, the energy that fueled it had come from the wrong place and the desire to succeed was in many ways for the wrong reasons. It had all been about getting away, as far away as possible, from the island that had nearly killed her and her siblings. And far away she had gone. No, the island had not killed her. On the contrary, it had made her remarkably resolute and strong, but it had robbed her of her childhood and shown her the ugliest side of mankind. That they all survived was just short of miraculous.

As Sophia entered her painting world her surroundings became silent. It was then that the world stood there to be analyzed and the past dared step forward. While her busy hands worked, her active mind began its dance. Why had she blamed the island in the first place for all that had happened? It was never the island; the fault lay with those who had surrounded her. So simple to understand, but it had taken her nearly forty years to get there. It had taken her nearly that long to set foot on the island again. At the age of twenty-two she had left, never to return, and with a world of aspiration in her heart.

Sounds of the ocean would occasionally seep through and break her stream of thought. Sophia would look up from her painting, be rewarded by the view and smile. The ocean had always been an innocent friend, she thought. It had always been a sanctuary, a comfort, an ally when despair was at its richest. It had served as the invisible conduit when she'd cry out for help to her father, a seaman who rode on those same waves, somewhere faraway.

Now as she looked out over the waves of an ocean so deep, she smiled, knowing that they were the same waves of her youth. They had never stopped rolling in and the tall swaying palm trees in sight had stood guard all that time, waiting for her to mature and understand. She was aware that what had taken her a lifetime to realize was nothing but a sigh in a wind, a spray in an eternal ocean, a laugh from old man time himself.

She continued painting. The contrast of values would be stark and the bright daylight would jump off the canvas. It was starting to happen. As her mind wandered into the corridors of her past, her painting was going in the right direction.

2

MEDICINE

"VIENES A MI MEMORIA" ~ "YOU COME TO MIND"
Caminando por una vereda sola, ~ Walking along a path alone,
Mil bellezas de compañía, ~ A thousand beauties for company,
Las hojas crujen al caminar, ~ Leaves crunch as I walk,
Marcan mi paso, ~ Marking my path,
Y la fragancia del aire, ~ And I breathe in the fragrance of
Puro respiro. ~ Pure air.

HOSPITAL VARGAS, CARACAS, VENEZUELA, NOVEMBER 1981

The murmur of excitement was all around the drab hospital room and everyone, protagonists and witnesses alike, could feel it. On that day physicians were godlier than ever, as they made rounds deciding the immediate future of their disciples. Medical students stood vulnerable and wilting or strong and invincible, awaiting the arrival of what felt like the Inquisition: their final oral exams. One student per patient, four physicians per student, and the moment was harrowing. Eyes were opened a little wider than usual and most were filled with visible expectations and fear. Breathing in general seemed unusually intentional and white faces glared with anoxia.

Standing beside a patient, a young medical student in a crisp, white coat tried to relax and gather her wits. She was nervous, too nervous. It was apparent in her hands which moved too quickly and in the sound of her voice which cracked when she said to no one in particular,

"My name? What's my name?" That absurd question had been wrapped in a nervous laugh.

"*Calmese, doctorcita.* Calm down, doctor," said the sympathetic and quiet voice of the patient lying in the bed.

The sound of the old lady's voice, who had volunteered as a patient for the exams, immediately grounded Sophia and she reached out to pat her arm, saying,

"Yes! Let's get on with this," as, robot-like, she reached for the medical history form and secured it to her clipboard. Reaching into her pocket for a pen, she began,

"What is your name?"

"María Joséfa Ruíz."

"How old are you?"

"Sixty three."

"Why are you here?"

"I have a pain all over my belly."

"With one finger, I want you to touch your pain."

The patient's finger, crooked with arthritis, attempted to follow the doctor's instructions and then with a shy smile she revealed the decay of yet another problem.

Standing in high heels the *Doctora* looked tall. Her white coat boasted neatly embroidered bold letters stating that she was "Dr. James." As she stood writing out the medical history with her stethoscope nestled comfortably around her neck, her confidence and knowledge returned. She spoke in a caring manner and her patients felt better just by seeing her smile. She played off of that to relax each of them.

"Is that pain an old friend of yours or is it the first time you have ever had it?"

"Oh! No, Doctorcita, I have had this pain many times before. It's no friend but we sure do know each other. It goes away, but lasts hours and I feel so bad until it leaves me."

The hospital was run down, dirty and corrupt in so many ways, but it was Sophia James' hospital. It was the place that was getting her closer to the completion of a dream, of a goal that had been forged into her brain since she was an infant learning to speak.

MEDICINE 7

For three years Sophia had worked tirelessly at getting into the medical school at the University Central of Venezuela. There were two medical schools in Caracas and they were both branches of the UCV. The Luis Razetti Medical School was within the confines of the University's main campus and the second medical school, José María Vargas, had its main structure in the Plaza San Lorenzo in the small town of San José. San José—really more of a slum than a town—was in the northeast quadrant of the valley of Caracas. It was poor, very poor, with makeshift houses built almost on top of each other, many of them with nothing but dirt floors. Around the school itself, all that remained were wasted vestiges of what once were beautiful and elaborate structures built a century ago. The town had fallen into a mass of disrepair, its unsightly hovels having been snatched up by small businesses happily chasing a livelihood. A pencil and notebooks shop here, an arepa shop there; one door down was a stall for making keys and next to it a tire repair shop. Entrepreneurship was the game and a mismatch of enterprises the result. However, within the confines of chaotic surroundings, a palpable and genuine joy prevailed in those who bartered and negotiated day in and day out. Sophia James loved *El Vargas* and in her eyes, every soul that lived in San José was a friend.

Venezuela had been a happenstance; Sophia had arrived there in 1976 to begin her married life. It was there, in the terraced city of Caracas, shouldered on its northern side by the magnificent Avila Mountains, that Sophia would first know stability and happiness.

There, where the old played off the new—and vice versa—a cosmopolitan whirlpool of activity and enterprise flourished. Caracas, shrouded within old world values, resulted in a great melting pot of diversity sweetened by a lack of prejudices. A proud, shining city on a hill, so to speak, as it had just come into unimaginable riches. Oil . . . black, heavy and dark crude . . . worth everything. Everything? The gift from above that appeared from below would not really be free; over time, Venezuela would pay dearly for its overindulgence. But that fact would be appreciated years later. In the meantime, those Sophia encountered were a well-spoken and proud lot. These South Americans were better educated and cultivated than most throughout the continent. At least that was the touted line, often supported by the playful mimicking and mocking of the Spanish accent spoken by rival Argentineans. For Sophia, Venezuelan pride was palpable and visible at every turn. It was apparent from their everyday dress which was proper whether leaving a castle or a small shanty. Without failure, Venezuelans were polite and constantly greeted anyone that came within earshot with, *"Buenos días, buenas tardes, buenas noches, buen provecho."* The melody of the Spanish language created an habitual song that was inviting and friendly. Sophia felt safe.

Her husband was a successful business man that ran a multinational company. He was deeply in love with Sophia and provided everything his bride needed including a sense of security she had never known. With a nice home in Las Mercedes and a membership at the Valle Arriba Golf Club, Sophia was free to learn and play. However, best of all was his belief in her potential to accomplish whatever she set out to do. For Sophia, his endless trust nurtured her drive and those ambitions and she loved him for it.

The three years invested in her quest to acquire acceptance at the medical school had proven the strength of her backbone to anyone who crossed paths with her. As impressed as they were by her assertiveness and relentless commitment, no one could ever guess what had made her that way. Her devastating childhood, filled with pain and sorrow, had been replaced by a survivor that was in love with life and grateful for every opportunity that came her way. Yes, her backbone was strong but only because too many had tried to break it. She approached most everything in life with fire in her belly and a lack of fear in her heart. That determination would become her life's trademark.

"Why would you want to study at our university, when you have so many wonderful schools in the United States?" asked the director of admissions. "When we have so few spaces available, why should we give one to you? Won't you soon be leaving our country and then our investment will be in vain? You should go back to your country and study there!"

The questions were continuous and the elicited response was a repetitive denial. Still, nothing fazed Sophia and she would not give up.

"I live here; this is now my home and so this is where I need to study. You have many thousands of students studying in the United States on scholarship, I know about Fundayacucho." Sophia referred to the Fundación Gran Mariscal de Ayacucho Scholarship, founded in 1975 to help aid academically eligible students pursue their dreams abroad. "Well, I ask you to give one seat to an American for all of those seats America gives to Venezuelans."

Sophia believed in her pursuit and that her request was just. She would chase after her dream until she won; she would not be denied. Along the way she met others that understood this and then they became her allies. However, with all the understanding and hand wringing, there seemed to be no one able to make her entry to the school any easier.

She established a pattern, a program that would keep her busy while her husband worked long hours. She found a job, made a little money and still wholeheartedly pursued entry at the university. The job was part time, mornings only, and it was with Roberto Delfino, a paper company founded by a man of the same name. Arriving early each morning, Sophia displayed her abilities as someone responsible and accurate. She served as executive secretary for the owner's son, Patrick.

With afternoons open to pursue her goal of entry at the medical school, her first step was to request an interview to meet the rector of the university, the Honorable Dr. Miguel Larysse. Sophia sat opposite the gentleman and eloquently laid out the story of her plight. She found that he was very receptive and sympathetic. "I understand your request, but you must understand that there are procedures . . . ."

"Oh yes, I do; I have met all your requirements, but I still continue to wait, to lose time and be denied. I have completed my pre-medical studies and should be ready to go straight into clinical courses, yet I am being denied; and there is no valid reason except—perhaps—prejudice as I am not a Venezuelan."

The promise of looking into Sophia's situation was firm and sincere and the young woman's step felt light and quick as she descended the stairwell leaving the presence of the university's most influential and powerful man. However, a month later she sought another interview and again found full understanding and . . . "I will look into it."

Time continued to pass, and as she felt forgotten and hopeless, she decided to take on yet another part-time job. Every afternoon, nicely dressed, she would present herself to "guard" the rector's office door. It would become Sophia's afternoon "job," one she would, sadly, hold for a very long time.

On that first day, as Sophia took up what would become her post, standing at the rector's door, she saw the man as he approached to enter his office. He looked at her in a friendly but bewildered manner and acknowledged her, "Hello, are you here to see me?" he kindly asked.

"Well, I do not have an appointment, but I am here so that you will see me and remember me." Sophia said with a smile and a plea in her eyes. The man raised his eyebrows in surprise and a bit taken aback, said, "Yes, I will remember you."

For an entire year Sophia stood at that door. Every day she was there when Rector Larysse arrived. At first he would give her a nod, but as time went by, he would try to avoid looking in her direction.

Then a trip came up and Sophia was whisked away to Europe. It was a glorious time, a time where other dreams she held were met. She loved the Old World and she reveled in being there and seeing it. Nevertheless, upon returning, she immediately went back to her post at the rector's door.

"Don't think I didn't notice your absence." The gentleman stated as he arrived to enter his office.

"I was in Europe these last three weeks," replied Sophia with a smile.

"Oh! You were in Europe? You wouldn't have been able to go, if you had been in school."

"A sacrifice I would gladly make, if you give me entrance." He smiled knowingly. The man knew how much Sophia was fighting to get into the University and most likely it was with heavy heart that he invited her into his office one day.

"Sophia James, I am sorry that I have not been able to oversee your entrance to the university and now my tenure has come to an end."

Sophia had entered the man's office with wide eyes and a sudden expectation of receiving the greatest news. However, upon hearing his words, Sophia, the proud girl with the straight back, slumped into a heap of sorrow and began to cry.

"You are leaving? I have stood at your door for over a year and now you are leaving? Who will be the next rector? He won't know me, he won't know what this means to me. I will mean nothing to him. I will have to start all over again."

The rector, with genuine sorrow, had watched the young woman collapse in tears before him. "The University denies thousands of worthy students every year, so to give admittance to you, an American that comes from a country where there are so many schools, is extremely difficult."

"But, I live here. I live here. I don't live there. My husband is here; this is where I must stay. I have got to get in."

"Dr. Carlos Moro Guersi will hear about you. Don't give up hope, Sophia. I trust you will be admitted."

It had been a blow. Sophia's expectations had soared for a moment; now she found herself sobbing uncontrollably. She would take a break from the afternoon "job," and once the new rector was installed, would introduce herself and let him know that she was not going to give up. She would not go away; she was going to become a doctor and deserved to study there, as she would most likely serve in Venezuela for years to come,.

The unexpected trip to Europe had been motive for her to leave her position with Roberto Delfino. It was a job she hated to lose, but was ready to move on to something different: employment at the British Embassy. There Sophia James would be Secretary to the British Council General. The new job was interesting and after she had been there a few months, a new Council General rotated in. It was this new boss who would soon become a nuisance and complicate things. The married man, a father of three, fell head-over-heels for Sophia.

"I would leave everything for you!"

At first Sophia tried to laugh it off, thinking that it was dry, English humor. However, too soon she realized that the man was most serious and obsessive. Sophia tried to be honest and reason with him,

"Look, please, no hard feelings but I am never going to be with you. I really love my husband. I am not going to leave him. Please, can't you stop acting this way? I like it here, but you're going to make me leave." It was ridiculous and it didn't stop, so Sophia resigned.

But as luck would have it, she didn't resign because of the Council General; she resigned because of a phone call from Dr. Miguel Yaber Pérez, one of the most distinguished physicians in the Venezuelan medical profession. He had been the director of the University Hospital of Caracas and one of its founders. Sophia had met him, and he too understood her situation and had promised to stay informed. Every now and then Sophia would drop in on him and tell him that she had not given up and was still hopeful.

CHAPTER 2

It was a bright sunny morning, the morning Sophia received the phone call to her desk at the Embassy. "Council General's office, this is Sophia, may I help you?"

"Sophia, this is Dr. Yaber," Sophia stopped breathing. She could feel her heart wildly begin pounding against its walls."

"Yes! Dr Yaber! Yes?"

Through a fog, as if in a dream, Sophia heard the words come to her in slow motion,

"Sophia, you won't have to stand in front of Dr. Moro Guersi's door today. You have been given admittance to the Medical School José María Vargas of the Universidad Central de Venezuela."

"Thank you! Thank you!" flew out of her mouth and she hung up. She didn't know if she had replied properly. Had she thanked him? It was all a blur. She was going to go to school! She looked up and in a loud voice called out to everyone in the office, "I have just been admitted to the Medical School!"

Sophia immersed herself in the wide world of medicine and loved it there. It was a time of great dedication as medicine would have it no other way. The profession gobbled her up and tucked her away in a world of its own. For Sophia, the challenge was enormous, as being married offered a distraction most others didn't have. Then after a couple of years of studying, the desire to begin a family took center stage and meticulously a plan was hatched. If the pregnancy took, the baby would arrive just as they celebrated their sixth wedding anniversary. Sophia was twenty eight and her husband thirty four. They were ready.

It was 1981, a cool November morning, but not in the already overheated auditorium packed with clinical students waiting for a lecture to begin. Sophia, sitting among her usual friends, leaned over to Rafael Alfonzo Sotillo and said, "Rafa, don't call me this weekend, we'll be busy making the baby." She said it with a big smile and a wink.

The class had known when Sophia had gotten off her contraceptives and the medical group speculated on if the "Americana," would really get pregnant. "That's not so easy. You don't just up and decide when exactly you're going to get pregnant," Leo had said.

"Of course we can; if we can't be precise, who could? It's called counting and planning. I figure I can give birth in between semesters and my chances are real good. I got off contraceptives over five months now so I know that my uterus is ripe and ready! I'm ready to catch anything Blondie sends my way." Sophia laughed and because of her candor turned a little pink, and then piled on, "Oh! Yes, and we are going to make a little boy." She winked full out giggling.

"Yeah, right! If you do, your husband is going to have to come over here and give classes!" Sure enough later that day, as classes were over and everyone was heading for the parking lot, Sophia's wicked good friend Rafa teased her by yelling at the top of his lungs for all ears to hear, "No one call Sophia this weekend! She's making the baaabb-byyyyyy!!!!!!"

Right on schedule, in the summer of 1982, Sophia became a mother, having given birth to a son. In five years, the couple produced four children. Though the first child had been the product of a perfectly executed plan, life had a great surprise in store for them. The second child was a girl, and life was blissful. Then Tommy arrived, teaching the family things they had never known. It was precisely because of Tommy that a fourth child became a part of the master plan and with the arrival of a beautiful baby girl their nest was complete.

⸺

Sophia had been at the canvas for a while and went over to a chair to rest her legs and back. She was a fast painter but only the bare bones were there; they were good bones, and she smiled. As her body reclined on the comfortable seat, the thread of her thoughts stuck with her. She remembered clearly how fiercely she had clung to her Tommy and how much protecting that special child had meant to her. All of her children had meant so much to her. Being a good mother and wife were her greatest ambitions in life. She closed her eyes for a moment and remembered a day twenty years ago when her children were still quite young.

3

THE ESSENCE: THE CORE

"NO ME COMPARES CON UNA ROSA" ~ "DON'T COMPARE ME TO A ROSE"
Pétalos de una rosa, frescas y puras ~ Petals of a rose, fresh and pure
Cuando abre el capullo, con ternura. ~ When the bud, tenderly opens.
El tiempo que no vacila, ~ Time which never hesitates,
Y nunca está dormido. ~ And never lies sleeping,
A pesar de su belleza, ~ Regardless of its beauty,
La rosa es consumida. ~ The rose is consumed.
No me compares con una rosa, ~ Don't compare me to a rose,
Que yo soy de fibra. ~ I'm made out of fiber.
No me compares con una rosa, ~ Don't compare me to a rose,
Que soy dulce pero dura. ~ I'm sweet but I'm tough.
No me compares con una rosa, ~ Don't compare me to a rose,
Flor tan bella pero tan frágil, ~ Such a beautiful flower but so fragile,
No me compares con una rosa ~ Don't compare me to a rose,
Que aún yo amo. ~ For I, still love.

"Come on, stop the car, stop the car, I want them to see it." In a quick maneuver the car came to a stop on the shoulder of the old country road. Sophia jumped out and opened the rear door while the children protested.

"Oh, Mommy, do we really have to get out, can't we just see it from here?"

"Come on. It'll be worthwhile. You'll learn something. Come on. Everybody get out on this side. Cars are too fast over there. Don't open that door."

The four children reluctantly climbed out of the car and followed their mother to the edge of the fields.

"You see that long, tall stalk? That's the cane stalk. That's it. There it is. Now come and touch the leaf. See how stiff and sharp it is? " The children leaned forward touching the leaf with growing curiosity. "Those nice long leaves can really cut you up if you just start walking into that field. Now, look carefully. See those little hairs on that long leaf? Can you see the little hairs?" she repeated as she pulled the leaf down lower for the youngest one to see. "They'll make you itch like crazy." The woman was excited and was injecting enthusiasm into the children. She angled around so as to grab a stalk.

"Sweetheart, do we have a knife in the car?" Her husband smiled at her knowing that nothing was going to stop her, so he went back to find a knife.

"See how close and tall it all grows together? If you ever did go into a sugarcane field, you'd have to wear a long-sleeve shirt and hold your arms above your face so that a leaf wouldn't get into your eyes and hurt you."

"Oh Mommy, this stuff looks awful. . . . Ouch!"

"Careful, careful. You're right, it doesn't look too friendly, does it? But it's where sugar comes from."

Her husband was handing her a little pocketknife. "Thanks, Babe." She said with an excited smile.

"OK, the stalk is going to be hard to cut off with this little thing, and cane doesn't snap off. Unless you cut it off, you'll never free it." The woman bent down on one knee and began struggling to cut the cane free. The little knife was ineffective and she decided to not run the risk of losing her children's attention.

"Look, I don't need to completely free the cane I'll just open it a little for you. I want you to taste it straight from the fields and then we'll go." It was obvious that she knew what she was doing. She tore away at the tough outer layer by sliding her knife just under its cover.

"See how white? See the juice?" She began hacking out chunks and was offering them to the children. "Hmmm, go ahead, see how sweet it is." The children reached out, now curious, wanting to know what the flavor was like.

"Mmmm, I like it, Mommy. It's really sweet!"

"Well, kids, this is the stuff I grew up with. It was all around my house...."

That twenty-year-old memory was of a trip on which Sophia had tried to introduce her four children to a tropical world similar to the one she had grown up in. The trip had been an attempt at reconciliation with the island of her youth, but it had proven futile for her; its soil still felt hostile. It would take yet another twenty years for the self-imposed exile to end.

Reliably, time dealt with the gnawing pain that, for too long, hovered near the surface of her soul and she had finally been freed of it. The importance of it all had dulled, becoming somewhat of a blur as the drive it had nourished no longer was the engine and the strength obtained from it had long been used up. She had other sources from which to draw now, ones that derived from love and not from anger. Sophia James had prevailed. She would no longer suffer for the wrongdoing of others when she was but an innocent child.

Sophia had learned how to embrace the positives of life. She knew that in her blood lay a line full of adventurers. Those adventures were not for the faint of heart, but for the strong and brave, as in the case of her grandmother, Odelia Nobriga. The woman was born on the island of Oahu, Hawaii, shortly after her parents arrived there from Madeira and the Azores, Portugal. In the late 1890s, there was no steam crossing the Magellan Straits; it was a life-risking adventure sailing around Cape Horn of South America. The treacherous waters of the Horn, known as the sailor's graveyard, delivered a scary ride—and their last one, for far too many. On the other side, her Grandfather George Jones's family went back and forth from Scotland sailing across the Atlantic to Canada in the early eighteen hundreds. They were true pioneers, people with gumption, who, rather than staying put and safe, dared to venture out seeking a better life for themselves and their families.

Sophia's father, Anthony Ferguson James, was a Californian, born in 1922. He also had courage, acquiring much of it from a terrible car crash he was in at the age of six. Back in those days cars were owned by few and walking great distances was a part of life. One day while running an errand for his mother, a neighbor stopped to give him a ride. A few moments later he was flying through the windshield, landing on his face and disfiguring part of it. It was a terrible thing and the soft tissues of his young face were badly damaged. His life, as his face, was scarred forever and though it made life miserable in many respects, it also forced his character to become stronger than it otherwise might have. He had graduated from high school and wanted to proceed to college, but like for so many, the Great Depression and his father's death, made him drop education for work. He was sixteen when he took the birth certificate of a deceased brother, a couple years older, and got on his first ship. His first two years at sea coincided with the beginning of World War II and he found himself barely seventeen in the middle of a dangerous ocean. He quickly rose to become chief electrician on board any vessel that needed one. It was a hard and dangerous job that demanded an intelligent and reliable type. He was that type. He had a strong spirit, and a sense of duty and responsibility. He would pass those strengths of character on to his children. He taught them how to believe in themselves and how to play the best game with the cards dealt, while holding on to honesty and traditions. That would be his greatest legacy.

Sophia's mother was a different story. She proved correct the old adage that "opposites attract." She was the true opposite of Sophia's father and, sadly, the weak link in Sophia's life. She was from the island of Puerto Rico, an attractive fifteen year old when she came to the mainland with her mother. She had received little schooling, spoke little English, but had a great smile. She had netted the young Mr. James, ten years her senior, shortly after arriving. They married and she had their first child by the age of seventeen. She then proceeded to have child after child until six were born. Her days were lost cleaning children and house. Time for personal growth was never there. During Sophia's early years she could remember a kind and caring person that kept house beautifully and loved her children. Though a genuine bond of understanding never developed between mother and daughter, her early childhood years were happy ones.

Sophia James was born in Sacramento, California, and growing up there in the late 50s, was to witness times when segregation laws were being tested all over the nation. The struggle for equal rights and civil liberties was in full force. However, the world's concerns were not a part of her Christmas in 1958, when Sophia was only five years old. It was a joyful and memorable Christmas at the James's home that year. The house on Thirty-Fourth Street was decked out in lights, everyone was happy, and relatives were stopping by. Brightly wrapped gifts awaited everyone snug under a Christmas tree heavy with tinsel and soon the excited ripping and tearing of Christmas paper began. On that occasion Sophia received one of the most precious gifts ever.

"An accordion!!!!!!!! An accordion!!!!!!" she cried. "Thank you Daddy, thank you Mommy, thank you, thank you, thank you, I love you, I love you, I love you," running to give them both hugs and kisses before pulling the accordion straps around her shoulders. With her small left wrist held tight in the bellows belt, and her right hand going up and down the keyboard at full speed, she was making nonsense music of her own, with a big smile on her face. It was a joy and Sophia knew that she would learn how to play, as the promise of lessons came with the instrument. However, the accordion had not come without sacrifice and the slight expression of apprehension on her father's face, the moment she opened the accordion box, was one she never forgot.

The little girl had been asking for a piano and her father, who at that time was a home contractor going through hard times, like so many others, couldn't afford one. He had tried, had looked into the possibility, and had had to bow to the fact that with four children and another on the way, he just couldn't swing it. His "I hope you like it," and then to see him share in the honest joy of the moment remained with Sophia always.

The dilemma of resolving the need for accordion lessons is one of the few precious and kind memories Sophia held of her mother. The family was in a tight spot and paying for lessons presented a problem. Sophia's mother resolved the matter by arranging to give Spanish lessons to the music teacher in exchange for accordion lessons for Sophia. In no time, Sophia was playing "Let's Dance the Polka" and some of Lawrence Welk's favorites. Playing the accordion was wonderful and she practiced all the time, quickly outgrowing one size and needing a more capable one and soon after, still another. Before long, the accordion was bigger than she was and the little girl would play it, almost entirely hidden, balancing it on her lap. Her left wrist soon needed to be bound in a brace for added strength, in pulling at the large bellows. Opening them wide and closing them quickly required power. Her right hand would fly up and down the keyboard in quick, polka staccato and everyone around would keep tempo by tapping the floor with their shoes. It was the best of times in her home and Sophia felt security and love. There was balance.

The James family was middle class when it came to economic wealth, but when it came to important values and strong principles they were wealthy indeed. Mr. James had wanted a large family and like most parents, he had hopes of seeing each of his children succeed where he had not. Good manners, being polite, never lying and being honest always, were drilled into the children from birth. He did not hope that his children would absorb this through some sort of osmosis, but instead, painstakingly and unwaveringly took an active role in teaching them these things by example and constancy. Of course, this was during the early years when Sophia was very young and others were yet to be born. So Sophia benefitted by being the eldest and had developed a strong core of values by the time school began.

The beginning of her education came with a dispute, a sort of "big bang" caused by racial segregation. As the first day of school drew near so did anticipation in the James household. Sophia's family had moved to a new neighborhood, two blocks away from what was considered a great elementary school. During long, carefree summer days, she and her siblings would get permission to play in the school yard. For hours, Sophia would wander around the big, beautiful, clean school that would soon open and be hers. It was a dream come true and she was ready. The little girl had been studying with her father on most evenings—since always it seemed—and could read and write and had a good grasp on math. Her father had always addressed her as an adult. She had no memories of him ever babying her. On the contrary, in his mind she had never been too young to learn. When she was five, her father gave her a microscope; and when she turned six, he gave her a real chemistry set. Those gifts did not lie idle, as father and child spent hours exploring and smearing slides, seeing that there is more to things than what appears on the surface. As the hours of wondrous discovery passed, Sophia's father would talk about studying medicine. He was brainwashing her . . . deliberately.

"There is nothing like it, Sophia. To be able to help someone in need. To be able to take someone's pain away. To be a doctor is a wonderful thing." he would say.

THE ESSENCE: THE CORE

Yes, she was ready to start school and by the age of five she knew that she was going to study medicine, be a plastic surgeon and specialize in burns. However, first she had to start first grade. Just a matter of a couple more weeks and the summer would be over.

A few days before the first day of school arrived, the James family received a notification in the mail. It was from the County School Board advising them that Sophia was not to attend the school nearby. Instead each morning she was to board a bus, bright and early and be bussed over to another county. Her place in her beloved school was to be taken by another child that would likewise be bussed over from some other county.

Upon receiving this notification Sophia's father was infuriated. In fact, the little girl had seldom seen him ranting, raving and cursing the way he did that day. "What in the hell does this God damn government think it is! I'm a God damn law-abiding, taxpaying citizen, and now they are just going to push us around? Well I'll be God damned if I don't send Sophia to Fruitvale and all of her brothers and sisters afterwards!" Whew! The cursing and raving went on for hours and by the time her dad calmed down, she knew all about the problem and what his course of action was going to be. Sophia was a bit afraid for her father because she understood that he was aiming to do something that he was asked not to. But he never swayed an inch and by the time the first day of school arrived, she was silently scared stiff about going.

Sophia's mother got her up nice and early that first day of school. Though the child had no appetite whatsoever, her mother made her eat a good, wholesome breakfast. Then combing her daughter's long, light hair into lovely braids, she helped her into a darling, new, pastel-blue dress. With matching ribbons at the tip of her braids, Sophia left her house that morning holding her father's hand very firmly. She was marched to school to experience what was to become her first difficult situation in life—and to learn a huge lesson.

Mr. James also had dressed nicely and with a friendly smile on his face went into the school's main office. The office was large and had two desks. One was labeled "Registrar" and the other "Secretary." To the right of the entrance, there was a small visitor's area consisting of three chairs and a small coffee table with magazines on it. Also visible was a door with a sign that said "Principal."

Mr. James approached the lady registrar and announced, "Good morning, I'm Mr. James and I've brought this lovely young student for your school." He looked down at Sophia with obvious pride.

"Oh! How nice. How are you?" said the welcoming voice as the smiling face looked directly at the little girl. Quickly Sophia smiled back and surely her very large eyes opened a little wider. Actually, on the inside, she had a serious tummy ache. She had eaten all that breakfast without wanting it, but now the thought of her Daddy getting into trouble made her stomach feel upside down. Nevertheless, she stood still and straight, and smiled the whole while. Everything was going quite smoothly, the comments of "What a lovely dress," and "Such long braids," were accompanied by kindness. Forms were quickly being filled out and she started to breathe more evenly until the question, "Your address please?"

Mr. James, not blinking an eye and with the look of complete innocence on his face, gave his address. Well . . . that's where it all started.

"Oh! Mr. James, we are so sorry but little Sophia cannot come to this school. She has been assigned to . . . let me look up what county Sophia's school is in, so that you can report there." The registrar began her alphabetical search repeating "J . . . J" while Sophia's face suddenly drained of color.

"Oh! Yes," said her father "I did receive a notification on that decision, but I was not in agreement. As you know, we can see the school from our house and I don't want my little girl up early traveling on a bus to another county, just because someone has dreamt up such foolishness."

"Oh, believe me Mr. James, we know how you feel, but she cannot stay here; you must take her to her assigned school. Now if you will just give me a moment I can tell you where she has been assigned."

At this point Mr. James took Sophia by the hand and led her to one of the three visitor chairs in the office. He tenderly knelt down on one knee and looked into her eyes saying, "Sophia, do not move from this seat. Wait for me to come back and I'll be here for you when school is out."

The Registrar and the Secretary were both watching incredulously, but it was only after Mr. James stood up and headed for the door that they reacted. "Mr. James you can't just . . ." That was all he heard. He was gone.

It was a long day, but little Sophia with her hands folded in her lap did not move. People went in and out of the office. Some smiled at her and others looked at her curiously as they had seen her there earlier. Sophia felt uncomfortable; this certainly was not the first day she had dreamt of. She could hear the laughter of children in the hallways and it was tiring to just sit in that chair. However, her father had said 'stay' and so stay she would.

The next day the same scene was repeated. Her father grasped her by the hand, placed her in the same chair in the main office and again walked out. On this day, one of the secretaries passed by at snack time and gave the well-behaved, quiet child an apple. Sophia found her voice and most politely thanked the lady. She was glad for the attention. Again, her father came as the day ended and took her home. On that day he sat down and explained to Sophia the reasons for his actions.

"Sophia, I know it's hard for you to understand how I just leave you in that chair, but you see, I believe that Fruitvale is the right school for you. I also believe, Sophia, that we live in a free country and as your father who knows what's best for you, I want you to go to the school of my choosing and not to the school that our very faraway government in Washington—that knows nothing about you—has chosen. I'm sorry about all of this, my sweet Sophia." He put his arm around her and said, "You might as well learn right now that there are times when you must stand up for what you believe is right . . . and this, Sophia, is one of those times."

So, once again, on the third day, Sophia, holding her father's hand tight, entered the main office to sit at her newly-acquired post. However, this time things went differently. Upon arrival, the principal's secretary asked Mr. James to wait for the principal as he wanted to speak with him.

"Mr. James, what you are doing is quite illegal, sir." said the Principal.

"Why?" said Mr. James, comfortably seated in a chair in front of the principal's desk. "I am bringing her to school every day. You are the one that is not allowing her to receive an education."

The principal, a Mr. Faust, was a nice-looking man in his early fifties and experience had made him perceptive. He could see that Mr. James was not going to budge. He sat, squinting his eyes at him for a moment, as if thinking, *Do I fight or do I give in?* He lowered his gaze, loudly exhaled and gave in. For this alone Sophia was grateful; she knew that her father could be a very stubborn man when he was convinced of being right about something.

Sophia had silently harbored fears that her Daddy was really getting into trouble; maybe they would put him in jail. Despite all of her fears, everything had turned in an instant. The principal got up from his seat, came around his desk toward Mr. James and, with a pat on the back ushered him toward the door.

"I can't really blame you Mr. James," said the principal. "I'd probably be doing the same thing. It's a crazy law—forcing children to go to schools far away from home. It's even dangerous. I'm going to have trouble for this decision, but that'll be my problem." He glanced at the little girl whom he had seen day after day sit in that chair without moving. He extended his arm to touch the crown of her head, "Sophia, welcome to Fruitvale Elementary School."

Those words sounded heavenly and with a beaming smile Sophia watched the principal give instructions to the registrar. Then, looking at his secretary, he said, "Clara, please take Miss James over to Mrs. McMullen's class when the paperwork is completed." With that, the kindly gentleman turned around and returned to his office. The secretary winked at Sophia as she took her hand and led her to her long-awaited first day of school.

Sophia fell in love instantly with everything she saw. The classroom was beautiful. There were many windows and the colors of drawings on the wall made the room cheerful and fun. Yes, she fell in love with everything, but most of all, with the face of her teacher. She loved Mrs. McMullen from that very first moment, and perhaps because of it, excelled in every way possible so that Mrs. McMullen would love her too.

Sophia's inner core was forming and it was becoming strong. That first year of school remained forever the safest and happiest memory of her entire childhood.

4

RURAL LIFE, SMOKE AND ASHES

"ACOMPÁÑAME O LLÉVAME" ~ "COME WITH ME OR TAKE ME"
Una pradera abierta, ~ An open field,
Llena de flores para ti, ~ Filled with flowers for you,
Quiero ir a recogerlas, ~ I want to go pick them,
Para hacerte sonreír. ~ Just to make you smile.
Tu rostro siempre me acompaña, ~ Your face is always with me,
Tu risa baila en el aire, ~ Your laughter dances in the air,
Quiero tomarte las manos, ~ I want to take you by the hands,
Poner el mundo a tus pies. ~ And put the world at your feet.

It was 1960, a good year for the James family. Mr. James's business was doing well and that year he bought a brand new Chrysler station wagon. It was a honey of a car souped up with electric windows, a third back seat that faced the rear and the prize of it all, an RCA Victor record player. It was a bonafide record player, a new invention capable of playing in a moving vehicle. Their car was one of the first to have it installed; it went in front, beneath the dash board. It played 45-rpm vinyl records. Going down the road in their new red station wagon, listening to "Wheels," "Yellow Bird," and "It's Almost Tomorrow," was wonderful until they hit train tracks. Then it skipped!

A couple of years later, the James family had no choice but to move away. McClellan Air Force Base in North Highlands, Sacramento, was expanding and needed more land for its growth. The Base bought up several properties including the James's, paid them a fair price and gave them plenty of time to vacate. With Sacramento growing at a fast pace, Mr. James decided to move out of city limits and into a rural area. His guess was that rural property would appreciate rapidly, as city expansion continued. Also, the outskirts would stretch their dollar giving them more land for their buck.

"Land! God's gift to mankind." Mr. James would frequently say. "We'll find ourselves a nice piece of land and plant it with fruit trees. No matter what comes and goes, kids, we'll always have that." Little did Mr. James know that he was almost being prophetic.

The white house Mr. James bought was smaller than their former home and needed work done on it. Otherwise, it was fine and attractive. The front of the house had a wide, spacious, covered porch with large picture windows on each side. Empty flower boxes skirted the porch, waiting to be filled with bright red geraniums, and the front lawn lay thirsty, with the promise of turning green. The potential was there and, with a little work, it would be made to look nice. Best of all, was the potential for fun that the house had with the twenty acres that surrounded it. On one side of the house there was a red swing with dirt dug deep under it, tracks left behind by children who had previously played there. Still the greatest attraction was the open space—the meadow that surrounded the house. It was beautiful, and it was theirs. The meadow was a bright orange when they moved in, covered by billions of poppies.

Their work was cut out for them and within a short time the porch had an inviting swing seat, flower boxes boasted the beautiful red geraniums, and the lawn was turning greener by the day. The place was coming around and looking cared for. Anyone passing by would know children lived there as Mr. James, with saw and hammer, had immediately added necessary play items. A long see-saw sat right next to a high swing and further back, a tether pole. With bicycles at hand and poppies to pick, the James children had it all and were excited about life in the country.

Mr. and Mrs. James were also excited about their new surroundings. They had gotten a good price for their former home and, by moving out of Sacramento, felt that financially they were doing well. The infrastructure of their new surroundings was quite simple: mostly dirt roads and a lot of dust. Their property, however, was strategically placed directly across from the local school house. The little, two-room public school house was almost one of a kind, with only a few like it left in the United States. Mr. James, being a romantic at heart, upon seeing the whitewashed school with its noticeable bell tower, had been sold on the location. It was a beautiful area with an occasional large, old eucalyptus tree standing guard, as if welcoming newcomers. Expansive golden fields of barley stretched outward as far as the eye could reach. Light yellow fields crisscrossed dirt roads where a handful of cars and trucks transited daily. Each car clearly defined its existence in the distance by the inevitable cloud of dust that followed. There was a sense of freedom in this new place and Sophia, with a mind full of imagination, would at times take off running for no real reason. She would feel like a pony or imagine that, with the great expanse before her, if she ran fast enough she might be able to lift off. Instead, her fast legs would take her to an ancient eucalyptus tree that stood in the middle of the field directly in front of her house. There in its cool shade, she would lie in the sweet, tall grass and recapture her breath. She would close her eyes and see herself lifting off the ground just as she was about to reach a barbed wired fence. She would soar into the sky and, like a bird gliding with outward-stretched arms, look down at their new home. She could see her mother on the porch, busy shaking out a small rug, and her siblings playing in the yard. The family car would be gone as her father would be at work. Sophia loved the country, loved the land and loved the smell in the air. After a while, she would let out a giggle, get up from the cool grass under the eucalyptus tree, shake out her dress and come running back home. Only she would ever know that she could fly.

Those long, hot, summer days before school started went by with the family united and working hard to make their new house feel like home. As a long day would come to an end the heat would subside and a breeze could be felt that refreshed everyone. On such an evening the family hiked over to a stream where frogs could be found and, among the cotton tails, Mr. James showed the children how to catch them. Everyone ran around trying to catch a bright green frog. They were successful and returned home with several. However, the children were horrified to know that the frogs were to be eaten. Their father appreciated the delicacy of frog legs but found it very difficult to convince the children to join him. Sophia wouldn't touch one. She looked at the nicely fried leg, gagged and turned pale. With pleading eyes she looked at Mr. James for a dismissal. Sophia and the rest of the children ran from the table.

On future frog hunting evenings, Sophia would devote her energies to cutting and gathering cotton tails. She would take them home and paint their heads with every paint color she had. She would get a vase from her mother and present them to her. They were beautiful and would last for months decorating the top of the television or some lonely corner.

With ten days of summer left before school started, the James family began planning a small vacation. They had all been working hard moving, repairing, cleaning and painting; work, work, work, was what they did all summer long. The work was not over either, for some furnishings still remained in storage and needed to be moved into the house. However, Mr. James also was tired and much to everyone's joy he decided that the rest could wait for their return.

Sophia's favorite uncle, her father's oldest brother, Uncle George decided that he too would join in on the adventure and would bring his family on the trip. The two brothers quickly made plans and the small vacation turned into a wonderful camping trip to the Grand Canyon. Uncle George was a handsome man with fine features. His hair was jet black and he wore it like Elvis Presley. He was tall and slender and had a prominent Adam's apple. Uncle George seemed always full of energy and had a playful and fun disposition. He always made time for his nieces and nephews. Often he would show off his athleticism by walking up and down stairs on his hands. The strong, large muscles in his arms were readily made available for all the kids to touch and feel how strong and hard they were. No matter how much each one tried, no one could ever put a dent into one of those muscles. Uncle George was kind and sweet and having him come on the trip would only make it more fun.

Both families would travel by car, caravanning all the way. They would carry tents and stop to camp out at camping sites. They packed carefully, making sure that all the ingredients for true camping were carried by one family or the other. Uncle George brought his guitar, Mr. James his harmonica, and Sophia her accordion. Excitement was everywhere. Like busy bees, everyone helped get ready for the trip. A few days later, the Jameses drove away from their nice-looking home in their large, red station wagon, packed in tight and riding low.

Memories made on that trip became for Sophia among her most treasured. Little did she or her family know that as they drove away from their lovely home, they were driving away from a secure and happy life which would be forever lost. This trip would mark the beginning of what would develop into a tragic childhood for Sophia and her brothers and sisters.

They had come back home. The weeklong trip to the Grand Canyon had been wonderful. As their car pulled to a stop the abrupt silence of the humming engine made little Sophia stir to life from a deep sleep in the back seat. The even, purring sound had suddenly been replaced by something like a muffled cry and Sophia felt alarmed. It was the crack of dawn and light was just breaking enough to let her see the silhouette of her mother bent over crying.

Automatically, Sophia dazed from sleep and alert from fear said, "Don't cry Mommy, everything will be all right." Sophia didn't know what had happened, for her brain—still too groggy from sleep—wouldn't register very much. She kept repeating that everything would be all right and to not cry, Mommy, when suddenly, the view in the background hit the foreground of her brain. They were home but she couldn't see the house. She bolted up stiff in her seat and began wiping her blurry eyes searching for the house. She couldn't see it. Her house was supposed to be there but it wasn't. Instead there was an ugly space filled with the charred remains of their dreams. Smoke was still rising from the ashes. The sight of the nearby swing set with nothing but limp chains and the charred new bike which had been left, leaning on the house, would be engraved in her memory always.

The fire had hurt the family. These were tough times for many people and now to be homeless was a real setback. However, in the face of adversity, Sophia repeatedly heard her father say, "We will all hold together.... We'll pull through."

For a month they lived in the cramped quarters of a motel room five miles away. All they had left in the world were a few things that had remained in storage, their camping gear, and the clothing they had packed. Everything else was gone. However, after friends read in the local newspapers about the fire, her old school, Fruitvale School, put on a fundraiser and collected clothing and all kinds of things that they could use. Sophia felt embarrassed when she went to her old school and saw her old classmates and teachers. They all were wonderful and so giving but still Sophia felt very awkward to now have nothing and having to take dresses from her old friends. It was indeed a great lesson in humility.

The profit that Mr. James had made on the house sale was now being used and one could see, by the strain on his face, that he was feeling great pressure. The next move Mr. James made was to put a large trailer home on his property, close to where the old house had stood. Mrs. James and the children took everything in stride and tried to make merry of the situation. After all, they found out that the house had exploded because of a gas leak. So all they could do was be thankful they had not arrived a day sooner. It was clear to all of them that the things lost were just things and that they were all unharmed, safe and together. With that comforting thought in their minds they were able to move forward with optimism and in no time the trailer home was just that: home.

To come to Alpha School after Fruitvale was like going back in time. The school was a small, A-frame with a bell tower, right out of "Little House on the Prairie." The main structure was divided into two rooms which housed the entire school population. One room was for first, second, third, and fourth graders and the other was for big kids: fifth, sixth, seventh, and eighth graders. Four rows of desks represented the four grades that were taught in each room. The first row was first grade; the second row was second grade, and so on. It was run in its entirety by Mr. and Mrs. Polli. They were teachers, administrators and principal, all in one. Mrs. Polli had the younger group and Mr. Polli taught the older grades and also was the principal. The Pollis were a middle-aged couple. They were very dedicated and stern, but also friendly and caring. Mrs. Polli, a very simple woman, was rail-thin. She was neat, with her clothes always nicely pressed, and wore her graying hair in a bun just above the nape of her neck. Her glasses were highly magnified giving her eyes a larger-than-real appearance. She rarely laughed but when she did, it was high-pitched and contagious. Anyone hearing her could not help but join in. Mr. Polli was quite different. He was a handsome man and his nicely parted hair was still very dark. He was tall and friendly, but his presence commanded respect. When he entered a room it would fall silent immediately. He was liked by all students, but feared by them too, since it was Mr. Polli who dispensed discipline—usually punishments—at Alpha School. When there was trouble, he would carry in his right hand a paddle and would publicly punish anyone deserving. Paddling was the maximum shame a student could endure and it was a badge of honor to get through school with a clean record of never being paddled.

The front of the building had a wide porch with seven steps leading to a front yard, lined with huge weeping willows. The back of the school was a big yard, mainly plain dirt with grass growing in patches. All the many playing shoes made it hard for grass to grow. There were several picnic tables, high swings, a couple of high slides, and an old jungle gym everyone fought over. A couple of old busses were parked in the back area, and, further out, there was a baseball field. With the school's setting, and just a little imagination, Sophia could see Tom Sawyer and Huck Finn running among her classmates. Alpha School would be great and Sophia was happy to start her fourth grade there along with her sister Karen in the second and brother Bobby in the first. There were three more James children at home, but they were all too small for school.

From the James's property, the school's backyard was clearly visible, so Mrs. James could often see her children running around and playing during recess. However, best of all, was the fact that she could watch her children walk to school. She could see them cross the dirt road directly in front of their trailer and head diagonally toward a small gate that offered a short cut to children that lived on that side of the school. She could see them go all the way toward the front of the school and then make a left and disappear around the front corner, toward the steps. Each morning at seven forty-five, the kids were out the door and at eight o'clock the Alpha School bell would toll.

It was impossible for young Sophia to know that her destiny did not lie in this safe haven and that she would be at Alpha School for only one year. Fortunately for her, she maximized every moment, and during that year she made her first friends. Those friends she would keep at her side forever in her memories. A girl by the name of Colleen Gray became her closest friend. Colleen was, perhaps, the prettiest girl in school. She wore stylish, short brown hair with bangs, was always nice and neat and had the brightest and warmest smile. On the first day of school, Colleen was the first one to approach Sophia and make her feel welcome.

"So your name is Sophia. That's a pretty name. I was wondering what it was. My name is Colleen Gray. It's good to finally meet you."

With that the sky opened, sun flooded through, and Sophia, with the widest smile, looked at her square in the eyes. Sophia had heard the friendly voice and now, in a glance, recognized that this was an intelligent and confident girl. By all means, Sophia would show her worth; she reciprocated by graciously extending her hand, "Why, thank you. It's really good to meet you too, Colleen. I'm so glad to finally make it to school."

Because of the fire, the James children had lost the first week of school. So they knew no one and felt out of place. They were behind in school tasks and had a lot of catching up to do. However, most important for them, was the social aspect of it all. Making friends was priority number one!

"I'm glad you did, too. You know I saw your house burning down Sophia. It was terrible."

"You did?"

"Yes, everyone did. When the fire broke out there was a big bang, and people started running over from everywhere. My dad jumped into his truck and I jumped in with him to see what was going on. It was just after dinnertime and everyone was afraid that your family might have been in the house. Your neighbor, Mrs. Stanford, assured everyone that the house was empty and that you were all on a trip somewhere."

"That's right, thank goodness for that. We were coming back from our camping trip to the Grand Canyon. When we actually arrived the house was still smoking. We lost everything Colleen; it was terrible. Heck, I'm wearing a dress somebody gave me."

As soon as she said it, she regretted it. What a blabbermouth—complaining. She tried to quickly fix it, "I mean…we're doing…just fine, actually."

Colleen was sensitive and she immediately was aware of Sophia's exposed pride, so she flashed her a smile, shrugging it off. "That's great. So . . . I'll show you my favorite places as soon as you catch up from all the work Mrs. Polli is going to give you!" She moved away with a chuckle that had the ring of 'I know Mrs. Polli, and you're in for it.'

Sure enough, Colleen and Sophia became fast friends and sometimes during recess they would run over to the James's trailer for lemonade. Mr. and Mrs. James got to know Colleen and had no objections when Sophia told them about an invitation and asked for permission to sleep over at the Gray's. Colleen's family was considered wealthier than most as they owned a nursery where all locals went for fruit trees and plants. A good portion of the countryside was theirs and their farmhouse had barns and silos. The night Sophia slept over was the first time ever she slept away from her family.

Where they would sleep was decided around the dinner table, when Colleen's father volunteered, "So girls, are you sleeping in Colleen's room, or would you like me to fix up the loft out in the barn?" Colleen started to giggle and Sophia let out a gasp of excitement.

"Really?" she said looking at Colleen who was now laughing at Sophia's expression.

"Could we really sleep in the barn? Oh! My gosh!!!! I'd love to sleep in the loft. What about you Colleen?"

"Sure, silly. Daddy will make it real nice for us and we'll take plenty of blankets and a flashlight and it'll be great. I love to sleep there."

"Oh, thank you, Mr. Gray. That is so nice of you. Thank you so much."

Colleen's expression changed to mischief when she said, "You do know that there are mice in the barn that like to nibble on your toes while you're sleeping, right?"

Sophia's face went dark and her eyes opened wide. "Mice? They'll be in the loft with us?"

Everyone around the table started to laugh and Mrs. Gray said, "Now, now, Colleen stop teasing Sophia."

Then she looked at Sophia with a grin on her face and said, "Sure there are mice. We have them everywhere. But we have cats around here so that we can keep the place clean. Now, don't you worry at all, no mice are going to bother you because there aren't any in the barn."

"Oh, good" said Sophia trying to sound polite and at the same time relieved.

Mr. Gray prepared the loft for them. Stacks of bailed hay were piled high and toward the center of the loft was a small area where they would sleep. There Mr. Gray had spread a neat pile of loose hay for their bed; on top of it he had stretched out blankets and placed a couple of pillows. Once in pajamas and with teeth brushed Colleen yelled out, "I'll race ya" and started running, giggling wildly. Sophia was right behind her, out the back screen door with a crash, with a flashlight in hand

CHAPTER 4

and feet struggling to stay in their slippers the girls made it to the barn and ran for the ladder. Up and up they went making a racket and when they were both at the top they threw themselves onto the soft mound of hay. It was wonderfully fluffy and the smell of hay was sweet and cool.

"Oh Colleen, this is wonderful, I can't believe I'm up in a real loft, about to sleep on hay." Sophia was saying this as she stretched herself out to look over the edge. There was a small light on in the barn and she could see three horses in their stalls.

"I like it a lot too." Colleen had said smiling.

"Do you sleep here whenever you want to?"

"No, just when I have a cousin over or a friend like you. I mean it's great and all, but it's not much fun if you're all alone. So I don't get to do it very often."

Sophia was still looking over the edge and taking in everything below. "So what about those horses, do you ever ride them?"

Colleen snuggled up next to her and also was looking down. "Just Andy, the one to the left, he's the oldest one and I trust him more. The others can get too rowdy and I'm a little afraid of them."

"I've ridden a horse before," Sophia said as she moved away from the edge and lay on her back, reaching for a piece of straw, "at the county fair. I love horses."

"You do! Well I know of someone that loves you too!" As Colleen said these words she flashed a huge smile and raised her eyebrows. Sophia sat up saying, "What are you talking about?"

"Well, I'm talking about Ricky Richardson, of course."

"What do you mean, 'of course?' I didn't know he liked me. My gosh, he's in sixth grade! I didn't even know he had noticed me."

"Well he has; he told me so himself. Do you like him?"

"No. I really like Ronnie."

"Ronnie Thompson? Are you kidding?"

"Nope, I'm not kidding. I like Ronnie and I'm not sure why." She paused a second as if considering the matter. "Maybe it's the way he rides his bicycle so fast. I just know that Ricky has too many freckles and I don't like freckles." As Sophia said this her head went down on her pillow and she exhaled.

Colleen proceeded to put her head down too. "Well yesterday, at lunch time, you walked by and that is what Ricky told me: that he was in love with you."

"Sorry, but no way, not interested, nope, no way, no way. . . ." Then, without realizing it, Sophia drifted off.

Living in the tight trailer made privacy difficult, and inadvertently Sophia would hear conversations by her parents that were not meant for her. More and more she was hearing the words *Puerto Rico*. Sophia's parents always argued, and when they fought, they would insult each other, yelling with ugly, foul language, and being very hurtful. Sophia hated being around when this happened and she would try to get the kids out and get busy. More and more, with the increased arguing going on between their parents, the children would head over to the huge, old, eucalyptus tree that stood like a sentinel, a refuge, in the field in front of their home. The tree must have been 200 years old, and everyone loved it. It was where all the kids in the neighborhood would come together and play. Its trunk was carved with everyone's name and a hundred hearts told the story of who was in love with who. Its ancient wide branches, dressed in dense foliage, provided wonderful shade on hot summer days. The old majestic eucalyptus tree captured everyone's imagination and was a true friend that forgave them all when they played for hours upon its branches. However, one day Sophia's father was not as forgiving and on that day she was in trouble.

The whole gang was there. It was a stifling Saturday afternoon and everyone was trying to make the best of it. The fact that so many friends were there—including some of Sophia's favorites, Jane, Colleen, Sammy, Alice, Ricky and Ronnie—prompted them to play a game which depended on a high number of participants. It was team work that made the game possible and it was smarts that kept everyone safe. A group of kids would climb up the tree and, with their combined weight, would manage to make a flexible limb droop toward the ground. Because the eucalyptus limbs were so vast, it took a good number of kids to make up enough weight for this to happen. On the ground another group of kids would be ready to grab the limb and then hold on to it while the kids up in the tree climbed back down. Then everyone would help hold the limb to the ground while someone would call out a name. Once a name was called the counting would begin, and on the count of, "One . . . two . . . three!" everyone, except for the one called, would let go. The kid hanging on would be thrown into the air screaming and laughing, courtesy of a tummy flip-flop. As soon as the ride was over, the kids on the ground would reach up and grab the dangling participant by his feet, then his legs, and so on. They would get him down safely and again secure the branch for the next countdown. This game was played for hours, everybody laughing and having a ton of fun—not realizing that they were all becoming experts in organizational team work.

Now, not all the kids were allowed to play. From the James family it had been decided, by older kids in the neighborhood, that only Sophia and Karen were big enough to play this game. However, on this day, Bobby cried and begged to please be given a chance. "I will hold on tight, Sophia. I won't let go, I promise," he wailed. For the longest time everyone tried to ignore him and then they tried to make him understand that he was too small in size for such adventure, that he had to wait to grow bigger. But he begged and begged until the group of kids gave up and gave him a shot at the big leagues.

"OK, Bobby, don't let go, whatever you do, don't let go. One . . . two . . . three!" and all the kids holding the branch let go of it. With Bobby's light weight, the limb shot up like a whip and seemed to propel him to the sky. With terror, Sophia watched and, much to her relief, she could see that Bobby hadn't let go. However, since he was so small, the limb did not come back to them and Bobby was left hanging way up high in the tree. The kids on the ground were scared. They could see trouble and kept calling to Bobby to keep holding on.

Desperately the older kids began scrambling up the tree to try and reach for him. However, he was out on the tip of the limb and they couldn't reach that far. As some kids tried to make it out onto the limb others stood on the ground frantically directing. Not enough of them had reacted fast enough and so the few up in the tree were not heavy enough to bring the branch down. Bobby was crying for help and warning that he was about to fall and everyone was screaming as they knew that he was going to fall from way up high any second.

At that moment Mr. James was just arriving home and heard the screams. He looked up over at the old eucalyptus tree and saw what was going on. He started running, and kept picking up speed. He looked frightened. He too was calling, "Hang on Bobby, hang on!" Just then Bobby, who couldn't hold any longer, came down with a thud. He hadn't hit his head and no bones were broken, but he lay on the ground crying, more out of fear than damage. Mr. James consoled him and checked him out and then looked at Sophia. He stood up, took a few steps away from the stiff, silent crowd and reached for a switch stick. Sophia's blood ran cold and she backed away knowing that her Dad was about to give it to her. He started with Karen grabbing her by her right arm and giving her one switch of the stick on the back of her legs. She gave out a terrible screech. He let her go and headed over to Sophia who stood petrified and mortified that Ronnie and Ricky, as well as the whole gang, were watching. Sophia looked at him with pleading eyes but he was heading straight for her. He grabbed her by an arm, swung her around and started swinging—one, two, three, four—with the blasted stick. Sophia did not make a sound. She silently limped away from her friends, who watched the whole ordeal in muted stupefaction. She was humiliated and embarrassed more than hurt by the swats on the back of her legs. It was an awful day.

Her father later felt remorse and asked, "Why didn't you cry out like your sister Karen did? I would've stopped right away." Not Sophia, She was the oldest; she would never cry out. Never! She was too proud and strong. On that day the telltale signs of her inner core were visible.

A few months after the fire, as Mr. James tried to recuperate financially, he continued to support his family with his work in construction. He was in the right place and time when an opportunity presented itself to bid on a house that was up for auction. To get his family out of the cramped trailer was a priority and it prompted Mr. James to snatch up the house. The construction of the house was sound and he knew that it would withstand a move, once all the necessary permits were secured.

"Mrs. Polli, it's coming!" called the school gardener from the door.

Mrs. Polli turned to the class and cheerfully said, "OK, everyone can go outside, the house is coming!"

Immediately the children were up and running and suddenly the school day felt like a holiday. Neighbors also joined in as they too were on the lookout to see the house come rolling home. Everyone knew what happened to the James Family and to now see them get a real house back was a joy shared by everyone. People could only imagine how tough it was for a family of six young children to live in the cramped trailer. So much excitement was in the air when in the distance they saw yellow caution lights flashing from city trucks helping the home slowly move down the road toward them.

Kids were squealing with delight and calling out to Sophia. "Sophia!! Sophia your house is coming! Your house is coming!!"

However, no one was happier than Sophia, Karen and Bobby. They ran to the farthest point possible on school property, out in right field, alongside the road within the school fence. They all watched the procession with fascination and curiosity.

The house was white and kind of looked like the one that had burnt down. Coming down the road the way it was, made it look very big to the children and since they were impressed, they'd pat Sophia on the shoulder and congratulate her. Sophia was smiling so much her jaws ached, but she just continued to smile more. There was a smaller truck out in front that appeared to be guiding the old flatbed truck that was hauling the house. The smaller truck was also clearing the way. Working men trimmed a branch here and there from big trees alongside the road to allow the house through. They stopped and filled holes on the side of the road when necessary. All other traffic on the two lane country road was detoured, as the truck's load took up every bit of space. Everything was going smoothly.

Slowly but surely, the house crept down the road. The main spectators, all the school kids perched halfway up the fence, were right there every step of the way, calling out instructions: "Be careful, there's another big branch; it's going to get the roof over there." They clapped, they howled, they whistled, they gave words of encouragement, "Great job! Wow! You missed that branch!" Everyone turned the corner with the house and from the back schoolyard they all watched it until it was resting on its new foundation. It looked beautiful.

The details of how deep in debt Mr. James had become were not known to Sophia. All she knew was that her father was in serious financial trouble. The struggle between her mother and father on what to do next prompted Mr. James to decide, in search of economic relief, to go back to sea. He would take up his old job as a seaman and try to get himself out of debt. The construction business was in a huge slump and the pay that he could get by going overseas at this time would far exceed anything he could realistically make at home. For a seaman to find a job on a ship was an easy task in those days because of the ongoing war in Vietnam. There were more jobs than men and so the pay was real good. However, the dangers involved in transporting ordnance, munitions and explosives over the Pacific were great and Mr. James counted on having lady luck at his side. The James family moved into the house just before Christmas. Just after the holiday, Mr. James left for the ocean.

Sophia in particular was suffering from the absence of her daddy. After all, he was more than a dad. He was her best teacher and she missed their quiet times of sharing and learning. Life for the James children was changing dramatically ever since the move to the countryside. The wonderful intentions were not matched by luck and they bounced from one difficult moment to the next. Along the way, they were learning how to survive and make do with what they had, great or little. They were learning not to complain, but to help each other. They were learning that sometimes things don't go one's way and yet life goes on and one must never give up. They were gathering strength and didn't know it. They also didn't know that this staging ground would serve as a basis for their survival. They actually had been lucky to have had tough experiences to learn from. If life had been too cushy, they might not have been mature enough to handle the challenges they would soon face.

Sophia's mom was everything now and the bigger children all helped around the house with chores. Being an American, but coming from the island of Puerto Rico, made her different, and as Sophia grew up, she learned very little about her mother's mysterious birthplace. She knew that the Spanish language was spoken there and when she would ask her mother to speak it, Sophia was always captivated by its beautiful sound. The language moved, it fluctuated rhythmically and was rich with innate melody. Beautiful as well were her mother's looks. She was not your everyday woman; she was quite exceptional. Her wavy, jet-black hair and large, dark eyes contrasted with her white skin and made her face jump out. She had a lovely smile, framed by full, red lips and bright white teeth. Yes, Sophia thought her mother to be beautiful.

With Mr. James away for months at a time, it became apparent that Sophia's mother began to feel loneliness and despair over the burden of raising six children alone. More frequently the children could hear comments of "We should all move to Puerto Rico. It's so beautiful there and I have family that will help us."

When Mr. James returned from his first trip, three months later, the concept of moving to Puerto Rico was firmly in her mother's mind. After that, day and night she would hound him about moving there. "You might even find work there," she would tell Sophia's dad.

Sophia didn't want to go, though no one was asking her. She had her friends; she loved Alpha school and was making A's in all of her classes.

She was clearly aware that they were going through a tough patch, but nevertheless, she was confident that if her daddy had a little more time, things would get better.

However, her parents were thinking about it, and as days passed they thought about it more and more seriously. Sophia's mother was painting the island of Puerto Rico with a very colorful brush. The relatives that she never wrote to, or sought to contact, overnight became wonderful and loving people who missed her very much and whom she could no longer bear being away from. She incessantly talked about moving until Mr. James broke down and said the words that Sophia had begun to fear. "Children, how about if we move to Puerto Rico this summer?"

It was a question that knew its own answer. It was a voiced decision.

5

VENEZUELA IN TURMOIL

"MAGIA" ~ "MAGIC"
"*Magia tiene tu mirada,* ~ Magic is in your gaze,
"*Cuando me miras,* ~ When you look at me,
" *Sentimientos concentrados,* ~ Concentrated feelings,
" *Son transferidos en un instante,* ~ Are transferred in an instant,
" *En un instante.* ~ In an instant.
"*Magia, magia tienes,* ~ Magic, magic you have,
" *Magia, magia eres tu,* ~ Magic, magic you are.
" *Te adueñaste de mi vida.* ~ You took over my life.
" *Magia en tu sonrisa,* ~ Magic in your smile,
" *Magia en tu alegría,* ~ Magic in your joy,
" *Me contagio de tu magia,* ~ I'm enraptured by your magic,
" *Y tu risa es mía.* ~ And your smile is mine.

Sophia looked up at the canvas, trying to extricate herself from where her mind had been. The painting was moving along and she assessed her progress. She could aim for a different section or stay put. Yes, the white fluffy cumulus clouds in the cerulean blue sky had settled just enough for her to safely knife in the palm trees. *They must stand out powerfully yet appear pliable*, she thought. She got up from the chair and resolutely took up the knife. A dab into the sap green, a bold stroke upward, and the first palm frond was there. On and on she worked the higher reaches of the canvas, as her mind meandered back to Tommy's birth.

Tommy was the first of her children to be born in Venezuela and he came a few weeks early and without medical assistance.

His arrival was so unexpected and urgent that Sophia was afraid that she would not make it to the hospital. It was rush hour in Caracas and traffic was up. Her obstetrician was there, a quick exam, and in an hour it would all be over. Off went the Doctor for a water fountain and off went Sophia into dramatic, sudden labor. Alone, she began calling, trying to alert someone that she was giving birth, right then and there. Her husband, frantically ran for the doctor. Meanwhile, a bright yellow shirt, probably an expecting father himself, stood at the door announcing to the world, "Yes, she is right! The baby is coming out!"

Good grief! There lay Sophia delivering her baby with a stranger watching every detail when, a moment too late, the cavalry arrived. Her husband ran in just ahead of the doctor, only to find that the baby was out and lying on the bed among the bloodied sheets.

What a show that had been! But it was a few hours later, when the family pediatrician, Dr. Elias Milgram, came to see her, that joy would turn to sorrow. She greeted him with her usual smile and found that his was lacking. Instead, the kindly man she liked so much was reaching for her hand and leaning forward so as to sit on her bed. This was not his normal behavior, and it set off every alarm within Sophia's body.

"No, don't touch me. What's wrong? What is going on here?" said Sophia almost choking with an instant fear that had grabbed at her throat.

With a calming and caring voice, Dr. Milgram said, "Sophia, I have every reason to believe, after evaluating the baby, that he has Down syndrome."

Those were the last words Sophia heard as the world turned dark around her and she folded over unconscious. It was only momentary, and soon she reopened her eyes, regaining her posture and with a face so pale whispered, "Are you sure?"

He was.

While some panicked and fretted and tried to give her consoling words and advice, Sophia hung on to her little baby, just a little tighter than the others. There was a frailty there and she was his mother. Oh, how well she knew what it meant to not have a strong mother. How well she knew the pain and sorrow when a mother was missed. Sophia James would protect this child like no other and those family members and friends that accepted and loved him, would be loved back. Those that didn't would be forgotten.

Soon everyone knew that Tommy was a fighter; his progress was much better than many predicted. True, from the onset he was bombarded with therapies of everything the young caring mother could think of, but it was his perseverant spirit that shined through. Her medical knowledge was a key influence to expediency; she was very aware that for him, more than most, time was truly of the essence. Tommy walked early for a child with Down syndrome, was potty trained way before expected and could handle a spoon and feed himself as messily as any other. His downfall was speech. It was long in coming and when it came there was little to show for his efforts. However, he was big on communication. Not a defined sign language, but a combination of mimicking and facial gestures. Providing the best for Tommy was a challenge. However, from the beginning, the family didn't complain or ask why; they just took one step at a time and tried to use time wisely. Tommy grew up as a beautiful and happy child and Sophia's entire family was all the better because of him.

Three was the number of children Sophia expected to have, but with Tommy being a special child, she felt that he needed a sibling who would sandwich him in. He needed someone else to be the "baby;" he already had the title of "special." So talks began with Sophia lobbying for a fourth child. She spoke with her loving husband and she spoke with God, humbly asking for him to send them the child their particular family needed. He did. The fourth child was a little girl and she made for the perfect caboose.

During the five years while Sophia was having babies, she alternated between children at home and children at the Children's Hospital, "José Manuel de los Ríos." It was an exhausting time but a rewarding one that was only made possible by her husband's support. As an executive he had excelled and additional hands were made available to help care for their children. Medicine had been a long and torturous road but Sophia never gave up. As completion was to take place, fate stepped in and sent Sophia down a different path.

The country of Venezuela was seeing difficult times. There was growing unrest caused by many factors, with widespread corruption within the government paramount. On February 27, 1989, emotions came to a head and exploded in what was later known as the *Caracazo*.

This event would, in fact, be the trigger that sent the whole country spiraling down a different road. On that fateful date, death was everywhere, and numbers were mounting. "Three hundred," declared the government.

"Three thousand." declared the American Embassy and Sophia declared double. It was retching, scary, sad beyond words and threatening. Every negative adjective imaginable fit the description; the *Caracazo* was a vile response from citizens toward government and government toward citizens.

The spark that ignited the initial rioting was the increase in the price of gasoline which in turn would increase the cost of public transportation and most everything else. There were many policies developed by President Carlos Andres Pérez in his attempt to pay down the foreign debt Venezuela had, and comply with requirements of the International Monetary Fund. Too many of those policies were repudiated by the Venezuelan masses, as they represented sacrifice for them, while government corruption was openly rampant. However, it was that gas hike that triggered all the pent up hatred of citizens toward the government. The ferocity with which people came down from the hills surrounding Caracas to loot and riot, elicited a response from authorities that resulted in the massacre. It was the worst massacre in Venezuelan history and it left an indelible print of fear on Sophia.

Sophia was on call at the Hospital Vargas when the wounded starting coming in. The number outweighed possibilities of treatment and with injuries so severe that soon the wounded were becoming cadavers; bodies started piling up. It was a frantic mess, blood everywhere, screams and wailing, "Doctor help, he's dying!" There was not enough of anything to help treat the sudden influx of patients. Hospital Vargas always had a shortage of basic necessities, gauze, syringes and antiseptics. Daily, doctors and students arrived with their own contributions to help those who would arrive during their watch. However, in an emergency situation such as the one on that fateful day, the hospital was entirely and completely inadequate. Alongside the crying of those dying and those hurt, cries of powerless and frantic doctors and nurses could be heard. They were ineffective and in despair watched the amassing dead accumulate. Sophia stayed, like everyone else, and did all she could until no more could be done. Then she went home to her husband and children, fully aware that their world had dramatically changed. She had just seen the costly result of hatred and witnessed the horror of brothers killing brothers. The thousands killed were killed by soldiers under orders. They had chosen to obey those orders and kill their countrymen. The fact that anti-Americanism was flaunted by the burning of the American flag in the streets of Caracas confused and terrified Sophia. With great introspection, Sophia realized and accepted that her children needed a mother to protect them and not a doctor. Shortly after those fateful days, she never returned—ever again—to her beloved Hospital Vargas.

The episode of the *Caracazo* seriously scarred Sophia with a fear of living in Venezuela. She decided to take her children off the big yellow American school bus that drove through the valley of Caracas, delivering little American children to their homes. She could almost see a target drawn on the side of the bus, as if inviting disaster. She would drive them herself. She went back to Scout leadership for girls and boys and threw her heart and soul into it. For the next four years she would be the President of English Speaking Girl Scout Troops on Foreign Soil for Venezuela. Around that time she was invited onto the board of directors of *Colegio Internacional de Caracas*, the International School of Caracas (CIC), which enabled her to promote and develop the implementation of a special ed program. Sophia took full advantage of it, and built an alliance with the National Down Syndrome Congress out of Atlanta. She set up teacher seminars on how to work with children of special needs, and soon, handicapped kids who previously had no life beyond their homes, were coming out and going to school. It was a beautiful thing and Sophia was excited about these endeavors. She was contributing to the wellbeing of society and, at the same time, watching closely over her children.

After the *Caracazo* in 1989 and two coups d'état in 1992, followed by food shortages and frequent rioting, Sophia and her husband decided that it was time to leave Venezuela and return home to the United States. They left Venezuela on September 23, 1993.

With a heavy heart Sophia packed up eighteen years of living and took with her only a small portion which would represent those years of growth and happiness. After long days of packing and organizing, selling belongings that could not accompany them, finally the family—all but her husband who had gone ahead to settle things at the other end—boarded their one way flight. Just getting the four children, their large collie Prince and a truck load of suitcases to the airport had been hectic. With the dog in the airplane's belly and her four children around her, entertained with crayons and coloring books, Sophia leaned her head back and relaxed in the leather first class seat. Yes, her life since she had taken charge of it was first class. There was no lamenting or a search for excuses to not accomplish whatever needed being done. She was an optimist that believed in going forward, on her own efforts and would not wait for someone's cue. The misery and constant sorrow of her childhood and that of the children that surrounded her then—her siblings—were buried. It would never touch the children she had next to her, at this time in life. She would fiercely shield them from all of that. These children were lucky. They had the Sophia all children needed, the responsible adult. Sophia took a peek at them, they were content and consumed by their coloring. It seemed Sophia had always been raising children, one set then, and one set now. On that day, as on this one, her mind was lured into traveling back, to another one way flight. One she took as a child, thirty years earlier. A flight that would introduce her to a world she could have never imagined existed.

6

PUERTO RICO, ANOTHER WORLD

"SIMPLEMENTE QUIMERA" ~ "SIMPLY CHIMERA"
Desde pequeños con los pies descalzos, ~ From childhood with bare feet,
Comandamos y mandamos, ~ We command and demand,
Confundimos lo que es ganarnos, ~ We confuse what it is to earn,
Un pedacito de pan. ~ A little piece of bread.
Vivimos en eterna utopía, ~ We live in an eternal utopia,
Nuestro mundo es girasol, ~ Our world is a sunflower,
Y creemos ser merecedores, ~ And we believe we deserve
De todo, todo, todo lo mejor. ~ Everything, everything that is the best.
Pero las cosas no son así, ~ But things aren't that way,
Porque no sabemos lo que es todo, ~ Because we don't know what
everything is,
Cuando es que debemos dejar, ~ When is it that we should stop,
De desear para apreciar. ~ Wanting to appreciating.

JUNE 3, 1963

The plane landed just as the sun was going down and the glow of its brightest orange reflected upon the landing strip, making it look like a super highway from some science fiction movie. The image caught the children's imagination and they drew in their breath in anticipation of the beauty that lay ahead. Indeed, beyond the landing strip lay the ocean, framed by a sandy beach outlined by tall, bending palm trees.

Sophia smiled at the beautiful palm trees which stood everywhere, bowing their trunks as if in permanent salute and welcoming them as they took their first steps onto foreign soil.

Though the trip had been exhausting, the James family and everyone on board seemed happy. That was openly demonstrated the moment the plane, hesitantly and almost reluctantly, placed both wheels on the runway, by the explosion of applause, whistles and laughter that erupted on board. People were making the sign of the cross on their chest and kissing crossed fingers, something Sophia had never seen before, but understood that God was being thanked. Seemingly, no one believed that they would land safely and were all joyful they had. The Spanish language flowed like a stream on a mission and it made for wide eyes and big smiles among the James children. Everything was new. As they descended from the aircraft and walked across the tarmac they could hear music playing with the sounds of a rhythm they had never heard before. The landscape was flat, with a shimmering ocean in the distance, and the air felt wet and sticky. People also appeared to be different. Their dress was formal and elegant and Sophia felt that their appearance was incongruent with their relaxed and friendly mannerisms. It was a whole new and different world and the children were very curious about everything around them.

After Mr. James gathered their luggage, they all exited, hoping to find Mrs. James's father who had promised to be there. He was. A very short and stocky figure stood at the gate wearing a friendly and welcoming smile. The introductions all began after Mrs. James had embraced her father and cried tears of joy for seeing him. He was very friendly toward all of them and after giving each one a hug, they started the trip to the town of Arecibo, which is where he lived.

The trip was a long one. For five hours they bounced around in a large station wagon which the grandfather had rented. There was very little space left for the children once all their luggage was in. So they piled up on top of the luggage, stretched out across it, and onto each other, while trying not to hit the roof with every bump. The trip was real tough but no one complained. Every now and then one of the boys might say, "Come on, move your elbow, it's killing me," but that was about it. They behaved like few others might have and made themselves proud.

It was pitch black when they arrived at a small house in the countryside surrounded by fields of what later they would find out was sugarcane. The children were all quite timid and very curious. They had understood nothing of what was spoken during the long drive, since the main conversation was held in Spanish. No one except Mrs. James understood what was being said and only occasionally would she translate something for them. The five children and the baby in Sophia's arms were all huddled together tightly, while the car was being unloaded and the Spanish rattled on and on.

Finally, they were all invited into the tiny house. It was a house like none Sophia had ever seen. Its white windows were made out of horizontal, aluminum slats that opened with a little crank handle. The bedrooms were right off of the small main living area and had no doors to them. Instead, they were guarded by long, and what once were colorful, curtains. Concrete floors were covered by what appeared to be large, smooth gravel tiles and their opaque and indifferent color bore the markings of having been scrubbed many times. From the ceiling, in the center of the main room hung a bare light bulb from a thin and cob webbed wire. The walls were dirty with neglect and the accumulation of time. In the middle of the room stood an old woman that must have been shy of four feet and very round. Her ankles were visible below her long skirt and were twice their size with swelling. When she moved it was more like a torturous shuffle than a walk. Besides her heavy weight the old woman was burdened with a large hunchback, which made it hard for her to turn her head. Her tanned face was wrinkled beyond imagination and there were large bags beneath her small, unexpectedly, sky-blue eyes. She did not have a friendly, or kind looking face. In fact, in the eyes of a child she was quite a scary-looking person. From the first moment they met her, she made it clear, not by words but gestures that they were not welcome and that she was not happy to have them there. The children stood huddled, petrified and muted. Suddenly Sophia realized that she was not the only one in shock. With the baby still in her arms, the rest of them were hanging on to her dress with whitened knuckles and their young eyes so very wide with curiosity and fear.

It was Karen on that very first night, a year and half younger than Sophia, who unknowingly gave the James family their first alert signal. Had it not been lost in time and circumstance, Mr. James might have plucked up his family and left immediately, but no one saw the signal or no one wanted to see it.

"Mommy, Mommy please, I've got to go potty now," said Karen with urgency.

At the sound of this petition a great commotion ensued among the many people that had been arriving. Sophia could see a roll of toilet paper traveling from the back of the house from hand to hand toward Karen. Finally the roll was given to Karen and suddenly she was being led out of the room and out the back door! Sophia, who had seen her exit, was completely bewildered and did not understand what was going on. The frenzied sound of loud, cackling laughter was so foreign to her and the toothless smiles speaking words she didn't understand as they grabbed her hair and touched her dress was unnerving. Almost as quickly as she had left, little Ketty, which was Karen's nickname, returned crying and demanded that Sophia go with her. Immediately, Sophia handed the baby to her Dad and grabbed Karen's hand. Out into the dark night they went, guided by another girl their own age. The night air was humid on Sophia's skin and the moon was covered by a cloud adding to the night's darkness. They had just enough light for her to see the path they were to follow. After a few more steps the smell of the outhouse became their guide. Ketty cried harder as they got closer. Sophia put her arm around her little sister and felt like crying with her. She wouldn't; crying never helped.

"Sophia, is that the potty? Is that where we're supposed to go?"

"I think so Ketty, I don't see any other place."

"But it stinks so bad."

"Look, I'll help you. You just kinda lean over the seat and let it out while I hold your hand so you don't fall in."

"Oh, Sophia, I want to go home. I don't want to be here," Karen cried.

"Home is too far away. Now don't sit down. It might be full of mess or something."

At that point they opened a squeaky, rickety half door that didn't make it to the floor nor to the roof, it just hung somewhere in the middle covering the essentials. As soon as they opened the door to the little shack, the stench hit them full on. Cockroaches dived back into the black hole and the girls knew they had arrived at the wrong place.

That first night, five of the six children shared a double size bed and that night Sophia prayed that her father would soon take them back home. Back home to California.

The next few days were absorbed in discovering the many new things that were to be found on a tropical island. The warm climate invited flowers to grow everywhere, no designed pattern or landscaping, just literally everywhere. There was a whole array of new fruits to be discovered and tasted. And then there was the sugarcane. Crops of sugarcane occupied field after field and absorbed the lives of the people of that region. The island was truly innately beautiful and that helped uplift the family from its initial shock.

Sophia's maternal grandfather was not poverty stricken as most that lived around them. For one he owned a small grocery store that supplied the neighborhood with all essentials. Also, he owned much land on the island and had several homes. Sophia soon came to realize that the house where they were staying was one of the nicest around. Most of the surrounding dwellings were not of concrete, as the one he had built for his mother, but shacks built of wood with leaky tin roofs. Her grandfather was indeed a devoted son who put his mother's comforts and needs before anyone else's, including his own. In fact his latest almost wife—for he never actually married—who had borne him four sons, lived in a tiny wooden house. Their arrangement was rather strange as he only slept at that house on weekends, spending weekdays in his mother's house, so that she wouldn't be lonely. The grandfather had a total of ten children. Nine were sons and Sophia's mother was the only daughter. Every time one of his children married he would give them a piece of land, around three acres, and help them build on it. Because of this, the Risorios seemed to form a clan, all living close by. With so many sons, the Risorio clan begot Risorios. To Sophia it seemed that her supply of cousins was endless. Sophia was extracting many lessons from the new environment. The amount of poverty she could see was a great lesson but more of a lesson was the fact that people didn't seem to be aware of it.

An outhouse or latrine and an outdoor bathhouse for taking showers were all anyone had in that part of the island. Indoor plumbing had yet to arrive. However Sophia's grandfather and neighbors felt very rich, for electricity and running water had just made it to them a couple of years before. A faucet out in the yard was the miracle that several families shared. Life was dealt in buckets: a bucket for cooking, a bucket for washing dishes outdoors on a filthy slab of concrete, and a tilting bucket for showers. Most people were illiterate, any vehicle was a jalopy owned by a "rich" person, and superstitions abounded. However, the gentle people of Puerto Rico made merry of anything and everything was an excuse to make merry.

For Sophia, Puerto Rico was like a different planet. Her father was also shocked by the backwardness of the place and the situation in which he had put his family. Angry arguments were a constant between Sophia's parents. He felt deceived by his wife. However, it was not true. She had not deliberately deceived him. Mrs. James was an uneducated person herself and had fantasized all the troubles away. In her mind she was convinced that modernization would have arrived in her little town, as it had everywhere else. When Mrs. James's mother had taken her off the island, years earlier, it was in search of a better life. They were striving to get away from their hopeless existence. However, time played its game on Mrs. James and so many of the things that she had tried to escape from were forgotten—or replaced by unrealistic fantasies. She too, was silently and hopelessly disappointed to see that her old home was nearly as she had left it, forgotten by time.

Sophia's grandfather Casiano, was a respected man in their small *barrio*. Being the owner of a grocery store, owning some land, and being literate, all gave him stature and prestige amongst his neighbors. He enjoyed politics and was a stout republican, thus very pro-United States. He hoped that the island would one day become the fifty-first state and exhibited flags and mementoes to that effect. His favorite pastime was cock fighting which was the national pastime of the island. Cock fighting was practiced throughout all the rural areas and it fascinated Sophia. It was not an inexpensive sport, as fighting cocks were worth a lot of money. These special birds required much attention and only a disciplined individual could care for them. Every morning, of every single day, just before light, Casiano would bathe his fighting roosters. They were beautiful birds that required devotion and Casiano, like every cock owner, devoted a lot of time to them. The cocks were groomed and preened constantly. The one faucet that existed in the yard had been placed at about three feet off the ground, with the cleaning of the cocks in mind. Many times Sophia got up early in the morning, still dark, to watch him wash the birds. He would hold them tight under an arm and dunk them under the rushing cold and fresh water. Allow them to shake and dunk them again. He did it in a ritualistic manner, counting the times he dunked each bird and each bird was dunked the exact same amount of times. He had about a dozen cocks and after bathing each one he would dry them, massage them profusely and exercise them. Only after each one had received the same amount of everything, would he return it to a cage and feed it. Each cock had its feathers removed from its legs and Sophia would watch in amazement as he plucked and plucked until none were left. Then he would begin to file down the spur or the *espuela* which was the cock's main weapon. The huge spur that protruded from the inner sides of what was the ankle area of a rooster's foot, was filed to a sharp point. Like a knife it could easily puncture a hole into its opponent's torso when placed in a fighting ring. During the day Casiano would visit the roosters and go through a "spooking" exercise that was meant to train them to be fierce. Fighting roosters were very fierce, and when Casiano handled them, they all had their pointed nail wrapped in a small rag to avoid being hurt or hurting him. He would also watch out for their beaks as a swift peck would easily draw blood from his arms if he weren't careful. Those fierce fighting cocks were of great beauty. Bright reds, orange, blue and green colors were on display in the long plumage around their necks. When they were placed in the fighting ring they would attack by jumping and kicking their feet forward as if trying to poke the other bird with their *espuela*. However, when watching a fight, it was their flying plumage which mostly captivated Sophia. Too soon the beauty of strength and swiftness was replaced by flying blood turning the whole affair of cock fighting into an ugly sight for the young girl. The beautiful birds would become bloodied around their heads from the pecking and their colorful plumage would turn dark, wet and sticky, taking all remnants of color with it. They fought to their death and in a few moments a magnificent specimen would be reduced to a heap of non-moving feathers. For Sophia it was hard to understand how her grandfather, who got up so early every morning to care for the birds, could so easily send them off to be pecked to death. If his bird won the fight, he won the purse. However if his bird lost, he would shrug, scratch his head and laugh.

From the roosters Casiano would head over to the cows and begin milking. The cows were not as novel to Sophia as the roosters were. Nevertheless, it was her opportunity to learn how to milk them. Whenever she approached her grandfather, while he was milking a cow, he would point the cow's teat at her and the stream of milk would fly. The distance milk could travel, after one knowledgeable tug on a teat of a full udder, was impressive.

The first summer there, yielded an unlimited amount of things to learn about on the island. On one hot summer day, Don Casiano called all children within sight to approach him. Everyone gathered round him to find out what was going on. He was out to hire anybody that was willing to do a little work. He would pay them a few coins to pick annatto seeds. Sophia was willing to do the picking. The fee was a quarter an hour. She was game and agreed to do the picking before she even knew what *achiote* was. Everyone laughed at her and pointed to a very large bush nearby. Casiano walked over to it and picked from a branch a fat looking, oval pod. It was more or less the size of an egg and on its surface it had soft thick protrusions that looked like long, thick hairs. It was a weird looking thing that hung all over the tree. Sophia had noticed it earlier and expected it to bloom. With time Sophia would learn that it was one of the islands most prized condiments. Puerto Rican cooking does not happen without *achiote*. The pod contained hundreds of small, bright, moist, red achiote seeds. The seeds were mostly used to add coloring to sauces and rice. It gives food a reddish orange appearance and definitely adds a distinct flavor to the cooking. Sophia was hired on the spot as the grandfather knew that she would be an avid and hard worker. Early the next morning she was out with an old wooden ladder, pulling the *achiote* pods off the tree, and filling a basket with them. She wore old clothes, and was advised that by the end of the day she would be red from head to toe from the *achiote* picking. Any clothing touched by *achiote* would be stained forever. With her braids crisscrossed as a crown on the top of her head, to help her stay cool, she wore tennis shoes without socks, an old t-shirt, and pants. The pod of the *achiote* is furry and while picking, if any of the fur comes off and falls on the picker's face, the itching begins. After a while the itching combined with the hot sun and sweat can make a picker quite miserable. Soon the *achiote* picker's face would take on a bloodied appearance, as red hands—too many times—would reach up, trying to relieve the torture. Sophia was red everywhere by the end of the day. She had worked real hard and taken every pod off the few trees around. Casiano had come by a few times throughout the day to see how she was doing and would laugh to see how stubborn and determined she was to finish the task. At the end of the day, with two and half dollars in her pocket, she limped away to scrub the red off, determined to never do that sorry job again.

Though Sophia and her siblings were learning about life on an island, the desire to return home to California was foremost in their thoughts. The children would huddle around Sophia and Bobby would ask, "When are we going back home? Sophia, I really miss home." It was a question that had no answer. As the weeks went by, the possibilities of leaving the island became dimmer. Plans that would keep Sophia's family there, for many years to come, were taking shape. For one, their car was bouncing somewhere out in the ocean, making its way to them and secondly, the grandfather, trying to help them get out of the little house, came forward with an acre of land encouraging Mr. James to build on it. Too soon, Mr. James decided that he would build and voiced his decision to the family. It was not happily accepted by the children and Sophia led the gang in whining and begging their father to return them to California. It all fell on deaf ears. They were to stay in Puerto Rico.

Work on the property began immediately. Sophia's father along with several workers or *obreros*, had gone to work on clearing the land. Within two weeks the foundation was laid and the building site became the new-found gathering place for neighbors. Everyone was in awe at the speed with which things were happening. On the sleepy island of Puerto Rico, everything happened, *mañana*, tomorrow, tomorrow.

Houses on the island, if not of wood, were made of cement blocks. One block placed on top of another formed a thick, solid wall that was most appropriate for the tropical climate. Once a house was finished the blocks served as a great buffer keeping the coolness within and the scorching heat outside. Also, cement blocks held strong against severe tropical storms and hurricanes which frequently hit the Caribbean. However, Mr. James, a builder out of California, was not used to building with blocks, so he began building the home with a wooden frame and would subsequently use sheetrock for the interior. Soon Mr. James realized that to build this way on the island of Puerto Rico, at that time, was going to require much imagination. There was no such thing as sheetrock on the island. Being of the mindset that one did not let a little thing like sheetrock stand in ones way of the primary objective, he improvised and built the house in a rather fascinating way.

The first step was to recruit all of his children and have them collect bottle caps. Day after day the children searched alongside dirt roads, near trash areas around bars and little stores picking up every bottle cap in sight. Unintentionally, they were doing the biggest cleanup act that region of the island had ever seen. They were ridding it of beer caps *Cerveza Corona* and *Cerveza India*, Coke, 7UP, Malta, Royal Crown, Kola Champagne—whatever caps they could find. Before the house was finished, thousands of them were used.

Secondly, he went off in search of cardboard boxes. He would open the box and use it as flat cardboard. Next, he bought rolls and rolls of chicken wire. The idea was that he would place cardboard onto the wooden structure and on top of the cardboard he nailed the chicken wire. That is where the bottle caps came in to play. He inserted a cap in between the wire and the cardboard and then nailed it down. This was slowly done by stages on both sides of the wooden structure. The purpose of inserting the bottle caps in between the wire and cardboard assured that the wire was kept lifted off the cardboard and therefore when he was ready to apply cement it would have something to grab on to. The concept was actually quite ingenious and it caught the attention of everyone around. The *Americano*, as he was called, was doing his thing his way, and everyone around seemed anxious to see how the house would look in the end.

Since arriving on the island Sophia had met all of her maternal relatives. There were many. Almost anyone real young was a cousin and anyone a little older was an aunt or an uncle. All of them were very nice to the James family and took pride in telling everyone that these *Americanos* were their relatives. Of all the cousins and family, there were two girls, Sylvana and Erica, that were Sophia's favorites. Sylvana was the eldest and the prettiest by far. She was a year older than Sophia and had a long, curly braid of jet black hair. Erica was Sophia's age, a tomboy of sorts, who mostly was a tag along, as she wasn't very mature. The two girls, the youngest of four sisters, lived in a small wooden house close by, and with them Sophia learned all about what it was to be a girl growing up in that region. They helped her learn Spanish by writing out the lyrics to popular songs on the radio. With the written words Sophia, who loved to sing, would memorize the songs, not even knowing what they were about. Nevertheless, she would sing them as if she knew the language fluently.

One day, shortly after arriving on the island, Sophia played a prank on her grandfather. She walked up to him and, upon seeing her, he asked her in Spanish as he did not know English, his usual question,

"Have you learned Spanish yet?"

She smiled wide and said, "*Si*," and then proceeded to sing a whole song to him in Spanish with near-perfect pronunciation. The old man looked perplexed and quite impressed and went on to say, "You sure did learn fast."

Sophia smiled again and said, "*Si*."

He added, "Your pronunciation is terrific."

She smiled again and said, "*Si*."

At that he smiled back and said, "How is it that you have learned Spanish so quickly?" When she said, *Si*, he laughed out loud and shook his finger at her saying, "You sure had me fooled."

The house that her cousins lived in was like many around, however it was the first of its type that Sophia had ever seen inside. The small, wooden house sat high up on stilts and five concrete steps led up to a small porch with a railing. The walls were made of single horizontal boards that not always fit well and so there were cracks. Where a knot in the wood had fallen out, a hole would be there. The front door was small and someone like Mr. James, who stood just over six feet tall, had to bow his head to enter.

Once in the main living room, which was a very small space, one could see the cooking area toward the back and beyond it a window. This window served another purpose as well as it was geared to be the area where the family washed their dishes. The window consisted of two shutters that opened outwardly from the center. Built on to the ledge of the window was a wide shelf covered in tin that supported two basins, one for soapy water and one for rinse water. The rest of the small space was where the dishes dripped dry. Only one person could fit in that space so there was no sharing the task. The person there was usually the hard working Panchita, the adopted daughter. The containers that held the soapy water and the rinse water were not actual bowls. They were *guiras*, huge, brown, tropical seeds that grew abundantly. As soon as the gourds were big enough, they were picked, carefully cut in half—all contents emptied from them—and set out to dry. They made for reliable bowls, just as good as plastic. Things like this mesmerized Sophia. She was aware of what she was seeing. She understood that these people lived in extreme poverty, but she also could see the practicality of it all and the recycling that was going on. She looked beyond the surface and accepted the people for themselves and not their possessions.

After two months on the island their big, green, shiny 1959 Plymouth Savoy 4-door sedan finally arrived. It had been shipped from Florida at great expense and never was an investment more worthwhile. Their car was a salvation. It gave them freedom they sorely needed and the opportunity to pile in and learn more about what was beyond their surroundings. With the arrival of the car, Mr. James was as excited as the children. The coast line was breathtaking with inviting beaches everywhere and almost every weekend they'd swim in the ocean. Different cousins came along and the car would be packed up until it seemed it might burst. However, no one cared if they were squashed during the ride; the fun ahead was always worth it.

The interior of the island was very mountainous and not easily accessible because the roads were narrow, cliff-hangers. Nevertheless, to go up into the lush rain forests adorned with beautiful orchids was exciting. National parks had picnic tables and caves were in abundance. These caves were not equipped for tourists; they were untouched and natural. Often the James kids would dare creep into the darkness of one, go in a few steps, and come out screaming because someone slid a cold wet hand up a shirt or brushed someone's leg with a light stick.

The countryside was the best. It was where one could see for miles and miles the greatest achievement of the people they lived amongst. The calming sight of the hunter green colored sugarcane was the most beautiful sight of all. The tall, beautiful fields of cane gave the island beauty, gave the island work and gave the island its greatest income. Sugar was their life and there was a true sweetness about the coexistence of people and their cane. There was a respect, a caring, and a preservation of traditions that never died as long as the cane lived.

However, the car's arrival, more than for recreational purposes, was instrumental in facilitating the building effort. To jump in it and take off for the hardware store made things so much easier than having to go out and stop a public car. Time and money were at a premium in the lives of the James family, even though it seemed that everyone else around them managed to take in a *siesta*.

Weeks turned into months and the family continued in the small house that belonged to the grandfather. In the room where the children slept, another bed had been placed. With the placement of that second bed the room was completely filled, so it was a matter of climbing up onto the bed from the curtained doorway. For the parents, Mr. James was allowed to build a temporary partition in the kitchen, the size of a bed, which gave them a place to sleep. There they slept with little Evy. Evy at this time was only five months old and on many nights her cries could be heard throughout the small sleeping house.

Soon Mr. James faced reality and acknowledged that he was running out of money. Getting his family into the new house was going to have to wait for him to come back with more. With the promise of only making a short trip, he took a boat off the island and ended up going to Madagascar. He had been gone one week when Sophia became seriously ill. A pain in her right side made her moan and her eyes and skin had taken on a yellowish tinge. She became very weak and lay in bed day after day complaining to her mother, whenever she was near. Mrs. James at first, knowing Sophia to be a strong girl, thought that whatever it was would go away. However, after a week Sophia was at a standstill and could not get up. Seeing her color look so awkward and ugly Mrs. James finally took her to a doctor. The diagnosis was serious and immediate.

"Hepatitis, Señora James, that is what your daughter has."

"What is that? Is it bad?"

"Yes, it is a serious condition that will keep her in bed for a minimum of seven weeks. Her liver has been compromised and is swollen; she must take medication and stay in bed so that her liver does not worsen. This is life threatening, señora; you must take good care of this little girl."

"Mrs. James, looked afraid and worried, "But…how did she get this?"

"The girl ate something unsanitary; you must make sure that she is in a clean environment, where food is carefully prepared. Every time you use a bathroom you must wash your hands before touching food."

Mrs. James's eyes were wide as if not understanding and the Dr. looked at her and snapped in clear Spanish, "She ate ¡*Mierda, Señora*! Something that had filth on it!"

Mrs. James looked disgusted and said, "My God that is terrible; I don't know what to say."

"Don't say anything," said the doctor showing disgust of his own. "Just make sure that things get cleaned up and make sure that you keep this child away from others. Hepatitis is contagious."

The seven weeks in bed were eternal for Sophia. She was placed in the area that her father had partitioned off in the kitchen. It was where she best could be away from others. Though cooking continued only steps away, done mostly by the old great grandmother, Sophia lay in bed with the curtain drawn trying to not bother at all. She spent many hours drawing and many hours reflecting on how the world that she had entered was so different than the world she was from. She understood how she had become ill and viewed this episode as yet another indication of how they should leave the island as soon as possible. Sophia knew that her family was a great imposition on the people of this little house. The great grandmother worked tirelessly cooking for everyone in that tiny furnace of a kitchen.

From what Sophia could see, cleanliness was unknown to most of the people around her. The old great grandmother knew nothing about personal hygiene and always smelled of urine. When she wanted to urinate she would shuffle outdoors, widen her stance and anyone present could see a pool of pee foaming around her feet. It was grotesque and Sophia would remember that one of the few times she saw the old lady laugh, was when she peed in front of Sophia and saw the little girl open her mouth in shock. Grime and filth were everywhere. Dirty dishes were washed outside on a concrete slab that held two large gourds, one with a little soapy water and the other for rinsing. However, too soon the soapy water would turn brown and murky and then sour and smelly but dishes continued to be washed there. The old lady herself had never known anything about the outside world. She had been conceived from the rape of a native girl by a blue eyed Spaniard. She lived her life within the confines of ignorance and then was raped herself, producing the one son that was Sophia's grandfather. Sophia knew how she had gotten hepatitis; she was just glad that she was the only one.

Six months later her daddy returned to find that his wife was desperate, hating the conditions they were in, and neglecting the children. Sophia, completely recuperated from the hepatitis, ran around with Karen, their long hair in a mangle and most of the time with bare feet. The boys had holes in their pants and looked like orphans. Mrs. James on the other hand, had joined politics. It was an outlet for her, a way to escape the dreariness of the world she had put her family in. She invested much of the monies sent home in a wardrobe for herself. Sophia's father was alarmed with all of this. Going away to work was not optional but while he was gone he was counting on Sophia's mother to hold down the fort, and do the best she could. True enough that the circumstances in which he expected her to be her best were appalling, but mothering her children was her duty.

The day after Mr. James arrived they all piled into the car and made the five hour trip into San Juan, the capital of the island. The mission: to buy a television. The children were all ecstatic with joy. Bobby more than any of them, had voiced missing his Saturday morning cartoons. For Sophia it was a touch of civilization coming back into their lives and she was glad for it. Upon returning to the old great-grandmother's home with the television, Mr. James presented it as a gift from him to her. He told her that he hoped she liked it and that later, when they moved out, he would get another one for his family. The kind gesture was met with some opposition. She wasn't sure about having other people come into her house. After all, these were strangers. The James's however, decided to let the television speak for itself and once it was plugged in, she was the most fascinated of them all. Bringing the TV into her world brought about changes in her that were witnessed by everyone. The old lady took to putting on nice clothing in the evenings after her shower. She would be in a hurry to finish up in the kitchen and sit down as family members arrived each evening at eight o'clock sharp to watch yet another episode of a soap opera. She, like everyone else, was soon hooked on the televised novels known as *telenovelas*. At times she'd laugh out loud and now she had found something to talk about during the day. Yes, the television had transformed her in many ways bringing into her life a world full of things she had no idea existed. However, it was more than amusing when sitting down to watch her soap opera with everyone else, she would check the girls and admonish them, "Sit down nicely. Can't you see that he can look up your dress?"

The girls would softly giggle and quickly adjust their dresses to a position below their knees.

The simple inclusion of a TV in their life enhanced it considerably. However it did not diminish in any way Mr. James's determination to finish the house and get everyone into it as soon as humanly possible. Sophia's father worked day and night and as fast as he could, but it was not fast enough to avoid sharing the small house with yet another visitor.

A long-lost brother of Sophia's mother returned to the nest to visit his old father. Ismael was a handsome man, with dark hair. In many ways he resembled his sister. He was about thirty-five years old and had been away from the island for the last fifteen years. During that time no one knew his whereabouts, or what he made of his life. He just left the island and now out of the blue he showed up on his father's doorstep. He was welcomed and everyone showered him with kindness and attention. All members of his extended family immediately came to visit him and welcome him back after so many years.

The new uncle was friendly and full of fascinating stories. The children sat with wide eyes, as close as they could to the grownups, hoping that he would throw a little English their way. For Sophia it was a joy to hear someone speak of the mainland. Being tucked away out in the countryside of the tiny island, made the years in California almost seem unreal, like an intangible dream. That night the children were allowed to stay up a little later. Yet, when the order was given to go to bed, without hesitation they all marched off.

The new uncle was to sleep on a couch in the living room, which in effect was only a breath away. Sophia was in a deep sleep when she was gradually brought out of it by the awareness of a hand slipping up her nightgown and tugging at her underpants. There was a form bending over her, she could feel the person's breath on her cheek. Terror grabbed hold of her so tightly that she couldn't move and felt paralyzed. Her eyes were glued shut and her breath seemed to be caught in her throat. She could hear herself screaming inside, but no sound was coming out. The hand had gotten inside of her underwear and a finger was being thrust up into her vagina. Finally with a burning sensation in her tender tissues a whimper fought its way out of her throat and the hand immediately withdrew. She still lay there paralyzed with fright as she felt the person reaching out toward her sister Karen. Karen reacted quicker; she cried out just with the tugging of the underpants, and the hand and the person were gone. Sophia lay completely awake and trembling. She knew who it had been. She had clearly heard the couch make noises as the new uncle returned to his sleeping place.

The next morning Sophia awoke her sister and asked her if she had remembered what had happened during the night. She hadn't and when Sophia told her, she giggled. Karen was immature for her eight years and hadn't understood the importance of what had happened. Now Sophia began to cry, and grabbed Karen tightly by the arm.

"Karen, what that man did, sneaking around when Daddy and Mommy were asleep to touch our privates is a very, very bad thing. He is a dangerous man and so you had better stay away from him. Don't get near him ever again Karen. Are you listening to me?" Karen's smile had completely disappeared and she looked frightened as she nodded her head at Sophia.

Sophia took longer than ever getting ready for school that morning. First of all she didn't even want to go out of the room. She knew that he was right on the other side of that ugly cloth curtain and she was afraid to look at him. She finally went out of the room and avoided meeting his eyes. She made her way out to the tiny outhouse, which her father had improved by putting a real toilet seat around the hole, and when she urinated the stinging made her cry out loud. She was so afraid and ashamed she didn't know what to do. So she did the only thing she could do, which was to go to her mother.

Her mother listened with unbelieving ears. "It can't be," she said "he'd never hurt you. He's my brother."

"But Mommy, it stung bad when I tinkled." At this she reacted turning pale, worried and scared all in one. She rounded up Karen and grabbing each girl by an arm took them over to their Dad, who had been working since dawn on the house. She made them wait at some distance while she spoke to their father. In a matter of seconds Mr. James was up, looking mad and coming toward the girls.

"Sophia, my God, why didn't you scream?" He grabbed her by the shoulders and was shaking her.

"I was too scared Daddy, I couldn't move," replied Sophia with tears sliding down her face. At this explanation Karen let out a soft giggle and Mr. James's hand flew out and hit her on the side of the head. It wasn't a hard hit, but the smile on Karen's face disappeared in a hurry. Sophia's father was enraged. He dropped the hammer that was in his left hand and in quick strides made it over to where the man still lay sleeping. Sophia's mother was calling out to him, trying to calm him down, but nothing could. He looked like if he were going to kill him. Sophia and Karen, peering through a front window, saw when their Dad grabbed him by the shirt and punched him. The old great grandmother was screaming and everything was chaos. The uncle tried to get off the floor and Mr. James punched him again. At this point, Mrs. James was able to hold him back as, between swearing and cursing, the father warned him to never get near his children again.

It was a silent ride to the doctor's office. Sophia's father insisted that she be checked by a physician to confirm the extent of what had happened. In the meantime he was determined to take action. "I am going to press charges and send the dirty son of a b---- to jail."

The doctor confirmed that little Sophia had indeed been molested and that Karen had not been. He was a kind doctor and spoke with Sophia reassuring her that she was not to be blamed and that she could continue to grow normally, etc., etc. This ugly and sad incident changed Sophia's outlook in many ways. She became more guarded and less trusting and more than ever hoped that her daddy would see the signs. There were so many warning signs and reasons to pack them up and take them back home to the US. But, all signs were ignored and the uncle left the island, as if nothing had happened. In the meantime, a house that should have never been started and would tie them there for a long time was getting finished.

Not considering for a moment the option of leaving the island, Mr. James focused with renewed fury on building the house. Because of his desire to get the children into the house as fast as humanly possible, he went ahead and moved everyone in before it was finished. From the outside it looked pretty much done. The cardboard and wire had been placed and he was able to apply the plaster. Once it dried he then had painted the house yellow and orange. The design was most attractive for a tropical environment. The rectangular shape was wrapped around on three sides by a porch that boasted arches. At about every eight feet there was an arch. Making the arches had been yet another trick Mr. James pulled off. He had taken thin wood and soaked it, softening it so it would become pliable and bend. Everyone was in disbelief and even jealous at how he had so quickly been able to make such of a pretty house and the only one around with arches. At that time, no one had them. Though the inside was only a shell, nothing mattered; everyone was relieved to be there and hoping for better days to come.

But life in general had become a chimera, a mirage, a wish for something better that would never be. They all played the game pretending that it was better, but in reality—close beneath the surface—their world was crumbling. They were on a slippery slope heading in the wrong direction and braving it. They were doomed; they had not changed course when they could have.

While the house was being built and the children were running around looking for bottle caps, their first year of school was being completed on the island of Puerto Rico in the little town of Arecibo. Her cousin Erica, who was in Sophia's same classroom, had helped her during that first year of school. With Sophia speaking whatever Spanish she had picked up that first summer, she felt lost half the time. She did not understand what teachers wanted when they pointed at her. Assignments also would have been a nightmare without Erica translating in her halting English.

Through interaction with other children, the Jameses soon were learning the language. Spanish is very much a phonetic language, so words are pronounced just as they are written. However, on the island it is a *Spanglish* that is spoken, a mixture of Spanish with English words thrown in every now and then. If you wanted to speak about the roof, you pointed to the roof and said roofo. It sounded funny, but it worked. Many a time, during that first year, the kids took their English, added an *o* and called it Spanish.

The James children were something of a novelty in the country town. People were kind to them and very giving, and at school, teachers were considerate and understanding of their struggle. When it was learned that Sophia could play the accordion, she was invited to participate in her first Christmas show. It was a thrill for her and everyone applauded and laughed as they stamped their feet to the strange polka music. To be in a foreign place was tough for the children so teachers made them feel welcome by practicing their own English with them. Although, school was quite a challenge because of the language barrier, Sophia did not suffer. She was smart, quick to learn, and her fourth grade math was far beyond what was being taught in her fifth grade. As

Erica helped Sophia by translating, Sophia helped Erica with math and, before they knew it, nearly a year had passed.

Life did improve for the James family once they were in the house; and Mr. James continued to improve it daily. There were four bedrooms just like in their homes back in California. The girls would share one, the older boys would share one, one for the babies and one for parents. The layout of the kitchen was open and had a counter top in between it and the dining room. All windows had screens and both doors had screen doors. However, the greatest thing about the house, even though it was far from finished, was the fact that it had running water. The children were able to use a real toilet. To not have to go into the awful, smelly outhouse and to once again have a few basic necessities in their life was an improvement. Sophia thought that the house had real possibility; it just was in the wrong place. Location, location, location was an important concept that Sophia became aware of very early in life.

As time went by, money ran out and soon Mr. James was talking about "When I get back . . . ." Sophia, who by now was ten, was very mature for her age. Not much got by her without her understanding or knowing when to pick up her ears. The pattern was clear to her. Go off to sea, bring back money, stay till it was gone and then leave again. She really did not like the last part and would have loved to have her daddy find work on the island. She was sure that some company would want a smart American, already on the island, to work for them. At times she would tell her daddy what she thought, but he had little self-confidence and allowed his scarred face to unnerve him and prevent him from going into uncharted waters. There was more than the concern of missing him. Sophia knew that the relationship between her parents was changing. Sophia's mother had become bolder in her native home and, though that was a good thing, it was an unbalanced boldness. It was not used to shield, guard, and protect her family but for her own independence. Sophia knew that it was too early for her mother to be gone all the time playing politics. The children were too small and they really needed her at home taking care of them. So Sophia would kiss her father goodbye and in her heart silently make a prayer for him as well as one for her mother.

Once Mr. James had left, Sophia spent a lot of time with her cousins, Sylvana and Erica. With school out and summer ahead, the children only had time on their hands. One day Erica, bored and looking mischievous said to Sophia, "Hey, Sophia, want to try smoking?"

Sophia looked surprised and said, "Are you serious?"

"Sure I am, we could do it tomorrow night when everyone is watching the *telenovela.*"

"My God, Erica, we could get caught and besides where are you going to get the cigarettes?" asked Sophia thinking that she had diffused her ambitions.

"I've got it all figured out, I just need a little help."

"What do you need me to do?" asked Sophia becoming curious.

"Well, we'll go to grandpa's store together and then you'll strike up a conversation with him. Once you've got his attention, I'll sneak around back and grab a pack."

"You mean we're going to steal them?"

"Sure, how else do you think we could get cigarettes, by just asking him? Hey, grandpa can you give Sophia and me some cigarettes so that we can go try them out? Of course not! He won't just give them to us, so we gotta take them. But don't worry Sophia, all you have to do is get his attention, I'll be the one that actually grabs them."

"Oh, Erica we don't really have to do this, do we? I mean, what if he catches us, can you imagine the trouble we'd be in?"

"Come on, Sophia let's do it. It'll be fun."

Sophia wasn't happy about the whole idea, but decided to please Erica. After, all Erica had always done anything Sophia wanted to do. The next morning Sophia had an upset stomach with the thought of having to go into the store and pull off a "job." The girls got together right after lunch and for hours schemed on how they would do it. It was around three o'clock in the afternoon of that sunny Saturday when they finally got enough guts to actually walk into the store to grab the cigarettes. Old Casiano was sitting on a bench just inside the counter with his beloved *Reader's Digest* in hand. *Reader's Digest* was his fountain of knowledge; it educated him and fed his ego. Few people around the barrio knew how to read, let alone have a book imported specifically for him to catch up on "intellectual" topics. Yes, the book was his life, and it actually gave him one. The two girls walked into the store through the back door. As they did so, Don Casiano, turned around in his seat and over his spectacles checked them out, acknowledged them with a small grunt, and turned back in his seat to continue his reading. The girls went up to the counter and looked at each other, with the look of... 'Well . . . do it!' Everything seemed perfect, the fact that he was immersed in his reading and that there were no patrons in the store at that moment. As the girls just stood there, the silence became heavier and they knew that any moment their grandfather was going to look up and ask them what they wanted. Sophia approached him, peered over his shoulder to see what he was reading, breathed in and said, "Grandpa, I'm going to sweep the store clean, OK?" The old man just nodded and Sophia hurried herself over to where the brooms were kept. Furiously, she attacked the job. The sound of her sweeping was the only sound made. She was focused on the task when Erica, who after a while had gone outside, caught her attention and nodded, indicating that she had accomplished the mission. This signal only made Sophia sweep harder. Guilt had her reverently devoted to the task which had created a light cloud of dust. When the store was nicely swept, she went up to her grandfather, who continued immersed in a story about crocodile hunting in Leticia, Colombia. She called out, "All done!" The old man jumped at the sound of her voice. The sweeping had become an agreeable, rhythmic, constant sound lost in the background. With the lack of customers and the good story, he was absorbed into another world, where lights flashed in the night searching for the roaming eyes of a crocodile lurking on the surface waiting to jump on him. Through eyes that appeared glazed over by rampant imagination, he distractedly waved his goodbyes.

It had been done. Erica was lying in the tall grass that was off to one side of the store, after she keeled over with laughter. "My God! You took forever. You swept the whole place, you dope. Ha, ha, ha. I thought you were going to ask for the mop!" She laughed even harder. Sophia wasn't laughing but instead patiently let Erica enjoy herself.

"OK, OK, so did you get them? She asked in a low voice. That only brought more laughter out of Erica.

"You mean you didn't even see me? Relax, Sophia. Look here." She lifted her skirt and retrieved the pack from the side of her underwear. Yes, she had them, a spanking new red and white box of Winstons.

Sophia reacted, "Put them away. Someone might see. So now, when are we going to smoke them?"

"Tonight when everyone is watching *'La Renuncia,'* I'll come over and get you." *La Renuncia* was the hottest soap opera ever made; at least that's what everyone seemed to think. In the little town of Arecibo, streets became deserted while it was airing. In factories, working places, public cars and in bars, laughter and raised eyebrows was heard and seen everywhere as people mulled over every episode bit by bit. The town loved their *telenovela* and since not everyone had a television it brought families and neighbors together every evening, for an hour of enthralling, often sappy—but wonderful—entertainment.

It was on such a night, when everyone was deep into the novel, that Erica came over to Sophia's house and the two of them slipped away.

"Where were you? I thought the novel was going to end and you didn't arrive."

"I told Mom I was going to visit you and so she gave me some *gandules* (pigeon peas) to shell. I did some and slipped away. We don't have too much time now."

"So, where are we going to do this?" asked Sophia

"How about if we hide in the sugarcane field?"

Sophia agreed and they both started running toward the field. The full moon overhead gave them light and they could see the proud cane glistening in it. As they approached the field they entered carefully as the almost ripe sugarcane stood tall and dense making it hard to penetrate. The leaf, like a blade, could slice ones skin if it caught it at just the right angle and would leave a person itching for days. With the light of the moon the girls easily picked their way through the cane to a safe place somewhere in the center. They crushed some stalks sideways to open a space where they knelt down, and both started giggling. Even though they were frightened of being caught, it was an adventure and they were really going to have their smoke. They quickly tried to quiet each other down for fear that their laughter might float over the sea of cane and tell tales.

"Ready?" asked Erica, once she had halfheartedly controlled her laughter.

"Let's do it." said Sophia.

Erica, now down to business, deftly opened the package and dealt out the two cigarettes. She lit one and handed it to Sophia. Then she lit another for herself. The two girls waited for each other and smiling inhaled a looooong deep one. Fire! Burning up, dying, Oh! My God! Explosion of coughs choked both of them as they gagged, spit, waved toward their mouth and throughout all of this an awful taste was developing in their taste buds. *So this was it*, thought Sophia.

"Erica," she said choking, and full of tears, "This is terrible, I can hardly breathe, this is the worst thing I've ever tasted in my life. I hate it. It's miserable." While Sophia was trying to regain composure, Erica on the other hand, succeeded at getting over that first breath of smoke reasonably well and had taken another puff.

While Sophia was complaining, Erica was starting to smile, "Oh, quit it, it's not that bad. That first taste wasn't the greatest, but you've got to give it a chance."

"To heck with that idea, I hate the stuff and I don't want anymore. Come on, let's go back in before we're missed anyway," said Sophia as she got up from her squatting position. Erica didn't budge, "You go ahead. I'm going to stay for a little while longer. Don't forget to cover for me, if someone mentions me."

"Whatever," said Sophia as she turned to leave the tight, uncomfortable enclosure.

It was almost nine thirty and Sophia went straight to bed. She had been disappointed with the experience. All of that planning to rip off their grandfather of those lousy cigarettes and then she'd almost choked to death on them. She vowed that would be the end of cigarettes for her. She would never be a smoker, period. Promising herself that she'd never be talked into something, she really didn't think was right, was the last thing she did before falling into a deep sleep.

The usual sounds did not wake her the following morning. Instead, there was a commotion that was loud and continuous. The urgency of the voices actually frightened her. She jumped out of bed and ran outside in pajamas. She could not believe her eyes. The whole sugarcane field was gone; it had literally gone up in smoke! Her shock had been quite authentic, but it only took her a few seconds to put two and two together. After that, she remained very much on the wings of conversations listening to the speculation of others. The conclusion was that no one had a guess in hell as to how the fire could have possibly started and Sophia was as mum as a corpse. After a conservative amount of time around the grownups, she went back inside got into her clothes and then went running out to find Erica. Sophia didn't have to make it to her cousin's house; Erica was standing at the blackened edge of the burnt fields along with a group of neighbors that were all giving their best guess as to how it could have happened.

"Those guys that went by speeding—they were drunk. One of them probably threw a lit cigarette," said one neighbor.

"Why you know that Doña Petra is losing it, maybe she started the fire on purpose, you know she's always trying to pick a fight." And so the gossip began with Erica standing right in the middle of it, agreeing with every possibility. As Sophia approached, Erica looked at her with a smile and winked. She was silently saying *shut up and smile*. After a while, Sophia and Erica left the crowd.

As soon as possible Sophia said, "What happened? How did it happen Erica? I can't believe it."

"Well . . . after you left, I went ahead and smoked myself three more cigarettes. You know, I'm a complete expert now. I'll show you later."

"Oh, no you won't." shot back Sophia. "Now, tell me how did the fire start? I still can't believe it!"

"Yeah, yeah; look, I was lighting my fourth one and my match kept going out on me. So, I decided to get a few dry leaves and make myself a bigger match. Well, the dry leaves went up so fast, and the ones nearby caught fire before I could do anything. I was so terrified, that I just started to run out. I couldn't stop the fire and I sure didn't want to be caught in it. I really am sorry this happened. You aren't going to tell anyone are you?"

"Tell anyone? Are you crazy? I don't know anything about this. You are the one that better keep your mouth shut," said Sophia angrily. "If you ever start boasting and it slips, I promise you I'll beat you up." Sophia stalked off; she was furious and had no intentions of sharing anything with Erica for a while.

7

MASK OF DECEPTION

"LA SOLEDAD" ~ "SOLITUDE"
La vida tiene sus decepciones, ~ Life has its disappointments,
Y alegrías que te ven guiando, ~ And joys that guide you,
Y con cada una de ellas, ~ And with each one of them,
Tu vida se va formando te vas formando. ~ Your life and you begin to form.
La soledad se acerca y te invita, ~ Solitude comes near and invites you,
A disfrutar de su paz y calma, ~ To enjoy its peace and calm,
Te promete compañía, ~ He promises you company,
Te cuidará, te vivirá, ~ Will take care of you, live off of you,
En silencio. ~ In silence.
Soledad ya no eres mi amigo. ~ Solitude you are no longer my friend,
Porque me quieres ahogada en llanto. ~ Because you want me drowning in sorrow.
Eres amante celoso como tú, ~ You are a jealous lover, like you,
No hay otro igual, Soledad. ~ There is no other, Solitude.

As soon as Mr. James departed, Mrs. James jumped with both feet right back into the political arena. She met a man who hosted a radio show and was running for mayor of Arecibo. With a wealth of experience acquired abroad, fluency in English, a husband working away that always sent a paycheck home allowing her to dress well, a nice car, and good looks, she was an attractive package. The man hired her on the spot to be his secretary. Since now she was a working woman, she had all the reason in the world to not be home around the noisy, always hungry and dirty kids. In the morning Sophia would get up and feed her sisters and brothers some cereal, while her mother looking like a model in yet another new outfit, would waltz out of her bedroom to ask, "How do I look?"

Sophia would try to smile and say, "Great!" in a joyful way, but she couldn't. Resentment was building and it grew with every passing day. Her mother was no longer the woman she loved as she was filled with her ego and no longer appeared to care about her little ones. She constantly depended, more and more, on Sophia to take care of the kids while she was out all day long "working." Since Sophia didn't know how to cook, canned food became the substitute for a nice, hot homemade meal. The old great-grandmother came to the rescue, as she could see the children motherless most of the time. She began cooking larger amounts of food every day and had the children file in every evening to eat. She criticized their mother for not tending to the children and with the eyes of one who had seen this before, would shake her head in shame. Regardless of her feelings for Mrs. James, for a while, the old great-grandmother became the true lifesaver for the children. Mrs. James, who had begun living a reckless life, used the old woman's kindness to her benefit. She spent even more time away, knowing that someone else had adopted a portion of what was supposed to be her responsibility. The protected and well-guided life that Sophia had lived in her first years was shattering before her eyes and she could do nothing about it. It was wrong, it wasn't fair. However, she at least had had the benefit of a mother and father for nine years. Baby Evy had none. She was just over a year old.

The relationship between mother and daughter grew more distant with each passing day. Sophia tried to be loving and kind to her small siblings, but there was so much anger building up in her. Her mother now was gone every day from morning till night. She was impeccably dressed all the time while the children looked more and more like abandoned orphans.

It was Sophia's eleventh birthday and the day had not started out any differently. As her mother prepared to leave, Sophia wondered if she had remembered it. Soon enough, Sophia was convinced that she hadn't.

With her usual, "Take care, everybody," she was out the door. Sophia's brothers and sisters did remember that it was her birthday and the day before had made cards, decorating them by sticking leaves on and drawing hearts and such. The children loved each other and though they did not see or understand as much as Sophia, they knew that these were bad times and so they clung together even more fiercely. The baby was now walking and after being prompted by Karen, she very proudly carried a rose, picked from someone's garden, and gave it to Sophia saying Fia!! Sophia treasured this rose and kept it for many years among the pages of one of her favorite stories, *The Adventures of Tom Sawyer*.

As it turned out, the birthday would have more than a lovely rose for which to be remembered. A neighbor by the name of Esther had heard about Sophia's birthday and decided to bake her a cake. She packed it up, along with her four children, and carried it over to the Jameses. It was a joy when the kids saw Esther at the door and they all laughed and hugged as she came in with her tribe. They all huddled around the cake and started to sing *Happy Birthday* in Spanish. For a moment Sophia was completely happy. Then Sylvana, her older cousin, dropped by and things chilled down real fast.

The pretty, dark-haired Sylvana had been unfriendly toward Sophia for the last few months. Sophia believed that it was jealousy though she couldn't understand why; nevertheless, recognizing she was a target she avoided her. It had become routine to hear Sylvana poking fun at Sophia's Spanish, or criticizing her clothing or making fun of her gait, her smile, her anything. On this day, Sylvana had heard the stream of laughter flowing from the James's house and showed up to poison the good time being had. She gave a small knock and opened the screen door entering without waiting for an answer. Screens were a novelty to everyone in the small town. People had never seen anything like them before and were quite fascinated when Mr. James ordered them from the mainland. As Sophia looked up and saw that the new arrival was Sylvana, the memory of the look on her face when she had first seen the screen door, made a smile creep onto Sophia's lips.

As their eyes met Sophia, who had begun cutting the cake, gave her a welcoming smile and said, "It's my birthday and Esther has made me a cake, would you like a slice?" Sylvana's eyebrows were beautiful; they were remarkably thick and jet black. Often she involuntarily arched them incredibly high almost forming a true question mark with them, whenever there was a question on her mind.

She did just that as Sophia spoke to her and replied, "No thank you, Sophia. You enjoy it, and Happy Birthday." She had actually sounded sincere and kind. Sophia's heart warmed and she smiled at her again. Big mistake! Sophia should have felt disaster coming and the extra smile only invited it head on. Sylvana made her way over to Sophia and now stood beside her.

"So, have you heard the latest?"

"About what?" Sophia asked as she continued to cut slices of cake for the others.

"Why about your mother?" Sophia stopped cutting. Esther listening to the exchange said, "Let me keep cutting that for you," taking the knife out of Sophia's hand.

"What do you have to say about my mother, Sylvana?"

"Well, that Don Francisco Rivera saw her at the *Pozita* today with her boyfriend. You know, her boss." Sophia's heart rate increased and she was beginning to feel heat rising in her face. "Anyway," continued Sylvana, "apparently he was all over her, in fact he saw . . ." and that was as much as she got out when Sophia, who had become crimson with pain and anger grabbed, at arm's length, a very ripe avocado that had been resting on the kitchen counter and smashed it into her face. Sylvana squealed, and removing a portion of the avocado mush from her face, proceeded to cover Sophia in it.

Karen jumped up to defend Sophia and said, "How dare you do that to my sister?" and ended up with a hair full. Little baby Evy, standing close by, started to cry and got some thrown into her hair too. It was a mess, avocado was thrown everywhere. Karen and Evy were crying and Esther who witnessed the whole thing, overhearing the ugly remark made by Sylvana, had gone outside while the avocado was being flung around and called out to Sylvana's mother. Aunt Luisa and Sylvana's eldest sister Sila came running and were out of breath when they reached what a few moments earlier had been a happy celebration. Sophia was on her knees consoling her baby sister Evy as she told Sylvana's mother what had happened.

Aunt Luisa glaring into Sylvana's eyes, took a quick glance at Esther who stood nodding her head saying, "Yes, that's how it happened." Sylvana's mother suddenly reached out and with her knuckles gave

Sylvana a good wallop on the head. She pushed her out the door and grabbing her by her thick braid, dragged her home. As they made their way down the lane, Aunt Luisa called out to her oldest daughter, "Sila, you stay and wash the girls' hair. Also, help pick up the avocado mess on the floor. When you've finished, I want you straight back at the house."

Sila took Karen out under a mango tree and started washing her hair with a hose. When she finished with her, she began with baby Evy. Sophia didn't have much to say while all of this was going on. She was angry and hurt. She felt at times her eyes welling up with tears and looking upwards she managed to keep them in. She knew she would cry but she didn't want to do it around anyone. If it was true that her mother was out making a fool of herself and all of them, she didn't want anyone to think she believed this possible, for even one minute. Though Sophia did hold her head high, until everyone left, there was fear in her heart.

Many nights when her mother returned late from "work," she would ask her, "Why do you come home so late?" Often the answers didn't make sense to her. Nevertheless, the thought of learning about a truth as ugly as the one she suspected would keep her from asking. The *Pozita* that Sylvana had mentioned was a small beach. It had a parking area which was a popular hangout for couples hiding from spouses, parents or teachers. It had a bad reputation and anyone seen at the *Pozita*, got just that.

On the other hand the beach itself was lovely. It was a small cove that harbored a deep, safe pool surrounded by high rocks making it a great place for diving. So though the *Pozita* had its dark reputation, it was visited by many because it was conveniently close to town and easy for anyone to have a quick swim. The James children had been there many times as it was where Mr. James had taken them to learn how to swim and dive.

That night, when it was ten o'clock and her mother still had not returned, Sophia decided that she would confront her. She needed the truth. What was going on? Was she in love with someone else? Did she not love her daddy anymore? What was she planning to do, if she was in love with someone else? A million questions gnawed at her brain and her stomach was upset with anxiety.

She opened the screen door and went outside to sit in a rocking chair, in a dark corner of the porch. Her hands were cold and clammy as she chewed on her fingernails and pulled at the cuticles. She thought of how messy the house was. They had cleaned up the mashed avocado that was thrown around, but the garbage had yet to be thrown out and clothes in the laundry area were piled in a smelly mound. She thought of how she had to get better organized so that the kids could help more and they could keep the house cleaner. Sophia sat quietly on the porch waiting and waiting. With her feet up on the seat of the rocker, she hugged her knees and cried. She tried to reason for an explanation; why was her mother so late? Didn't she care for any of them anymore? Had she gone crazy? Didn't her mother realize that she was only a little girl and that there were five younger than her that needed love and attention? Didn't she understand that Sophia couldn't do everything? That she didn't know how to do everything? Didn't she know that she wanted to play, to be hugged, to be listened to and laughed with? She scratched her lice-infected head and continued crying. She hated that selfish woman. She hated her, and though she tried to make her mind remember how kind and caring she could be, there was a mental block that would not allow that to happen. The kind memories seemed now very far away, the little bits of them belonging to some far away time.

The sound of the Plymouth brought her back to the dark corner on the porch. She had arrived! *Oh! My God! Please help me, please help me. Let there be some logical explanation. Please tell me that you love me and that there is nothing wrong and that it's all in my imagination*, were the only thoughts racing through her mind as her heart beat wildly and her knees felt weakened. The car door opened and the full moonlit night allowed Sophia to see her mother's high heeled shoes coming out, followed by a very shapely leg. Sophia had always considered her mother's legs as striking. She was wearing a snug-fitting, red, linen dress. It was a nice dress, one that enhanced her figure, thought Sophia.

She walked toward the porch carrying her purse and saw the little girl. "Why, Sophia, what are you doing out here? Why aren't you in bed? Is everyone all right? 'Oh! Music to my ears,' thought Sophia. Those were the caring questions that Sophia so badly wanted to hear. A concerned mother obviously couldn't be having boyfriends and be cheating on her father . . . .

"Mommy, I need to talk to you; it's real important and I don't want the other kids to hear, so that's why I waited for you out here."

"Well, hurry it up, I'm tired. What is it?" said Mrs. James lifting an eyebrow and looking impatient.

"Today was a pretty bad day for me, Mommy. Did you know that it was my birthday?" she asked, looking briefly into her mother's face and saw the look of surprise. Sophia quickly continued, "Well, there was so much to do around the house and I didn't know if maybe you had planned something special, so the kids and I were trying to clean up, when Esther and her kids arrived with a birthday cake she had baked for me. Anyway, the house was still a mess but there was nothing I could do at that point. Everyone was happy and singing *Happy Birthday* to me when Sylvana came over."

Sophia paused for air and tears started rolling down her face. Her mother, who had quietly been listening, squinted her face a little as if giving her full attention.

"Well, uhm, Sylvana said something terrible about you and a big fight started. All of us had mashed avocado all over us and everyone was screaming and crying so bad that Aunt Luisa and Sila came running over to see what was going on."

"Oh! For Christ sake," said her mother, putting her hand dramatically to her forehead. Sophia quickly taking another breath said, "Anyway, Sila helped Karen and Evy wash their hair and wash the avocado off. But . . . I haven't been able to get what Sylvana said to me out of my head."

"Nonsense!" said Mrs. James pulling cigarettes out of her purse. Thrusting one into her mouth she proceeded to light it as she looked into Sophia's face asking her, "Did Luisa actually come in? Did she see the mess the house is in?"

"You don't understand; we were all fighting. I had slapped Sylvana across the face and covered her in avocado, so Aunt Luisa came running in. Of course she came in and so did Sila."

In a low voice profanities started streaming from her mother's mouth. It surprised Sophia as she wasn't used to hearing her mother say bad words.

"Mommy, I don't know if they had time to see the house. They were trying to calm us down and to find out why we were fighting. When Sylvana repeated to her mother what she had told me every one became silent and then Aunt Luisa gave Sylvana another whack and took her home. Then she told Sila to wash our hair up and Sila did it outside under the mango tree."

Mrs. James in a matter-of-fact way, as if she didn't really care, asked, "So, what was it that Sylvana said?"

"She said that Don Francisco Rivera was at the *Pozita* today and saw you there. He said that he had seen you with your boyfriend . . . you know, your boss. She said that he was all over you and . . . . That's when I jumped her. Please, Mommy, tell me it's not true, that you don't do these things. That she just made this up to hurt us."

Sophia's mother put her hands on Sophia's shoulder and looking into her eyes said, "That was very mean of Sylvana. I'm glad her mother walloped her. And NO, there is no truth to any of it. Mr. Perez and I work together and we have become close friends but that's all, Sophia. How could I possibly have a boyfriend when I'm a married lady?"

As she looked into Sophia's face, Sophia was agreeing completely, of course. How could such a thing be possible? Yes, it was all a mistake, her mother wouldn't do that and, in fact, couldn't do anything wrong. No, there was nothing to worry about. There had been no truth to it and that was all there was. Nothing.

The following day there was a big change. Mrs. James decided to not go to her job and instead stayed home cleaning, washing clothes and making a nice dinner. Sophia was surprised and happy, but still a little guarded. A couple of days earlier they had received a letter from Mr. James telling them that he would be home within the month. So it was time to get everything in order. Why, after all, it would do no good to have the neighborhood gossiping about Mrs. James. These thoughts led her to quit the job and so that was the end of that. She got her act together and for the few weeks until Mr. James arrived home she was a good mother again.

It was dusk, the sun was almost gone and although the light was dim, there was just enough of it left for the children to recognize the lonely figure heading toward them. He was still faraway down the dirt, palm-lined, narrow road but the gait was his, it was their father! "Daddy, Daddy, Daddy," they screamed as they all ran barefoot toward him. Their shrieks reflected the sheer happiness of having him back. In a second they were all over him, pulling him down, jumping on him, laughing, crying and giggling.

He would always do that, just show up. Never a warning, so that they could be all cleaned up with hair combed. Instead, they were always dirty from play; hair rumpled but always with their faces lit up with love. Nothing else mattered; he was back and he loved them.

Mrs. James heard the cries and quickly passing a comb through her wavy hair, ran out to welcome him back as well. When Mr. James saw their mother running toward him, he let go of all the children to embrace her. It was a touching moment for all of them and Sophia smiled enjoying the moment and pushing away any other thoughts that tried to creep into her mind. They were all together again, and that was all that mattered.

On this trip their father had been to Africa and then to Brazil. As tradition would have it, on the evening of his arrival he would launch into storytelling, play a little harmonica and then tell another story. Photographs taken by shipmates would make the tales real and the children would marvel at the life their father lived. The pictures of natives from a small village in Africa standing around him with painted faces. Bare-chested women with long necklaces made out of seeds and in typical dress, stood next to him in another. Pictures like these were exciting and the children came to expect them. One after another, stories followed until, beaten by sleep, the children would go to bed and dream of the faraway places he so vividly described and they someday hoped to see.

With money in his pocket, Mr. James returned with the plan of finishing the inside of the home. However, he decided to work first on another project that needed to be done. A wide. circular driveway would be a true asset for their home. It would keep the environment cleaner and best of all it would provide a wonderful runway in which the children could roller skate.

He did not cut corners when it came to the driveway. He did make it long, circular and with walkways leading from it to the porch. All the children helped and in a couple of weeks it was done. Soon after, he piled all the children into the car and off they went to far-away San Juan in search of roller skates. The next day they were out on the driveway skating from the break of dawn till the dim light of dusk. They would place obstacles, jump, spin while jumping, fall, get bloody, cry and keep going. Knees around the house were nothing but a lump of soft scabs that night. The bigger and uglier the better and they all fought over whose was the biggest and the ugliest. They were having fun and as time passed, besides having scarred knees, they all became good skaters.

It was very quiet in the countryside where they lived, with not much exciting ever happening. In fact, they had been the entertainment for many since arriving. People thought that the *Americanos* were different. The greatest difference wasn't in their complexion but in the way that they always had something going on. The building of the home for one, had taken everyone aback. It was done with great speed and looked different from any house around. The nice green car looked very elegant, parked on the newly made driveway or in the garage. A sidewalk leading to the home and a sturdy fence surrounding the property were inspiring to others in the neighborhood. The *Americanos,* with their projects were amusing, but also silently were showing those around them a different way of doing things. More and more homes with arches started popping up and often someone would drop by and ask Mr. James for advice on this project or that.

Dusty days went by without much out of the ordinary ever happening. In fact bringing the small town to life sometimes depended on death. Sophia realized this to be true when an old man that lived about a mile away from the James's passed away. His death represented a whole new and vast learning experience for Sophia. The entire town jumped on this opportunity for distraction. It didn't matter that it was supposed to be sad distraction. It was a distraction, an excuse to take them away from everyday routines and into an "obligation to the dead." Upon hearing the news, everyone went into grieving mode and fell upon the grieving household which was already inundated by members of the immediate family. The old man had lived a very prolific life and was survived by a large family. He had fourteen children of his own of which twelve were alive and in attendance. Those children, in turn had their own families, each with many children. Neighbors and friends of a lifetime, all came. Some came to pay their respects, others to snoop, and then there were those that came to find romance. For one reason or another everyone came. They filled the house from wall to wall; out they spilled onto the rundown porch, into the front yard and out onto the narrow dirt road. Poor people most of them, but as was the custom, everyone arrived with something in hand. Thermos bottles filled with *café con leche,* were the most popular; together with bread, cold meats, bags of mangoes, and, of course, the bottle of spirits brought in via the back pocket. Soft, low voices deep in conversation could be heard as a vibrating hum throughout the area. In a corner of the yard the muffled sound of a radio surrounded by baseball fans, discreetly trying to keep track of the score. The common factor was the lack of color, black was everywhere. It covered women from the veil on their heads to the shoes on their feet. Everyone wore black with white being the only exception. Even the young girls were in black, and with ingenuity they faced the challenge of complying with tradition, while still remaining coquettish. So the skirts varied from all black, to black and white checks, to stripes, to tight fitting, to long, to short, to very short. Yes, this was an opportunity to meet someone and everyone had that in mind—besides, of course, mourning the deceased.

In the small living room of the house the old man lay for all to view, in an open coffin. Visitors would pay their respects before the casket, approaching with downcast eyes, making their way toward the widow with audible wailing and moaning. The widow in turn would seem to come out of reverie, to become comforter of those that were crying before her. For Sophia this was the first dead person, she had ever seen. She wasn't afraid to go and look at the body; instead she was filled with curiosity. Unobtrusively she edged her way up toward the coffin. When she looked at the face of the old man, whom she had seen sitting out on his old porch almost daily, on her trips to and from school, there was no feeling of fear, instead she looked quite inquisitively at him. How did he look different? There was a smile, it was wrong. In life she had never seen him smile. He'd make an acknowledging grunt when she went by, but definitely no smile. His hair was combed tightly down to the side and this also appeared wrong to Sophia who could see him in her mind's eye with his hair never combed and always kind of on end. His skin had a lot of make-up on it and seemed to cake in some spots. The color was wrong, he wasn't so pink, and instead his flesh was of a grayish tone. Now, he just was too rosy. Overall, he didn't look real, but sort of plastic, kind of like a mannequin. He did look comfortable though, the casket was out of wood and lined with shiny, puffy, white satin. As Sophia looked at him, she thought that he had probably never known what it was to lie in satin while he was alive. The thought saddened her and she promised herself that she would make sure to have a lot of satin in her life. She stared at him long and hard, though with no disrespect, just curiosity, until someone came to her side and nudged her away.

As she made it to a small vacant spot along the wall, she mulled over what she had just seen. She concluded that death was the grand unfair finale. To be laid out, on display, for everyone to see, not even looking like oneself was the pits. Sophia stood quietly, listening and watching and was fascinated at the human conduct displayed. As night grew near, she knew that she'd have to be going home soon, but the stories and the display of emotions kept her motionless at her new-found post. After a while of watching toothless faces laughing at some joke or hearing someone suddenly break down into horrific wailing, Sophia was summoned by her brother Bobby. "Time to come home, Sophia. Daddy's calling you." Sophia nodded and quickly made it through the crowds to where Bobby stood. As they started for home she put her arm over his shoulder and he put his arm around her waist.

As soon as she was home she secured permission to return to the wake. She didn't want to miss anything. This was her first "muerto," and she wanted to do him right. It was getting dark by the time Sophia returned to her spot along the wall in the home of the deceased man. She heard there was going to be a "Rosario," and she wanted to know what that was all about. In a loud voice a man called out for everyone to be silent because the "Rosario" was about to begin. At this, women started coming inside the little house, while the men inside stood up to go outside, making seats available. All chairs along the wall were taken so those without sat on the floor. Quickly everyone was settled and all became quiet. Sophia was watching every move and wondered what was next, when all of a sudden she jumped at the sound of a loud, shrieking voice that shattered the silence. The voice belonged to the oldest woman there and it was like a crackling cry. Sophia had never heard a sound quite like that one. She began with a chant, and though Sophia now spoke Spanish, she could not understand anything said by the woman. After a while the ritual developed a rhythm. The old woman's voice led and everyone in the room followed intermittently with other corresponding chants. After a while, Sophia's ear would pick out a word here and there and the verses began making sense. Soon she knew when to expect the chorus to fall in and what it would say. It was fascinating and soon after Sophia was mouthing parts of the rosary:

> *Santa, Santa Maria, Madre de Dios,*
> *Ruega por nosotros,*
> *Nosotros los pecadores,*
> *Ahora y en la hora de nuestra muerte. Amen.*

The singing chant of the religious verses went on and on. At one point Sophia's father, the "Americano," showed up, and seeing how his daughter was sitting enthralled on the floor, in the midst of it all, let her stay. The wake lasted until dawn. A couple of breaks were taken during the night, in which hot chocolate and Ritz crackers loaded with guava jelly and white cheese, all held together with a toothpick, were passed around. During these breaks, people would stretch, slip out for fresh air, or just slouch in their sitting positions and fall asleep. Sophia felt light headed. She had never spent the whole night up before and her body had a strange tingling feeling to it; still she did not allow herself to fall asleep. At six in the morning she went home along with a big crowd of people. The deed was done; the old dead man had been watched during the first night of his death as was the custom. He was prayed for so that all of his earthly sins would be forgiven and he would go to heaven. Everyone would be at the burial in the afternoon and after that they would wait for a week to pass and then begin a new praying session. Another session would take place, once the man had been dead for ninety days. Again at the first anniversary of his death, there would be a mass at the main cathedral in town and another all night praying vigil. That's what Sophia found out, and she was amazed at all the praying that was yet to take place. After all, she had never seen the man in church, so she didn't think of him as being very religious. However, a custom was a custom and so she kept those thoughts to herself and only nodded and smiled at her informer.

Sophia's dad was expected to leave again for a long trip; he had one month left at home with his children when Sophia began to develop frequent stomach aches. She was silently dreading his departure, and all along she kept quiet about her mother's previous behavior. However, now as his departure grew near, she was filled with fear of bad things to come and of the added responsibilities that she might again have to assume. The last time her father was gone and her mother was, too—most the time—she had hardly been able to cope with all of her school work. It had taken a toll on her grades and this too affected her because being an excellent student was important to her. The stomach aches could not be ignored; they grew as her fear grew and by the time his departure was imminent, she needed medical attention. Sophia's dad was quite concerned about her the day he took her to the doctor. For the last couple of days she began crying at anything, and the pain kept her away from school, confirming in Mr. James's view that indeed there was an illness. Gastritis was diagnosed accompanied by a thousand questions, which from Sophia's perspective, would never be answered truthfully. She knew why she was ill, she just couldn't tell.

Sophia's dad left and three weeks had passed. All the children were adjusting once again to life without him, and it wasn't easy. They all missed that spark of light that he added to their lives. He injected happiness into their home and there was always a project to be accomplished. There were books to be read and stories to be told. There was a wealth of knowledge flowing through the house that was lost once he departed. Sophia's mom tried to fill his shoes, but they were too big for her. The house had become gloomy and had become an "entertain yourself," environment. Mrs. James lacked creativity and interest which was so easily detected by the children. She failed in her attempts of communication and didn't seek a substitute, like being affectionate, so the distance between mother and children widened. Sophia, who was so much like her Dad, was at eleven, a far better communicator than her mother. So the children tended to gravitate around her for entertainment. Mrs. James' prior behavioral patterns, that Sophia continued to expect at any time, began to resurface and with them Sophia's gastritis flared up. It became difficult for her to eat which in turn exacerbated a loss of appetite. Already thin, Sophia's weight began dropping. The times ahead were going to be very dark and Sophia could literally sense it in her stomach.

"Sophia!" rang her mother's voice through the house early one Saturday morning. "I'm going into town and I won't be back until late. I've got my hair to do and other errands to run. You look after the kids. If anyone gets hungry, there's sandwich stuff and you can always open up a Campbell soup, OK?" She flashed a big smile with her straight, white teeth and walked out the door. Sophia hadn't had time to answer, but of course everything was going to be *yes* and *yes*. It had all started again. Sure enough, Mrs. James returned after dark. When she came home Sophia pretended to be asleep, and so they didn't speak.

Days went by and Mrs. James became absent more frequently. She was once again forgetting the children but they made the best of things trying to not notice the fact. At school a party was being organized for Valentine's Day and Sophia had been caught up in the excitement. She kept herself busy with plans and volunteered to help decorate the school. Hundreds of red hearts were cut out and stapled together making decorative garlands that were placed all around the room. Red and white balloons were being donated by a toy store from town. Centerpieces for tables were to be assembled at school the night before the party. Sophia wanted to help. She wanted to have something social to do. With the situation at home being so unstable and suffering from the gastritis, Sophia hadn't been thrilled over something in a long time. Three days before the party Sophia waited for her mother to return from a day away at her latest hang out, a neighbor's house. Mrs. James would visit these neighbors frequently and sometimes she'd take the children with her. The Valena family had one son. He was nineteen and quite cute Sophia thought.

Sophia faced her mother to remind her about the party and make sure that she had permission to go.

"Mommy," said Sophia, "you know about the Valentine's Day party we're having at school? . . . . Well, I want to know if I can go the night before the party and help out with decorations? There are going to be several teachers there and some of my friends are going." Before Mrs. James could get in an answer she continued "Also, Mom, I would like to have a new dress for the party; my dresses have gotten too tight and they don't look very nice anymore."

"Sophia, you know that I don't want you out at night. Besides . . . when did you say that this party is?"

"It's in a week. Next Saturday." A little fear started to grab Sophia and she quickly said, "We are going to have a great time. I've been in charge of making the garlands and they look beautiful, but there is still so much to be done." As Sophia said this she gave her mother a big smile.

Sophia's mother had a somber look on her face and did not seem to be participating at all in Sophia's outwardly attempt at happiness. In a dismissive tone her mother said, "You know that Daddy's check comes to us every two weeks and so we don't have any money to go out and buy you a dress now. It's just too bad. You should have asked me before.

So I don't see how you're going to be able to go to that party. Also, I have a commitment for that night and I need you here to take care of the kids." Sophia had been turning red and tears were welling up in her eyes. She could feel a huge ball forming in her throat and it was beginning to hurt. She wanted to run away and cry, and cry. Instead she started screaming and wouldn't stop.

"No, no, I don't want to stay home and take care of the kids, I'm always doing that for you. These are your kids, not mine. I want to go to the party and have fun. I've been working so hard and always cleaning the house. I won't stay, I won't stay, I won't do it! I wanna go to the party and have a new dress. I deserve it! You buy yourself clothes all the time. I need a new dress NOOOOOOW," she screamed.

Sophia's mother walked up to her and slapped her hard across the face. She then, grabbed her by the shoulders and began shaking her, "You can completely forget about the party now. You'll stay home like it or not and you'll do as you're told."

Sophia ran to her bedroom and cried herself to sleep that night. As she sobbed she prayed that her father would return quickly and save them from the trap they were in. She felt that her dreams of great things to come were beginning to fade and this made her angrier. Sophia had always believed that she would live an interesting life because she would make it that way. She had her goals; she had always had them and knew that it would take the very best of her to achieve them. This thought kept her excited and always made her demand more of herself. However, as much as she tried to go with the flow of things, she was very much aware that growing up in a small town, isolated in backwardness on the small island, was going to only make her goals in life harder to achieve. She knew that the education she was receiving was substandard. Where were her refined role models? Where was the fine music she longed for somewhere deep inside? How would she ever find it amongst the loud, deafening nonsensical stuff she heard daily on their radio? How would she succeed when each day brought more responsibilities to bear? She fell asleep knowing that she would not go to the party and that instead she would stay home and take care of her siblings. It would be all right, she would play along, and trust that time and endurance would bring rewards someday and somehow.

Three months had gone by since Mr. James had left and another three would pass before he returned. Mrs. James was gone all the time and spent on herself most of the money that Mr. James sent home. She continued to frequent the neighbor's house, but no one realized that most of the time spent at the Valena's was when the son was there alone. Sophia did not consider her mother very old but certainly she was not young. However, in reality, she was quite young, with six children and a husband far away. Mrs. James was only twenty-nine years old. With no sense of duty toward her children, she sought out the young guy that lived close by. The eager youth, seeking new experiences, lived with unsuspecting elderly parents. They had a small house, placed far back from the road, private and solitary. A perfect place, where she could park her car out of sight and no one would suspect. The affair had begun.

It was her mother's constant absence from her home and duties that made Sophia suspicious. Her mother was too happy when she came home in the evenings. What was there to be so happy about? Sophia would wonder. She knew that often her mother was at the neighbor's house but Sophia noticed that lately she was dressing up too much just to go over to see Ramón's family. Lately, Ramón Valena was also visiting the James's house.

Sophia liked Ramón. He was friendly, polite and her young mind did not suspect him of any wrongdoing. His visits became increasingly frequent and her mother was more and more concerned about her presence in a nervous and silly way. She would go into a cleaning frenzy, before he arrived and she actually began baking again. The children looked ragged and abandoned, but she either didn't notice that or just didn't care. She was wrapped up in herself and though she smiled at her children she did not see them or know them. It took a while before the seed of suspicion began to germinate in Sophia. She started suspecting that her mother had something going on with Ramón, but she refused to accept it. The thought made her sick. Her mother was old compared to this grown up kid. Besides, it just couldn't be; he was too close to home. She could never be so naive to think that she could have an affair with him and not have everyone find out. Impossible! However, the doubt grew as days passed and now that Sophia was suspicious of them, she kept a closer eye on her mother.

Sophia didn't feel well one morning and instead of jumping up for school she lay under the covers, trying to talk herself into functioning.

Her muscles hurt and her throat felt sore, she was definitely coming down with a cold.

"Sophia time for school," her mother called from her doorway.

"I can't go, I'm sick, I'm getting a cold, and my throat hurts . . . everything hurts."

"Well that's too bad, you've got to go to school. You can't just miss."

"Mommy, I'm sick. Don't you understand? Besides, I miss school all the time when you need me. Please help me; can I have some aspirin?"

"Well, I won't be here today, I have something to do," answered her mother without sympathy.

"Where are you going to be?" bounced out of Sophia's mouth. Her mother, not prepared to answer this question, quickly fished for an answer.

"Just things, just things that I've got to do."

"Well, I can take care of myself, that's OK."

Her mother didn't look comfortable as she left the room and the very expression on her face, is what made Sophia's mind start racing. Her mother wasn't concerned at all about Sophia—she never was. Sophia lived daily with painful stomach aches, needing to see a doctor and needing a little medicine to help, and she never cared. No, it was not concern that Sophia read on her face; it was inconvenience. She had a plan and Sophia, by staying home, was interfering with it.

As soon as all the children left for school Mrs. James was out the door. She had not even said good-bye to Sophia. Now, Sophia all alone, cuddled deep under the covers searching for relief and sleep. However, sleep never came. An idea popped into her head and she couldn't get it out. She would walk over to Ramón's house to confirm that her mother was not there. The suspicions of Ramón sickened her and this was her chance to get rid of them. Her body ached as she got up and dressed, but she was not to be deterred from her decision.

The warm air felt cool on Sophia's arms as she went outside. She began to shiver and knew that she had a fever. Nevertheless, the intrigue she had webbed in her brain excited her, and with every step down the road in the direction of Ramón's house her hands became clammier. Far back from the road in amongst some ancient and very large trees, sat the small, neat, wooden house of the Valena family. The long, dusty driveway that led to the house was lined on both sides by tall palm trees. The beautiful slender palms canopied most of the road and, even as sick as Sophia was, she could not ignore the beauty around her. On and on went Sophia as the house became larger with each step. Upon arriving she had the feeling that there was no one home. The silence was complete, including that of the dog Sato. His bark had never failed before but on this mid-morning he walked up to Sophia, sniffed and retreated back into the shadow of a tree to continue his siesta. Sophia inched her way toward the porch. She went up several steps to knock on the door, when she heard a distant sound of laughter. She stopped in her tracks. Her heart beating wildly felt as if it would pound itself out of her chest. Now, no longer the visitor, but the spy, she carefully went back down the steps she had climbed and went around the side of the house toward the rear. The muffled voices were becoming more distinct. She could hear some words. They were isolated, surrounded by indistinct sounds. She could not grab on to a whole sentence. There was a rhythmic sound of urgency, derived from pleasure or struggle that sent Sophia's head reeling. She felt as if she would faint from fear. She knew. She knew it was her mother. She was there. She could hear her voice. She could recognize it. She also had recognized the other voice. She stumbled to the back of the house and saw the big green Plymouth. She wanted to cry, but she was too frightened. Her breath was uneven and her skin was wet with perspiration. She crouched down to her knees, feeling more secure closer to the ground. *Calm down Sophia, calm down. Take control of yourself. What are you going to do? Are you going to run home as fast as you can, before they discover you? Are you going to knock on the door and confront them? No, no, no, run, just run, run and don't stop. Run Sophia!* As her mind juggled with what to do, her legs, primed by fear, took off. Soon she was down the dirt driveway, running fast, fast toward her home.

In fifteen minutes she was in her house crying and vomiting. Sophia was confused; she had just turned eleven and was innocent. She didn't know exactly what the mechanics were in a sexual relationship, but she knew that she had just witnessed it. She knew that her mother had been in bed with Ramón. She knew first hand that her mother had betrayed her father. No stupid gossip from some stupid girl, but her own ears hearing the words that now seemed sickening, "Amor mío, te amo." She felt disgusted, sick to the bone and it had nothing to do with her recently acquired cold. She was outraged and wanted to scream out what she knew and instead she cried, and cried and cried. Sophia tucked herself away in her bed and slept a long and deep sleep. Her sleep was full of sorrow and awakening. In a few moments she had been introduced to the ugliest of worlds, a world of betrayal, lies and deceit. In a matter of moments, any remaining trust or love felt toward her mother vanished. Sophia felt completely betrayed.

Sophia's mother returned five hours later to find her daughter a changed person. Sophia was sitting outside on the porch, bathed, with hair combed and her small hands clasped together on her lap. As Mrs. James descended from the vehicle she attempted to flash a smile at her. The smile found only a look of contempt openly placed on Sophia's young face.

Sophia stood up and placed her small hands on her hips and said in a loud voice, "So where have you been all day?"

Her mother stared her down, "Be careful with the tone you use with me, Sophia."

Sophia unnerved, laughed a bit wildly, so unlike her, and yelled out, "Only the one you deserve! You're no mother!"

"You are going to get it, you lousy little s---! I'll fix you!" screamed back Mrs. James as she approached her with her hand in the air, ready to strike. Sophia looked her in the face and yelled back, "I saw you! I saw you. You were at the Valena's house and you were in bed with Ramón. I hate you with all my heart and I promise that I'll tell Daddy!"

The screaming stopped as the sound of laughter floated over from the street. Both mother and daughter raised their gaze to see the school children returning home. There was the usual gang of neighbors, the kids that Sophia walked home with every day. Mrs. James looked at Sophia and with a dangerous smile went past her into the house. Sophia sighed with relief thinking that the gang had saved her, but she was wrong. A few seconds later the screen door burst open with a bang and out came her mother with a wide leather belt. The kids from school were directly in front of Sophia's house when Mrs. James grabbed her by a sleeve and began belting her with the buckle of the belt on the shins of her legs. There was not a trace of pride that could prevent Sophia from screaming with pain. The hard buckle would slam against the bone of her thin legs which felt as if they were being shattered. Sophia fell to the floor while screaming and begging her to stop and the children in the street stood as stone watching the unimaginable: Sophia getting beaten. The motion of Sophia falling set the children running toward her. Their screaming and crying was what contained Mrs. James' rage and made her stop. She threw the belt down and went inside slamming the screen door behind her. Sophia lay on the floor, crumpled up in fear. Her exposed legs were bloodied by the cutting blows of the buckle and the long licks of purple were already beginning to form throughout.

For two days Sophia could hardly walk, she would not speak and would not eat. Besides the common cold which had her in a fever, the beating hurt her spirit and the core of her lay in recession. She couldn't think positively, or negatively, she couldn't think at all. For the next few days she was like an empty shell, devoid of feeling or substance, a wandering spirit without a soul. Though the beating was debilitating, it was short lived as Sophia's strong spirit and good soul would not succumb. What might have hurt her permanently only made her stronger.

It was out in the open, people overheard. A word in English caught by one, another word caught by another, put the gossiping tongues in overdrive and the argument between mother and daughter was pieced together.

"The wife of the *Americano* was having an affair with Ramón, the youngest and only son not married of the Valena family."

"The little girl had seen the mother in bed with him at the Valena's house."

"The little girl saw them making love on the porch at the Valena's house."

"No, I heard that she found them in the grass under the big mango tree in front of their house and they were both naked when she found them too!"

The little town was having a field day with the gossip and Sophia heard a lot of it. She kept to herself. She tried to concentrate on her sixth grade studies, on helping her brothers and sisters, and stayed indoors most the time. She hated being the object of people's pitiful stares or outright outrage. The older Valenas also became invisible. They immediately switched to a different public car stop to get to work each day. The one they had always used was only accessible by walking past Sophia's house. The one that did not become invisible and, in fact became even more visible, was Ramón. He had seldom been seen at Sophia's grandfather's store but now became an active patron. His visits to the James house became more frequent, after his parents told Mrs.

James that she was not welcomed to visit them anymore. Sophia remained silent, not commenting, not questioning. After the beating she was afraid of her mother. She knew that her mother was capable of hurting her badly or even worse. Self-preservation made her go along with anything. She saw Ramón, coming more frequently and each time more relaxed than the time before, inching his way into their lives, as if he had a right to. Sophia was trapped, she lived a daily nightmare, waiting with anxiety for the evening knock on the door when Ramón would arrive and her mother would go into a gush of smiles that would choke Sophia with revulsion. He'd be right at home the moment he entered and each day he gave himself more freedom. He'd go into the kitchen and open the fridge, drink whatever he wanted from it, or with a beer in his hand he'd go up to the television and change the channel regardless of who was watching and Sophia remained silent. She was sickened to the core and wanted to kick him out and her mother with him, but instead she'd remove herself and go into the privacy of her shared bedroom. She hated her home. She became fond of the dusty and dirty little school that she went to, just because it was an escape. Her mother ignored the gossip and the protesting words of her relatives. She continued her relationship with Ramón as if nothing was wrong. She just changed address. Now it took place out of the James's house.

Sophia controlled herself until one day when she came home and found Ramón taking a nap on her mother's bed. She exploded, "Hey, wake up, leave my house now. Who do you think you are? This is not your house and you don't belong here all the time. This is my house and I don't want you coming here. How dare you lie down on my father's bed. You get out of here. Leave my house and don't you come back! You're not welcome here. Get out of here!" All of these words came out of her mouth in one single cry of anguish.

"Shut up, Sophia, you God damn little brat. Get over here and say you're sorry right now," said Sophia's mother.

"Well I'm not sorry and I'm not going to say it. You can leave with him if you want to." That was as far as she got when her mother started hitting her. She was hitting her around the head and the ears. One of the slaps caught her square in the face and the diamond ring that her father had given her, hit one of Sophia's front teeth and gum. Blood started coming from her mouth and as Mrs. James continued to hit her, the blood smeared around her face. This caught Mrs. James's attention and she stopped. The baby Evy and the others were crying hysterically at seeing Sophia all bloodied. The house was filled with a crying chaos. Somewhere in the middle of all of this Ramón left the house. Sophia lay on the floor with the evidence of the beating on her face. Her lip had swollen and her cheek bone was turning blue. Her hair was twisted in every which way and she looked hurt. Sophia didn't feel too much pain. She felt rather numb. Her face seemed to pulsate all over. It felt like it got big, and then small, and then big again. She hadn't inspected her mouth, but knew that one of her front teeth was chipped. She couldn't help but worry about that. That could be serious. She knew that any bruise clears up and goes away with time but a scar or a lost tooth, would be a lifelong trace of her sufferings. She hoped that she could survive without one.

The children were clinging to Sophia showing their love and fear while hiding their eyes from the enraged woman. The next thing they knew, Mrs. James was starting up the car and pulling out of the driveway. They had no idea where she was going, but they finally raised their heads and the fear was gone. That evening with her face all battered, she went to visit her grandfather and great-grandmother. The old woman upon seeing her flew into a rage.

"How could she do this to my little girl? Come here, *mi niña*. Let me put some herbs on it. It'll feel better and help the swelling go down quicker. She is a *puta*, that daughter of yours!" The old lady had never showed love to Sophia but Sophia would forever remember her for the kindness of that night. She put a cold compress of bay leaves on her face and that, along with the attention, made Sophia feel better. Her grandfather listened to what had happened.

"Grandpa, please don't let that man come into our house. Please, can't you do something?" He never answered the question but got up and began swearing as he left the room.

More and more the girls were finding ways to take care of their needs without their mother. Their hair, which grew past their waist, needed to be done by someone that knew how. They tried to do it for each other, but the long and tangled mass just became more tangled. Someone must have seen the girls out in their yard trying to do their hair, because, soon after, a neighbor lady by the name of Tiba stepped forward. She was a kind person that invited the girls to come over to her home every Sunday where she would gladly wash their hair for them.

Tiba was in her mid-fifties and had three grown children of her own, two daughters and a son. The son was mentally disabled and could do nothing for himself. Tiba loved him and did everything for him with tenderness and care. Though he was fully grown the small woman was capable of lifting him when she needed to. Her oldest daughter Tina, was only a name to Sophia and Karen. She had left the island for New York, so they only knew her by photograph. She was very beautiful, her hair was a light auburn and she did not look Puerto Rican, but perhaps Irish. The younger of her children, Lilliana, was on the island and she was as wonderful and kind as her mother. She was in high school at the time and Sophia would see her walk by their house every day from school. There was always a friendly exchange and sometimes even a surprise bubble gum would come out of Lilliana's pocket. Tiba's family lived very modestly but they were quite wealthy in kindness and love. Luckily for the James children, they lavished some of it on them.

Most certainly, Tiba could guess what the kids were going through, but she never let on and she never asked questions. For Sophia getting her hair washed became an event which also meant freedom. She was free from all the little ones for a while. Her mother knew that Tiba would be washing the girl's hair that day, so rather than do it herself she was quite glad to have someone else do it for her. So, for a few hours on Sunday, Sophia could count on her mother watching the children. After their hair was done, Sophia would go home and open up the can number three thousand of Campbell soup. With that, along with bread and butter, the children would have dinner.

After the day Sophia kicked Ramón out, he stopped coming around. At least that is what Sophia thought until one night. It was about two in the morning, when all of a sudden she woke up during a nightmare. She lay silently afraid in the top bunk of her bunk bed, trying to get the awful images out of her head when she heard hushed voices. They were in the distance but she was sure that there was someone speaking. Hardly breathing and incredulous with a sinking feeling of fear, she got up. She had to see who was there. Could her daddy have returned? Her mind analyzed this possibility but rejected it. Something about the voices told her that it wasn't her daddy. That it was forbidden. That it was wrong. Sophia raised herself onto her elbows and the bed creaked, she stopped all breathing listening for an interruption in the smooth and soft flow of speech. There was none. Ever so gently she moved her legs toward the edge and guided them over all the while holding most of her weight with her arms. She managed to get down from the upper bunk in complete silence, and once on the floor she stood completely still listening. The flow of sounds continued uninterrupted and she imagined what was going on. She was sure it was Ramón in the house with her mother and she hated her with passion. Spying . . . how low of her, but she couldn't not do it; she needed to know who was stealing into their night. As she approached the living room and looked beyond she could see the light on in her mothers' bedroom. She reached the closed door and with breath at bay she put her ear to it. The voices were muffled, very hushed and she could not distinguish who owned them. She touched the door knob as the voices spoke, but out of fear, let go of it. One sound and she could be caught and then perhaps beat up again. Sophia backed away from the door, careful not to trip and ever so slowly made it back to her room. She climbed up into her bed and laid there listening and devising a plan. Tomorrow she would be ready. With the sound of those hushed voices coming from her mother's bed, Sophia fell into a sad sleep.

The warm sunlight came in through her window and the brightness awoke her. She felt as if she had been crying, as if her face was swollen but her face was dry. A sense of complete emptiness filled her young body and she knew that again her spirit was wounded. Quickly getting ready for school, she helped her brothers and sisters with breakfast. A few glances to her mother's innocent-looking face made her stomach upset. Every time her mother caught one of those glances, Sophia was quick to smile. Yes, she would not give herself away. She would wait to really know what was going on and who was stealing into her home.

That day at school was a terrible one as she could not concentrate at all on the lesson being taught. Even classmates noticed her distraction.

"Sophia, what's wrong with you? You seem so spaced out." Sophia looked at the two girls that approached her and stared at them for a moment and then broke down crying. She cried hard, she cried from within. Her nose began running and she was a complete mess, but she continued crying.

"What is it? What's the matter with you?" they asked, but Sophia just continued to cry, not uttering a word for an answer. A teacher who was in the yard, keeping an eye over recess, approached them and also echoed the questions. Sophia looked up at her and their eyes met. The pain that the teacher saw in Sophia's eyes led her to ask no more questions. Instead she gathered her up into her arms and held her gently, while Sophia cried and cried. By the time school was back in session, Sophia had relaxed, washed her face and quietly sat in her seat with her head high. True, she cried as she needed to, something she had not done in front of anyone in a long time, but she kept her dignity and had said nothing. Her classmates had a certain respect and admiration for her that they could not explain. They didn't understand it, but it was there.

The James's house had never been completely finished. On the occasions when their father was home, he worked alone, and mostly on the outside of the house and its surroundings. Therefore, the inside continued to have inner dividing walls still made out of card board, wire, and bottle caps. Plastering and then painting was what remained to be done. Also, the bedroom ceilings were not in, so there were spaces between the top of the dividing walls and the rafters. There weren't too many places in the house that were like this but the main bedroom of the house still had an unfinished portion on a wall. Sophia's mind could not think of anything but of the discovery she had made the night before. Besides the sorrow that Sophia felt there was a smoldering anger. How dare her mother? How could she bring a man into her bed, with her children right there in the house with her? She had no sense of decency. The thought tortured her. She must find out who the intruder was. She thought of the spot of unfinished wall and made a plan that could work. All she needed was a little time alone inside the house and she could carry it out. Once she knew for sure who it was, then she'd cautiously think of what the next best step would be. Sophia was not going to allow herself to get beat up again. This time she would make sure that she had some sort of protection.

By the time school was over that day and the walk home completed, Sophia fine tuned her plan and was excited to have a go at it. For once, she hoped that her mother would not be there when she arrived. Sure enough, she wasn't. Sophia threw her books down and told the kids, "OK, everybody what do you want to do? Go outside and play or stay inside and help clean up." They all chorused, "Go outside and play!"

"OK, then, go ahead. I'm gonna figure out what we can have for dinner." All the kids ran out as fast as they could. They were used to having Sophia tell them what to do. She had been doing it for some time now. The children loved her and trusted her. They knew that no matter what, she would think of a way to keep them safe. They knew that she would never let anyone hurt them.

In the most matter-of-fact way, she proceeded into the kitchen and searched for a long thin carving knife. Once she had it, she went to her mother's wall and searched for a spot where she might carve a little hole. Probing with the knife, she found a spot where there were no two-by-fours and managed to make a small hole clear through. Then she went inside the room and turned the dresser mirror just a bit—to an angle that enabled her to see the bed. Back and forth she went, making adjustments until she thought that she had a clear, visible shot. The hole was quite unobtrusive and she was sure that her mother would never notice it. There, it had been done. Now she would go about her chores, get her homework done, and wait for the night.

She couldn't fall asleep. She was too excited with fear and anxiety and also concerned that if she did fall asleep she wouldn't wake up till morning. She lay in bed wide awake, waiting and waiting until she heard the creaking sound of the front screen door opening. *Oh! My God, it's really happening, someone is coming in*, went through her mind as her body turned cold and her heart pounded with fear. At first she felt immobile and feared she would never dare move an inch. However, about twenty minutes later, she began to climb down, slowly, silently. As she approached her mother's bedroom door, the fear of a stumble or bumping into something made her walk holding her breath. *Calm down, Sophia, Calm down*, she repeated to herself over and over again. She was certain that her mother could hear her pounding chest coming closer. Ever so gently she approached the hole in the wall that she had carved out that afternoon. She was terrified to look, for it would be a one-way street; she could never back out. She hesitated, maybe it was best to actually not see—to kind of know but not really know—what was going on.

Never! Her mother could fool herself, but Sophia never would. She would know the truth and then she would condemn it. This was their home, where their father worked so hard. No one was going to trash it. Brushing all thoughts aside she looked into the lighted room through the hole. It had worked, the mirror showed her the bed and she could see her mother. However, the angle was not turned in enough. She was just short of seeing the person that lay next to her. She was mad at herself for not having judged the mirror angle better. Still she looked and stared at her mother as if she were looking at her through a dream. Sophia could see her beauty. She had always seen it. Her hair was so black on the pillow, her smile, her large eyes full of life and yes, youth. Sophia looked at her as if she were not her mother but some woman she didn't know and felt sorry for her. She realized that this person was lost. She didn't know what she wanted. She had a family, but couldn't meet their demands and now didn't want them. She wanted freedom, to laugh and feel young and have no responsibilities. She didn't want to wait long months for a man whose face she sometimes couldn't remember, while she was receiving attention from all who could see her desire to run. Sophia, as young as she was, truly understood this, and knew she would never forgive her for not being a good mother. Lost in her thoughts she continued to watch and slightly jumped at the sight of a man's hand raised gently to caress her face. He had reached over and touched her right cheek and the act shocked Sophia. She knew, of course, that someone was in bed with her mother, but she had not seen him. Now, she had seen his hand and the presence of another person lying in her mother's bed was visually confirmed. She knew it, but to actually see the hand caressing her mother's face, sent her stepping backwards and, semiconsciously, she was careful not to make noise. The sight of the hand made her feel sick and dizzy. She wondered what would happen to her when she saw the whole person. Sophia went back to her bed and listened with anger. Each second carved away at a widening gap, between mother and daughter, that not even time would overcome.

    The alarm clock rang and Sophia felt as if she had just put her head down. It was going to be a tough day. She would do the best she could with it and wait for the time when she came home and angled the mirror more. She was becoming obsessed; she could think of nothing else but seeing with her own eyes, her mother and her lover. All day long she could see the hand reaching out from nowhere and touching her mother's face. A few times her eyes became moist because she had allowed herself to think of when that face was hers too. She remembered how she hugged and kissed her mother before bed at night. In what now seemed like years ago, she remembered going to her mother to seek comfort after being hurt. How did the good times become so lost? How would the good times ever return?

It took a minute to angle the mirror a little more and she did it as soon as she got home. Sophia tried to be herself, but it was hard. After a meal of rice and corned beef, Sophia started with the dishes while the smaller ones started with baths. Mrs. James was determined to get the house silent as early as possible these days, so by the stroke of eight, lights were out. Sophia usually protested but on this night she was the first one under the covers. She was so sleepy, because of the long day and the lack of sleep the night before, that, for a while, she struggled to not fall asleep. The unseen visitor arrived early. It was only eleven when Sophia heard the now familiar squeak of the screen door and the hushed voices begin. She was much bolder on this night than the night before. She descended from her bed without all the slow, painstaking care she had taken previously. She was sure that she could not be heard even if she did make a little noise.

With bolder steps, encouraged by the sounds of a hushed conversation, she peeked through the hole that she had made. At first she couldn't understand what she was seeing; she had angled the mirror and had tested the view carefully. Whoever lay in bed next to her mother should have been completely in view. *Oh! My God!* Finally her brain recognized what she was seeing. The mirror was draped with a towel. *She knew! She had realized and still pursued having him in their home and in her bed even knowing that someone knew. What a hateful, uncaring person !* screamed Sophia's mind. Sophia blindly took off backwards in an attempt to get away from sin, anger and hatred. She didn't know or understand her feelings. She wasn't sure if it was hatred for her mother or anger at not being able to see. In her confused state she backed right into a rocking chair. The sound was loud and clear, she was horrified. The congenial murmuring that had been going on abruptly stopped and she stood, glued in time, but for only a second. Quickly, without a thought, she ran on her tiptoes down the hall to her bed as noiselessly as she could. She climbed up into her bed and froze. She tried to hear over the sound of her heart beats and could hear nothing. It seemed as if no one had come after her. She was safe for now but she didn't know for how long. As Sophia lay in bed she thought of how her mother had noticed the telltale signs left behind: the turned mirror, the small hole in between the two-by-fours. She had found them, she knew that Sophia knew, and she shamelessly carried on. She could have turned the mirror back into place, but no, she placed the towel, so as to say; "*I know you know and I don't care.*"

In the morning, Sophia quickly and quietly got ready for school. She was afraid of trouble that could only end in her being hurt. She avoided her mother's eyes and filled in the gaps by helping the others. "Did you have a good night sleep, Sophia?" came suddenly out of her mother's mouth. Sophia jumped at the question and looked up into her mother's smiling face. She looked back down at the shoes she was tying. "No, I didn't." She looked up at Johnny: "All ready, Johnny. Go get your notebooks," Sophia said with love to her little brother. As Sophia walked to school she knew that she would think of a way to see who it was, or confirm it was Ramón, that was entering her home at night. The plan that she hatched next had to do with climbing up to peer over the bedrooms' dividing wall. Since the bedroom ceilings were not in, there was a space between the top of the dividing wall and the rafters in the roof. This incomplete portion of the house was her last possibility, and it presented some problems. Almost at the top of that wall Mr. James had built a big, wide shelf. This shelf was a storage area that was packed to the brim with odds and ends that most people keep in attics: old suitcases filled with souvenirs and memories long gone; boxes filled with items that should have been given away. In conclusion. a lot of junk. Nevertheless, there it was, taking up every bit of space. How would she clear it up enough to have space for herself and how could she do it without it being noticeable? She was sure that her mother would be keeping an eye on that area and trying to stay a step ahead of her. It was a relief for Sophia to come home that day and see the Plymouth not parked in the driveway. Yes! Her mother was out and she could breathe freely and not worry about having to pretend things she did not feel. Sophia considered herself a good and honest person, but all of this deceit, lying, and cheating made her feel dirty. She had not asked for any of it; the whole situation was thrown at her and she was just coping. Becoming a spy bothered her but she had no choice. She would see who the person was with her own eyes and when things got real bad— as she knew they would—she would be a witness to the truth. Just guessing who had been in bed with her mother wouldn't do.

To even reach the shelf was an effort. She had to put a big chair in the middle of the room and then try to balance a smaller one onto it. This trick she would have to perform in the dark: placing the chairs on top of each other in complete silence. She wondered how she could possibly do it, but the thought didn't deter her. She made it up to the shelf, high enough to actually climb onto it if there were enough space. But there wasn't. She would have to clear it out a little so that she could fit onto it. Quickly she grabbed a few things and made her way down with them and hid them under the bed. She took only things from the back, things that could not be seen from down below. She didn't want to disturb anything in plain view, for fear of giving herself away. Once again she tackled the chairs and by pushing things around a bit, she was able to climb onto the shelf and peer into her mother's bedroom. The view was full and complete. She smiled at herself, but it was only a fleeting smile as fear of being caught seized her. Quickly she was down and arranging everything as it had been, except for the empty space in the back. Sophia rushed to her room, took off her school uniform and, buttoning an old dress with her left hand, she quickly patted her hair into place with her right hand. Sophia then rushed into the kitchen and started preparing a simple meal. Her mother hadn't caught her, but she was invaded with fear. Maybe she would notice something out of place. Maybe she would kill her.

Sophia's imagination was racing and she was close to tears when little Frankie came into the house and said, "Sophia, look at what I found; maybe I can save it and go fishing. Would you go fishing with me?" Sophia looked down and saw a long, skinny worm dangling from his fingers. She looked at her little brother's innocent and dirty face and thoughts of fear for herself dissipated. She wished she could be carefree like this little guy and have no adult fears constantly menacing and robbing her of her innocence. To be Frankie or little Evy or even the bigger ones who knew nothing, would have been better than being herself at this time. Still she had no control of what was happening and when she knelt to accept Frankie's invitation she said, "I'll go anywhere with you, buddy." And instead of looking at the worm she grabbed him and gave him a hug and he hugged her back. They both needed love so desperately, the hug turned into a long one. When they let go, they smiled into each other's faces.

Little Frankie said, "You're silly. Sophia," and she laughed realizing that she hadn't done that in a while.

Like so many nights, Sophia again lay thinking instead of sleeping. Sleep deprivation was really becoming a problem. Just recently she had fallen asleep on her desk at school. Later she was told that the kids had giggled a bit and someone even lifted one of her braids high into the air, but she didn't awaken. The social studies teacher, whom everyone so fondly referred to as Mrs. *Boca Chula*, which meant "cute mouth," had stopped the kids from poking fun and allowed Sophia to remain asleep.

After class was over, with the hustle and bustle of the class leaving, Sophia awoke and found her teacher standing over her. Sophia had given her a blank look as if not knowing where she was. It took her just a few seconds to realize what had happened and a stream of apologies began to flow from her. Mrs. *Boca Chula* made a silencing gesture and put her hand on Sophia's shoulder.

"Sophia, you're a good girl and you work hard with your Spanish. I'm proud of you and I like you very much. I want you to know that you can come to me if you need to speak with someone; I will always be here for you." Sophia was staring at her while listening carefully, "I won't ask you to tell me what your problem is, but I do know that you have a problem. I've seen you too tired lately and you have lost weight since school started. If you need help of any type, come to me, Sophia, and I will help you." Sophia was so touched by the teacher's sincere kindness, that in a second her eyes filled up with tears and she began to cry. She cried again, as she had done so often recently and felt embarrassed that it was in front of her teacher.

As her nose began to run and her face to puff up, she blurted out, "Thank you, thank you, but I can't tell you, I could never tell you," and she ran outside with her heart torn. She skipped the next class, which is something she had never done before. She couldn't face her classmates and her next teacher with her face and nose screaming out, *I've been crying*. It was around two in the afternoon, that lazy and drowsy hour of the day, when falling asleep is easy even if one is not sleepy.

Sophia went outside into the warm sunny day and looked around for a place to sit. Pickings were slim. *Escuela Primaria de Factor* or Factor Elementary School was a scattered mess of buildings constructed on the high ground of a large piece of land. It faced Highway #2 which was the main road that crisscrossed the island from east to west. In between the school buildings and the highway were the low lands, occupied by playing fields for baseball and soccer. Factor School was a poor public school. It was in great disrepair, needing paint and running water. Toilets were smelly outhouses and the lone faucet in the middle of the school yard corridor always had, in between classes, a long line of kids waiting to put their mouths under it to catch a sip of water. Children ran, loaded down by books from one structure to another, in what was a pancake of dust or a bowl of mud, depending on the weather. There was very little vegetation around the school and concrete sidewalks were unheard of. The ground baked in the dusty, hot, humid sun or flooded in torrential rains, but still this was not a miserable place. On the contrary, among the small, dilapidated buildings, Factor School had a cafeteria. There was food at midday for everyone. It was pretty awful, tasteless, and ugly, but it filled growling tummies with something warm. The cafeteria was always jammed-packed with kids ready to eat. There was a lot of poverty in this region and a free meal in an empty and gnawing stomach was not to be wasted. For many, the cafeteria alone was a good reason to keep kids in school.

Sophia found herself heading toward the scant shade of a small tree. She gathered her skirt around her and settled on a large stone under its few branches. Leaning on its trunk she felt a light breeze and it, in itself, made her feel better. She knew she shouldn't be out there and that she could even be seen by her teacher, but she really didn't care. She needed to calm down, to have a moment of quiet, and relax. As she sat there leaning on the little tree, all stretched out and trying to think of nothing, she inspected her legs. She thought she was lucky to have nice ones. She frowned at the little brown hairs that primly stood up everywhere on them. She hated hairy legs, but she contented herself by thinking that her legs weren't very hairy at all. Nevertheless, she fantasized about spreading a soft and smooth cream all over them and then gently and carefully removing all of those little brown hairs, with a scary razor blade. She knew just how to do it; she had watched her mother do it so many times.

NO. She would not think about her mother. She would concentrate on her legs. Oh, yes, that little ugly scar. It seemed so many years ago when she was playing hide and seek with her cousin Ricky on 34th Street, back in Sacramento. It must have been another life, but no, not really, for precisely there was the little scar recording the moment forever. Sophia smiled as her mind raced back to the dark evening when giggles were heard everywhere and scampering feet carried them off in search of a safe haven. A little spot where Ricky who was "it," wouldn't find them. Sophia had found a nice little dark corner on the front unlit porch of her house. There were bushes that encroached upon the area and if Sophia could get down low enough, she would be completely concealed. When she crouched down into a squatting position she suddenly felt an unexpected pain in her right leg. Her leg had rammed into the broken neck of a glass Coke bottle that had been carelessly left there. Blood had flowed and her dad prepared homemade butterfly stitches and closed it up on the spot. Sophia had been filled with admiration for him. As she sat in the cool shade staring at the scar in the most intense and critical way, she thought that it should have been properly stitched.

Now it was late and the sudden squeaking of the screen door brought her back to her scary reality. She recognized all the subsequent sounds; the intruder was there and her mother was quietly guiding him into her bedroom. Sophia lay still, waiting to be brave enough to venture out of the protection of her bed. Little by little, as she had done before, she made her way down onto the floor and once again the alert and scared little girl tiptoed toward her mother's room. She went into the boy's bedroom and began in complete silence to place the smaller chair onto the larger one, as she had practiced earlier. All was going well. She began climbing and made it to the ledge without a sound. The murmuring sounds in the room next door continued unsuspectingly and Sophia had started pushing the boxes that were to the front of the shelf toward the back. Slowly, slowly, ever so carefully, ever so gently she had made enough space to fit onto the shelf. She grabbed onto an exposed beam and that helped her pull herself upwards. The wood had not creaked and the thin little girl, swinging, made it up onto the shelf, virtually without breaking the silence. Sophia sat motionless on the edge of the shelf for several minutes. She was trying to stabilize her breathing and her heart beats. This was it, the moment that she had been kept awake night after night for. Now she would see who it was, but fear invaded her and she needed to regroup her thoughts so that she could find the courage to look. Moments continued to pass and all of a sudden a small giggle from the room provoked enough anger in her, to give her that courage. She got up on her knees and leaned toward the opening. There she was under the yellow and rose printed sheets and next to her on his side was Ramón. They both were covered, but Sophia could see that they had no clothing on. The whole scene made her want to scream in rage and as she fought with her brain for silence, a small cry escaped. It was heard and in a flash her mother saw her. She screamed to Ramón, *"Mira!"* As the word flew out of her, her arm sprung up to point at Sophia who sat motionless and hopelessly discovered. Sophia didn't try to flee, she didn't pronounce a word nor remove her eyes from the bizarre scene. Her mother was hysterical and was about to run from the bed and get her when she realized that indeed she had nothing on.

She stopped panicking and looked up at the expressionless set of eyes. In a cold voice she said, "Sophia get down this minute, I'm going to kill you." Sophia gave her and then Ramón one last direct look, turned and quietly got down. She went straight to her own bed and lay waiting for whatever was to come. She felt hollow and devoid of feelings. What was to come didn't seem to matter much. The bedroom door opened but no footsteps came running to kill her, instead she heard the screen door open and shut. A minute later she heard her mother's car start up and drive away. Sophia turned over and went to sleep.

When Sophia woke up the next morning, it was about nine o'clock, all the kids except Bobby were awake and parked in front of the Saturday morning cartoons. Sophia headed for the kitchen and looked through the window to see if her mother's car was there. It wasn't, she hadn't returned.

"Karen, have you seen Mommy?" called out Sophia.

"No, she's not here," responded Karen.

Sophia's brow furrowed. Though she was glad to not have to face her mother, it was pretty incredible that she would just go off and not return throughout the entire night. Sophia went to work. She got everyone to eat some cereal and then started sweeping the house. She kept busy so as to ingratiate herself with her mother by cleaning. She was afraid of being hurt. She didn't know what to expect. She didn't want to be beaten and need to hide wounds from prying eyes at school. She was sure that her teachers knew when she had been beaten in the past. Gossip ran rampant and Sophia's high socks could only hide so much.

However, they had said nothing and had not asked questions; but Sophia saw a change. All of her teachers thereafter became more gentle and kind with her.

All day Saturday, Sophia's mother did not return. The children had entertained themselves with play or fight and Sophia made sure that everyone ate something when they were hungry. Night came and still her mother had not returned. By nine o'clock all the children were in bed. By eleven o'clock, Sophia heard the screen door open.

Sophia never uttered a word about what she knew to her brothers or sisters. She saw no value in hurting and worrying them. However, Sophia had lost much of her innocence. She knew about deceit, about lust, and she knew about hatred. Sophia was always mature for her age but as a witness to lies and hypocrisy, her wisdom grew. At the age of eleven she decided what she wanted out of life and what she would reject and protect herself from, as long as she lived. Sophia's young soul had been scarred repeatedly in the last year, but luckily she had avoided physical scars. Her mother never did beat her for what happened that night; instead she used her. She made her work and made her stay home from school anytime, on what seemed a whim. Sophia knew that she was being used and played to the beat of that drum. It was called *self-preservation*. More than anything else, she avoided—as much as possible—being hurt and visibly scared. A scar would be a witness to her sad childhood. It could handicap her for the rest of her life and Sophia knew that she had to put this entire hurt away, so as to move forward in life and succeed. These thoughts kept the young girl filled with hope and made her stronger than ever. Yes, she would have a good life someday. A life filled with honor and honesty. She would be a wonderful wife to a wonderful man. She would have children of her own and be the most devoted, loving, and caring mother ever. She would protect her children's childhood and innocence with her life. Yes, her future was beautiful and she would unwaveringly head toward it.

Things were quiet around the house for a couple of weeks. Interaction between mother and children seemed improved. There was breakfast in the morning before going to school and dinner after the long walk home. Sophia didn't know what to make of this sudden and unexpected change. She never guessed that their situation would improve after knowing what she knew. If anything she thought that all hell would break loose. Later, she was to realize that this period was only a reprieve—like a time out—to let things cool down.

Sure enough, it was about a month later when those dreaded and awful familiar sounds again awoke her. Drowsy from sleep, Sophia jumped with a jolt and felt an ache in her stomach. "No, no it can't be. Please God, no." she whispered under her covers. The sounds were real and again they were coming from her mother's bedroom. Sophia didn't know what to do. She sat straight up rigid in her bed, feeling helpless and lost. She swung her legs across the bed in complete silence and again tiptoed in bare feet toward the living room. There she could see that the light was on in her mother's bedroom. *The nerve, the bastard, how dare he come in here? I hate you Mom, you lousy miserable woman*, thought Sophia. She crept back to her room and lay awake, listening and thinking. She didn't know what to do but she realized that she needed to be real careful. Her mother was completely out of control and in a moment of rage could really hurt her or maybe even kill her. Sophia tried to keep this in mind, but nevertheless, she would find a way to defend her home. She wasn't going to stand by and allow another man to come in and take her father's place.

The same episode repeated itself the following night and the one after that. Sophia decided to go to that spot high up on the wall and peer over to make sure that it still was Ramón. Maybe her mother now was bringing in others? She didn't know, but she could believe anything. After agonizing minutes of working in silence she made it onto the shelf and was able to peer over. No, she would not see who was there. Her mother had suspended a rope across the room and draped a sheet from it. This improvised curtain was well placed and blocked out a direct line of sight.

Sophia continued to go to school trying to do homework and concentrate. However, she found herself seeing over and over again those long fingers caressing her mother's face, the nude bodies under the sheet of her father's bed. She was so completely exhausted all the time and her young stressed body was taking her chronic gastritis to a full-out gastroenteritis. The constant pain that gnawed at her stomach and tummy didn't let her eat. Again she was losing weight and her face was pale with blackish areas under her large eyes. She needed to sleep, to have peace and not lay there listening to every noise, every sound, every night. She needed to make it stop.

"When I come and wake you up, I want you to follow me. You have to be real quiet, I mean quieter than you have ever been in your life. Then, when I give you a signal, you've got to bang that can as loud and as hard as possible and scream; scream as loud as you can too. Now look at me...we can do this. Mommy has another man coming into our house at night and that is bad. Daddy is our dad and that is his bed and nobody else gets to sleep in it with our mother. It's a terrible thing and we have to stop it. You have to stay real quiet about this, Karen, Bobby and Johnny. If she knows anything about this plan, she'll beat me and, maybe this time, even kill me, and then just keep bringing him into our house at night when you are sleeping."

"Who is it?" asked Bobby for once very serious and fully alert.

"I think I know who it is, but I'm not sure. We'll find out soon, probably tonight."

This was the plan she devised. She thought and thought about it and hated it, but she couldn't see another way out. She didn't want to tell the other children and she knew that her mother knew that. Since Sophia was keeping the secret for her, she would continue committing the crime as long as she wanted to. Sophia felt she had no choice.

The house was very quiet. The singing Coquí, a tiny frog indigenous to the island, could clearly be heard. The world outside seemed peaceful. In Sophia's body however, there was a raging battle. She lay trying to differentiate the sounds from outside of her body and the real world. Still, motionless, she lay listening to every single sound that came from every single place. There it was, just after midnight, the sound of the front screen door, squeaking as it opened. A feeling of satisfaction overcame her. The wait had paid off. Tonight it would be out in the open, no longer her secret to keep and suffer over. Tonight everyone would know how her mother had neglected her family. How she was cheating on her hard working husband. Tonight would be the last time Ramón Valena—if that's who it was—would go through their doors to disturb their lives.

Sophia waited, not moving, but with all of her senses on alert. She wanted to give them time to get in bed, she wanted to make sure that he didn't get away. Half an hour later, she made her move.

She first went to her sister, and whispered, "Karen, Karen, be quiet, get up, he's in the room with her now." They went for the boys. Silently the James children picked up the cans and pot covers that were carefully laid out the night before and gathered in front of their parent's room. A silent Sophia counted down with her arms, leading the group as if she were a conductor and they were a band about to rip the silence. That is what they did. Crash! Screams!! Clang, bang; it was total chaos, deafening, mayhem, continuous and non-relenting. The door opened, the door closed, Mrs. James and her lover were jumping around not knowing what to do. A minute passed and then two, as the continued screams and can beating went on. Then it happened, the first neighbor arrived, then another, and another.

The door was closed, they were in there, trapped, caught, and then the grandfather arrived. "She's in there with a man in bed with her," screamed the children.

"He's in there right now, he's in there!" One of the neighbors said, "Let's kick the door down."

At that, the door opened. Out came Mrs. James trying to quickly put on her mask of deception "What's going on? There's nobody here." By now, even people from houses further away came running into the melee to see who was getting killed. Sophia went up to her mother and peeked past her, seeing Ramón's reflection in the mirror. He was lying on the floor next to the bed. He didn't fit under it.

Sophia screamed, "There he is!! He's on the floor by the bed." Don Casiano, the grandfather, went in, along with a couple of other men, and pushed him out of the house wearing just his underwear.

8

MUSIC

"AÑORANZA A VENEZUELA" ~ "LONGING FOR VENEZUELA"
Dicen que se me pasa, se me pasa, ~ They say I'll get over it, I'll get over it,
Que el tiempo todo cura, eso es locura, ~ That time heals everything, that's madness,
Que pronto se me olvida, se me olvida, ~ That soon I'll forget, I'll forget,
A mi Venezuela. ~ My Venezuela.
Pero no se me quitan las ganas, ~ But I don't lose the desire,
De ver tus calles llenas de tu gente, ~ Of seeing streets filled with your people,
De encontrarme rodeada, de tu Avila, ~ Of being surrounded, by your Avila,
Tan bella y tan grandiosa. ~ So beautiful and so grandiose.
Añoranza, tengo de ti Venezuela, ~ Longing, is what I have for you Venezuela,
No te saco de mi mente un momento, ~ You are not out of my mind for a moment,
Añoranza de compartir contigo, ~ Longing to share with you,
Todos tus problemas, todos tus dilemas, ~ All of your problems, all your dilemmas,
Y todo tu amor. ~ And all of your love.

The doorbell rang and Sophia set her large palette, which was resting on her lap, onto a table nearby. She limped away from the bench as her body, frozen into one position for a long while, had tightened up.

"Coming, coming!" She hurried to the door and smiled happily to see a friend and began pulling off her painting apron. "Lola! Lola! What a surprise, come on in!" Sophia liked Lola. She had met her recently and found her to be interesting and grounded. Lola Gonzalez de Roig was a prominent person in her own right. Born into Puerto Rican high society, she was the granddaughter of a man by the name of Keelan, a Bostonian educator whose family had been involved in the founding of Boston College. Lola was a published poet and was married to a man belonging to one of the island's most powerful and prominent families, the Roigs. Antonio Roig, on his father's side, was the heir apparent to a wealthy landowner and sugar baron. His family had held a position of leadership throughout the east side of the island in the sugarcane industry for a century. Their refinery, Central Roig, was among the last to shut down in the year 2000. On his mother's side, Roig was a Ferré. A name known mainly for embracing the political machinery, as his uncle, industrialist Luis Ferré, became the third governor of the island and founded the New Progressive Party which advocated statehood for the island.

"No, no, don't take off your apron, I don't want to interrupt you, I just happened to be nearby and wanted to say hello and see what you are up to."

"Well, good! I'm glad you did! I am up to wonderful things, Lola. Come and I'll show you." Sophia had mischief on her face and Lola happily followed while enjoying the intrigue.

"Lola, I've started it! I'm so excited! I believe it will be wonderful, but I've only just started, so there isn't much to show for yet."

"But my goodness! This is a huge painting! Sophia, it is going to be gorgeous! Ladies on horses? It is like in colonial times, I love it!"

"I got the idea from seeing the Three Kings Day parade—the Paso Fino horses and their beautiful steps and every one decked out in the attire of that period. I couldn't get the scene out of my mind, so I'm painting it and putting it to rest. This painting will have much meaning for me." Sophia said those words with an inadvertent tone of introspection. Lola would never know how much truth lay in what she had heard.

"Well! What are you doing tonight? Nothing important! So, we must celebrate that you have begun this mission."

"Oh! Lola, no, no, no, I have nothing to show yet," said Sophia a little self-consciously.

"Yes, yes, yes, I can bring a tray of cheese and some lovely wines and we can call a few over, you know the philosopher types and have a small *"tertulia"* and we will toast for the beginning of this magnificent work of art!" Lola was laughing, the perfect socialite, thankfully á la lite, who loved a gathering. Any reason was a good reason for a good time. She was from Puerto Rico, and that is the Puerto Rican way.

Sophia smiled and tilted her head, as if saying, *Are you sure?*

Lola only laughed harder and said, "OK, OK. We will do it when it is finished! For sure!"

The next morning, with threatening cloudy skies, Sophia quickly was up and off to the beach. That early morning brisk walk was essential in helping keep her weight in check. Puerto Rico's cooking was savory and often irresistible, which made it quite dangerous for a woman's figure.

She quickly showered and looked forward to picking up her palette and advancing the painting. A little coffee with her husband, a little attention for her Tommy, and she would find herself squirting more oils onto her depleted palette.

'Some nice clean turpentine, so there will be no contamination of colors, she thought as she picked up the large white plastic container of odorless turp, on the bottom shelf of her painting closet. She carefully poured some into a clean jar. Casting a glance over at the roll of paper towels nearby to make sure she had it, she smiled. She had everything! She moved over to her painting bench, picked up the apron left there the night before, and eased herself to a place in front of the canvas. Picking up her palette knife, she generously gathered paint and spread it thick onto the canvas. Sophia liked thick paint, no little smudges here and there, but bold strokes of heavy paint. *Nice trunk on that palm tree,* she thought happily, and the day began.

Soon she was humming. It was one of her old songs. She started to remember the day she recorded it and how the whole world of music had become an important part of her life. Georgia was on her mind.

1993 ATLANTA, GEORGIA

Atlanta, Georgia, where everything seems to start with "Peachtree,"—Peachtree Street, Peachtree Rd., Peachtree Blvd, on and on—was their chosen city to return to when they left Venezuela. Sophia's husband was a Georgia Tech graduate and old friends and Sigma Nu brothers welcomed him, ready to pick up where they had left off three decades earlier. A band of brothers, with a bond never to be broken, was what Sophia saw. She loved seeing her husband among his old friends and the obvious pleasure it gave him to renew those old ties. However, silently, she found herself deeply missing Venezuela.

Life in Atlanta was busy as children settled into a new routine and became accustomed to their new surroundings. Their home was at the edge of a lake and daily sunsets would shine upon those waters, making the world the most amazing place. It was a different life, different in so many ways and as with every change it took time for the family to adjust. Life in Venezuela had been ensconced in sophistication as the country held fiercely to traditions of elegance and formality or to appearance and superficiality. Sophia's children grew up under that way of life where dressing properly and displaying good manners became a part of who they were. The *buenos días, buenas tardes,* and *buenas noches* constantly heard, had become a part of their lexicon as well. However, the US was different. Everything was more relaxed, yet life was lived at an accelerated pace. There was not much time to worry about formality and there was no real dress code; it was a new 'anything goes,' atmosphere. It was during this time that boys began wearing pants below the belt line, displaying underwear. This appearance and attitude was incomprehensible to the family but it didn't matter much to them as they were distracted by megastores filled with toys and overflowing grocery stores. The sense of security, nice highways, and parks made their new life a fun place, and everyone was happy and ready to explore.

The USA was home, and every one of Sophia's children clearly understood that. It was a fact that Sophia and their father had emphasized from birth, with yearly travel to the US to visit grandparents or Georgia Tech homecomings. While in Caracas, it had become a family tradition to head over to the US Ambassador's residence every Fourth of July to celebrate Independence Day by wearing red, white and blue.

With little American flags clutched in their hands, Sophia's children, depending on their age, said or mouthed the pledge of allegiance. With their right hand on their heart they listened to and learned the Star Spangled Banner. That was one thing about living abroad: sometimes expats became more patriotic than mainlanders. The absence of the homeland would make the heart fonder and the tendency to grasp at any display of patriotism was relished. Those celebratory moments reminded them of their identity and tightened the link that bonded them with their nation.

Always in search for activities to keep everyone engaged and busy, Sophia came across some 'breaking news,' on the television. There had been an incident at an ice skating rink where a top skater was attacked. Someone had clubbed one of her knees, causing an injury that could deprive her of competing for the US on the Olympic team. It had been the Kerrigan-Harding saga. Sophia shook her head in disbelief and suddenly a light bulb inside her brain went on. It was a Thursday and right after her children climbed off their respective school bus, she cried out, "Kids, would you like to go ice skating?" A chorus of approval greeted her and on that following Saturday, January 8, 1994 they went. Never in a million years could Sophia have guessed that the outing was the beginning of a wonderful life-changing event for their family.

The dank and cold ice skating rink was filled with carnival music and flashing lights. Tons of people, young and old, were haplessly going around in circles. Some skated by with certain fluidity but most looked reckless and about to fall any moment. However, toward the center of the ice the more experienced skaters could be seen attempting scratch spins, spirals and a myriad of awkward jumps.

The first on the slippery surface was her oldest child Chip who charged forward like a bull in a china shop. Arms going round and round, somehow he managed to stay on his feet and laugh out loud the entire time. Soon he had it down and was going around in circles, racing others he didn't know. The second child, Colleen, approached the ice in a much different manner. Slowly and thoughtfully she stepped out onto the ice, and gently glided forward. Her balance was there and at that very first instant she looked comfortable and poised. Sophia inhaled and knew what she had seen. She said nothing, but intently watched her little girl go around the rink. In a few moments she was doing what she had seen on television. Lifting her right leg high into the air and gliding forward on her left. As she went by her mother, she stopped and said "Mommy, I like skating. I'd like to come again." She did skate again and nearly every day for the next eleven years. The beautiful little tropical bird, Colleen, would train all those years with Olympic figure skating coach Don Laws and become an international figure skater, harboring all the hopes and dreams of an Olympian.

Sophia's days, like for so many moms, revolved around driving from one sport to another and getting each child where he or she needed to be. She was living the American dream. Gone were the chauffeurs and all the domestic help, replaced by a race that never ended. At times Sophia would ponder her new reality and silently give credit to the way in which South American women got the same things done. Nevertheless, she was happy to be so closely involved in the development of her children. They were learning, excited and happy.

It was the time wasted in between her children's practices that became an itch. The daily demands placed upon Sophia were plentiful, but very basic. There was no real challenge and she was aware of the enemy found in boredom. Conversations around the rink were elementary and always turned toward, "So how old is your daughter?" "How long has she been skating?" "Oh! When is her birthday?"

The lust, the desire, the jealousies were ridiculous. Children were learning how to skate and parents were engrossed in every move they made and also that made by any possible competitor. Yes, the competitive spirit was alive, but not well. Instead, it was damning and Sophia was sickened by it.

"How long has she been doing that jump?" "How many jumps does she have?" "What blade does she use on her skates?" "Oh! It must be the blade!"

Sophia couldn't take it and began not entering the rink. She hoped her little girl would do well, but that was not within her control. Her daughter would excel or she wouldn't—time would tell. As long as she was safe and happy, Sophia would support her at anything.

For Sophia some things were very clear. It always came back to that inner sense, that individual drive. If a person had it, the individual was guided by it. The person that did not have it wasn't exactly cut out for that specific pursuit. From the beginning Sophia laid down the law. Since courting a career in Figure Skating was very demanding, it would take a united and loving family to meet the challenges they would face.

"Colleen, getting up at four thirty every morning to be at the rink at five thirty for figures, and then heading out to school, is going to take a lot of discipline on your part. You are going to need a lot of help from your dad and me. Now, I promise that I will drive you there and back every morning, but you have to come to my bed and wake me up. I will not wake you up, Colleen. If you want this, I'll help you make it happen, but it has to come from you." And so it had been said, and so it was carried out.

Every day the little girl, still in her pajamas, came into her parents' room and woke up her mother, "Mommy, it's time." The race to be out the door began and with it, the forging of a bond that would hold them together forever.

For Sophia, a woman so driven to become a doctor—a person able to respond in an instant to a crisis—life had become quite simplified. Not for a moment did she resent this. The gift and meaning of motherhood was clear to her because of the heartbreak of her own childhood. She loved mothering above everything else in life and to have her children love her back was the greatest gift life could offer. Nevertheless, she needed a challenge. She needed to find something . . . something.

Avoiding the worthless gossiping innards of the rink, Sophia sat inside her car on those frozen and dark winter mornings, wrapped in a heavy coat. She pined over Venezuela, missing the place and friends she had made over her eighteen years there. Her medical career still fresh in her mind captivated much of her thoughts and she considered the possibility of revalidating her studies in the US. However, she resisted doing that. Medicine would dictate hours away from home when her family needed her. She would fill those empty gaps of time, while getting the children to their activities, with something constructive and exciting. Sophia would not only do something worthwhile but she would be showing her children that productivity and happiness do not lie within idle hands.

On one of those cold mornings, while Colleen worked with her coach inside the rink, Sophia sat pondering as she tried to keep warm. Suddenly—just like that—a melody and a few words popped into her head. She began humming, fumbled for a pencil and wrote down the words. Those words and that melody would be the first of over a hundred songs that Sophia would write and put to music. That cold morning marked the beginning of a dynamic and successful career as a recording artist which spanned the next five years.

"*Añoranza a Venezuela*," Longing for Venezuela, was the very first song she composed and it created a great excitement in Sophia, something she had been missing since leaving Venezuela. She felt like a receptor, an antenna that stood ready and waiting for any sound or signal to jump, write and create. She wasn't quite sure about how to continue forward with her songs once they were completed, as she had never met a composer. However, she did know a singer—in fact, a wonderful and famous singer, Chucho Avellanet. He was a Puerto Rican who had married a Venezuelan girl and lived in Caracas. His son and Sophia's son were in the same classroom and though Sophia had never told Chucho, he had unknowingly helped her learn Spanish. Sophia would listen to his wonderful voice and learn his ballads way back when she was a young girl. Sophia contacted Chucho and he agreed to see her in Caracas. Maybe, just maybe, he would sing *Añoranza.*

It had been eight months, an eternity, since Sophia had left Venezuela and now she was flying back, because she had written a song for the country. She was proud and happy and anyone noticing her, as she waltzed through the airport, could see it. She had completed the first leg of her Atlanta-Caracas flight and was making her way through the Miami airport. Her next flight would take her directly into Venezuela. With her heart racing and a smile that wouldn't quit, she chose a seat at the gate and sat down. It was hard for her to sit still and conceal her euphoria, so she tried to become distracted by surveying passengers. As her eyes roamed from one passenger to another she knew that none of them could ever guess the reason for her excitement. She was returning to a place she loved and had missed so dearly. She had not had a conversation in Spanish for as long as she had been away and suddenly, there she was, surrounded by all of those that knew where she was going. They probably shared the same malls, the same bank, the same Avila Mountain.

She no longer could contain herself and suddenly stood up and in a loud voice said, "Hello, hello, please, I know that most of you here are from Venezuela. I want to tell you that I love your country and I am returning now, to take a song that I have composed for you." She halted briefly, continued smiling radiantly and said, "I am now going to sing you my song." Newspapers that had been held high had begun dropping along with lower jawbones of those passengers listening. Sophia, without another thought, began singing her love song. She sang loud and with great passion, she sang it without interruption and she sang it from the heart, while looking them in the eye. When she finished she stood laughing, as a loud and sustained applause engulfed her gate and those around it.

"Thank you for your beautiful song."

"We loved your song."

"Gracias por la canción, que bella la canción," were the words Sophia heard over and over, along with pats on the back as she made her way toward the rear of the plane. Sophia was queen.

As it would be, the trip to Venezuela had been good timing. Her meeting with Chucho, the great and famous singer—who teased her about never having had someone come from *so far away, to sing to me*—would serve as an incentive to move forward. He would not sing Sophia's song, because *Longing for Venezuela* did not have appropriate lyrics for him. At the time he was about to divorce his Venezuelan wife and then move back to Puerto Rico. Nevertheless, he encouraged Sophia to continue writing and producing music. She would take his advice to heart and embrace music with all her might.

Lyrics and melody with catchy rhythms would come to her anytime, unexpectedly, through the air neatly packaged, invading her senses. Those moments would send her on a mad dash for the voice recorder, which had come to live at her side. Each instrument came to her as if in a separate envelope and was singled out and defined by its own musical line. The process was enthralling and Sophia was creating. Every spare moment was invested in developing her music until the day she was ready to meet Phil Thomson. He was southerner through and through who lived, breathed, and literally ate in his small recording studio. Phil had a good ear, a lot of experience in recording music and a willingness to please a client. He also had a lot of cats. Sophia wasn't a cat person but he came with cats, take him or leave him, and along with his kind heart, Sophia decided to take him. Phil was great at getting that special sound, unique tempo, and finding first-class musicians. Problem was that most of them also were southerners and country music was the brew they were accustomed to. However, the music Sophia had been writing was full out Latin. Nevertheless, musicians eat, drink and sleep music. So because those southern boys had a little good will and a whole lot of talent, Sophia had them whipped up in no time, and pounding out that Latin beat.

Sophia began to live the most fun and engaging time of her life, as she took to singing her songs. She had no illusions about being a great singer; she wasn't. However, in Atlanta, no matter how much she asked around, not even Phil could come up with a good Spanish singer. So she decided that if it was going to be less than great, she could do that herself. With each song, she relaxed a little more and, along with her confidence, her voice seemed to improve. She got better at the process overall and when she would meet with musicians to lay down tracks, she knew just what she wanted for each of her songs.

"You sound great, but it's just not quite what I'm hearing. Give it another try like this," going on to sound out the imaginary trumpet she held in her hands, *ta .. ta .. ta .. tatata*! Do it like that, but take it up an octave and give me four."

Gregg the trumpet player laughed and shaking his head said, "You've got to be kidding me. You're killing me!"

"Naw, you can do it Gregg, let me hear ya." The music would flow and he would hit the high notes needed.

"Great, you got it! You're amazing. Now take that last note and hold it, show me a real fermata."

There was no more lost time in Sophia's life; she was as active as she could be. All the "in between" time spent in the van during ice-hockey meets for Chip, skating lessons and ballet for Colleen, speech therapy and tennis for Tommy, and violin classes for Ali, was being maximized. Not to mention, scouts. Girl Scouts for the girls and Boy Scouts for Chip, they all, except Tommy, had been scouts. Tommy was gobbled up by the Special Olympics. The vehicle was hopping with music, imagination and hope. Creativity was king and though no one could see Sophia's tiara, she was wearing one.

Yet there was that one person that always treated her as if he could see it, her husband. The man she married was the true constant in her life, that honest and good person she could blindly depend on. He would pick up the slack if need be and do it while encouraging and enabling. Sophia loved him and nothing in the whole world meant more to her than her family. Sure, the music was fun, the discovery of it, exciting, but neither it, nor anything, held a candle to the importance of her family.

MUSIC

The first album was developed with music rich in strings and passionate poetic ballads alongside fast beats filled with tease. Sophia completed it quickly, within that first year, hoping to garner attention from the music industry. It worked. She signed with an agent and a promotional package followed with television interviews at home, in the US, and back in Venezuela. Articles and reviews were written about the American woman who wrote and composed the album "Latinoamericano, Devolviendo un Poco," It was that sense of "giving back" that enchanted many and attracted them into looking deeper into Sophia. She was making headway in spite of repeatedly being told to not dare venture into the world of music.

"You could never cut it; it's all about skin." However, how could she *not* listen to the rhythms that flooded her every moment? Indeed she listened wholeheartedly and made her music irresistible.

The first album led to a second, a third and a fourth. The wonderful group of musicians she had found and assembled as "her own" were always loyal, but the demand for a true salsa beat had become the next challenge. For that, Sophia's agent Tony Sabournin had her recording in Miami at The Gentleman's Studio. There, on the same board where Ricky Martin, earlier in the day, laid down "Livin' La Vida Loca," Sophia put to bed, "Se Me Va A Oxidar."

It was eight o'clock in the evening when Sophia, her agent and a PR person reached The Gentleman's recording studio. It was large, with lighting that showed the rich contrast of mahogany surfaces against the black-buffered, sound-proof walls. There was a nice leather sofa for visitors or witnesses, depending on who would view the session through the large window into the adjacent sound room. Introductions were friendly but speedy, every second was money, and without further preamble, Sophia was invited to enter and begin singing. For Sophia, it was the big leagues and she was surprised at her lack of intimidation. Sophia entered the sound room and went directly to the single bench in front of the mic, where headphones were resting. She placed them on her head and said into the mic, "One," the mic was real hot and everyone jumped.

"Sorry" mouthed Sophia, revealing a little shyness.

"Try it now" said the voice in her ear.

"One, two, three. Whew! That's better," said Sophia. For the next few minutes the sound technician busied himself and Sophia, before beginning, announced that she needed to take off her shoes to sing.

"Sure, whatever it takes," said the technician, while through the glass Sophia could see how the comment had caused amusement, with someone saying . . . *a real diva*. It meant nothing to her. She was focused.

Sophia took off her shoes, buried her toes into the cold plush carpet and closed her eyes. No sounds, everyone waited. She opened her eyes, looked directly at the sound man and nodded. The intro of her music began and, at the precise moment she was supposed to, she began singing in her best voice. There was not one single interruption. There was not another take. The song was in the can and Sophia could see how her agent and the others were slapping each other on the back. Sabournin entered the sound room flamboyantly laughing and profusely began thanking her for her professionalism. The experience was new for Sophia, she had yet to learn that it was usually not done that way. A spoiled singer—a diva—would need many takes and everyone would brace themselves to patiently deal with the singer until they had what they needed. However, Sophia had approached it all as *This is it! It better be good!* and it was.

That song would make top ten nationwide on Latin charts and lend some serious credibility to Sophia's capabilities.

With credibility came opportunities and soon Sophia was flying off, with a filming crew, to Mexico City, where a video for MTV Latino would be produced. The experience was surreal and for Sophia absolutely amusing. Bodyguards, makeup crew, lights, camera, action and her own large trailer parked on Zócalo property. *How did that happen?* wondered Sophia. Singing on a stage, singing in the park, running in one outfit, dancing in another, signing autographs on city streets and being covered from head to toe in silver paint. Everything she did with a laugh and a kick knowing that it was all superfluous, but admitting she was having a blast.

The success of Sophia's song was great joy for her and her family. It never fazed her at all and her determination to continue on only grew. When she wasn't recording, she was doing her motherly chores, and most people who knew her had no idea of what she was up to in between those chores. Her trips to Miami were maximized. She would arrive, start working, recording, writing—whatever had to be done—

and quickly turn around, return home to relieve her husband and pick up where she had left off. For Sophia it was clear that without the selfless prompting and loving support of the man she married, high adventure of this nature would never be possible while responsibly raising four children. She was so grateful to him and loved him so. He was her knight in shining armor and her adored hero.

It was during those hot Georgian summer days, when staying out in the car while her daughter Colleen skated, was to risk being baked to a well-done crisp. Sophia, with a bright red smile and red face to match would, with no other choice, resume entering the rink. What a place! In the summertime, the cool welcoming air made it paradise.

Then reality would hit, as she saw the lack of smiles in those that incessantly watched. On those days when Don Laws, Colleen's coach, would see Sophia enter the rink, he would approach her and say, "So, you dared enter the snake pit today?"

Sophia would smile back, "I am treading lightly." The wink and laughter shared with him and the joy of watching her daughter float on ice, like an angel in flight, were the rewards. Bundled up in a heavy coat she would avoid the coffee shop, aka "the snake pit," and enter the freezing rink area where coaches and students worked tirelessly. It was invigorating. It was a place where dreams were tangible and announced in every jump, in every fall, and in every getting up to bravely try again. The speed of the skater, aloof in his constant balancing act, fascinated Sophia. The reward of seeing her daughter's confidence grow and her determination become stronger, nurtured Sophia's happiness.

However, within that world of speed and daring finesse, the mother of some young talented skater would come in and show the ugly side of the sport. The heavyset, uncombed woman would stand at the ice's door with her hand on her hip and screech for all to hear, "Get up! What's the matter with you? You are supposed to . . ." and then the mother, who surely was incapable of standing on ice, let alone skating on it, would proceed to tell the young prodigy how to do it. Sophia couldn't—nor did she try—to mask her distaste when looking at the heartless and disheveled woman. She could see that the suffering child who had just fallen was hurting and needed a smile or a nod of encouragement from her mother but got instead a mouth full of ugliness.

Sophia got up from the bench in front of her painting and headed toward the kitchen for a glass of water. The house was quiet and suddenly the sounds of the ever-present ocean took over. Sophia stood with her glass in hand drinking while critically surveying her work. She stood as far away as the room would allow and could see that proportions on the canvas were sound and congruent.

"Yes! Yes! You are going to be beautiful!" she said out loud and it felt as good as a tennis player who, after winning a point, pumps his fist. Sophia was on a roll and with confidence she again positioned herself in front of the canvas and continued painting.

Thoughts of the days when Colleen skated stuck with her. In her mind's eye she could see her skating toward the exit door at full speed, transitioning onto the outer rubber surface with not more than a hop. *That maneuver alone would have probably sent me crashing,* thought Sophia with an audible chuckle.

"Mommy, what did you think? Did you like that last double loop?" asked Colleen with a bright smile on her face.

"Oh! It was wonderful. I'm so proud of you!" said Sophia sliding off the bleachers and putting her arm around her daughter as they walked out. "Come on, let's get those skates off."

Colleen was thriving. She had by chance found a dream early in life. She knew that she was good at it and her spirit was happy, strong and confident. Skating had become the entity that would bond Sophia and her oldest daughter forever. Sharing those early morning drives and the thousands of hours of conversations and laughs, made them tighter than twine.

Because of that closeness, a few years—later when Colleen's coach told Sophia that he was moving away from Georgia and heading to Maryland—Sophia was quick to make an important decision. As the coach outlined details of his intentions, Sophia's brain distanced itself, shutting him off, and beginning to dissect what the devastating news meant for Colleen's future in skating. Her mind was reeling, *How could this be? What should be done?*

"Sophia, I must go full circle. Maryland is my home and you mustn't worry about Colleen. We will find a wonderful family there that can keep her." Sophia said nothing; she knew that would never happen. She would never send her precious daughter away to live with anyone. The caring coach continued to speak, and Sophia could see his lips moving but she was too far removed to hear him. She was carefully and quickly evaluating each child individually. How would each one fare if they too were to move? Alison's school was overcrowded to a point where children no longer fit in classrooms and occupied trailers all day. Tommy was about to be switched over to a special program that required being bused to another county. Chip was already up at Avon Old Farms in Connecticut, so it didn't matter much to him. Her husband was flexible with his work. He could continue managing family investments and such from any address. In moments the answer was clear. Each child would be fine or even benefit from such a move. They would all do fine. She looked up at Don Laws and said, "Well then, I guess it's decided, we too are going to move. Where are we going?"

The coach audibly inhaled, looked closely into Sophia's face and burst out laughing. "The rink is in Laurel, Maryland!"

She smiled knowing that her decision was the correct one, though it was clear that what would be lost in the shuffle was her music. Her musicians, her mainstays, were in Atlanta. Maybe she could go back and forth for a while, but in her heart she knew that she was saying *goodbye* to a very special time. However, she never flinched, there was not a flicker of doubt that moving was the right thing to do for her family. Their children's needs, whatever they might be, came first. That was the deal she had so mindfully signed on to when she married and became a mother. How well she knew the devastation that could be brought into a child's life if a parent forgot that simple and basic promise.

9

FRUITS OF DECEIT

"ME TUMBARÁS" ~ "YOU'LL KNOCK ME DOWN"
Sabes lo que quieres y sabes pensar, ~ You know what you want and how to think,
El éxito te espera, sabes agarrar, ~ Success awaits you, you know how to seize,
Muchos se te acercan, oportunidad, ~ Many approach you, opportunity,
De nadie te confías, y te oigo gritar, ~ You trust no one, and I hear you scream,
(Coro) ~ (Chorus)
Me tumbarás, y me levanto, ~ You'll knock me down, and I'll get up,
Me tumbarás y me devuelvo, ~ You'll knock me down and I'll come back,
Me tumbarás, no tengo miedo, ~ You'll knock me down, I'm not afraid,
Me tumbas y me paro y me vuelvo parar. ~ Knock me down, and I'll get up and I'll get up again.

It was a Saturday, and must have been around ten o'clock in the morning, when a woman selling house smocks stopped in at the James's house. Sophia's mother and the woman sat outside on the porch as Mrs. James admired every smock in the bag. When the woman happily left, Mrs. James called for Sophia to show off her new purchases. The little girl stood looking at the nine smocks her mother had bought. She couldn't believe that she bought so many of them. She tried to smile and be interested, but instead she felt resentment rising in her throat. The selfish woman wouldn't buy them any clothes, and had just bought herself a boatload of the awful, baggy things.

"They're nice, but so many?"

Her mother looked at her seriously and said, "Sophia, I need to feel comfortable these days, you see I didn't know it until now, but we are going to have another baby in our family." Sophia's jaw almost fell off her face, she stood staring, "What did you say?"

"That, I'm expecting a baby, Sophia."

Sophia was young but no one's fool. The realization made her blurt out,

"My God, my God, how could you do this? This is really going to kill Daddy? He always loved you and always tried to make you happy. Oh, my God! Oh, my God, what's going to happen?"

Sophia was nearly hysterical. She was blinded by tears and seemed to be speaking to herself. Mrs. James's attitude changed and she tried to look offended by the assumption of such a possibility. "Stop it! What are you saying? Of course your Daddy is the father of this baby." Sophia stopped dead and stared her in the face, throwing all caution to the wind and seemed to spit out the words with venom when she spoke, "You stop it! Do you really think anyone could believe that? Daddy has been gone for almost five months. Do you really think that he is going to swallow that? It's not his and you have a big problem because he is going to know it. Do you think he can't count? Oh! My God what are we going to do? Daddy might leave us. You will have hurt him so badly and he has always been so good to us. We're on this island because you wanted to come back and I never could understand it after meeting your family. They don't love you! There never was anything here for us but your selfishness. You have become nothing. I hate you. I wish you were dead!"

Sophia ran off to her room; she cried and cried until she could cry no more. The young girl was wise enough to foresee all the pain that was still to come. She cried for herself, for her brothers and sisters, and then she cried for her father. She knew that his heart would be shattered.

The relationship between mother and daughter had broken down entirely, since that awful night in the mother's bedroom. Sophia answered her mother when spoken to but never offered to speak to her first. Only on a few occasions after learning about the pregnancy did Sophia, who was consumed by worry, involuntarily touch the subject.

"What will Dad do to Ramón when he finds out?" Mrs. James's reply sounded almost childish and she seemed to believe it, "He is not going to find out about Ramón, because no one will dare tell him. Besides, this child belongs to your daddy and is your little sister or brother and that is all there is to it."

It took a matter of days for Mrs. James's condition to become noticeable. She wore the awful smocks around the house and when she went out she tried to wear baggy things. Nevertheless, tongues waggled. No one mentioned anything to Sophia nor asked her questions about the night of the banging pots. She didn't give anyone the opportunity either. The only neighbor Sophia continued to visit was Tiba, on Sundays, for her Sunday hair-washing session. It truly became more like a therapy, not just a mere cleansing of one's hair but an unspoken cleansing of one's soul. Sophia relaxed with Tiba as she gently and affectionately tended to her. The sweet Tiba would not ask questions, so Sophia did not have to put up her guard. She could be completely quiet during a visit and feel when she left that the kind woman understood everything. But always upon leaving Tiba, who was a devout Catholic, would say "God bless you, child," and would give Sophia and Karen each, a much needed hug.

It was with fear instead of joy that Sophia awaited the arrival of her father. He was due anytime now. His six months away were over, and though Sophia and all the children needed him so desperately, she dreaded his arrival. Her gastroenteritis, the inflammation that she had in the stomach and throughout her intestines, which caused her so much pain, flared up. Without medication and her mother lost to her, the little girl would curl up at night in a fetal position, tight, tight, tight until the pain subsided. Sophia became very slim and her large eyes appeared enormous. At school her nickname was *Cow Eyes*. She ate very little, trying to avoid the pain that seized her after intake. Worry kept her hunger at bay.

'What would happen? How furious could her Daddy become? What if he killed her mother out of anger for being betrayed? What if he sought out Ramón and killed him? Would he spend the rest of his life in prison? Would he just turn his back and leave them all to rot on that island? What would become of their lives if they were forgotten by their

Daddy? Their lives would be lost. *No! No! My life will never be lost, unless I let it be*, she told herself over and over again, trying to remember it, trying to believe it.

It was a hot and humid Wednesday with a pop quiz on punctuation in Sophia's sixth grade class. Sophia aced it and was bored by it. Finally, the end of the school day bell saved her and she was quickly out the door. The four James children that were in school always met up to walk home together. Everyone with their own friends, but always within ear shot of each other. That was the rule. On days when their mother was out, they came home to find someone who had been paid a couple dollars, caring for the small ones. As soon as Sophia had thrown down her heavy load of books, exhausted from the three-mile walk, the sitter would be out the door, leaving her to change the smelly diaper. Sophia felt angry to always be doing a mother's job. However, knowing that a bomb was about to hit them, she was more loving and patient than ever toward her siblings.

On this afternoon the homeward-bound children could see from a distance that the shiny green Plymouth was home. Sophia let out a sigh of relief, thinking that maybe she would be able to get started on a project for school. The boys were running ahead with sweat pouring down their faces, racing each other to see who would be first to get the glass of water at the other end. Sophia saw them racing each other and a smile came to her face and then her heart stopped. In a panic she began running as fast as she could toward the house. She didn't know what was happening but she could hear the boys screaming out of their minds. Only once she reached the house did she realize that the cries were of delight and in one second she was staring into her daddy's smiling face. His arms were outstretched and the children, in a rowdy session of laughter and joy, all fought to be in those strong and protecting arms. Sophia was so glad to see her father, she also lunged forward to get into those loving arms and as she hugged her Daddy she looked into his eyes and the world came crashing inside of her. He was smiling but she knew that he knew. *Oh Daddy, I'm so sorry*, raced through her brain. Sophia looked away from his eyes and began to quietly cry in his embrace. She held on to him so tightly, that her Daddy grabbed her by both arms and separating her enough to look into her face said, "Come on, my little Sophia, you couldn't have missed me so much."

"Yes, I did, Daddy. Yes, I did."

His smiling eyes looked a little deeper and he said in a quiet and trustworthy voice, "I'm home now, everything will be fine." *Did he know? Yes!* She thought, *I think he knows.*

Dinner was filled with stories and her dad even pulled out his harmonica, but beneath all the apparent happiness, Sophia could sense a fire smoldering. Masking her feelings the best she could, she kept every thought to herself and played along. The inevitable would happen soon enough and so they might as well enjoy the moment.

It was two-thirty in the morning when Sophia's mother came to her bed and awoke her. She was crying. The blinding light shone brightly into Sophia's face, keeping her eyes from opening, as she lay on the top bunk above her sister Karen. She was awakened from a deep sleep, a restful, peaceful, and long-awaited sleep.

"Sophia, look, look at what your father has done to me. Look, look at me," said Sophia's mother as she stood next to her crying.

Finally sleep gave way to reality and as her eyes became accustomed to the brightness, she was able to open them and stare into the crying face of her mother.

"Look at me, my hair, he's cut it all off!" It was a pitiful sight. Indeed Sophia's father cut her hair off and did a miserable job of it too. It was coarsely chopped and presented bald patches throughout. Sophia stared and didn't utter a word. Her mother pleaded with her,

"Your father did this to me!"

"You're lucky that's all he did to you." Sophia heard herself say those words and felt sorry for having said them. Her mother looked totally dejected and Sophia, almost feeling as if someone else spoke for her, went on to say, "It could have been so much worse. If you were married to some guy from around here he would have cut your throat, not your hair, for having someone else's baby. I'm sorry, I just can't cry for you. You have hurt us all so much with this. Please go away, I've got school tomorrow." Her mother still crying left the room and turned off the light. Sophia lay in the dark with her eyes wide open and silently cried, *My God, am I tough? Or am I just mean?*

Sophia tried to keep her life together as best she could as the turmoil of her parents' difficulties swirled around her. Her mother now constantly sported a scarf and hardly ever exchanged a word with their father. Mr. James was silent a lot these days and Sophia knew that he was debating on what to do. Mrs. James's belly continued to grow and the question of who was the father, in moments of heated discussion, could be overheard by all. Her father knew that the baby was not his but her mother had not told him who she was spending time with. At times when Sophia would walk in on an argument, the look of *Don't even think of telling*, would be all over her mother's face.

Coming home from school one day, about a week later, Sophia found her mother crying. She was sprawled over her bed and made no attempt to stop when Sophia came in. How hopelessly little she looked, how completely lost and even immature she seemed to Sophia.

"What happened? Why are you crying?" and for the first time in a long time Sophia reached out to touch her leg, in a gesture of consolation. "Where's Daddy?"

"I don't know, he left a couple of hours ago. He might not come back." She answered in a despairing way, as if she cared. Tightness grabbed Sophia around the throat and filled with alarm, she asked, "Why? What happened? Were you fighting again?"

"Ramón, he knows everything about Ramón; he threatened to kill him and then he left." She said while sobbing into her pillow. Sophia stood there looking at her as if carved in stone. The most fearful of all of her fears had engulfed her once again. She could feel a desire to vomit overtake her as blood seemed to drain from her body. The clamminess in her hands and an overall cold sweat made her feel nauseous and ill. No, she wouldn't scream and cry like her foolish mother. Instead she quietly waited and hoped that on this day Ramón be somewhere safe, far away from them. Payback time was nearing. She knew it and it terrified her.

About an hour later Sophia heard the car roll into the driveway. With more fear than anything else she ran out to meet her daddy and found that he returned with lumber sticking out of the rear window. The children out in the yard beat her to him, crying out, "Daddy, Daddy, what's the wood for? Daddy, why did you buy so much wood? Can I help you build whatever you're building, Daddy? Can I? Can I?"

"Let's get the wood out of the car first," he replied. Sophia looked at her Daddy and their eyes met. Her face did not have a look of excitement but of love and fear.

She nudged up to him and hugged him, "Daddy, please never leave us, we need you so much." As she said those words tears began to well up in her eyes and her dad then understood the extent of her knowledge.

He hugged her back, "Oh, my little Sophia, I'll never do that, I love you too much." His heart ached for the little girl. Since her birth, he had harbored so many hopes for her. In an instant they were back at the dining room table, in Sacramento, going over all the pieces included in the new chemistry set. Gently he pushed Sophia aside and told the children with a glimmer of excitement in his eyes, "We are going to build a tree house, right up in that tree." He pointed to the oldest tree in the front yard, the only one that was on the property before he built the house.

All the trees around the James house were very young and most of them were accidentals. They all began as fence posts. On many Sundays, while Mr. James was building the house, he spent time at a local bar, offering rounds of cold beers and having laughs in his broken Spanish. After a few beers, and some jokes he couldn't understand, he and a bunch of guys would pile into somebody's pickup truck. Off they'd go with machetes to Lafunia and La Boca, to *help the Americano* cut limbs off of large trees, destined to be used as fence posts. The posts weren't very big, but they were sturdy and did a fine job of holding up the cyclone wire mesh fence. As time went by, it was beautiful to see so many of them just break out and sprout limbs, adding their light, lush, yellowish-green to the empty land. With time, they would become very big and beautiful *Araguaneys*, covered in bright orange and yellow blossoms. They were the island's national tree.

"It's going to be so great. We'll have a trap door in the floor, so that you can climb in, and a window on every side with shutters that can open and close. When it's all finished, we'll paint it!" The children cheered with delight and their dad got down on one knee, flashing a wink at Sophia and trying to embrace all of them in one big bear hug. He loved his kids and wouldn't hide it. Sophia realized that this was his way of telling the children that he was theirs forever, no matter what the future brought.

Finishing the inside of the house was not a priority for Mr. James. It seemed that building the tree house with the children was the priority. Work started that weekend, the kids nearby, waiting and hoping for their name to be called out.

"Hand me the hammer, Frankie."

"Johnny, bring me the saw, be careful with it now."

"Bobby, hand me the nails." The kids ran back and forth, proud to be needed. It worked like clockwork. Earlier Mr. James would call out for something and all three boys would race as fast as they could to the object.

A tug of war would ensue, followed with cries of, "I got here first." "No! Let go, it's mine," and Mr. James would have to stop work to restore order. With each job specifically assigned, all fights ended and work continued swiftly. The work began in a feverish way and quickly the little structure, perched up in the widespread tree, was taking form.

Every day in Puerto Rico was warm. Flowers bloomed year round and meadows never looked dry, but lush and green. When there were droughts they never lasted long enough for the color to recede. The island seemed so beautiful at times, a true paradise, arrayed in its virgin, tropical, lavish flora. During those days in which the James family built their little tree house, there was joy for the children. Sophia allowed her imagination to run away and she, like the others, enjoying each moment of sunshine, wanting to believe that all was well and safe.

Building the tree house was a project owned by children and father. While the children were at school their father worked inside their home on areas that needed to be finished. However, every day once the kids were home from school—and all day Saturdays and Sundays—Mr. James and the children worked on the tree house. Learning how to saw and use a hammer without bending the nail were all parts of the experience. If Sophia's father had taken up the challenge, to get away from the problem, it was working. After about two weekends, the tree house was almost completely finished. Everyone was excited to vote on the paint color. It was going to be a yellow house with pink around the windows. It was during the paint job that disaster struck again.

Down the dirt road, still at some distance, Sophia saw a tall lanky figure approach. She recognized Ramón immediately and in the same second felt faint. He was going to defiantly walk right by their home in broad daylight. She knew instantly that her father would react and as her shocked silent stare went from the dusty road to her father, he too watched the distant figure. The world around her took on a different dimension and everything went into slow motion. Sounds were muffled and with a beating weight in her chest she saw her father move forward with long reaching strides.

In a wave of panic Sophia could hear her dad say, "So you think you're going to just walk by the front of our house? You dirty son of a bitch!" As soon as he said those words he punched him in the face. Ramón fell with the blow and while he was down on the ground he fumbled in his pocket for a knife. He got it out and opened it. It was old, curved and about four inches long. It looked dangerous and the children were screaming in terror. Mr. James bent down to pick up a piece of wood, as bystanders came running with all the commotion, and lunged forward to prevent Ramón from getting close to Mr. James with the knife. Ramón's face was dark and menacing as he yelled death threats, while being dragged away. The James children did their job and pulled and yanked at their father to get him back home and away from danger. There was no more building on that day. The young ones had experienced something they had never seen before—their father hitting another man—and it was something they would never forget.

The court room had an unpleasant smell, made by years and years of sweat and tears. The room was large and filled with hard wooden benches. The judge's seat at the front looked foreboding. Sophia could recognize many faces and knew that people were looking forward to a juicy tale to take home. The James family, all nicely dressed sat together. From the youngest to the eldest, they understood the seriousness of their whereabouts. With straight backs and clammy hands they were, without a doubt, scared into being on their best behavior. Eyes intent on every movement in the room, they all sat patiently awaiting the judge's arrival.

In he came, a white-haired man wearing glasses, a black robe, and a visible kindness on his face. He spoke clearly and firmly but Sophia did not fear him. On the contrary, after one look at him, she felt that he was someone that could be trusted.

Sophia had groomed herself extra carefully that morning. She had never been inside the court house before and she was going to testify. She knew her facts. She knew what she saw but nevertheless was afraid that maybe they wouldn't win the case and then there would be so much more fear in the future.

"State your name please."

"Sophia James."

"Raise your right hand. Do you solemnly swear to tell the truth, the whole truth and nothing but the truth, so help you God?"

"I will."

Sophia climbed up the steps and sat up straight and as tall as an eleven-year-old could. The defense attorney was very gentle and convivial. He asked Sophia to repeat her name and identify her father. Finally he wanted to hear the details of what happened on the day of the fight.

"It was a beautiful day. We were all outside working on the tree house that our dad is building for us . . . ." She continued clearly and intelligently to recount the details of what happened. During her statement she turned and looked at the judge as if telling the details directly to him. He in turn looked at her kindly as if urging her to continue. The lawyer asked her if she actually saw the knife with her own eyes and she replied that she had.

He then asked her, "How long do you think that curved knife was?"

Sophia said without hesitation, "About six inches long, sir." The defense attorney went on and asked Sophia to explain how the fight was stopped?

Once she answered, he advised her to remain seated while, "That other attorney over there wants to ask you some more questions."

Sophia smiled at the prosecutor as he approached her and he smiled back.

"So, Sophia were you afraid on the day that your father attacked Mr. Valena?"

"Oh, yes, I was, sir," said Sophia feeling all eyes of the court on her.

"Tell us why you were afraid."

"Well sir, I knew there was going to be trouble, the moment I saw Ram. . . Mr. Valena coming down the street. Then when my father hit him and he pulled out the knife, it was terrible. I didn't want anyone to get hurt, sir."

"Do you know why your father hit Mr. Valena?"

"Sure, I do." Answered Sophia quite confidently and glancing over at the judge.

"Would you tell us why?"

"Well, it's a long and terrible story but believe me he had it coming." To this the court room broke into a muffled laugh and Sophia shot a glance at the judge.

Looking at Sophia the judge asked, "Are you afraid of Mr. Valena?"

To this Sophia looked at the judge in earnest, as if only speaking to him, "Your honor, I'm not afraid of him, but he has caused our family a lot of pain and I know that anytime we see him, there could be trouble. On the day that the fight broke out, your honor, I was so afraid for my father. He is such a good person. He is all we have in the world, your honor, the only person to take care of us and we need him. We are six kids, your honor." The judge looked down and began writing; he didn't look up for a long time. Meanwhile the prosecutor continued asking Sophia questions.

"So you say that the knife was about six inches long?"

"Yes," replied Sophia.

"Could you show me with your fingers, on this surface, what that length is? Sophia immediately placed her two pointers on the wooden slab in front of her. The lawyer asked her to not move her fingers, while he reached for a ruler sitting on the stenographer's desk. With a flair for the melodrama he measured the distance between Sophia's fingers and called out, "Seven inches!" With a bit of ridiculous flamboyance, he moved around the courtroom relishing the moment. "Such a pocket knife does not exist! In fact there isn't a six-inch pocket knife manufactured either." Sophia looked confused and straight at him. The lawyer looked at the young girl, sitting straight in the witness seat, "You said that you had seen a knife, but there was no such knife at all, was there? He didn't really pull out any knife from his pocket, now did he?" Sophia felt hot, her heart was skipping beats and she heard her voice say, "What?"

"You were afraid for your Dad. You wanted the fight to stop, so you started screaming 'Knife!' didn't you? However, there really was no knife at all. Isn't that the truth?"

To this Sophia looked up at the judge and said, "Your honor, I don't know what's wrong with him. Of course there was a knife. I saw it and so did a lot of other people that are sitting right here, waiting to see what happens. He had a knife and it was big for a pocket knife and curved. Maybe they don't make'em any more or something, but he sure had one, and as long as I showed you, too!"

"I understand," said the judge.

Sophia was dismissed. She turned to smile at the judge and returned to her seat alongside her father, brothers, and sisters. Every one of the

Jameses, except for their mother, was there, even little Evy. As Sophia returned to sit amongst them, all the kids flashed her big smiles.

The judge didn't take too long to make up his mind. He had heard enough and then he called for Ramón to come up to the stand. In a clear, loud and forceful voice, allowing all to hear, he said, "You may not come near the James family. You may not walk by their home. Take a different street. I want you to avoid being around them. Much has not been said here in this court house today, nevertheless, I have read about it in the file. Your irresponsible acts, young man, have caused a lot of damage and I will not have this family suffer anymore by you taunting them and thinking that you can just go on your merry way. You avoid them and if I have any complaints of you walking past their house, I'll change your address and you can be a guest in my jail and see how you like it!"

That was the end of it. They never, ever saw Ramón walk by their home again. The day in court proved to have all the rich gossip in the world, enough to hold the townspeople for a long time. At first the version went around pretty much as it had happened, but as time went by, the story changed. It had been a bloody fight and Ramón spent time in jail for it.

Mr. James's stay came to an end. Money ran out and it was time for him to go back to sea. Sophia silently hoped that he would somehow find work close by: a job at a factory, maybe construction work, or anything to keep him from leaving. His last visit was painful, but Sophia had been safe from her mother's beatings and there had been no sleepless nights filled with fear or fury. There was a truce of sorts between parents. They would remain married and once Mrs. James gave birth to the baby, Mr. James would adopt the child as if it were his own. What had happened was part of the past and it would and must be considered a mistake worth forgiving. Too many lives were at stake; too many children needed her to be their mother. Yes, it was all logical; Sophia had heard the whole plan. Still the ugly woman that would beat her was fresh in her mind, and the lovely mother they needed seemed too far away for this plan to be plausible, or even logical.

Departure was always tough but this one was like no other. He reassured his children that everything would be fine, that he loved them, and that he would come back. He would definitely come back, were the only words that mattered to Sophia.

FRUITS OF DECEIT 141

With Mr. James's departure all was fair game again. The mother's gentler mask came right off immediately. This time there was no grace period. It was again replaced by her calm and calculating mask of deception. Sophia was fearful and took care to stay out of her way as much as possible.

Along with the growth of the child in the mother's womb, grew the distance between mother and children. There was no love to be found anywhere except among the children themselves. There were no conversations, and questions, when asked, were seldom answered. Over a short period of time Sophia's mother began collecting boxes. Big brown ones like the ones discarded in dumpsters by department stores. Mrs. James was packing, really cleaning up the place. The nicest things they owned were being placed in those boxes for 'safe keeping.' It was a surprise to the children when the little night lamps with the Spanish Flamenco dancer holding castanets from Spain, also were put away. They missed them. They had always been there and now they, too, were hidden in boxes. Everything was being packed away. She was filling up the home with boxes of all sizes and Sophia didn't know how to make sense of it. Very seldom did the young girl approach her mother to speak, however, on one morning while her mother sat in front of a mirror, Sophia inquired about the accumulation of all the boxes.

"Mom, why are you bringing so many boxes into the house?"

"I was wondering when you were going to ask. We're moving," she said without even a glance.

"Moving?" Said Sophia with apprehension. "It can't be. We've been working so hard on the house and on our tree house. This is home, where are we going to go?" All of a sudden her heart gave a leap of joy and with the trace of a smile she couldn't hold back, she said, "Are we going back to California?"

"No, no, we are not moving back to California," said the mother with sarcasm. "We are moving away from this house, not forever, but it was part of the agreement between your father and me. This house isn't finished and I'm sick and tired of living in it like this. So, we are moving out. When we're out, your Dad is going to have some men come in and finish it for us. Once it's finished then we'll be back." Sophia just stood there with her mouth open. She didn't know what to say. She didn't feel particularly happy and couldn't imagine that such of an important event was going to take place and she had not heard anything about it.

"Oh, I hadn't heard anything. I didn't know anything. I guess we should all help pack up."

Her mother looked at her through the mirror and said, "I'll tell you when to help me. I'll be packing while you kids are at school. We aren't in a terrible hurry. Enough of that, don't you have homework?"

As days went by the packing was taking place. It was obvious, but it was being done in a random way. Items that were necessary while they were still in the house were being packed first and that seemed senseless to Sophia. One evening when the night lights in Sophia's room vanished, Sophia spoke with her mother.

"Where did our little lamps go?"

"What lamps?"

"The ones from Spain that Daddy brought us, the ones with the little bull heads?"

"Oh! Those . . . I put them away for safe keeping."

"But, we use them all the time, we need them, if not it's too dark in the room."

"Forget it, they're packed" she answered roughly. More and more Sophia could sense that something was really wrong. She didn't know what, but her mother's demeanor was threatening and mysterious.

The house was being reduced to complete bareness. One day coming home from school, as they got close enough to see their home, they saw a large van and men carrying furniture from the house into it. They started running down the barren, dirt road and quickly realized that it was their beds and dressers that were going into the van. Sophia ran to her mother, "What's going on? Why are they taking our furniture?"

"Get out of the way! They're taking things to our new house." With that she ignored the children and stood watching with a blank look on her face. The truck left and she carried on as if it had never been there. All along the children were huddling close to Sophia. They had all watched in silence as their beds and dressers were lifted and taken, wondering where they were going to sleep? Where were they going to put their clothes?

"Mommy," said Sophia very carefully, with the children standing around her.

"Where is our new house?"

"Don't ask me a single question. Don't do it Sophia." The voice was cutting and the threat was clear. Johnny immediately moved forward and grabbed Sophia by the hand.

"Sophia, come inside now. I need you to help me with something." The children all moved away with Sophia in the center. They understood that anything Sophia said at that moment could cause her to be beaten and they didn't want to see her hurt. As they entered the house, they held their breaths looking at the mess created by the movers. With the beds gone, dusty boxes that had been stored under them, were visible. Clothing from drawers was thrown in a pile on the floor next to where the dressers had been. Sophia sat down on the floor of one room and without a word stared and stared.

Bobby sat next to her. In a hushed voice he said, "I can find some boxes for our clothes, Sophia. Don't worry about it, it'll be all right."

The house was in boxes and nearly bare, and to make matters worse, Sophia wasn't feeling well. She didn't know that she had been bitten by a bad mosquito. That evening she was running a fever; it was the beginning of dengue fever, a terrible, debilitating and life-threatening virus that begins with one little mosquito bite. Every joint and muscle in her body ached and for two days she did not eat. She was rolled up in old blankets on the floor where her bed used to be, and through those delirious days she could hear people coming and going. Items were being carried out and then one day turned into night and no lights came on. The house was dark, candles were lit and she could feel the kids moving around, and trying to find comfort on the floor next to her. Dengue would take the life of many on the island of Puerto Rico but thankfully, Sophia was too hearty a soul to be defeated by dengue. Alone, she weathered the illness without food, medicines, or care, spending several days lost in sleep and hallucinations. Her hallucinations were very scary and she would find herself sitting up crying for help. Little men, all dressed up as soldiers, would be everywhere in her room. Their objective seemed to be to get close to her. They wanted to attack her, she was sure of it, and the threat of so many of them terrified her. They were climbing up her sheets as if in a military drill, thousands of them ready to cover her up and kill her with their tiny bayonets, Nooooooooo!!!, she would cry out in her hallucinating stupor. On the morning her fever broke her mother woke her up; on bent knee she nudged Sophia awake. She awoke, immersed in sweat-soaked sheets, with her hair matted to her head. Seeing through blurry eyes as if looking through a prism, she deciphered her mother's face. Slowly awakening, Sophia gathered that she was alive and being spoken to. The words were hitting her. She could hear noise but could not decipher what they meant.

Sophia kept saying, "What? What?" Her mother kept speaking and then words, syllables got through to her brain and she understood their meaning.

"I'm leaving. I'm leaving, Sophia." Yes, the words got through and she could hear them, but could not understand their meaning.

She continued to say, "What? What?"

Then she saw her mother get up and say, "Goodbye, Sophia." Sophia didn't know what was happening but began to mouth the words. "Please, don't go. Please, don't leave us. Please, don't go." she cried out in a small voice. From the wet bedding on the floor, she extended an arm trying to reach for her, as the firm sound of her high heels faded away. That was it. She walked out, as if she were going to the grocery store, but in reality she walked right out of the lives of six young children.

Many long years would pass before Sophia, or any of them, ever saw or heard of her again.

10

THE FACE OF EVIL

"TOMA TU AMADA" ~ "TAKE YOUR LOVE"
Conocer el amor, importa tanto, ~ To know love, matters so much,
Nutre tu alma con calor. ~ It nurtures your soul with warmth.
Un gran amor, no viene de la nada, ~ A great love, doesn't come from a void,
Es pura y es bella. ~ It is pure and it is beautiful.
Toma tu amada o toma tu amado, ~ Take her or take him,
Con un gesto, dile te quiero, ~ With a gesture say, I love you,
Cuida ese amante, tan preciado tesoro, ~ Care for that love, such a precious treasure,
No lo descuides, no lo pierdas. ~ Don't neglect it, don't lose it.
Porque un amor es un regalo, ~ Because love is a gift,
Del destino de la vida, ~ From destiny, from life,
No es un hecho dado. ~ It is not, a given.
Porque amor es privilegio, ~ Because love is a privilege,
Una suerte, cuando es encontrada. ~ A stroke of luck, when found.
Un amor nace en el cielo, ~ Love is born in heaven,
Y llega a la tierra virgen pura esperanza, ~ And reaches earth, as virgin, pure hope,
Dulcemente ella espera a que dos almas gemelas, ~ Sweetly it awaits for two soul mates,
La hagan crecer. ~ To make it grow.

Sophia's greatest fear was worse than she could have ever imagined, and it now was their reality. They were completely abandoned and left in a loveless world. Their mother was never packing to move them to another home, but instead was collecting everything they owned to sell. She stopped payment on everything so furniture was repossessed. Electricity and water were all turned off, as she hoarded all monies until she had enough to begin somewhere else on her own. She left her six children in the worst of ways, on the floor, in a shell of a house. No bed to sleep on, no chairs to sit in, without electricity, no water, without plates or utensils. To avoid a showdown she cowardly left when Sophia was being ravaged by dengue. She left all of her children to fend for themselves.

> ANTHONY YOUR CHILDREN ARE ALONE STOP
> YOU MUST COME HOME IMMEDIATELY STOP
> YOUR SISTER GLADYS STOP.

The words glared back at Mr. James as he read them from a telegram. The last port his ship left was the port of Alexandria in Egypt, and he was somewhere in the middle of the Red Sea when it was handed to him. He couldn't get off and fly home, so the telegram only took peace away from him. There was nothing for him to do but conclude his itinerary. He had to get back to his home port and find his way back to the Caribbean, and it would take months.

It seemed to Sophia that no one in the world cared that they were left alone. She contacted an aunt out in California, who in return promised to try and locate her father, but that was all she ever heard from that side of the family. Days without electricity or water were scary and hungry, but nights were scarier and hungrier. Sophia became stronger after defeating dengue fever, and the realization of being left alone sunk in. She took on the role of guide and gathered her little brothers and sisters around her. Sophia wasn't twelve yet and Evy the youngest wasn't two, but they would survive. She was determined that they would. That was the message she gave her siblings: "We all have to help each other now more than ever. We all have to stay close and we're going to be OK." The kids did just that. They believed in their sister, Sophia, and they all hung tight. Food at the beginning was bad and mostly made up of potato chips and Vienna sausages. Sophia didn't really know how to cook. What she did in the past was mostly can-opening. However, without electricity they couldn't even heat up a can of soup. They somehow coped every day. They "borrowed" water by the bucket from a neighbor to drink and when things got too bad, they used some to flush the toilet. They ate mangoes. They ate bananas. They spoke with the grandfather and he gave them food on credit. That was all the help that the grandfather offered them. He did not put on their electricity nor give them any money at all. Each long day turned into night and after two months they heard the sweet sound of their father's voice trying to get into the house at about three in the morning. He finally had made his way back from so far away and in an instant there was hope, there was joy and there was blessed laughter. However, most of all there was an adult, someone responsible, someone that would take the burden off of Sophia's shoulders.

Mr. James returned with money and began putting things in order. Having electricity was the most cherished of improvements. Sleeping on the floor wasn't half as bad as the misery of darkness. Carrying candles was awful and dangerous but the real humiliation was having everyone in the neighborhood pity them. On days when Sophia could make it to school she would be teased about living in "the dark house." Mockery was hard to bear but during the whole time that they were so alone, Sophia marveled at how adults that knew of their situation, managed to look the other way and never offer a helping hand. All members of the Risorio family took the grandfather's lead and ignored it all. Sylvana and Erica stopped speaking to the James children. Their mother, Aunt Luisa, knew of Mrs. James's behavior and she didn't want her daughters "contaminated," or anywhere near the scandal. The many uncles and aunts pretended to not know, that there were six children abandoned in the dark house next to them. No one stepped forward with a hot meal for them or a kindness. Sophia always thought that they were a miserable lot and every day they proved her right.

After the lights, he got the children off the floor and back into beds. He didn't go out and buy beds, he made them. They were very simple and made out of four posts from which a narrow metallic mesh was suspended. A mattress lay over the wired mesh to make a bed that was comfortable. Each child had one and their young little bodies felt the relief of getting off the hard concrete floor. With electricity, hot meals started to fill the children's tummies. They had all lost weight, and were not much more than skin and bones, a fact that had not gone by unnoticed by Mr. James. On that first night upon his arrival, after the initial hugs and kisses, he took a good look into his children's gaunt little faces and broke down and cried with them.

It was time for planning, a time in which to accept realities and work together to go forward and survive the cruelty of being young and motherless. Sophia began to learn how to cook. Her first rice was hard, her second was sloppy but after a few attempts she started to get the knack of it, for which everyone was grateful. The boys, ever hungry, would compliment Sophia on every dish she conquered and the sounds of mmmmmm..., would go on and on. These times, though real tough, were not unhappy. They had their daddy. They constantly were filled with some project or another trying to improve their lives and trying to prepare for the unutterable words "When Daddy leaves . . . ." The thought would give Sophia stomach pains. No matter how practical, realistic, and grown up she tried to be, she couldn't control the visceral pain that those words caused her.

Sitting on the floor around their father, they all had discussed everything over and over again. The goal was clear, they must not be separated. They would stick together and not end up in the welfare system or be split up among foster homes. Those possibilities had to be avoided at all cost. Though the Jameses were lacking everything else at that moment, they never were short on pride or love. It was clear that the only option was for Sophia to grow up in a hurry and become the head of the family. Mr. James had to return to the ocean to earn a living and there simply was no other adult to take charge. The father explained that as long as they were in Puerto Rico they would be left alone. There were too many poor people on the island for authorities to be too concerned about one family. The kids would fend for themselves and no one would really care. Back home on the US mainland it would be impossible. Social Services would climb all over them and never let it happen. They would come knocking and decide everyone's future. In the blink of an eye, the six James children would be split up, placed into foster care and only God knew if they'd ever meet again. The conclusion was that eleven-year-old Sophia, would find herself alone and in command of five younger children.

With the immediate future defined, Mr. James went into action gearing Sophia up with essential survival tools. She would need to manage money. With this in mind, Mr. James headed into town and sat down with the manager of the *Banco Popular* and explained the situation. Full cooperation was given for the little girl to be the executor of an account. A couple of days later, Mr. James, walked into the bank with Sophia and introduced her. She was warmly welcomed and quickly given a few pointers on how business was conducted at the bank. With kindness, and a few stares of amazement by bank employees, she was shown, by the manager himself, how to deposit a check and how to take money out of the account when needed. It all was simple enough and Sophia knew she could handle it.

Next on the list, was something not as easy: learning how to drive. At first the thought was scary but there was no time for scary. The 1959 green Plymouth was an elegant and long vehicle. It was designed with big fins over its back wheels and long, horizontal stoplights. It was a real nice car, and the one that the James family drove across the United States and shipped over from Miami. That car was a challenge for any adult to drive because of its size, but for a little girl to do it was nearly unimaginable. The car was not an automatic but a standard shift and to change gears was real tough for Sophia. It was an incredible sight to see: the little girl sitting up high on a pillow in the drivers' seat, barely able to see the road over the steering wheel, while reaching down with all her might to push in the clutch. Her Dad was patient and encouraged her constantly to not be afraid. She understood that knowing how to drive the car could be a life saver. Setting fear aside, she learned right there and then how to drive the monstrously huge vehicle. In just a few short months, there was very little left of the little girl in Sophia.

With all the training, and all the warnings, on what to do if a specific incident occurred, time flew. Before they knew it, three months passed and Mr. James needed to go back to work. Going back to work meant going back to a sea, faraway. Sophia dreaded his departure more than he would ever know. She always played tough and brave. She always acted up to the task, but deep inside she was quite afraid of being alone, of being the one everyone looked to when a question needed answering. She would be the one they ran to, when they had a bad dream, hurt themselves, or just needed a hug. She would be the one they would hide behind if there was danger. Sophia's feelings were compounded, for she not only held dread but held resentment. Dread to be alone, dread to hear sounds in the night that would scare her, dread to not have someone to protect her, someone to love her. The resentment was a new feeling, one she never before had felt toward her dad. It developed as time for his departure neared and he began to prepare for it. He, unlike them, was able to escape the island which trapped them all. He was able to leave and hear English all around him and see familiar sights—sights that Sophia longed for since she was taken away from California.

The evening Mr. James left was one to be remembered forever, as he pulled himself away from his six children, all clinging to him. Sophia didn't want to be a part of that, but there she was, like the rest crying and saying "Daddy, please don't go." The chorus was constant and it rose to a crescendo as the driver of the *carro público* placed his bags in the trunk. When the car actually backed up the children pushed forward in unison crying and begging. When the car started down the old dirt road, in the twilight one could see Mr. James put his waving arm out the window and the silhouette of the boys running after the car. The boys returned to where Sophia, Karen and little Evy stood in the middle of the road, with nothing but lights in the distance. They all hung onto each other and cried out loud beneath the palm trees.

The nightmare began the very next day, at five o'clock in the morning, when the pounding sound of a hammer awoke Sophia. With swollen eye lids after all the crying from the night before, she peered out the white levered windows and saw in the early morning light her grandfather talking to another man. She continued to watch and saw that the man was doing something with their fence. She quickly grabbed a towel and wrapped it about her shoulders and ran out onto the porch.

"What are you doing?" she said loudly, and the grandfather spoke quickly saying, "Go inside, this is not your business."

"What do you mean it's not my business? This is our fence, what are you doing to it?" The grandfather replied impatiently, "I'm moving the entrance. You may no longer enter where you have the driveway now. It's going to be through here from now on." With that he turned around and continued to give the man the orders to remove the fence. Sophia became furious and started screaming.

"You can't do that. Listen *señor*, don't touch that fence." said Sophia to the worker. The man stopped, looked at Casiano and then laughed.

"*Que nena ésta*. What a kid." said the worker with apparent amusement, and resumed working.

THE FACE OF EVIL

"I will go to the police right now, if you don't stop!" Casiano's grin disappeared and he headed toward the existing gate and entered their yard. Sophia saw him coming at a threatening pace and did not move but warned him, "Don't you try to hit me. If you hit me, then you'll really be in trouble with the police, because I'll have more to denounce you for."

The man showed her the knuckles of his closed fist but did not come closer. He turned around and, with his face red with anger, told the man in a rough way to continue working. At this point a couple of younger ones awoke and came outside to hold on to Sophia. Sophia stood still watching the man resume his job. She turned around, ushered the children inside and quickly changed into street clothes.

She told the children, "You can watch through the window, but don't go outside and don't say a word. When I leave, lock the door behind me." In no time Sophia was running down the street to the corner called *La Marina*, where one would wait for a public car to come. A public car was usually a station wagon with three or even four rows of seats. People knew the drill and everyone tried to avoid the last seat in the back, known as "La Cocina." The kitchen, as the last seat was called, got its name because it was the hottest place in the vehicle. Windows back there didn't open and with a car filled with passengers ventilation was all but absent. Shock absorbers were usually worn down, so the bumping around was something terrible. Also, the possibility of being squashed by a large passenger was very real. All in all, one wanted to avoid "the kitchen." On that morning Sophia was willing to ride on the hood. The ride into town was about forty minutes long. She thought about driving the car, as it was for emergencies, and this certainly was one. However, going to the police department driving, underage and without a driver's license, could only bring her more problems.

As she bounced around in "the kitchen" of the public car, she thought of what just happened. Casiano Risorio was the patriarch of the family. He was a short man in stature, quite large around the waist and not handsome at all. At the beginning of their arrival on the island, he every now and then showed a kindness toward his only daughter's children. However, love he had never given them. He seemed to resent the fact that they were *Americanos*. He would call them that, and whenever he would say the word, he would laugh and sneer. He seemed to rejoice in ridiculing the children. Over time his hostile attitude worsened and any kindness was gone. Sophia was convinced that they were nothing but an unwanted nuisance to him. She also realized that they were living proof of his shame. His only daughter abandoned her children and he did nothing to help them. He would have been happy to see them all leave, and the fact that they hadn't, only filled him with an anger that increased with each passing day.

At the police station, officers gave her their full attention and were gentle and caring. Quickly, it was decided that she was to be taken over to the court house, where a judge could decide what best should be done. Sophia, in the back seat of a police car, was at the courthouse, ten minutes later. The friendly officer led her to the office of a judge, and because of the escort, she was able to see him quickly. The judge was the kind-looking grey-haired man that had presided over the case with Ramón Valena. What a joy for Sophia to see him. She remembered the serenity and comfort his presence gave her. In turn the judge remembered the little girl that had sat tall in his courtroom and spoken eloquently. Judge Fuentes was interested in knowing what brought Sophia back into the courthouse. Patiently he listened to her story. Sophia explained that she visited the police station and repeated what she told the officer. He noted that Sophia's name was an English name, and began speaking with Sophia in English.

"So who is the man that is tearing down your fence?"

"The man is, Casiano Risorio, he is . . . well, he is my grandfather."

"Why would he do that?" asked the judge very interested and with a friendly manner.

"He gave my family some land, so that we could build a house on it, but now that we are all alone, he tries to take advantage and make changes any way he likes. My father was here until yesterday, but he didn't tell him anything. He waited for us kids to be alone and then do with us as he wishes."

"So you children are all alone?"

Suddenly, Sophia felt a little fear and she began explaining everything in a rushed manner. She was speaking quickly trying to get everything in, and answered in one constant stream of words.

"Yes, your honor, we are. You see, we have no choice, our mother ran away and our father is a sailor. I am going to take care of my brothers and sisters. My father supports us, and will send us money every two weeks, and we will be fine. My problem is that these people that are supposed to be our family only make life more difficult. This man, my grandfather, I think he hates us. Please, your honor, understand that my daddy left us because he believes that I can do the job, and I can sir, and also because he had to go to work. He has to go make money for us to live. Can you stop my grandfather from knocking down our fence?"

The judge came from around his desk and leaned on it, directly in front of Sophia. His attitude was kind and he gently asked, "Don't you have family in the United States that you could go live with?"

"Yes, your honor, we do have many relatives, but no one has offered help. My brothers and sisters are my closest family and we must stay together. If we go back to the United States we will be separated, one living here and one living there. We have to stay together and if everyone would just leave us alone, we will do just fine."

The judge looked seriously into Sophia's eyes and she, sitting in the chair before him, stared right back at him. He could see her determination. He lifted himself from the desk and went back to his seat. He reached for a pen and began to write. As he slowly got up from his chair, he again stared into Sophia's eyes. She never blinked and staring back into his, gave him a smile. He headed for the door and asked the officer, who was standing outside, to come in.

"Officer, I want you to take this young lady in your car back to her home and I want you to hand this citation to Mr. Risorio. He is to desist from the work that he is doing on the fence in question and report to me later today."

The officer nodded and replied, "Yes, your honor."

Then looking at Sophia, Judge Fuentes addressed her, "Sophia, I want you to come back this afternoon as well. I have something to tell Mr. Risorio and I want you to hear it."

The back seat of the patrol car was comfortable enough, but as Sophia approached her neighborhood, she felt rather odd to have people look into the advancing cop car and see her sitting in the back seat, as if she were a criminal. Feeling very self-conscious she tried to hold her head up high and have a pleasant look on her face.

It was with great relief that she got out of the vehicle. The work on the fence was going on and a good portion of it was down. She walked with the officer toward the fence and heard him tell the worker to stop working immediately. The man, who just a few hours earlier had snickered at her, now looked the little girl up and down and quickly threw his hammer to the ground. While this happened, a small congregation of people from the neighborhood, who had followed the police car, gathered around to watch. Oh, yes! They were going to have a juicy tale to spread around that week.

The officer looked back at Sophia and asked, "Which is your grandfather?"

"He's not here, he must be inside the store." Sophia led the way for the officer. Though her hands were clammy and her heart was beating wildly she went around to the front of the store and entered it, as if she were going to introduce a long lost uncle.

The officer followed her into the store and approached Casiano. "*Buenos días*, are you *señor* Casiano Risorio?"

"Yes, I am," exhaling a huge breath and looking like he might explode any moment, he leaned forward on the counter. Sophia could see the anger, barely beneath the surface, and it filled her with fear.

"Mr. Risorio, you are summoned by Judge Fuentes to be at the courthouse this afternoon at 2:00 pm sharp. You may not touch the fence that surrounds the house where this child lives." With that the officer glanced at Sophia. He must have seen fear reflected in her face because the officer immediately turned back to Casiano and said, "Under no circumstances may you approach this child or any of the children that live in that house, until you speak with the judge today." It was Sophia who now looked at the officer and silently thanked him. The officer gently put his arm on Sophia's slender shoulder and guided her toward the door.

No, Casiano did not approach Sophia, but she and the whole island must have heard him screaming, once the patrol car drove away. Never in her life had Sophia seen him so mad. He went outside and around toward the back of the store and stood in front of Sophia's house where the fence had been torn down and kicked at the dirt and dust.

"Who in the hell do you think you are, taking me, MEEEEE, to the courthouse? Never in my life has anyone ever dared to do such a thing and now I am going to have this mucous-faced, lice-filled kid having the judge order me to the courthouse! Why you are a little ----- and you better not come around me asking me for help, you God Damn -----" He took his hat off and threw it to the ground. He cursed every bad word Sophia ever heard and then more. The kids in the house watched through the white levered windows, which were opened just a crack, just enough to see it all. They were first terrified and shocked but the more and more Casiano kicked, the more ridiculous he looked, and the children exploded in laughter. War had begun.

The courthouse was a large white and intimidating structure in the shape of a cube. Once inside the foreboding edifice, a large courtyard surrounded by long balconies, was visible. It was attractive; however, the design with the open structure allowed feuding parties to view each other at a distance. It was known that often shouting matches and disputes would begin in the hallways and would have to be broken up.

Sophia was back at the courthouse early that afternoon. By one thirty she was standing outside of the judge's room, when across the way she saw Casiano arrive. He walked slowly, was nicely dressed and had his consort on his arm. She too was wearing Sunday's best and looked at Sophia disapprovingly, shaking her head silently. Sophia looked at them directly but didn't move to approach them, or speak to them. She quietly stayed to her side of the doorway and didn't budge, dreading everything and hating to go through with it all; but she had no choice. She would not have her grandfather or anyone coming to their home and doing just anything they wanted to do. She was in charge now, the children and her home were her responsibility and she would stand up for all of them.

An officer approached the doorway with a bunch of papers in hand and called their names. This time the judge was not in his office, but was in a courtroom filled with rows of benches. Behind a large desk toward the front of the room, dressed in his robes, Judge Fuentes summoned Sophia and her grandfather to the front.

"Mr. Risorio, is this young girl your granddaughter?"

"Yes, sir." Replied Sophia's grandfather as he stood in front of the judge.

"Were you taking down a fence that surrounds her home this morning without permission from her father?"

"Well, her father is not on the island and I have the need to . . ."

In a stern voice, that meant that he was not playing games, the judge quite loudly said, "Answer the question please. Were you or were you not taking down a fence that surrounds her home this morning?"

"Not personally, I had an employee begin the work."

"Why didn't you ask her father before he left the island?"

"I didn't realize that I was going to need to do this so soon."

"Is it true that this little girl lives alone with her brothers and sisters in this house?"

"Yes, it is."

"Mr. Risorio, do you love your granddaughter?" To this Mr. Risorio looked so bewildered and out of place, he fumbled for words and the judge called out "Speak up, I'm waiting."

"Why, sure I do; she is my granddaughter!"

"Then why are you here? Why aren't you helping these children that are all alone? Why instead do you wait for her father to leave, and then do as you please behind his back?"

The judge paused and looked at Mr. Risorio with obvious disdain on his face. Mr. Risorio on the other hand looked most uncomfortable and for once seemed to be without words.

Judge Fuentes reached for his glasses and took them off, looking at Sophia's grandfather he spoke to him as if trying to reason with him.

"Mr. Risorio, you may not remove that fence. Do you understand? This court will not fine you at this time but you are to replace what has been torn down immediately and leave the entrance to the home where it is. When Mr. James returns, you and he can settle what will be done. While he is gone, this little girl has enough to do without having to fight with you. I want to know that you are helping these children, Mr. Risorio. I will be keeping an eye on you, Sophia. I want Mr. Risorio to know that I am ordering you to come to me if you have any more problems with this gentleman or with any other person. You are dismissed and I never want to see you again in my courtroom, Mr. Risorio."

With those words booming through the courthouse, Sophia looked at the judge and with a smile of gratitude waved goodbye. That is when she turned around and noticed that the courthouse had people from the barrio. The word quickly spread and people made their way into town to see for themselves how Mr. Risorio was taken to court by his little granddaughter. That evening everyone gossiped about the event,

"Why imagine, his own granddaughter took him to court!"

"He didn't look so high and mighty as the judge put him in his place."

For Sophia, inadvertently she was doing as her father had done, when in first grade he made her sit in the principal's office for three days. She had a taken a stand and was showing her siblings, through example, what sometimes needs to be done. The great lesson she learned as a child when her father stood up against the ruling to bus children across county lines in the interest of segregation, would forever accompany her. Sophia was acquiring a reputation that would help keep them safe. 'Don't mess with the *Americanita*, she will take you to court!'

For the James family, life had always been a roller coaster when it came to the topic of money. Times were great, when they had some or times were dismal, when they had none. Their daddy would come home with plenty and stay until there was nothing; always extremes. Sophia realized early that the concept of *money management* was a concept her dad did not practice well. Her logical brain realized that some people understood the secrets of money and others could live long lives and never quite get it. For Sophia, some had money because they wanted it, worked for it, lusted for it, saved it and grew it. For others it was very difficult to obtain and even more difficult to save or make grow, even if they had some.

Money became an issue and took on a unique importance. Money was something a child went to a parent for, to buy a piece of candy. Real money was never really handled by a child for matters such as buying clothing, shoes, or real food. Now all of a sudden it was. Money took on a completely new meaning and it made life miserable. There never was enough of it and once they had some of it, it slipped away too easily. Their grandfather was responsible for the lessons in money; he kept reminding them how much they owed him.

A check for their support arrived biweekly from their father. However, no matter how Sophia tried to make sure that everything necessary was bought, and that nothing was owed to anyone, having a little left over was impossible. In part, it was because their grandfather kept tabs on their purchases. Casiano's little wooden shack was the nearest grocery store in the area and he had a monopoly of all goods sold to neighbors. His bookkeeping system was worthwhile to the buyer, if he trusted Casiano completely. In the case of the James children he kept track of all their purchases. After a short period of time, Sophia clearly knew that he was making the most of the situation. When Sophia kept track of expenditures and presented her tally at the end of the two weeks, he laughed and said, "You're a child, you don't know anything about numbers and the amount that I say is what you owe me" Period.

He was God! There was no discussing it with him. The amount really owed was only known by him.

Sophia knew that they would never be able to save money this way, but she had no choice. So after a short while, their purchases could not be covered by the checks arriving and the debt with Casiano grew and grew. He, of course, was doing the children a service. How good of him. He would boast of helping the children out and not cutting off their credit. For Sophia it was an uphill battle and she knew that when her father came she would be in debt. For the time being there was nothing she could do about it. They needed to eat and his was the only store around.

It was about a month later that the reason for the grandfather to want to move the location of the entry to the James home was made clear to everyone. Since the day Sophia took him to court, the only contact the children had with him was through the purchase of their groceries. They were totally alone as far as he was concerned. For Sophia that was fine. She didn't trust him or like him and was glad to have little to do with him. All of Sophia's negative feelings toward him were justified, once his real intentions for removing the fence were known.

It was a sunny day like any other with nice, blue skies, and a few fluffy white clouds thrown in, just to make the heavens more beautiful. The children were out in the yard playing and enjoying that Saturday. Bobby and Frankie made an obstacle course on the driveway and were skating through it like maniacs. Karen was out on the swing, and Sophia could see her through the kitchen window, reaching real high with her legs. Mr. James had made sure to build the swing as high as possible, so that the ride was a wonderful, far-reaching flight. Johnny was at his favorite place in the shade of the front porch, by the eternal little stream made by the kitchen drain. That little body of running water, over time, created banks at its edges. It was a perfect place for a regiment's encampment, protecting battlefields beyond. Johnny had a whole garrison set up on one side and an enemy posted on the other. With roads for sophisticated tank movements and mounds where battalion units huddled, Johnny was preparing for a major attack. Little Evy was pushing a baby cart around with her current most favorite doll. Everything was fine, noisy but safe, so Sophia continued with her needle and thread to try and hem a hand-me-down for little Evy.

THE FACE OF EVIL

Suddenly, the perspicacious Johnny came in,

"Sophia, look out the window, there are some men taking measurements. See how they are laying foundation strings down?" Sophia went to the window, looked out and her stomach turned over.

"Oh! My God! Trouble." Were the words that jumped out of her mouth. Sophia looked at Johnny and he looked back at her with wide, intelligent eyes. With all the construction they saw they knew when preparations were being made for the construction of something.

"Oh Johnny, this is bad, this is the beginning of something bad. Now what? dear God, now what?"

Johnny said, "I'm going to walk over there and just kind of ask them, what they're doing. What are they going to build?"

"OK, good, go ahead; see what you can find out." Sophia watched Johnny walk over to the men that were laying down the foundation lines. He got into a crouched down position and quietly watched. As Sophia watched Johnny she saw his old long pants with faded green stripes and big holes in the knees; he was barefoot and shirtless. His long, straight, brown hair almost covered his eyes. Johnny was a skinny fellow. After a while he must have asked a question for one of the men turned toward him and spoke to him. Watching, Sophia took in the size of what was being outlined. It was big. It was about ten feet from their fence, went all the way to the street and extended itself back as far as the James home did. In other words, it was like a monster, that if built where the string lay, would cover their home and engulf any view completely. Sophia watched bewildered and felt scared of what was coming.

Soon after, Johnny came back into the house. In his quiet manner he said, "Sophia, Casiano is building a new store and it is going to be more than just a store, it is going to be a bar."

Sophia started crying. "Why is he so hateful? Why would he do that? To put a bar right on top of us like that, did you see how big the thing is going to be and how close to us it will be?"

"I sure did. It'll cover up the house completely." Sophia sat down trying to think and Johnny watched out the window.

"OK, on Monday instead of going to school, I'll go and look for Judge Fuentes. He told me to come by anytime we might need him. So if I can find him, I'll tell him what's going on and maybe he can do something."

"Do you want me to go with you, Sophia?"

"No Johnny, you go to school. Don't miss the day."

On Monday, first thing in the morning, Sophia was heading out to the courthouse in search of Judge Fuentes. It didn't take long for her to find him. Judge Fuentes knew of their plight and often thought of the young James children.

"Hello, Sophia James, what is happening? What brings you to my chambers?" he asked in English.

"Well, your honor, first of all, thank you for seeing me."

"That's quite all right. Now, what's happening?"

"Well, sir, remember my grandfather, Mr. Risorio?"

"Yes, of course I remember him. What is he up to now?"

"Well, right in that spot where he was trying to tear down our fence and change the entrance, he now is building a store and bar. Right there in front of us, real close to our fence and across our entire yard. A bar!" Sophia looked down, shaking her head in obvious frustration..

"How do you know this? Has he started building?"

"Well, just this Saturday he had some men out there laying down foundation lines and one of my little brothers went over and asked them what they were doing and they told him about the bar. Judge Fuentes, I came to you because I don't want him to build a bar in front of us like that. You know that we are all alone, but if we are going to have drunks around us now, it is going to be more unsafe. I was just hoping that maybe there was something I could do, or you could do . . . to stop him."

"What a man." the judge said despicably. "OK, Sophia, this is what we're going to do. I'll have Mr. Risorio come in informally to speak with him. If the land he wants to build on is his property and he abides by building codes, legally my hands are tied. However, let me have a talk with him and see what I can do.

"Thank you, your honor. I'm sorry to bother you with our problems."

"That's quite all right, young lady. You come to me anytime. Is that understood?"

"Yes sir," said Sophia with a smile, "and thank you very much. Bye."

Sophia was on her way back home and knew that she did all that she could do. How she despised the wicked man that made the place even more insufferable.

Sure enough the building was on its way to becoming a reality. A comment here and there told her that the judge had spoken to her grandfather. However, he was within his legal rights and could not be stopped. Sophia did not speak to him about it. She knew that it would be futile. Silently and powerlessly the James children watched the building rise. It was the monster she and Johnny foresaw. She knew that any words spoken or music played, would be within earshot. It was way too close.

As the construction proceeded and the concrete blocks began to identify windows and doors, Sophia realized that a huge window at the closest point to their fence was in the plan. On that day she went to her grandfather.

"Please grandfather, I see that you are putting a window right in front of our home. Please don't do that, if you do, then we will have drunks watching us all the time. Maybe someone will try to hurt us girls. The children won't even be able to play out in the yard without eyes watching every movement. Please, please, don't do that."

The old man's ugly face laughed. "So now, it's, 'Please, please, Grandfather.' Well, forget it, kid. Now maybe I'll put in a bigger one and you and your judge can do nothing about it."

Sophia knew that she was looking into the face of evil. Again she decided to go speak with the judge and tell him what was happening. Again the judge summoned Mr. Risorio, but this time he had all the James children come in too. The Judge knew that he could legally do nothing. The man could put a window any place he wanted. He would just try to appeal to the man's sense of dignity, to see if he had any at all in him.

"Mr. Risorio, you are correct. You have the legal right to put a window anywhere you want. However, these children are becoming endangered by having a bar so close to their home. A window giving your patrons visual access to them will only endanger them further. You don't want to endanger these children anymore, do you? They are the children of your daughter, are they not?"

"Yes, that is true, but I didn't ask them to come to live in Puerto Rico, so they can leave anytime they want to."

"But while they're here, trying to exist all alone, without a parent, you should be helping them and not trying to make it more dangerous for them."

"That is your opinion, your honor." said Mr. Risorio with complete absence of emotion.

"Get out of here, Mr. Risorio. You bring shame to yourself," said the judge with contempt.

After Mr. Risorio walked out, the judge looked at the six James children. He took in their wide eyes and handsome faces; he took in their good manners and behavior. He shook his head and said, "Children, I'm sorry that I cannot force Mr. Risorio into being a caring human being. You have great obstacles ahead. Hang tight, listen to your sister and in any way I can help you, please come to me anytime." The judge looked miserable. His mouth hung as if he had something rotten in it. Being in the presence of their grandfather had done it.

With the completion of a fully equipped bar and pool room, the James home, which not long ago was built in quiet, green pastures, was now in the center of Factor's 'grand central.' The window that opened up onto their home was a double window with shutters; it was not louvered. So when it was open, it was really open.

The children lived with their living room windows mostly shut. The swing, the teeter totter, the tether pole, the skating, any and all of it, became a show for the men drinking at the bar. They would all huddle around the window to watch the children "perform." The window took spontaneous fun out of their lives and replaced it with self-conscious fear. The girls, if ever outside, were met by whistles and calls from those drinking at the bar. Not long after the bar was inaugurated Sophia assembled the children and made a plan.

"OK, kids, I've been thinking that we need to plant a whole lot of trees and bushes so that we can block out the bar." The kids all agreed and went to work planting trees that would grow tall. They knew that instant gratification was not possible and that they had to wait for the trees to grow. However, they knew that the trees would grow and then they would get some of their privacy back.

Sophia was aware that planting trees and bushes gave them their much needed privacy. However, she silently feared giving the house too much cover. Yes, fear was always present, for one reason or another.

11

SILENT HEROES

"THE NIGHT" ~ "LA NOCHE"
A little girl lay wide awake, ~ Una niñita acostada y despierta,
Her covers shoulder high, ~ Con su cobija hasta sus hombros,
Her life unfolding only ten, ~ Comenzando su vida, solo de diez,
She was wise. ~ Era juiciosa.
Her mom had passed, ~ Su mamá había pasado,
Her daddy gone, ~ Su papá se había ido,
Five younger as a test. ~ Cinco más jóvenes de prueba.
In command, beyond her years, ~ Al mando, más allá de su edad,
Then, then came night. ~ Entonces venía la noche.
Shadows played games everywhere, ~ Las sombras jugaban juegos por doquier,
And the house became alive, ~ Y la casa recobraba vida,
Many sounds belonging there, ~ Muchos sonidos que pertenecían,
But so many uninvited. ~ Pero tantos más no invitados.
The little girl lay still, ~ La pequeña niña permanecía quieta,
And her breath was hard to come by, ~ Y su respiración se le dificultaba,
Afraid to open up her eyes, ~ Con miedo de abrir sus ojos,
She would cry into the night, ~ A la noche le lloraba,
And she'd pray. ~ Y entonces rezaba.
(Chorus) ~ (Coro)
Oh! Dear God up in heaven, ~ Oh! Querido Dios que estás en los cielos,
Come to me tonight, ~ Ven a mí esta noche,

163

> *Keep us safe and keep us warm, ~ Salvaguárdanos y dénos calor,*
> *Till the morning light, ~ Hasta que llegue el amanecer,*
> *Oh! dear God up in heaven, ~ Oh! Querido Dios que estás en los cielos,*
> *I've been so brave and strong, ~ He sido tan valiente y fuerte,*
> *But now it's dark, and I'm in charge, ~ Pero ahora está obscuro y yo estoy a cargo,*
> *And yet I've so much fear, ~ Y tengo tanto miedo,*
> *Oh! dear Lord, ~ Oh! Querido Señor.*
> *The tide began to rise, ~ La marea comenzó a subir,*
> *And a wave would gently greet her, ~ Y una ola con gentileza la saludó.*
> *Her feet deep in wet sand, ~ Sus pies profundos en arena mojada,*
> *Like her mind, caressed by sleep, ~ Como su mente, acariciada por el sueño,*
> *Would sail away and have no fear, ~ Navegaría lejos y no tendría miedo,*
> *Just the cool breeze arms embracing, ~ Con solo el abrazo de la brisa fresca,*
> *And a bird would fly close by ~ Y un pájaro se acercaría,*
> *And would say, "Close your eyes, ~ Y le diría, "Cierra los ojos,*
> *Rest my child." ~ Descansa mi niña."*
> *Chorus ~ (Se repite el coro)*

The James children settled into a life where grownups were scarce or dangerous and survival depended exclusively on them. As time went by they developed routines that helped keep them safe and gave them joy. However, no matter how strong they became, people at times need people, and the James children, over the years, at times needed help. Within their difficult life there were a few that stood up and answered their call. A few that refused to ignore the injustices and abuse they saw. A few that didn't mind being inconvenienced and lent their needed hand. Those few with a conscience and love in their hearts that stepped forward to help the abandoned children were, without doubt, their silent heroes.

Down the road, a five-minute walk away, in a small corner house made of unpainted wood and with a tin roof, lived Esther, the mother of three children. She was a tiny woman in size with rough and worn hands that weren't usually noticed because of her big smile. She often wore her fine, long-braided, light hair crisscrossed like a crown on the top of her head. Esther's smile was wide and bright, something few people had in those parts where so many were missing teeth. Her children were all close in age, very young, and all at home. It was Esther who had brought joy to Sophia in the past. She was the one that brought her a birthday cake on the day of the fight with Sylvana. On many occasions Esther came by with one kindness or another. Soon after Sophia's father left and the whole court issue with the grandfather happened, she visited the James's home carrying a bag full of mangoes. Esther was a seamstress and a well-known one. She sewed anything for anyone and did it all by sight. No patterns. If you had a dress and you wanted another, all you had to do was bring her the fabric and a dress that fit. She would take the person's sizes from the dress and listen to the wish. Then she'd start cutting away. She was smart without being schooled. She was fast on her feet which kept her slim and she was innately kind. Esther, like everyone else in the barrio, knew what happened to the American family. Though she was not of a gossiping nature, in a small barrio like Factor, there was nothing to do but gossip, or listen. Her visit was very timely for the James children, as summer would be over in a couple of weeks and plans had to be made on how to get everything done and still have everyone go to school. Important issues such as this, Mr. James had not left resolved. Instead he trusted that somehow Sophia would work it out. The younger children were out in the yard as Esther approached calling out, "Hi, kids, how's it going?"

Sophia, from within the house, heard her and quickly went to the door. She said "Esther, hello, come on in, sit down, sit down."

"Hola, Sophia, let me sit out here on the porch." Sophia pulled a rocker up toward her and Esther made it onto the porch and sat down.

"I brought you these mangoes," she said laughing and setting the bag down. The kids immediately crushed forward trying to see what was in the bag.

Mangoes were common fare but always appreciated and so everyone looked at Sophia and she nodded saying, "Go ahead, everybody take one and say 'thank you' to Esther." The boys all chorused their 'thank you' and ran off with dust flying everywhere. Karen sat with one leg off the porch, leaning on a pillar, listening to the conversation. Sophia had great affection for Esther and began to tell her how hard everything was, how she needed to learn so much, but that she was learning and things were getting better every day.

"Of course, Esther, I still don't know when school starts how I'm going to manage. Frankie and Evy don't go to school yet and I can't leave them here alone. On the other hand I don't want to stop going to school. I can't. I'm going to be a doctor someday, so I must continue going to school. I really don't know what I'm going to do." Sophia's remark was more of a thought process, a spoken puzzle she was confronted with, than a whine.

"Well, that is why I came by, Sophia. I've been watching, hearing and thinking that with summer almost gone, you children are going to need someone to help you out, so I want to suggest something to you." At that, Esther looked down at Karen as if including her in what she was about to say. "You know that I have my three children at home still and I wouldn't mind having a couple more. So if you want, Sophia, you can drop those little ones over to me in the morning before school and then pick them up when you get home from school."

Sophia's eyes were popping out of her face and the wheels of her mind were turning at full throttle, *This would do it! This could be the solution!* "Oh, Esther how wonderful that you have come over here to offer us help like this. I will pay you though. How much should I pay you? This is wonderful; Oh, how wonderful!"

Sophia wanted to jump up and down, but she needed to behave adult like, so she controlled her desire to yell for happiness.

"OK, OK, we'll do it and you can pay me if you like, because it will cost me something to feed the children lunch and snacks. A couple dollars a day for each ought to be fair. What do you think?"

"Oh, Esther, I think you are wonderful!" With that Sophia put all formality aside and throwing caution to the wind, she thrust her arms around her, hugging her tight.

Esther did more than look after the young ones. For many years; she advised and helped the James children in many ways. On one Mother's Day, a couple of years later, when Sophia was in ninth grade, Esther received a new electric sewing machine as a gift from her husband. She was thrilled and sewed more than ever with her new toy. Often, when Sophia picked up Evy and Frankie she saw new dresses that Esther had just finished for someone. Sophia would admire them and while looking at them would figure out the pieces involved in making a dress. She looked at a dress as a puzzle and knew that she could sew if given the opportunity.

"Esther, now that you have that beautiful new sewing machine, what are you going to do with your old one?" Sophia timidly asked Esther.

"Oh, my, I haven't given that any thought. It's so old; I probably couldn't sell it if I wanted to."

"Well, if you decided that you wanted to try to sell it, how much do you think you could get for it?"

"Ah! Maybe twenty."

"I'll buy it from you, Esther. I've wanted to learn how to sew but I needed a sewing machine first."

"Well then, missy, you just bought yourself a sewing machine." said Esther with genuine laughter in her voice.

Sophia promised Esther that in a few days their check would come and then she'd have some money.

"OK, that's fine. You pay me when you can, but you can go ahead and take it out of here right now."

"Wow, Esther, I can't believe it: I have a sewing machine! I'll come by for it later with all the kids." Sophia skipped all the way back home with Evy and Frankie, skipping right beside her.

A little later that day, the kids went over with Sophia and they carried the sewing machine all the way home. As soon as it was in, Sophia said, "OK, who has the first pair of pants that needs to be fixed?"

They all yelled out, "I do!" and with that they all looked at each other and laughed.

In reality, the sewing machine that Esther sold to Sophia for so little was a gift. It opened up more possibilities than just being able to repair clothing at home easily. Esther was wonderful and very helpful, as she dropped in every now and then to show Sophia sewing tricks and check on her progress. Sophia's hands-on, fearless, approach—as if she were assembling a puzzle—helped her learn quickly. To keep it interesting she began refining her sewing, hiding seams, as well as finishing up with lovely bead work. Over time, Sophia became a fine and capable seamstress and in high school made money on the side with her sewing. Teachers at school realized how nice her work was and became patrons. Sophia was proud to sew for them and the extra money was heavenly.

It wasn't very often, but on a day when the James children truly needed help, it would be a neighbor, never a relative, who would come forth and offer a hand. Elias was a neighbor that owned a small bar close by. It was a friendly family bar and the oldest bar around. Sophia was convinced that Casiano was envious of Elias. After Casiano built his own bar, he still could never pull in the people that the kind hearted Elias could. Also, the clients that frequented Elias's bar remained loyal and stayed there. Elias's bar was more like a pool hall, where men drank beer and played pool. Like most small stores and bars, it had a juke box and also tables for dominoes. Domino games were big in Factor. In the evenings one could easily hear the slamming down of dominoes in passionate games filled with laughter and cries of "I told you so." Elias had a couple of kids of his own that were within the same age range as the James children. He had a large pot belly and a wide, dark mustache. He was a caring man that always waved at the *Americano* children on their way to and from school. Though he never told Sophia that she could count on him, somehow she knew she could.

Constantly situations came up that needed a decision and her attention. The children were good and Sophia got to know each of them in a much greater way than just as siblings. They knew she was in charge and they respected her and trusted her for guidance. Sophia played the grownup role, as best she could, and time kept passing with everyone still in one piece. Until one day, there was the first real emergency. It was a life-threatening injury, and it happened to Frankie.

It was toward the end of summer, just before school started, and Frankie was up in the tree house. The kids were all playing and having a good time and Frankie decided to climb out onto the roof of the little house, something he had done a hundred times before. On the day of the accident he fell and caught his arm on a pointed, loose wire of the cyclone fence. Right where his arm bends, he was torn wide open. A pulsating artery revealed itself and he was bleeding profusely as Sophia ran around screaming. She tried to take control of herself and think. She decided to drive him to the hospital. She wrapped his arm in a clean towel, "Karen, stay with the kids. Bobby, you come with me."

They jumped into the car and after turning the ignition there was no sound, just a click. She did it again and again. The car's battery was dead. She jumped out of the car and ran to the little house closest to them. It was the house of one of Mr. Risorio's sons, a half uncle. She called and his wife came out and claimed that he was sleeping and that he wasn't to be disturbed. Sophia begged, "No, please. get him up. This is no game Frankie could die. He could bleed to death, please help us, please." The wife turned around, shrugged her shoulders, and with a smile on her face closed her front door. Sophia got frantic and ran as fast as her legs could take her over to Elias' and straight into the bar. Now she was hysterically screaming and went straight to Elias, who was wiping down the counter.

"Don Elias, Don Elias, Frankie fell down, I can't start the car and he is going to bleed to death. Please, help me, please help me!" He threw the rag in his hand and ran for his car and on the way called out to his wife to tend the bar. In a minute they were rushing with Frankie to the hospital. It turned out to be a real lucky thing that Elias hadn't stopped to ask questions, because by the time they made it to the hospital, Frankie had lost a lot of blood and was quite pale. He was such a brave little boy in silence, without a wince, allowing the doctor to sew him up. In cold blood, no anesthesia at all, they put in over twenty stitches.

When his arm was all bandaged up he turned to Sophia and gave her a big smile, "We made it, Sophia!" He looked at Don Elias who stayed waiting for them. "*Gracias*, Don Elias." Don Elias put his hand on Frankie's head and gave him a pat.

"*Vamonos*," he said with a smile.

Those days of fear, when all the odds seemed stacked against them, only helped make Sophia—and all of them—stronger. She knew that her siblings were all good kids. They would complain and fight her sometimes, but they were loyal and would side with her at the drop of a hat.

School started and somehow the children managed to attend and keep things together. Perhaps the worst problem the James children faced, as they tried to exist without adult supervision, was the unfriendliness of their relatives. The open hostility was difficult to ignore because the James home was smack in amongst their homes. They had no love for the children and after Sophia took the grandfather to court, taunting the children became a pastime. One family member thought it funny to walk by with a hot lovely plate of food and holding up, call out to little Frankie or Johnny and say, 'smell,' and then walk away laughing. They were really ugly people—the ugliest Sophia could imagine.

Then one day, someone heard them talking about, 'the uncle.' Their mother's long-lost brother was once again coming back to the island. This was scary news. He was the dangerous, sick uncle who had molested Sophia. He was a real threat in Sophia's mind and she lived with fear that he might try to hurt one of them again. So Sophia sat down with the children and explained to them what happened when he was last on the island. Back then, the children had been too young to understand; now, to stay safe, they needed to know. They were a team, and holding together was the only way that they could protect each other and survive the dangers that seemed to be all around them. The children devised a plan to reinforce the doors at night. Besides the big wooden bar bracing the door, each night the children placed a chair wedged underneath the handle, 'just in case.' When it was time to go to bed they turned off all the lights and would sleep in their own small beds—except when storms came howling through. When winds were strong and big, bright lightning bolts exploded nearby, the children ran terrified, or laughing, depending on the size of the child, and huddled together. As a deafening crack of thunder rattled the house, they jumped into each other's beds. On those nights they all ended up in one room, giggling while trembling under covers. They were all learning how to deal with storms and hurricanes and the fear of having their roof blown off. The unforeseen situations were the ones that really terrified them.

Late at night, sounds of the world around them were transformed from scary, human sounds, to sweet sounds of nature. Every night, hours after the children sealed up their house nice and tight and turned off all the lights to try and sleep, the sounds of the juke box, men playing pool—drunks joking and laughing at Casiano's store—could clearly be heard. Sometime after midnight he would finally close up, and the sounds of the store would be exchanged for the call of the *coquí*.

The *coquí*, is a tiny little frog with huge vocals heard all over the island and considered a national treasure. Its call was everywhere and soared through the night leaving no silent gaps. Its unique lullaby can become distracting and one either surrenders and sleeps to it, or puzzles how such a loud sound could emanate from such a tiny creature.

One such night, its familiar din was replaced by a terrifying sound. Nothing natural about it, the sound was that of a man too close for comfort. It awoke Sophia from her sleep. The sound was calling her and came to her as if from a fog—from a great distance. The sound was rhythmic and pronounced in a slow slurred way. It was a man's voice and it was calling her name.

Sophia jumped up in fright, and then fear hit her. She knew that the voice belonged to the uncle that assaulted her. Shock and paralyzing fear grabbed her, as she stay frozen on her bed not knowing what to do. As the voice repeatedly called out, "Soo-phiiii-aaaaaaa, open the dooooooor," the little girl became emboldened and ran from bed to bed getting the others up. As they heard the voice they huddled around Sophia saying, "What are we going to do? Oh! My God! What if he gets in! Oh! My God!" Little Evy started to cry and they were all terrified.

With fear in her voice, Sophia cried out, "Go away! What do you want? Go away! Leave us alone! Leave us alone!"

"Sophia, open up, I'm coming in. If you don't open the door I'm going to break it down," he yelled back at her. The kids were pale with fear and Sophia's heart was beating violently in a terrified state. They heard the drunken and crazed man punch the white louvers of the window in the door, trying to break them in. As if it were in slow motion, in front of their wide eyes, they saw the first louver come off and be yanked out.

Dark, mad eyes peered through as the children huddled terrified, while Sophia screamed, "Get away from us, leave us alone!"

The man, hysterical with laughter, said, "I'm going to get you Sophiiii-aaaaaaa." As he said these words he continued banging and pulled off the second louver from the window in the door. Now his left arm— completely through up to his shoulder— was flailing around, reaching downwards trying to grab whatever was impeding him from getting the door open. He grabbed the chair that was placed under the knob and with a swing sent it crashing. Still the door held fast because of the wooden bar that held it firmly in place. Sophia in despair grabbed a mop and began hitting his arm. He grabbed the mop and threw it back at her.

"I'm going to get you, Sophiiiiaaaaa," said the voice that a moment earlier was filled with sexual overtones and now was filled with rage. It was Bobby, who after watching Sophia try to hit him with the mop, ran to his room and got his bat. Before Sophia knew it Bobby came running and swung it hitting his arm with a solid blow. A cry of pain and the arm was gone. The children stood huddled, trembling and wondering what was going to happen next. Their question was quickly answered when with laughter the man reappeared jamming a hose inside the house and saying, "I'm going to flood you out real good. Open up, *Carajo*!"

At this point Sophia told the children, "We are going to go to the corner facing Elias's house. At the count of three, we're all going to scream at the top of our lungs: 'Elias, help us!' and we'll keep on doing that until someone hears us." Turning their backs on the intruder, the children ran for the opposite corner of the house that faced Elias. In unison the children began to call him. The screams were loud and clear and it had shattered the night for many. With the arm of the drunkard hanging in through the window holding the running hose, the children's screams reflected their fear and urgency. Neighbors led by Elias ran toward them and soon the arm was gone and the sound of a fight could be heard. With lights switched on in the garage, the children crowded to peer through the gaping hole left by the absent louvers in the door. They could see that the man, falling over drunk, was wearing only white underwear. Out of complete viewing range, someone with an opened shirt and protruding belly threw a punch into the drunkard's face. Another gave him a kick; after that he was dragged away and the children could no longer see him. They never opened the door to thank anyone, nor did anyone stand around waiting to be thanked. It was over. Neighbors and strangers came running and with a sense of outrage and shame they dealt with him. It seemed that the *Americano* children were no one's responsibility and yet everyone's. Silently, through their actions, people near their home had spoken. They said that they were watching over them and were not going to stand by and let them be hurt. That night, as Sophia and the children tried to go back to sleep, she understood that people like Tiba, Esther and Elias were their silent heroes. Because of them, they would never be completely alone.

12

MALI, SINGAPORE, MADAGASCAR

"YO SOY DEL MUNDO" ~ "I'M OF THE WORLD"
Me preguntan, ¿De dónde soy? ~ I'm asked, where am I from?
¿Dónde nací yo? ~ Where was I born?
Todos quieren siempre adivinar, ~ Everyone always wants to guess,
Casi nunca lo pueden lograr. ~ They hardly ever can.
¿Donde pudiste tu nacer? ~ Where were you born?
¿De dónde soy yo? ~ Where am I from?
Eso no tiene mucho que ver, ~ It really doesn't matter much,
La llama viene del corazón. ~ The call comes from the heart.

Receiving a letter from their father was always a big deal. Actually, receiving any letter was quite an event and accomplishment, not only for the postal service, but for the children. The Garrochales Post Office was not too far away. Nevertheless, it was very hard to get to. No public transportation was available and so the ten miles were sometimes reached by bicycle, on a road too narrow for safety. Curves were too tight, and it was filled with pot holes and drivers going too fast. Nonetheless, the curvy asphalted road had its beauty, as it was lined on both sides by tall ancient palm trees. It was a trip hard for Sophia to enjoy because of the danger, so most of the time she tried to go by car. However, their big green Plymouth was not always reliable. Its V-8 engine was a gas guzzler, so Sophia would use it sparingly, which wasn't often enough. Because of the lack of use, the battery would die and that is when Sophia and the kids would turn the trip to the post office into an expedition. They would get on their bicycles and head down the road in a line. At the beginning Sophia, Karen, Bobby and Johnny would head out over cries of Frankie wanting to go. Back then, being so small, his three-wheeler just couldn't cut the distance and would slow them down too much. As time went by, he would eventually join them on his new, hand-me-down bike. All four of them heading down the road was a bonding experience. The greatest objective for Sophia was to get everyone there and back safely. As she peddled along, last one in line, she listened for oncoming cars, over Bobby's howls and laughter as he challenged everyone to go faster. Bobby's objective always seemed to be "the first" to arrive, to win the nonexistent race. Sophia constantly called for him to wait up, and he would ignore her calls, pretending to not hear. Riding with the children was a challenge for Sophia, as the worry of something bad happening gave her no peace.

It was when she made her trips alone that she truly could "see" her surroundings and enjoy the ride. On those times, she took notice of how the wind felt on her face, and it was surprising, as it almost felt cool on sweltering days. She would peddle hard for a bit just to feel that wind in her hair and on her skin and the feeling was so good. It made her feel clean and soft and for a moment completely free of worry. The road to the post office was not very inhabited and long stretches of time could go by before a car careened around her. During those stretches she enjoyed the quiet and the calmness of her surroundings. The countryside was all planted in sugarcane and its long stalks, with long, flimsy, innocent-looking leaves, glimmered as far as the eye could see. On a day with a strong breeze, the leaves all bent in unison and, in the sunlight, the blue-green sea of cane looked like the undulating waves of a vast ocean. The sound of stalks banging against each other increased proportionately with the winds and rose in a crescendo impossible to ignore. Along with the sound came the omnipresent smell of sugarcane, always there and lingering to announce the stage the cane was in. The vast fields of green would unfurl flowers at their tip tops and the world was then immersed in a flowery, clean scent. Then the cane would ripen and its time for a quick burn filled the world with ash and smoke. Then it was gone, all of it, leaving lanes and fields of green with open and barren spaces extending far, far, up to a mountain's skirt. The world would take on a barren look and the sweet, clean, wholesome smell of growth would dissipate and be replaced by a mild, rancid stench.

The sound of the wind, the enormity of the view, and the beautiful heads of palm trees made the long trip an escape. Sophia peddled hard, and then coasted as the wind and the view took her soul on a different journey. She would again commit herself to becoming the best she could be.

Rides to the post office were a reality check for Sophia and those excursions helped her grow wise. Riding alongside the ten-foot-tall seas of green sugarcane heightened her awareness of the land's greatness and brought home more forcefully the reality of the many that lived around it in squalor. These trips freed her spirit and allowed her to see from a detached perspective many a young girl pregnant in the tiny rickety shacks she passed along the way. Faces, once pretty, that smiled and waved back at her, as she passed them by. Faces that reflected acceptance and spirits that had never grown strong or ambitious enough to be broken, living simple lives without questions. Sophia would clearly see this and her resolve would strengthen. On these trips she promised herself to get out, to work hard and to not give up on her dreams, as long as she lived. She would not allow herself to be standing in a yard hanging endless amounts of clothes on lines above muddied soil; to be swollen with pregnancy time after time, having children without realizing that a family was being formed; to have children running around half naked and barefoot with tummies round with worms and parasites, would not happen to her.

She was able to recognize the contrast between the greatness of the rich land and the squalor of so many lives, because she had seen better. She had lived in California with caring parents long enough to have the advantage of memories that would allow her to compare. She remembered, she remembered it all, and would never let it go. The sanctuary of those memories kept her striving forward. It was so lovely feeling the air rush on her face.

Whenever the post office building finally came into sight, it was always a relief. After a while on the road, all curves looked alike and the post office building always seemed to just spring up on them. It was a tiny, cemented, square structure, painted with a wide row of pink at the bottom and the rest was a light blue. The old paint on the structure was dirty and peeling off, showing, beneath, a previous layer of what once was white. The old tin roof was curled and mashed in at a corner where it was hit repeatedly by high trucks. Smack in the center of this venerated eyesore was a door with a small window. Its front had neither awning nor porch of any sort, just the radiant hot dirt, that became hard enough to sweep—in dry weather—and muddy enough to ruin any good shoes when it rained. Dust formed whirlwinds in front of the structure with the passing of each car, promptly giving any visitor to the establishment a dusty, new hairdo.

Nevertheless, when the kids would come around that last bend they would start screaming for joy, "There it is! There it is!" as Sophia would head for the grimy little window. Those that came along raced for the nearby spigot and there, with face thrust under the rushing water, drank long and hard to cool down.

Bobby was always the first to make it to the faucet as Johnny pleaded, "Bobby, come on, I'm dying, let me have some. Hurry up! It's gonna dry up! Come on, it's my turn!" The pushing and the pleading eventually stopped. Johnny got his drink and they would throw themselves into the shade of a nearby tree, laughing.

Yes, on this day they could laugh because water had indeed gushed out of the faucet and was plentiful. However, on many occasions, the children ran for the faucet only to hear the hateful sound of air coming from within empty pipes. The croaking and gurgling sound of a pipe pushing empty air was always followed by sighs and moaning: "Maybe water will come. No, no, it's not coming, it's dry."

The kids would then wander over to the small window in the door and would look into the unsmiling face of the woman that sat perched on a stool year after year. As they would begin to ask for water she would break in with her usual response, "I have no water for you."

On those days Sophia would interrupt the letter collecting, approach a nearby house and politely call until someone answered. She then would ask if they could spare a glass of water for each of the children. She always ventured over to the same house to ask the favor. The white-haired lady knew what they wanted, whenever she saw them. She was kind and appeared to live alone, for they never saw another person respond to their calls. She would tell them to come in, come closer, and then she gave them water cooled from sitting inside of an indoor water tank. Many homes did not have running water, but those that did, had on their rooftops a large water tank. The tank captured rain water, and stored water, when the public water work's pressure was strong enough to send it up. Water delivery on the island was completely unreliable. It came and went for days at a time and forced people to resolve the problem by using the unsightly storage tanks.

Back at the post office window, the woman in her late forties awaited them. She was very overweight and always looked overheated. As she turned to collect mail, one could always spy a bag of *ajonjoli* close by. A favorite candy on the island *ajonjoli* was made out of sesame seeds and brown molasses. It was *so* good, but *so* high in calories for someone who moved *so* little. Sophia knew that her passive existence and the intake of sweets was the right combination to keep her round. No matter how many times the children had made it to her window, looking exhausted and sweaty from their long trip, they had never seen her smile. She must have been bitter with the boredom of her job. Many people would come at the end of the day to find mail, but in between lay many hours, and she must have resented her loneliness.

Finding mail from their dad was their greatest possible reward, and if that day brought them a wild-looking stamped envelope, they would throw themselves into the tall grass in some shade nearby, read the letter and dream. The bi-weekly check sent to the James children by the company that owned the vessel their father was on, was crucial, but there was nothing like a letter with foreign stamps which would reach them weeks after being sent. They were aware that they were reading old news, but that didn't matter at all. Any news was great and his letters always had high adventure in them. Postmarked from Bali, Singapore, Madagascar, South Africa, Brazil, Peru, Chile or Australia, the envelopes with the red and blue stripes on their edges, were what a long trip to the post office was all about. So many countries with names that, at the beginning, held no recognition to them, would lift them into a world so unlike anything around them. These letters were read with everyone sitting, wide-eyed and in silence, absorbing the tales. There was motivation upon returning home to find on the old globe where the country was located and, as time went by—without even noticing—the children had become good geographers. Oh, the stories, the color, the desire to fly away and see the world!

There was the story of Mr. James caring for zebras on his journey to the US from Africa. He would calm them down with lumps of sugar in their small, wooden cages on deck, when their loud stomps spoke of fear. From the trip into the Australian Outback he had managed to return home with a whole ostrich egg. After piercing, it was drained, and eaten by all. The many stone necklaces that he bought in Brazil and brought home for the girls to choose from made them giggle in anticipation. The tanks and firecrackers Mr. James would bring for Johnny's imaginary wars and the knick-knacks that filled his magical bag, were appreciated even more as each was accompanied by a story.

When Mr. James arrived it was like a holiday. He embodied so many things for the children, but most of all security and love. Awaiting his arrival between trips gave them a goal to hang on to and each of his letters represented hope. Hope was all they had and they tightly embraced it.

13

EVERYDAY STAPLE, TRADITIONS AND SUGARCANE

"RECUERDOS DE PUERTO RICO" ~ "MEMORIES OF PUERTO RICO"
Abro la ventana de mis recuerdos, ~ I open the window of my memories,
Un día soleado, Ay, le,lo,lai,le,lo,lai, ~ It's a sunny day, Ay,le,lo,lai,le,lo,lai,
Van con pecho desnudos, ~ They're passing by bare chested,
Muchos hombres forzudos, ~ Many strong men,
A picar la caña, Ay, le,lo,lai,le,lo,lai, ~ To cut the sugarcane, Ay, le,lo,lai,le,lo,lai.
Llevan termo en mano, rico cafecito, ~ They carry a thermos in hand, nice coffee,
Desayuno en fiambre, Ay, le,lo,lai,le,lo,lai. ~ Breakfast in lunchpail, Ay, le,lo,lai,le,lo,lai,
Y alguno va silbando, ~ And someone is whistling,
Y otro acompañando, ~ and another accompanying,
La música de Rafael Hernández, ~ To the music of Rafael Hernández,
Ay, le,lo,lai,le,lo,lai. ~ Ay, le,lo,lai,le,lo,lai.

It was a loud house on school mornings with everyone racing to the bathroom door. When the boys didn't make it first they would shrug and run outside. There they would quickly take a leak toward the field behind the house and brush their teeth with water from the hose.

Kitchen sink was second best, especially when it was nice n' empty, with no dishes left from the night before. The words, "Hurry it up" were repeated incessantly like the echo of a broken record. Soon plastic cups on the counter were grabbed and *Quick* chocolate powder was stirred into cold milk taking too long to dissolve. Along with a piece of rolled bread the dunking would begin, and it was good.

The bigger kids would take turns on running the little ones down the street to be watched over by Esther. Once the appointed member returned, they all set out together down the dusty road to school. Somehow they were surviving and doing harm to no one, just allowing time to pass and with some luck an adult would return and make life easier for them: feed them a tasty meal; wash their clothing that piled sky high when the washing machine would break down; or maybe, with some luck, give them a little love. Sophia missed love. There was really no one that paid them a kindness that involved hugging and she missed a caress, a kiss, a hug.

Sophia tried to remember that she had been luckier than her siblings. By being the oldest, for a short time, she had tasted a normal family life. She knew what it was to jump into her father's lap and ask him for a story, or to ask her mother to please put the yellow and not the blue ribbons into her clean and shiny long braids. At times when Sophia felt down, by all the demands that were made on her—by everyone and all the time—she forced herself to remember. To remember that Frankie, Evy and Johnnny, for just a short while, when they were too young to remember, had experienced having both parents. However, those thoughts hardly consoled her when she was supposed to come up with all the answers. There was no time out, no passing the hot potato on to someone older and more responsible.

At moments when sadness and burdens were too heavy, she would seek refuge to collect herself. Sophia, now twelve, would climb up into the tree house, sit in a corner away from the world and quietly remember. She clearly saw her orange meadow bright with poppies back home in California. Her friends, coming out of their homes, were heading out to the great eucalyptus tree. She could hear their laughter and wondered if, at that moment, on that day, they might be sitting and sharing stories and growing up together. She wanted to call out, tell them to wait up, that she was coming too, but she couldn't. She was trapped in another world and she couldn't get out. Nevertheless, she always held on to her sweet memories, running freely in the meadow across the street with her friends. She remembered her friend Colleen Grey, with her stylish haircut and toothy smile, and wondered what had become of her. She wondered if her friends ever remembered her. If they only knew what had happened to all of them, they wouldn't have believed it. She thought of Ricky, the boy that gave her a kiss on the cheek, as he ran by her calling out "I love you." She saw Ronnie with his clear, blue eyes and big smile racing past her on his bike. She had been in love with him. The happy memories made her cry and she longed for home, for Sacramento. During these little escapades where she relived and longed for the past, she became emboldened. Sophia promised herself to not surrender to the world that surrounded her. She would learn Spanish, learn it correctly and do it by reading. She had no role model and was capable enough to recognize that. She would do her duty, help her family stay together, be the best that she could be and then she would get out. She would work hard, keep her grades up no matter what, and she would go to college to become a doctor and leave the island that had trapped and stifled them all. No, she would not give up ever. She would make something of her life and she encouraged anyone that listened, to do the same. That was her goal and she would not waver.

Though their life was chaotic and many times downright miserable, it was important that they hang on to anything that made life beautiful. Sophia would keep traditions alive and by doing so, would instill strong values into the children. She now understood that the teachings her father had patiently and repeatedly given her in the past were protecting them. Making sure her siblings embraced those values and understood them was important for their life. Celebrating Thanksgiving, which was not celebrated in Puerto Rico, was important to remind them that they were Californians. Christmas was with a Christmas tree and Three Kings Day—well, they didn't know much about it—but they would. Easter had always been about the hunt for Easter eggs, but in Puerto Rico it was much more and they learned all about it. They would go to church, whatever church, and celebrate like good Christians, even if they didn't know what that meant. However, birthdays were the most important of all. A cake would be present and each and every birthday would be celebrated. Sophia tried her best to make this happen and together they did. Turkey was present during every Thanksgiving but one—the first one after they were left alone. Christmas, however, was a real challenge. The desire to have a Christmas tree was overwhelming. However, in Puerto Rico, the main celebration revolved around the nativity scene and the arrival of Three Kings Day on January 6. Still Sophia wanted her small siblings to know about Christmas and Santa Claus the way she had.

So on that first Christmas, the children set out to find a tree. They turned the activity into an excursion and went up into the back hills of Factor, beyond where Tiba lived and up into some land owned by their grandfather. The mission was about to be named "mission impossible" because all the trees were large and had no similarity to a pine of any sort. Reluctantly, thinking about giving up, they chanced upon a tree that had a bushy form to it. It was about six feet tall and its appearance, with some imagination, made them think of a Christmas tree. The main problem, about the tree, was that it was filled with large and awful thorns. As they got close to it and saw what they were up against, they all sat down on the ground, overheated, exhausted, and groaned. The debate began. It was going to be a mammoth effort to get that sucker out of the ground and down the hill. Just getting close enough to cut it at the base was going to hurt. So they all sat and stared at it hoping it would disappear. To have found it and not take it home would be accepting defeat. They were going to have to brave it. That was the conclusion and stubbornness won the day. They worked hard and each of them was poked and bloodied by the time they got home. They took the tree and shoved it into an empty, large tin can of *Galletas Maria*, a sweet and popular cracker. They filled it up with sand to hold the tree in place and it worked. They covered the can with aluminum tin foil and jazzed it up with a red bow. The tree itself stood near a wall in the center of their living room. The children had lights for it and prepared garlands out of loops of colorful paper. In the end it looked more funny than pretty, and the kids stood around admiring and laughing at their tree.

Colors and flavors of Christmas, indigenous to the island, inevitably spilled into the lives of the James children. It was a magical time that engulfed everyone. The religious aspects of Christmas were painstakingly observed everywhere. However, in Puerto Rico, Christmas was much more than church and a nativity scene. The island's inhabitants adopted a carefree attitude, working less and playing much more. Preparation of special typical dishes began and musicians reached for their instruments, loosening up stiff fingers in anticipation. December was a fun month with echoes of loud and festive tunes that each night carried to every corner of the island. Families rallied around kitchens actively preparing the holiday delicacies.

It was tradition that all women in a family would come together at a relative's home to make delicious *pasteles*. For two days, amidst jokes and loud laughter, *pasteles* would be prepared by organizing an assembly line. They were a huge undertaking and worth all the trouble. They were the most typical of all main dishes eaten on Christmas Eve, along with savory rice, filled with pigeon peas and roast pork. On that first Christmas the children spent alone, they were tortured by the delicious smells that floated on every air molecule. By the second Christmas, Sophia was determined that they would do more than just smell *pasteles*. There were six of them and they too could form their own assembly line.

"OK kids, do you want to eat *pasteles* this Christmas?" it was a question asked in earnest and Sophia watched for their spontaneous reaction.

"Yes!" was the loud reply accompanied by the sound of tongues licking chops and eyes popping out of every face. Sophia laughed. "Uhmmm, yes, Sophia, we want *pasteles*. Who's offered to make us some?" said the inquisitive Johnny with eyes shining with hope.

"Sorry, Johnny, but no one has volunteered yet. Soooo I thought we'd make 'em." said Sophia with her brightest smile, trying to inject enthusiasm into the proposal. The chorused sounds that bounced off her smile were more like a groan of disappointment. Still Sophia, continued, "Hey, guys, we can do it! Look, I'm gonna get everything we need. I'll ask around and find out how to do it and then we'll all get together and make them, like everybody else does."

"Yeah! Sophia, we can do them!" cried out Frankie, with a big, missing-a-front-tooth smile. The optimistic reply was appreciated, although the older children knew that *pasteles* were a major undertaking and their faces reflected doubt.

Sophia was on a mission. She and her siblings would have *pasteles* that Christmas. She asked around and found out how to make them and a few days before Christmas announced,

"Boys, I'm gonna need you to help make more shredders. Each of you go out and find a big lid off of a cracker can. No rust can be on the lid, you hear? When you come back I'll show you how to nail some holes into them so that we can all have something to work with, grinding the plantains tomorrow."

"Tomorrow?" asked Bobby.

"Yes, tomorrow, and the next day too!" She said with a bright smile "Tomorrow we begin making our pasteles!" The boys took off running. One over to Elias, someone over to Esther and after a while they were all back with a nail and rock in hand punching holes into their lids.

The following morning was filled with excitement and anticipation as the children paid close attention to find out which would be their assigned tasks.

"OK, everybody, we are going to be like an assembly line. Each of you will have your own job but we're all kind of working together here. We're a team. OK, let's start with peeling the bananas. Karen and Bobby wrap each hand in a plastic bag and using the knife carefully cut off the ends, and then rip their covers off. Afterwards, throw them into this bucket of water. I've already put salt into it."

"What's the salt for Sophia?" asked Frankie with a look of curiosity and interest.

"Oh, it's just to keep the bananas looking nice and white. You see, because they're so green, they're releasing a stain that will turn them black in no time."

"Sophia, I don't need to put my hand in plastic like some girl to peel bananas," said Bobby.

"Yeah, you're right, except that you're going to get that terrible black stain I was just talking about on your hands and it's gonna last you a long time."

"That's OK, who cares?" said Bobby with a smug grin.

"Johnny and Frankie, you guys are going to help grind down those bananas. OK? You know how to do that?"

"Sure, Sophia, we can do it!" the boys chorused.

"Evy, you come over here and sit down. Here, take this grinder and watch the boys and you can grind a banana into this bowl." Little Evy gave Sophia a big smile and grabbed onto her plastic bowl and lid as if they were gifts.

While the children were eagerly working on their tasks, Sophia, with a large knife, chopped up beef and pork and worked on a sauce. As time went by and all the bananas were done, the children began grinding plantains, taro root and yucca. These were then added into the ground banana mix.

The next day the wide-eyed children continued with the preparation of the *pasteles*. "Today we'll get the banana leaves ready. Grab a place around the table. We're going to wash each leaf and then we have to burn it."

"What do you mean burn it?" asked Johnny.

"Well, we're not going to really burn it too much, just enough so that the leaf will bend and not break when we are wrapping the *pasteles* into it. You'll see. Now wash the leaves carefully with the rag but do it gently so you don't break them. Do both sides. They have to be nice and clean or else our food we'll get dirty." Sophia took a leaf and showed them how she wanted them cleaned. She then took them over by the stove.

"OK, now see how the leaf is becoming shiny where the heat gets it. You have to keep moving the leaf around. As soon as you see it get shiny you move it over to the next spot. Now watch; see how I do it." The children crowded around, close to Sophia and got up on tippie toes to see.

"OK, we'll make our pile of clean, burnt leaves right over here, at this end of the table." Once the pile of leaves was ready, Sophia alerted everyone in an excited voice, "Now, let's do it! Let's begin assembling our *pasteles*."

Everyone again took their positions around the table and all the assembling tasks were assigned. Karen would scoop some of the ground bananas and mush it down in the center of a leaf. Johnny would put a smaller scoop of the meat sauce in the center of the banana mass. Frankie and little Evy would daintily put olives and red peppers on top of the meat. Sophia would fold the leaf over, making a little package. Bobby would then tie it up. By noon the *pasteles* were boiling in a big pot on the stove and the children roamed around smiling wide at the smells that were proudly coming out of their kitchen. An hour later the big moment came. Sophia called out, "OK, everybody, come on in, we're ready to taste one!" The mad dash from the swings, to the slamming screen door was on and within seconds everyone, even Toby their dog, was around the table watching the event unfold.

"Ouch! It's hot!" said Sophia. With scissors she cut off the string and carefully unfolded the *pastel*. It looked beautiful, the right color but when she proceeded to shove it off the leaf and into a plate it didn't move right. There was a problem. The *pastel* was hard, hard as a rock.

"Oh, No!" said Sophia with anxiety as she tried to cut into it. What was supposed to be a soft lovely shell of bananas with a yummy layer of meats within turned out to be so hard that Sophia needed a knife to cut it. With a look of shock and despair she took a taste of it and realized that it really wasn't good at all. Sophia was ashamed more than anything. She felt that she had failed the children.

She was about to begin crying when suddenly Frankie called out, "Look everybody, not even Toby wants some." Frankie was down on his knees offering one to the dog. "Wow! It's gotta really be bad!" With those words everyone began laughing. They all laughed hard and then they all hugged.

More than food, it was the *parrandas* that made Christmas on the island belong to everyone. A *parranda* was the tropical equivalent of Christmas caroling. It consisted of a group of people with instruments getting together with a group that wanted to sing. They would target a family and any time after midnight, a caravan of cars and singers would arrive at that family's doorstep. The James kids excitedly would gather up their sticks and carved maracas—the ones their dad brought from Brazil—and would join in. Sophia on such occasions drove the big Plymouth so as to have a quick escape if something other than music broke out. Quietly, with instruments in hand, everyone gathered as closely as possible to a bedroom window. After an unspoken count down, there would be a departure from silence into an explosion of sound. Everyone played something: from cans, sticks, tambourines, guiro, maracas, to guitars and, if lucky, an accordion. The thunderous sound filled every gap of space as singers and musicians played their lively music. The songs were all about 'Open up your door, so I can wish you a Merry Christmas.' With laughter and persistence the uninvited friends would sing until their would-be hosts opened their door. Once opened, the flooding would begin. Everyone would crowd into a large or small home, it didn't matter, while laughing, singing and playing music. Immediately, preparations of food and drink began. Most people prepared in advance and had food on hand, as they knew they could be "descended upon." Hot chocolate and coffee with trays of cheese, salami and crackers were passed around. After an hour, everyone would leave for another home and those from the first home would join in. Later those from the second home, after being "honored," would head out to the third home, and so on. It was a fun affair that only got better as the evening progressed and as the children grew older.

In years when it was possible, Easter was observed with the traditional egg hunt. The children boiled their eggs and painted them just as children do in the United States. On the morning of Easter Sunday they too would find on their bed a small basket with chocolates. The contents of those baskets disappeared before they were out of their beds. On holidays like Easter, they not only observed the American traditions, but also the traditions of the island. Puerto Rico was very Catholic and many processions and religious ceremonies were held during that time. The James children learned about them and observed them like everybody else. On *Viernes Santo*—Good Friday—the Friday just before Easter Sunday, the children would try to go to the large cathedral adjacent to Arecibo's main plaza. They wore their best clothing and each girl solemnly wore a veil covering her head, as all other females did. They had never received instruction on religion, but the children wanted to belong. Timidly they filed into the large church and sat among the approving eyes of neighbors. In respectful awe they would watch, listen and copy. When people kneeled, they would kneel. When they made the sign of the cross, the James children did the same. When it was time to receive the lovely wafer that melted in your mouth, not understanding that there were preconditions for participation, Sophia led and all six got in line.

"What are people saying to the priest before they get what he is putting in their mouth?" the children had asked her.

"I don't know; just mumble 'Amen,' close your eyes and open up. Watch me," replied Sophia in a hushed voice. Self-conscious and avoiding the priest's eyes they did just that. Religion was a mystery to them and Sophia did not know how to go about learning it herself or teaching it to her siblings.

She had attempted to explore religion with the children and they had gone to a small church that was walking distance from their house. It was not a Catholic church, but the children never really knew what religion it was. It had a pew and benches and a joyful choir. It was a lively place and the children sat down for the experience with wide eyes. Eyes that only got wider and wider as the place got louder and louder. The nicely dressed James children, would watch Sophia and would stand if she did, sit back, down, kneel, or whatever. However, things were so different than at the Catholic Church that Sophia was truly at a loss; parishioners at this place of worship, seemed unpredictable. The great dramatic moments did not happen in unison but were the sole activity of one individual that stood out, as the loudest, or the one that had received "it."

The children would hear people around them saying, "He's got it! or she's got it!" and then everyone proceeded to lift up their right arms, closing their eyes and mouthing something in a trance-like state. Meanwhile, the person with "it," writhed on the floor, having what might look like an epileptic attack. The children were stupefied and Sophia worried that the person might hit their head on the wooden benches. For Sophia, there was too much drama at that church, for real communion and she felt that the show took away from the sanctity of the moment.

But Frankie didn't think so, and kept saying, "Wow, did you see when he went over? Can we come again?"

For Sophia to watch the rituals performed within a church, whichever one, was a reminder of how families shared and learned together. Sophia felt that attending, whenever they could, was a good thing and an outward sign of respect for the traditions of those around them. So with tradition in mind, the six children would return home from church to prepare a meal of fish of some sort—even if it was dried and salted cod fish—or a can of sardines. For in their world, one never ate meat on Good Friday.

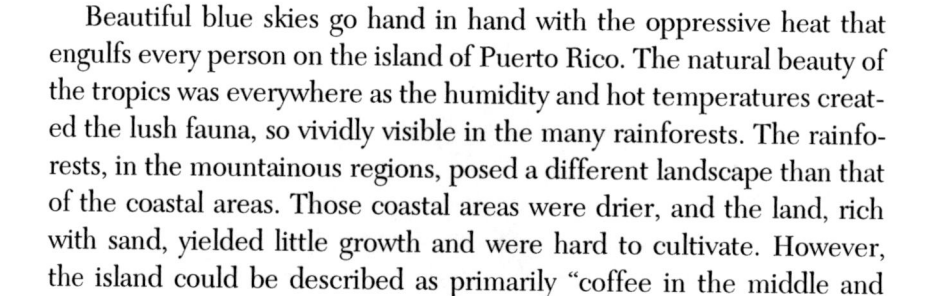

Beautiful blue skies go hand in hand with the oppressive heat that engulfs every person on the island of Puerto Rico. The natural beauty of the tropics was everywhere as the humidity and hot temperatures created the lush fauna, so vividly visible in the many rainforests. The rainforests, in the mountainous regions, posed a different landscape than that of the coastal areas. Those coastal areas were drier, and the land, rich with sand, yielded little growth and were hard to cultivate. However, the island could be described as primarily "coffee in the middle and sugarcane on the sides."

The barrio of Factor, where the James family lived, was on the eastern outskirts of Arecibo. It was basically made up of fields of sugarcane and great pastures of high grass where Holstein cows fed. The little roads of the countryside settlement were all dirt but so very beautiful, lined with tall palm trees that swayed and cooled down anyone walking in their shade. There were few privately owned vehicles and much of its traffic consisted of huge trucks weighted down by fresh-cut sugarcane.

Sugarcane was the life line of Factor. Many neighbors worked planting cane in the fields and then harvesting it when it was ready. Early in the morning, at the break of dawn, groups of workers would pass the James house on their way to the fields. If not wearing the typical straw hat, *la pava*, they would wear a rag around their head, to catch the sweat. With a coffee thermos in one hand to keep them going, in the other hand they carried the always-present long steel knife, the machete. In their pocket, you could bet your life, there would be a file. A file was for those left-over moments after lunch when they sat resting in the shade of their truck and busied themselves sharpening their machete. Planting and harvesting cane was hard work and it required scores of strong men to do it. Back then there was no harvesting sugarcane by machines. It all had to be done by hand. The planting of the sugarcane was a job held by men of all ages, but the actual cane cutters were mostly young and strong. Sugarcane was planted by placing small stalks of cane back into the ground. These stalks would grow roots and the cane would grow from that. However, this was only when a farmer was planting a parcel of land that did not previously have cane on it. Sugarcane did not need to be planted yearly, it was a perennial that grew back, year after year, from the undisturbed roots left in the ground during harvest. The cane grew high—eight to twelve feet—and when it was ready to be cut, it first would be burnt. A controlled, fast-moving, hot fire would quickly burn dry leaves and debris in the fields. At the same time it would seal the outside of the cane with its natural waxy coating and keep its sweetness locked in. Once this procedure was done, the cane would be ready for the cane cutters, *los picadores de caña*. A straight line of men would approach the wall of ripe-and-ready-to-cut sugarcane. Their pace would almost become rhythmic as they moved forward. Two cuts would produce a freed stalk. Raise the machete, catch a flash of light on the steel, cut down low at the stalk's birth and then cut the top off the stalk. Whack, whack! Whack, whack! Swinging their machetes back and forth, the *picadores,* all working in unison, trying to keep up. They would start the day with long sleeves protecting themselves from the cutting leaves that had not been burnt away. But as the hard labor and the beating sun would begin to roast them, shirts would come off and work would continue with bare chests. The island of Puerto Rico had no snakes, but workers were wary of yellow jackets and poisonous centipedes that would escape the initial burn. Often a centipede would crawl up a worker's pants and sting him causing much pain followed by fevers that would keep him home and out of work, endangering the family's welfare.

The cane-cutting process was fascinating. As the *picadores* cut the cane they would take a step back and throw it into a pile. Soon, row upon row of fallen cane would stack up in their tracks and then *los recogedores,* the gatherers, would take center stage. The *recogedores* were men that carried the cut cane and loaded it onto huge trucks. A couple of large planks with small cross boards, to prevent slippage, would be leaned on the truck and used as a ramp. The *recogedores* carrying their load would make it up the ramp as if it were nothing. Several men stood on the truck receiving the bundles. As the height of the stack grew, men would move to stand on top of the cane. Then they would begin standing many stalks vertically alongside the walls of the truck to help support the cane that would be stacked higher than the truck's guard rails.

To an observer, it might appear that the gatherers didn't know when to stop stacking cane onto a truck. The load would become so high, that often it was a wonder that the trucks managed to move. Finally, whistles and shouts of, *He, he he para, para, para eso, para eso*!!! Stop that! would be yelled out and the *recogedores* would target another truck. How the loads didn't fall off and those overloaded trucks avoided tipping over was a mystery. Occasionally, though, it did happen and the mess was awful. Those over-laden trucks would move at about three miles an hour, slowly balancing their enormous piles until reaching the mill.

However, not all farms had big trucks on which to transport the harvested cane to Arecibo's Cambalache Mill. Some small farmers still got their cane to the mill by oxen and carts. It wasn't often, but Sophia would see some go by on foot, steering the oxen that pulled their loaded-down cart.

Sugarcane absorbed everyone's life. Back home, wives or mothers of sugarcane cutters would spend the morning boiling rice, green bananas, breadfruit and codfish with olive oil and onions. By mid-morning, armies of small children or young wives could be seen heading for the fields carrying lunch to the workers. Lunch was carried in *fiambreras*, aluminum containers that vertically stacked two or three individual compartments. One compartment held white rice, another, breadfruit and bananas, and the third, beans or codfish. Meat was almost unheard of, excepting the occasional chicken, which was considered a delicacy by many of these poor sugarcane families. The lunch was a full meal and the men worked hard all morning waiting for the moment in which, in the shade of the huge truck, they'd sit and eat. After eating they'd lie down and take a catnap. In the countryside proper digestion of food was mandatory. People were superstitious and didn't understand the body very well. For them any pain might lead to death, something they saw plenty of. After the snooze they'd sit up, pull out their file and sharpen their machetes. A few minutes later, they would be back at it.

As well as any clock, time could be kept by sugarcane-related activities. Workers would go past the James house at five-thirty in the morning. Cane cutters would be up real early depending on how far they had to walk to fields or catch a ride. By nine-thirty, children were on their way with lunches and at three-thirty, workers walked by in the opposite direction, heading home. When they headed home at the end of a long day, they were all blackened by the burnt cane and the original color of a shirt could not be distinguished. However, again the next morning, their wives and mothers would take pride in sending them back nice and clean. As the harvesting season moved along, some men would continue to cut and would be transported to and from neighboring counties. They would all gather before day's light at a meeting place and jump on an empty flat-bed for the ride to work. In the afternoon they would ride by again on their way home. With their legs dangling, many times Sophia could hear them singing or laughing, obviously enjoying the ride and camaraderie. Hearing them, for some reason, always made Sophia feel good. They were simple people, to be sure, who did what they could to support their families. Most were illiterate and didn't ask for much out of life, but just went about doing what they knew, what they had seen their father and neighbors do before them. Their laughter and their demeanor told anyone listening that they loved life.

The Cambalache Mill was a lifeline for Arecibo. It had two main stacks, one the unpainted color of brick, the other painted white with huge black letters C A M B A L A C H E, written vertically large enough for everyone to see from miles away. The mill stood as a proud landmark with its surrounding large structures, tall and high, right off of Highway 2. The same road that went by the Factor Elementary School and crisscrossed the island. Anyone who lived to the east of Arecibo used Highway 2, as it was the only access road into town. Just before going by the Mill, train tracks were visible, reminding everyone of past times when trains existed all around the island. Sophia heard stories about them and how people missed them. They had been used mainly for the transportation of sugarcane but also served commuters until late in the fifties. They disappeared with the influx of automobiles.

Before reaching the entrance to the Central de Cambalache, a mile-long line of huge trucks, awaiting their turn to be unloaded, would sit parked on the shoulder of the road. On their way to that unloading line, those over-laden trucks had been dropping stalks of sugarcane along the way. With hundreds of trips and thousands of stalks falling and littering, an extra layer would develop on roads, courtesy of the fallen cane. It made for a bumpy ride causing cars to lose nuts and bolts and people to bite down to stop their rattling teeth. The closer one came to the mill, the more the hustle and bustle atmosphere could be felt. With some trucks idling, others would be switched off, all depending on how reliable their switch was. If a truck stalled out, the driver would quickly make the sign of the cross while whispering a prayer. If that didn't work, all truck drivers would head over and begin pushing. They knew that any day, they could be on the receiving end of that dreaded clicking sound. With trucks cued up down the road like a long slithering snake, drivers stood around in clusters talking and joking. Suddenly the line would begin to move forward, which triggered each small assembly to split, with the storyteller running off mid-sentence to move his truck up one space. Then without missing a beat he would run back, as would his listeners, and pick up the story right where he had left off. This gather-and-split motion occurred time and time again until they were admitted onto the grounds of the mill and came under the claw of the unloading crane. Being a truck driver was a good job; it required being literate, so it paid more, and was a lot easier than the hard work of the cane cutters.

Cambalache, like all mills on the island, was self-sufficient energy wise. The cane industry practiced the concept of recycling way before the word became known by most. One of the beautiful things about sugarcane is that once it reached the mill, everything was used and the cane itself generated sufficient power for the entire mill and more. As cane arrived it was put through a series of rollers that crushed it, extracting its sweet sucrose juices. What was left over, the by-product, was called *el bagazo*, the bagasse. Heaps of bagasse were laid out to dry and afterwards thrown into furnaces to fire huge boilers. The steam created would power turbines producing enough electricity for the entire mill.

The humming and buzzing of the active sugarcane mill ran parallel with the lives of those involved in the cane industry and was felt at all levels. After the cane had grown tall and strong, which took about twelve months, its harvesting began and with it, the purring of cane mills. Activity invaded everyone involved in the process of sugar making and they stayed active, working hard, until the harvest was over. With each acre producing approximately 40 tons, a cane cutter had to cut at least two tons a day to keep his job. Truck drivers took load after load, from field to mill; and once the sugar was in the sack, there was a crew of strong men stacking the 257-pound sacks high, way up high in a warehouse. In the mill, workers were equally on the run, unloading and processing the cane all the way through to the finished product. Then came *el tiempo muerto*, the dead time. It was when the mills went quiet, cane cutters looked for different work and homes recessed into soap operas. The dead time went by, as slowly as the slow growing cane took to ripen.

It was with a sigh of relief when a traveler would spy the Cambalache Mill, as it was a marker for anyone heading into town. It told the passenger that the town was about ten minutes away. For miles in both directions, until getting directly in front of the Mill, there was nothing but cane on both sides of the road, an omnipresent wall of green which actually seemed to cool down the ride, even when one was sitting in the hot "kitchen" of a public car. Sidewalks of cane, streets covered in cane, sugarcane was everything.

It was hard to keep order at the James's home. Besides the six children, the family had a dog, a horse and a pig to feed and take care of. It was Mr. James's idea of providing love, fun, and food, respectively. They all loved Tobi, the dog, but truthfully he was quite useless as he never barked when he should have. Dolly, the mare, had been a big mistake. Their father bought the horse in hopes of providing fun for the kids. He spoke with Elias, got him to allow the horse to graze in his pastures and it all seemed easy enough. However, as it often happens, at the beginning everyone loved to ride her, feed her, groom her, but after a while she represented work. Though everyone pitched in, Bobby was her primary caregiver. He was responsible for watering her before and after school and making sure that she was back in the James yard every night. Though there was moaning and groaning over Dolly, the family would have kept her, if it hadn't of been for what happened one night.

It was late at night when Sophia awoke from sounds outside. The world had gone quiet and for a while the night belonged to their dreams and the little coquí frogs. However, suddenly noises that did not belong there disturbed the peace and Sophia got up to look out of a window. Inside their yard, having jumped the fence, were four men that appeared to be drunk. They were holding Dolly and in a crazed manner were trying to copulate with her. It took Sophia awhile to figure out what the drunken men were trying to do, but once she had, filled with fear, she silently backed away from the window. The next day, without a second thought Sophia sold Dolly.

Raising a pig was a lot of work, and Sophia thought that her dad probably got the idea into his head after an evening of too many Corona beers. Pigs grow to be big and can even be dangerous. They all knew a neighbor lady that had a big sow bite into her thigh and maim her terribly. Yes, none of them felt comfortable once the pig had fully grown. Mr. James built a concrete corral for the pig, which had been a real cute little guy when he arrived. However, it took about six months to weigh over two hundred and fifty pounds and it no longer was cute. Mr. James returned home to find the pig just the right size and immediately set out to bring an expert over to the house. He wanted to show Sophia how a pig was slaughtered and everything from it, used. It became a lifelong lesson, only because Sophia could never forget it. However she never quite figured out what the lesson really was. On that day, Sophia watched the pig be killed and the ongoing madness that ensued. The expert immediately placed a basin to save every drop of blood leaking from the animal. Then in one awfully long, lengthwise slice of the abdomen, she removed its intestinal tract. She must have unraveled a mile and a half of tripe, proceeded to wash it and then turned inside out. It was placed in a huge aluminum tub along with guava leaves, for good odor! While it sat, the lady went on to put condiments into the bucket that held the blood and then she cut up small pieces of fat and mixed it all together. Then picking up the intestine she began the filling procedure. That was it! Sophia never, ever, was able to look at, or smell—let alone eat—blood sausage again.

So life was crazy, trying to take care of animals, and feed themselves; then there was housework. The omnipresent housework never went away and at times got completely out of hand. When that happened Sophia laid down the law and began by assigning specific jobs to everyone.

"Johnny and Frankie, you boys have the bathroom and then sweep out the garage. Karen, hit the clothes. I'll start ironing, and Bobby, you start raking the yard. I want to see all the grooves in the dirt. Wet it down. Come on, let's go, let's get going!"

"What shall I do, Sophia?" little Evy would ask wanting to be a part of it all.

"Here is a rag. You start dusting. Wherever you see dust, you go there and wipe it off, OK?"

Everyone had to pitch in and help the family. They were a team and at this time in their lives more than at any other time, past or future, it would be that way. They moved together, they worked together, they helped each other, watched out for each other, loved each other, laughed together, fought and cried together. They were a unit and they would survive all the misery without dwelling on it being so miserable. The cleaning process was endless but pressure especially grew around the time when Sophia knew that her father was about to return. She always wanted to show him how well she could take care of things, how he didn't have to worry. After all, Sophia knew that if their father decided sometime to not return, they would be lost, for surely her grandfather would sell her off to someone. She had no doubt of that!

Then there were the emergencies and with so many kids, it seemed that emergencies came up all the time. From a high fever, to a bump on the head, one could expect anything. Sophia would fly by the skin of her teeth; and everything got dealt with one way or another, from a kiss on the hurt spot, to a mad dash to the hospital.

Everything children can get, they got, and one by one, they licked them. One time someone brought the mumps home. Immediately Sophia knew who the visitor was. The swollen neck around the ears that turned the head and neck into one solid block, and the accompanying groaning and moaning of pain, were things Sophia had seen already.

Kids would go to school with the mumps, just to be sent home immediately by the angry teacher scolding, "Is your mother crazy? You are going to give that to everyone in school and if you run, that swollen neck is going to go down to your balls!" Oh! Yes, Sophia knew what the mumps were and how the person was to rest and stay still. She also knew that they were all doomed, that it would pass from one to another and so it did. The mumps ran through the James home as if it were a river.

The last to get it were Sophia and Karen and they got it on the same day. Knowing that they too would eventually become victims, the girls had supplied the house with liquids, straws and *Vicks VapoRub*. Vicks was the home remedy that cured everything. That is what everyone believed. So the two girls spread it heavily all over their swollen necks. Once the Vicks was applied they tied a handkerchief around their chin to the top of their heads so as to keep the sides of their heads snug with the glistening Vicks. This helped avoid getting it on their clothing. Vicks couldn't fail; if the penetration of the Vicks didn't help, the numbing distraction of the smell would be enough to forget about the pain for a while. On the morning that Sophia woke up with a fever, a swollen neck, and the misery of mumps, she was shocked to see that her sister Karen was in exactly the same condition. The two of them assessed each other and then, with their faces glued to a mirror, the greatest pain of all shot through them. The terrible pain was caused by laughter. Laughs and mumps don't mix. The muscles involved in laughter make the pain excruciating and so laughter begot pain and the funny looks of misery begot laughter. It all was terrible, but the more they hurt, the more they laughed—a painful vicious cycle triggered by a small glance at one another.

Amidst the tragedy of what had happened to the six children, they still had fun every chance they could. They hung on tight during tough times, but stayed optimistic, believing that good times were just around the corner. As time went by, Sophia became more capable and along with that everything improved. On a Saturday, when everyone was tired after a week of managing to not miss a school day, Sophia announced, "If everyone helps out today and we get the house cleaned up and clothes washed, tomorrow we're all going to the beach!"

"Yippee! Really Sophia? Promise?" and she promised. So after dealing out chores and driving everyone to get them done, Sophia and Karen, after dinner, went into the kitchen to start the real big cooking: the cooking for the beach! Preparations for a picnic on the beach were almost a ritual, and a guarantee that they were going.

As the cooking in the kitchen began, the smells of the fried chicken and the yummy potato salad kept the boys and Evy coming back asking for, "A little piece of chicken?"

"No," Sophia would say. "No, we can't eat it now or we won't have any for tomorrow." But it didn't matter, Bobby somehow managed to sneak a thigh and after that all she heard was "Sophiiiiiaaaaaa, Bobby is eating chicken! Can't I have one?" Sophia would give in and give everyone a piece and at that point she'd warn Bobby that if he took another piece that would be the end of the trip. Sophia knew that all of them would end up eating a piece of chicken during the frying process, so she always prepared for that and bought extra, making sure there was plenty for the next day. The food would hold overnight and in the morning, bright and early, they would head out to the beach.

The drive to the beach wasn't very long; it took just over half an hour to get there. Their lovely picnic was the first thing to be put into the vehicle followed by towels, beach ball, paddle ball, and a rope for some tug-a-war. Driving was not something that Sophia enjoyed. Though she was fourteen now and driving for a couple of years, she was still short and aware of being underage and that she could have trouble. However, she had come to consider policemen her friends. So on Beach Sundays she didn't think twice about sitting high on a pillow and heading down the road in the big green Plymouth. These were their happy times. The kids would ride in their bathing suits with all the windows open and feel the breeze. Someone would start a song and they would all take it up, singing loudly and laughing, somehow forgetting to fight and pester.

Beach days were long days. They left their house early in the morning and stayed swimming and playing for as long as the sun stayed warm. The picnic included a breakfast consisting of boiled eggs and mangoes. Then the lovely fried chicken and salad held them all day long. *La Pozita,* was the closest beach and always the one Sophia drove to. It was a beautiful pool of water protected by a natural barrier of rocks that protruded toward the ocean. It was shimmering blue, not too deep, and inviting. Beyond its mouth, however, the ocean was clearly visible and when waves were high, they crashed through the rocks, threatening to enter the calm pool. It was as safe as swimming at the beach could be, but still Sophia had little peace. She was just wired that way, a *worry-body* that would be constantly counting heads, then relaxing, and then counting heads again one minute later. She would watch them swim underwater and at times think that they were under too long. Jumping to her feet, heart thumping in her chest, she would run toward the water, when a head emerged with a huge giggle. At times the kids would all come out for a rest and throw themselves on the sand next to her.

After listening to, "I stepped on something sharp, I think it was a piece of glass," or "Did you see that huge wave? I rode it in for about a hundred feet," Sophia would tell everyone to stay out of the water and watch her dive. She would go to the rocks that protected the cove and after climbing to a position as high as possible, she would dive in, head first, concentrating on keeping her legs together. It was there, at *La Pozita*, that Sophia learned how to dive, and it was on those Beach Sundays that the younger James kids learned how to swim.

Beach Sundays were fun days indeed but not a rest for Sophia. On those days more than others she felt like the mother of the family. She felt responsible for all of them, and admitted to herself that they had become more than just siblings to her. On one particular Sunday she sat on a towel studying each of them. As she watched them swim and play she thought of how each one was showing individuality. She could see how they were maturing and developing their own personalities.

Her sister Karen had grown taller than she, and was thin and lanky which put her into that awkward-looking stage. Her body had grown too fast to know what to do with it. She was however, very beautiful, with a Snow White look of white, clear skin and rosy lips, surrounded by jet black hair. Her hair was soft and full; it had a lovely wave to it and was always healthy and shiny. Her eyelashes were long and thick and her eyes were large and striking. Overall, Karen looked a lot like Dad; in fact, all the children took their looks from his side. Karen loved dolls and despite it all had an innocence and naiveté about her. She didn't like to work, but she would. She helped like they all did and she was Sophia's right arm. Her finest characteristic was her kindness. She was always kind, frustrated at times like they all were, but genuine of heart and loving.

Bobby was lively and wanted to be free, running and jumping from birth. He was blond, rare for those parts of the island, and his handsome looks made him stand out. He was always a part of the action, whatever the action was, as long as it was play and fun. He didn't like working, but none of them did. However, when he did work, he did it well and took pride in it. Bobby was Sophia's greatest challenge. He was the hardest to rein in and he was the angriest. His nature was to be a loyal soul and being abandoned by his mother was unforgivable to him. He defended their home and those in it bravely and as a young boy he threatened to beat up anybody that might need it. The more Bobby grew up, the safer Sophia felt they all were.

Johnny was the quiet one. He had dark brown, straight-as-can-be hair, and a little darker complexion than the others. He was a good-looking boy with fine features, but the suffering was visible on him. He was way too thin. Sophia smiled as she watched him in the water and thought of how she would tease him about having parasites. However, he did not have a pot belly, just an insatiable hunger that was never satisfied. He was somewhat of a loner, with a wonderful inquisitive mind, and he used time wisely. He spent days building elaborate battle fields with his toy soldiers and tanks. His planned attacks were well thought out and Sophia knew that he was quite intelligent. He liked to study, was interested in geography, and the first to point out on the world globe the whereabouts of their father. Johnny could separate the important from the superfluous and that was almost an art form in their world. He was one they could count on.

Frankie was a ray of light, always smiling. He, too, was blond with bright rosy cheeks, a toothy, curious little boy that never made a fuss and always looked at the bright side of things. He was the first one to say with a big smile, "It'll be all right, Sophia." Everything was exciting to Frankie and he wanted to share it all. "Look at what I found!" and in he would bring a colorful caterpillar and show it like a prize. He wasn't bashful and when he wanted something he'd ask for it. "Sophia, give me hugs." Before she could answer, he'd be in her lap with his little arms around her neck. He was sweet and Sophia needed him so much to keep her sweet, too.

Baby Evy was beautiful. She was a picture-pretty little girl with soft curls of fine, blond hair, large wide eyes, that seemed to be forever looking for her lost mother. She spent much of her time chasing the bigger ones, wanting to hang out with them and then looking dejected because they avoided "the baby." Often Sophia awoke to find that she had crawled into bed with her and cuddled up. Too often neglected, needing attention, and only getting it when she cried, and too young to help herself, she was often a little rag-a-muffin looking for love. However, her cheerful disposition was innate; she was a happy child in spite of it all, and would smile over anything. Looking at Baby Evy always made Sophia wonder how a mother could leave her babies. It was a question without an answer or, if it had one, Sophia would never be able to understand it. Evy had outgrown diapers and her baby blanket and as Sophia watched her on that beautiful Beach Sunday, she was becoming a good swimmer. Sophia loved her as she truly loved them all, and would continue to try her best to protect them and survive.

Yes, on beach days Sophia only relaxed when the day of fun was over and they were on their way back home—all the James kids, nice and safe, asleep in the back seat.

14

POETRY AND A KISS

"EL BESO" ~ "THE KISS"
En la plaza del pueblo, ~ In the town square,
A una niña la besan, ~ A girl is being kissed
En la sombra de un árbol. ~ In the shade of a tree.
El mandado obligado, ~ The obligated errand,
Por la madre, espera, ~ For her mother, lies waiting,
Que sabroso está el beso. ~ How delicious is the kiss.
Ese beso el pueblo, si se la gozo. ~ The townsfolk sure did enjoy that kiss,
Ese beso, Uy! Ese beso Oh! ~ That kiss was Uy! That kiss was Oh!

Sophia was an attractive girl, but more than beauty, it was her distinctive poise that made her stand out among girls her age. There was a confidence, an assertiveness, about her that reflected maturity and pride, strong and fierce. Though not very tall, she *stood* tall and her eyes engaged, in a direct way, demanding attention. Her Spanish became excellent and fluent, yet it sounded unusual to those around her. Not so much because of an American accent, but for its correctness. She was determined from the beginning to learn the melodious language correctly and made a point of doing so by reading and learning her Spanish from books. Even though Sophia didn't know it, she was a poet, and the classics appealed to her. Early on, she began to distinguish what was correct from what was slang, in what she heard daily. She would speak without the horrible *Spanglish*, a combination of English and Spanish that slaughters the language and was spoken by so many on the island. Gabriel García Márquez, Miguel de Cervantes, Pablo Neruda and Federico García Lorca were among her many guides. These famous authors, if not their ideology, guided her Spanish well, and her vocabulary became extensive and mature. Sophia came to understand that first impressions define a person in many ways. She would not allow poor speech to handicap her, so she embraced the beautiful language and reveled in speaking it accurately.

It was no accident that Sophia acquired a true love for books. Her father was an avid reader and read to her when she was small. Every day, a good portion of him would be hidden behind the walls of the newspaper, one that had required a trip of some distance, before he could place his eager hands on it. The "San Juan Star," at the time, was the only English newspaper on the island and it was like water for the thirsty, for those that did not know Spanish. *Reading was key in a person's life*, was the perpetual message. It freed the mind to expand and find answers to unspoken questions. When Sophia's father packed up belongings that would make the trip with them from California to Puerto Rico, he couldn't help but bring a box with some of the classics. Those good and faithful books lay waiting in a box ready to teach and guide whoever reached in and freed them. They were like magic, transporting the reader to a different world and Sophia cherished their refuge. Reaching into that box and pulling out an Austen book was to enter the world of "Pride and Prejudice" or "Sense and Sensibility." The elegance, the correctness, the excitement helped form and protect Sophia's mind from the vulgarity that surrounded her. She identified with "Jane Eyre," the girl that would not quit, nor be less; and, when immersed in "Gone With the Wind," Sophia became Scarlett for a while. Reading always influenced Sophia and later, when she met Ayn Rand's writing, an ideological understanding of her own began to develop. When there was no one else, books and their teachings provided much-needed and cherished guidance for Sophia, and she loved them for it.

Over time, different opportunities and situations presented themselves and prompted Sophia to write. Those opportunities made Sophia aware of her creative mind and she began to appreciate and enjoy her own ability. Such an opportunity arose one weekend when a neighbor girl by the name of Rosa appeared at the James house. She was a tall, thin, young woman about twenty years old, a kind girl that made up for her lack of beauty by being neat and clean. Her teeth were bright white and perfectly straight and she constantly smiled. Her hair was her apparent nemesis. It was coarse, wiry and hard to control and she tried to hold it in place and make it attractive with flowered barrettes and such. Rosa was very poor and lived in a tiny wooden house. Sophia remembered being taken aback at the sight of her dwelling which was not more than 15 by 15 feet in size. The small house was up on stilts and four steps got you there. Each wall had a window except for the front which had the one and only door. The windows had two shutters, so they were either open or closed. In the back yard, an old and broken down latrine stood next to a small rickety out house made for bathing. Everything was visible from the dirt street that passed directly in front of the house, so anyone could easily see inside. A double-size bed was against the wall on the left side and in the right corner there was a stove and a table with two chairs. Rosa was raised by her grandmother and everything they owned in the world was within those thin walls. They both slept in the one and only bed that was visible from the dirt road and their main means of entertainment was an old radio.

Sophia and the kids began passing by Rosa's house on their journeys into town, once a new stop for public cars opened. It was closer than the old stop and they were happy to change the route. Often they would see a young woman, too tall for the dress she was wearing, sitting on the top step of her little square house. She would lift her hand and wave goodbye and call out "Adios" with a big smile. Sophia had the impression that she was a 'good girl,' as she never heard anyone say anything bad about Rosa. A reputation in a little barrio was all a person had. The only way to stay out of waggling tongues was to truly stay out of trouble. Any reason for gossip was scooped up in no time and magnified many times over.

To have Rosa show up at Sophia's house one day, and timidly knock at their door, was unexpected. None of the James children really knew her. At the sound of her knock someone raced from the TV to the door and opened it, calling for Sophia to come. Upon seeing Rosa, Sophia asked her to come in and as customary offered her something to drink.

"No, thank you. I don't care for anything right now," she said and then continued. "I have wanted to talk to you and maybe, if now is a good time . . ."

"Sure Rosa, would you like to sit outside where it's cooler and quieter. The kids are watching TV, so it's loud in here right now." Sophia and Rosa made themselves comfortable on the porch in a spot that was hidden from the street by bushes. The young woman that was at least six years older than Sophia, began to confide in her, and told her that she was in love. The object of her interest was a radio broadcaster who hosted an afternoon show every day. She listened to him always and had fallen in love with his voice and laughter. She began writing letters to him and in each letter she included a thin box of gum. Adams Chiclets was the most popular gum at the time, and its thin box lent itself well to being included in an envelope. What brought Rosa to the James's home was that a friend who had been helping her write letters had moved away and now, to continue corresponding with him, Rosa needed help.

"I have heard that you are very intelligent and I was hoping that you would help me write the letters." Sophia was amused and amazed and couldn't help but smile.

"No problem," she said, "Of course I'll help you, Rosa. We'll write him some letters that will make him fall in love with you, if he hasn't already." That response brought laughter to the shy Rosa and the following weekend she returned. The love letter writing began. For Sophia it was an opportunity to put her best Spanish forward.

She wrote poetically and before she would actually commit the words to paper she ran them by Rosa. Rosa's eyes would widen and she would say, "Yes! Oh, yes! That sounds so beautiful, Oh! Yes he will like that so much!" The two would sit, write and giggle and Sophia was learning about another side of herself. She was a romantic and her words had fire in them. They flowed with ease and with each letter Rosa was taking on more and more the literal meaning of her own name "Rose." Rosa was becoming quite the rose and she was enchanting the young man with the great voice that spoke daily on her radio. Every other week they huddled together and composed a letter that was mailed with the unfailing box of Chiclets. This went on for over a year and the letters grew in their intensity. For quite a while, the young man asked for a picture of Rosa. He wanted to see her. In Rosa's mind this was a problem, for she felt that once he saw her, he would not write again and his letters meant so much to her. Week after week the girls would make up an excuse to cover for the absent photo. Finally, the time came when the young man would not take 'no' for an answer and wanted to meet Rosa personally. Sophia tried to convince her that she was not ugly and that her beautiful soul made her beautiful too. But Rosa would not agree to meet the man she lost sleep over. As life would have it, around this time when Rosa was filled with conflict, her loving old grandmother passed away. If life had been austere for Rosa up to then, now she was completely alone. All letter writing ceased, along with Rosa's visits to the James's house. Only a couple months later word spread around the barrio that Rosa had married in a small ceremony at City Hall. The man she married was fifteen years her senior and a sugarcane cutter. He lived in a small house, just slightly larger than the tiny box of a house that Rosa had shared with her grandmother. Rosa's new address was not on a road that the James children used, so they rarely saw her. However, on a few occasions when they did pass by, Rosa would see them and run to the door waving and smiling her bright smile. Only Sophia knew the truth. Rosa loved, not the man she married, but a voice on the radio that would surely haunt her forever.

Writing love letters for Rosa was fun and the tragic sudden end to that episode was sad. Sophia had learned many things through that experience and a curiosity in her for love was also awakened. She was nearly fifteen and her options in the barrio were scant. It seemed to Sophia that all the "loves" she saw were like none she wanted. Boys were jealous and possessive and she was too mature to have someone less mature tell her what to do or what not to do. She was used to making decisions—calling the shots—and so any boyfriend she could have would be used by her for experience and would never own her, even if he thought he did. However, she did feel attracted to boys and at times was flirtatious. Anyone that attracted her attention was always considerably older, and she knew that she had to be careful. She wanted to have a love and to have her first kiss. But who? And how would that happen?

Once Sophia and Karen graduated from elementary school in Factor, they bypassed a school in a closer barrio for the bigger public school, the Muñoz Rivera Middle School in downtown Arecibo. It had a better academic reputation. While a private school was out of the question for them, Sophia was determined to find the most secure and academically sound school within their means. Of course, going to the school in town meant getting up earlier and depending on public transportation. In a world where very few owned a car, *carros publicos*—

public cars—thrived. The ride to school was thirty cents and the walk to the stop, even at a fast pace, was a good twenty minutes. A big old station wagon, riding low and looking heavy, with all kinds of things hanging from its front mirror, and fins over its wheels with signs saying *Tu Fiel Amigo,* Your Loyal Friend, or *Nunca es Tarde"* It's Never Too Late, would pull up. Everyone in it would begin piling out, so that the last ones could make their way into the dreaded "kitchen." With a moan or a groan of, *Ay, Dios Mio*! "Oh! My God!" the newcomer would make it to the back. However, if there was one thing Sophia always appreciated about Puerto Ricans, was their cleanliness. With it being so hot and life demanding close encounters, such as sitting in the dreaded back seat of the public car, passengers were all cleaned up, and dressed nicely to go into town. No matter how poor, everyone took a shower every evening; it was a matter of pride.

The Muñoz Rivera was a junior high school. It was large, old, a great structure with an impressive facade. The building sat high up and away from the street with a dozen steps leading to the first level. The classrooms were aligned along all walls surrounding a small courtyard. That configuration allowed for good ventilation. Like all schools it mandated that its students wear a uniform. All girls wore a white blouse with a gray skirt and vest. Around the collar a ribbon was worn and its color defined the student's grade: pink for 7th and burgundy for 8th. The one item that allowed for individuality was the little pin used to secure the crossed colored ribbon. That detail defined one's personality. Some wore a plain safety pin, but most had something coquettish or fun. Sophia always wore a little blue owl. The Muñoz Rivera School carried within its walls a more serious attitude towards education than Sophia had known since arriving in Puerto Rico. She was proud to call it her school and worked hard to do well and get good grades. Her efforts had not gone by unnoticed by Mrs. Pérez, her eighth grade Spanish teacher, who, like everyone else, seemed to know the story about the American children in Factor. She observed Sophia with curiosity when she entered her class. Sophia immediately liked her and, with quiet kindness, the teacher began giving her guidance.

It hadn't taken long when one day the teacher called Sophia over. "Sophia, after school today I would like you to come back to my classroom. I want to speak with you." She had said these words with warmth and her smile vanquished any apprehension in Sophia. As the school day came to an end, Sophia made her way back to Mrs. Pérez's room. She was curious to know what the meeting was all about.

"Sophia, you must be about fourteen now, right?"

"Yes, Ma'am, I'll be fifteen soon."

"Well, Sophia, I want you to know that I have heard an incredible story about you and your family." At those words Sophia felt her face become hot and she knew that she had turned red. "You are a very admirable young lady, Sophia, and I want you to know that I am proud to know you."

Sophia's eyes widened, began to moisten and she tried to stay in control of her emotions while she smiled at her teacher. Mrs. Pérez realized that she was walking a fine line and that Sophia's emotions were very close to the surface. Immediately, the insightful teacher turned her voice into a joyous laugh and blurted out, "I want you to come and spend a weekend at my home with my daughter and me. I am a widow and my daughter is a little older than you. There is something I want to show you Sophia. We'll have a fine time, I promise. What do you say? When can you come?"

She said these words with mischief and fun and Sophia wanted to hug her. But she didn't. Smiling wide she stared at her, almost unbelieving what she had heard. This was an invitation, something she had never heard since sleeping in the barn with Colleen Gray.

"Mrs. Pérez, wow, yes, I want to come, but I don't know when I can. I'm going to talk to everyone at home and see when I might be able to go home with you. It is very exciting to think of meeting your daughter and seeing your home. Thank you so much. I'll tell you soon when it could happen. Thank you, Mrs. Pérez. Thank you."

The thought of spending a night away at her teacher's house was an exciting thought. However, Sophia needed to make sure that everything would be all right at home. No one ever spent a night away and, even with the bar out front, Sophia always harbored fears of someone breaking into their house. How could she leave for a night and be sure that the children would be fine? Walking home from school toward the plaza to catch a public car that would take her to Factor, she pondered this question. The line for a car at the plaza was short and among those waiting was Tiba's daughter Lilliana. Sophia gladly approached her with the customary kiss on the cheek and sat next to her in the car. Finding Lilliana improved the tedious trip greatly, as Sophia liked her a lot, and spoke freely with her. She confided the conversation that she had had with her teacher that day. Lilliana was excited for her and said, "Sophia, go with her after school on Friday, and I will go over to your house early, make sure the kids have food and spend the night there. I'll stay until noon on Saturday and you get back as soon as you can. How about that?" she said smiling and giving her a nudge.

Sophia's eyes were wide and dreamy. "Really, you will?"

"Yes, and don't worry about anything. In fact, Mamá will probably come over with me!"

"Oh, Lilliana, that would be wonderful. I'll talk to my teacher tomorrow and see if I can go this Friday. I'll let you know right away, so that you can plan to come over. Thank you, Lilly" and Sophia squeezed her hand.

After school on Friday Sophia followed her teacher to her car. Feeling a bit intimidated and awkward, Sophia sat in the front seat beside her. She wondered if any friends from school saw her leave with the teacher. She hadn't mentioned it to anyone, usually keeping matters to herself. From school they headed over to the high school which was close by and picked up Mrs. Pérez's daughter. They then continued on their way to El Hatillo, a small town to the west of Arecibo. El Hatillo was just inland from the coastline, and lay in the opposite direction from Factor, which was to the east.

Mrs. Pérez's house was inviting from the moment Sophia entered. A small concrete home with a delightful rose garden out front and floors that shined clean and polished, the house was airy, smelled good and was filled with light. Mrs. Pérez immediately headed for the kitchen, and in no time squeezed some lemons, making a delicious glass of lemonade for each of them. Sophia felt welcomed and safe as Mrs. Pérez's daughter was, like her mother, sweet and kind. Maritza was taller than Sophia and after showing her around her home they busied themselves in the kitchen chatting and watching Mrs. Pérez prepare dinner.

The evening was surreal for Sophia. She tried to not give evidence of it, but a lovely mother preparing dinner in a clean home where laughter and pleasantries were spoken, touched Sophia's heart. She was experiencing what she so much knew existed, and that she had wanted and longed for. She lived the moment intensely, trying to sear every instant into her brain. Later, after dinner, the reason why Mrs. Pérez had invited Sophia to her home was revealed.

"Sophia, you must be wondering what it is I wanted to show you when I invited you to come for the night."

"Yes, Mrs. Pérez, I am, even though just being with you both for dinner has already been such a special event for me. My visit could end right now and I would be so grateful to you." Sophia's joy was palpable and Mrs. Pérez plunged forward.

"Well, Sophia, I want you to know that I have been watching you and you are growing up." As she said this, she smiled and glanced at her daughter who was sitting next to Sophia. With a small giggle Maritza reached over and grabbed Sophia's hand. Sophia too had a smile on her face intermixed with one of bewilderment. Mrs. Pérez's smile grew wider as she said, "Sophia, you are growing up! You are becoming a young lady!!And it's high time you got rid of those little girl dresses that you wear, whenever I've seen you out of uniform." Sophia's mouth dropped and she looked confused. Mrs. Pérez immediately continued. "Maritza has grown out of her clothing and we think that they would fit you. What do you say? Want to play dress up?"

Out came beautiful dresses, blouses and skirts, pants and shorts. They were like new and had been worn with care. Sophia put one on, then another and the *Ohhhs* and the *Ahhhhs* became a part of a magical evening where Sophia's appearance changed completely. The old dresses that she had long ago outgrown, with their waistlines up to her bust line and big bows tied in the back, were replaced by form-fitting clothes. Sophia felt beautiful, with her tight skirts and shiny heels. The kindness that Mrs. Pérez and Maritza showed Sophia forever became a treasured memory. For they not only gave her new clothing and shoes but greatly added to her self-confidence. Through their actions they told Sophia they believed in her and that she was worthwhile. These were the experiences and demonstrations of kindness that Sophia hung on to with all her might to preserve the best in her.

Hanging tough all the time wasn't easy, and daily life was one challenge after another, but somehow time kept passing and they stayed alive and unhurt. It became all about making the best of what they had and finding the bright side of things. Their life was constantly filled with fear, deprivation and work they hated, but every now and then, an exception would come along, and life would become fun.

The James children, like almost everyone else in Factor, were always starved for distraction. Every year *La Verbena de Factor* arrived and pulled people out of their homes and out of their lives, and, for one and all, was a sweet surrender. It was a much-awaited festival, celebrated in most small towns of the island. The *Verbena*, was an offshoot of the large *Fiestas Patronales*, which was devoted to the Patron Saint of the municipality. In the case of Arecibo, it was *Apóstol San Félipe*: Saint Philip the Apostle. The big fiestas were held in the Plaza Major of downtown Arecibo and were quite grand. However, for the James children, it was the *Verbena* out in the countryside that was theirs. Only an emergency could get Sophia to travel at night into Arecibo, and thankfully they had few of those.

The *Verbena* came around once a year. It was colorful and loud with typical music. Bands and trios from near and far, some known, but most unheard of, flexed their vocals and the promenading would begin. All rural communities anxiously waited for their *Verbenas*. It was an opportunity to put on the best show and outdo neighboring communities. So the goal was to have the best entertainment and of course the best Queen! Each coveted having the reputation of being the number one *Fiesta* around. With the reputation came money, as people would flood in from other counties and the fundraising *Verbena* would prove profitable. These *fiestas* absorbed everyone's imagination, and when it was *Verbena* time, there was time for little else.

People from Factor, competed fiercely to have their *Verbena* be the best one. Volunteers stepped forward, year after year, in hopes of making it better than the year before. So the search began to find the Queen. Every year, girls between the ages of fifteen and seventeen would step forward to compete and wear the Queen's crown. It was something that Sophia knew about but had never given a single thought. However, now, having turned fifteen, she was eligible and Karen, the boys, and people from the barrio, began encouraging her to run.

"Come on, Sophia you could win, you could be the queen of the *Verbena*!" Bobby had said.

The selection hinged on who sold the most tickets and Sophia knew that people could cheat. Each ticket cost $1.00 and so the candidate that collected the most money by selling more tickets than anyone else, was the winner. Bobby continued his push, "We'll help you sell tickets, Sophia. We'll sell more than anyone!"

"Sure, we can sell tickets all around the barrio and even to teachers at school," wistfully agreed Johnny.

"You'll be the prettiest queen ever!" said Frankie excitedly, already crowning her.

The whole matter sounded fun and distracting, so Sophia threw her hat into the ring and the race was on.

There were five contestants and two weeks in which tickets would be sold. On the last day they would turn over all monies, and the winner would be declared. Formalities began immediately, with pictures taken of all the contestants and announcements posted on bulletin boards everywhere, from the lumber yard to the local bakery. Sophia knew all the competing girls fairly well, but one of them was a friend. Lidia had studied in Sophia's same grade from day one. She was not known for her beauty, she was too heavy for that; however, she was liked by everyone because she was fun. Sophia and Lidia joked about beating each other.

The James kids were on a mission, and their weekends now had a goal. All of them got involved. The boys would stick together. They grabbed a batch of tickets and proudly went off telling everyone that their sister was in the race, "You can buy a ticket, or many, that's OK!" Frankie would say, with his big missing-a-front-tooth-smile. Sophia, Karen and little Evy, would get all dressed up and go from house to house selling tickets and thus collecting votes.

For Sophia, selling tickets was not an easy task. She didn't have the amount of time available to most girls. Nevertheless, she had her siblings all trying hard to help her win. They made a big effort and by the end of two weeks they had gathered over six hundred dollars. The children were very impressed when looking at all the money and were sure that Sophia would win. As it was, they weren't even close. Lidia had more than double their amount.

As the two weeks passed Sophia's desire to win had increased, so she was disappointed when she lost. She had come in second, and so Factor had Sophia as its First Princess. The theme that year was Constellations of the Universe and Sophia sewed herself the most beautiful dress. She was the Princess of the *"Via Lactea,"* the Milky Way, and her light sky-blue dress was covered with twinkling sequins. On the night of the coronation, the first Saturday night of the *Verbena*, Sophia also received a tiara, which she happily wore, as she proudly stood next to Queen Lidia.

The *Verbena* would last nine days, and would begin on a Friday night. It took over everyone's mind, time and money. It was like a fair, with all kinds of attractions and thrilling rides, stalls with food and games everywhere. Dollars were scooped up as fast as they could come out of a pocket and pockets were emptied too soon. The carnival was visible from the main road, as it was set up in the playing fields of the Factor School property. At dusk, the Ferris wheel's lights would flash on and the machine would begin turning. It was a signal announcing that the time for fun had arrived and everyone would start to head over. Loud music could be heard from far away and the overall atmosphere was convivial and exciting. People came from all over to the carnival and the James children came too. It was a carefree time, for there was no school during carnival, and days were long, extending into the night. The kids loved it. Having a few dollars to spend was very important as fun was not for free. Sophia would make sure that they had some. However, during the days the boys would be out trying to make money on their own, to have a little extra. They would collect pop and beer bottles and sell them for pennies, or they would pick up almonds, shell them and get a nickel for a small bag full. At dusk they all cleaned up and headed down the road to the carnival. A ride on most machines was a quarter and after working all day the boys would have extra coins in their pockets for a few extra rides. The James family was well known, everyone knew who they were, and their story. Sophia was called "*La Americanita,*" and everyone knew that she was in charge of the family. She was known to be tough, and though always polite and friendly, she was not to be fooled with, and no one did. Sophia always sensed respect from neighbors and men and it helped her fight silent fears of being abused or attacked. On this occasion however, Sophia was not only "the American girl," she was the *Princess of the Carnival.* Her name was out there on posters and strangers repeatedly called out her name, to say hello. The experience was strange and Sophia smiled at being recognized and also felt a little embarrassed to be drawing attention. Nonetheless, every night, she wore her tiara.

"OK, everybody, Bobby, Johnny and Frankie, you stay together at all times. Here is a dollar for you, and one for you, and one for you. Now don't spend it too quickly, boys. You know, when you run out of money, come back and find me. Karen, we will take turns with Evy, OK? While I have her, you can go off and meet up with your friends and then it'll be my turn to go off when you come back. Here is a dollar for you, and you take the first half hour. I'll be on the merry-go-round with her." The boys were gone before Sophia could blink an eye but Karen was in no hurry to run off. She didn't see anyone she knew immediately and so she hung around Sophia, watching Evy wave at them from the shiny white horse with beautiful flowers in its mane.

By the time Sophia was to have her half hour of freedom she had been spotted by a few girls from school. "Hi, Sophia, I saw you up on stage being crowned last night. You looked beautiful. You should have been our Queen and not fat Lidia,"

"Hey, now, don't say that. I can't think of a Queen I would like more. Well…myself, maybe." Sophia admitted with a giggle, and continued, "But Lidia sold more tickets, so she won fair and square. She's a great Queen! So what are you girls up to? I have a little free time right now."

"Are you going to get on any rides?" asked Sonia.

"Sure I am, I want to get on something scary. What about that one?" Sophia nodded toward the *Trabant*. Two of the girls shrieked, jumping at the idea. A third girl, Maritza, didn't want to do it.

"That ride makes me so dizzy, I want to throw up every time."

"Oh, come on, it looks like fun," said Sophia, "I'm going for it." She turned away heading for the ticket booth. The *Trabant* was a ride in the shape of a wheel. People, while standing, were attached to its sides. The wheel would begin rotating. At first slowly and then faster and faster as its sides would begin to lift, like a spinning saucer seeking its resting place. Many people would get sick while the *Trabant* was spinning, so crowds stood back, watching from a distance, to avoid the risk of being splattered by vomit.

Before the *Trabant* began its movement, Sophia had strapped herself in between the two friends that had wanted to go. Once standing there, filled with excitement, knowing that any moment it would start rotating, she looked around to see who else was riding. Straight across from her was a handsome, blond man she had seen before. He was looking right at her and self-consciously, Sophia looked away. She wasn't sure that he was looking at her or if it was at one of her friends. Surreptitiously, Sophia peeked at her friends, standing next to her.

They were laughing and yelling in anticipation of the ride and quite oblivious to the staring eyes, directly across from them.

All of a sudden, Sophia felt as if she were in a bubble, the whole world was looking at her. She dared to look across at the young man again, and this time he smiled. She held her head up high and smiled back, as if nothing at all, but there was a funny feeling in her tummy and her face felt very warm. She tried to not look at him anymore and just laugh with her friends when motion began. Nice and easy, round and round, then a little jolt and the machine was going faster, and faster still. Soon Sophia's head felt nailed to the back, as the centrifugal forces took over. Her dress was in place, around her knees, but it felt glued to her body. She knew that her dress was outlining every aspect of her. As the whirling machine continued to spin, rise and fall she again looked directly across at the young man, who had been staring at her. There he was comfortably, enjoying the ride with a friendly smile on his face and still looking straight at her. Her hair was a mangled mess and she forced her head to a side, trying to look comfortable, as she braved the machine and dominated her stomach. After a short time that felt endless, the *Trabant* began to slow down and Sophia, trying to look graceful, stumbled off the thing. The girls giggled, each catching their breath and organizing their hair while making their way to Maritza, who had been watching from the ground. Reeling with laughter, they told her about the guy that had vomited.

"Did you see him? He puked all over the place on his clothes and I think the girl next to him caught some too!"

"Oh! Yuck! It was so gross!" And the laughter just got louder as they regained their balance. Sophia noticed that the man who had been watching her was off to the side, talking with someone.

Sophia turned to the girls and asked, "Do any of you know who that guy is? He's wearing the blue, long-sleeve shirt and standing by José Rivera? I know that I have seen him before, but I can't remember."

"Oh, I know him, he's César Lugo." Carmen quickly replied.

"Why do you want to know?" she asked Sonia with curiosity dripping from her mouth. Sophia's guard went up. She certainly didn't want to give anyone anything to gossip about. "Oh, no reason, I was just wondering."

"Yeah! He lives close to the school but he doesn't come around the barrio very much because he's away at college. He's studying to become

POETRY AND A KISS

an engineer in Mayaguez." continued Carmen. Sophia listened and once she finished Sophia never mentioned him again.

Sophia returned to Karen, who had been with Evy, and was waiting for her turn to be free. At this point she had located a couple of friends and, after Sophia recommended *The Trabant*, they ran in its direction. As Sophia saw Karen run she noticed her long braid and quickly called out to her, "Karen, stick your braid in your dress, if it gets tangled on something it could be ripped off." Karen called out, "OK, Sophia, don't worry," and she was on her way, arm in arm with a school friend laughing and carefree.

The next evening was the same and the evening after that. The James kids would go to the carnival, get on their rides and have fun. Each night Sophia had seen César, and she had flirted with him, encouraging him to approach her. On the third night, just as Sophia was to get on the Ferris wheel, he cut in line and jumped on with her. As Sophia sat and turned to talk to her friend, she was shocked to see that César was there instead.

"Oh! My Gosh! I didn't see you get on, I thought María was behind me."

"She was, but at the last second I jumped in line to sit with you. I've wanted to talk to you, Sophia. You seem to always have your brothers and sisters around you, so I had to be bold," he said and flashed a smile. Sophia appreciated his insight and looked at him and smiled back with curiosity. She took notice of his light blue eyes and how the color of his light hair was the same as his mustache. Up close she could see that his bright smile showed front teeth that over lapped a tad. He was clean looking and seemed smart. She liked him.

He wanted to know more about her and they would talk in between shifts with Karen, while eating an ice cream or a *piragua de frambuesa*, a delicious strawberry snow cone. Bobby, Johnny and Frankie had taken notice of Sophia standing next to César and they went into alert mode. They saw her laugh or giggle, looking absorbed by whatever he was saying. They didn't like this—who was that guy anyway? So they started coming around and cutting into their conversation, as often as possible. Sophia understood what was happening and would give them more ride money to shoo them off. It would work for a little while and then they would be right back.

César was twenty-one and, as Carmen had said, was studying engineering. He sounded ambitious which was a quality Sophia liked. Each night as she arrived at the carnival, she would look around trying to spot him. Her girlfriends had noticed the budding romance and tried to pry information out of Sophia, but she wouldn't budge. She pretended to not be interested at all. Yet, every evening upon arriving at the Verbena, she would inconspicuously try to spot him in the crowds. He would be doing the same and, upon seeing her, would approach her and time would fly by. With Carnival winding down and only one night left, Sophia was looking forward to seeing César. He was without a doubt her first crush. There had been other boys, she had noticed and dreamt about, but they would turn out to be too silly or immature. César, however, was older and interesting, while respectful. On the last night of the Carnival, Sophia spotted him talking to some friends. He was wearing a light yellow shirt and khaki-colored slacks. He looked neat and handsome. She felt a flutter of excitement and then she saw a cigarette in his hand. It was her turn to stare and she watched as he raised his hand to his mouth comfortably and casually inhaled. That was the first sign of something she did not like. She hated smoke and could barely stand it when she was in a room with smokers. She would try to get out into the fresh air as soon as possible and let out her hair, hoping that it wouldn't be 'contaminated' by the awful smell. Now, here was César, a smoker. How sad. She pushed herself away, suddenly disappointed and went over to relieve Karen early. Karen had been giving her a chance to get to know César and had spent more than her fair share of time with little Evy.

"Hi Karen, go ahead and take off. I'll stay with Evy and you have some fun with your friends. No need to hurry back, I don't think that I am going to talk to César very much anymore."

"Oh, OK. Bye, I'll see you later," she took off running as she tucked her hair into the back of her dress.

Entertaining Evy was easy. At the time of the carnival she was a pretty little five year old with big, curious, wide eyes and a quick smile. Any attention made her happy and she always wanted to hold hands. She was shy around strangers and they seemed to frighten her. She would become introverted, very quiet and would stick four fingers into her mouth, while clinging to Sophia's skirt. However, most of the time at home she would run around with her long hair a mangled mess, chasing after a brother while laughing. She wasn't interested in learning her ABC's, and would stare at Sophia as if day dreaming, whenever she would try to get her to focus on them. As soon as Sophia released her from the torture, she would return to being happy and playful. At times when everything was quiet, Sophia would find little Evy sitting in a corner holding a doll so tight to her little body, that it told any bystander, 'I need love.' When Sophia or Karen took notice of these moments, they would stop what they were doing and sit with her in their lap, just holding her. She wasn't as mature as she should have been and Sophia felt that it was all her mother's fault. Sophia and Karen tried hard, each of them in her own way, but still Evy, the little girl, had needs that only a mother knew how to fulfill and she had missed out completely. Luckily, she was the baby—following three boys—and to survive, she had toughened up. Nevertheless, neither Sophia nor Karen would leave her alone. She was more than the baby, she was theirs. And being such a pretty one made her stand out in a crowd. 'How could a woman leave such of an angel before she was even two years old?' Sophia had asked herself that question a thousand times, and it was one of the reasons why her mother was, without question, quite dead to her.

César had been looking for Sophia and after a while he approached her and Evy.

"Hi, Sophia, how are you this evening?"

"I'm fine, César, I saw you earlier with some friends."

"Yes, they're some buddies from school and have just dropped in to enjoy the fiestas. I have spent enough time with them and I was hoping that you and I could go for a little walk. Could we?"

Sophia wanted to say, 'no,' but she saw his warm smile and she liked his company so much that "Yes," jumped out of her mouth before she could stop it, "I'd be happy to spend a little time with you but I must wait for Karen to come back. I can't leave Evy alone."

"Sure, I understand. So Evy, would you like to ride the Ferris wheel?" Sophia was surprised at how quickly Evy had answered with a transfer of hands and was ready to go off with him. Without hesitation, César quickly bought three tickets and Evy, in the middle, enjoyed riding the Ferris wheel for the first time.

After Karen had returned for duty, Sophia went off for a walk with César. It was a quiet moment and with the music not blaring in their ears they were able to talk without screaming and for the first time have a real conversation. Sophia was sharing a little about her dreams for the future. She was telling him that she was studying hard to earn a scholarship. She would go to the University in Río Piedras . . . . All of a sudden he pulled her towards him and kissed her full on the mouth. She was caught by surprise and she could feel how he was holding her tight. The sensation of the mustache, the wetness and the horrible taste of tobacco, made her hate it. She pulled herself away, so the ill-fated kiss was over, as fast as it had begun.

"That was awful!" Sophia said as she wiped her mouth with the back of her arm. "You shouldn't have done that César. You won't be kissing me again."

"What's wrong, Sophia, did I hurt you? Sophia, please come back." Sophia continued to walk away from César. She had wanted to be kissed, but this abrupt, terrible, cigarette-tasting, mushy kiss was not what she wanted. It was quite clear: she would not be kissing a smoker again.

15

A SPARKLE IN THE ROUGH

"DEVOLVIENDO UN POCO" ~ "GIVING A LITTLE BACK"
Devolviendo un poco, ~ Giving a little back,
De lo que me distes, ~ Of what you gave to me,
Devolviendo un poco, ~ Giving a little back,
Del amor que me llevé, ~ Of the love I took with me,
Devolviéndote un poco, ~ Giving you a little back,
Mientras canto mi añoranza, ~ While I sing my song of longing,
Devolviendo amor, con amor, ~ Giving back love, with love,
En mi canción. ~ In my song.

As time passed when Mr. James returned after a long absence he no longer was the only one telling stories. In those days stories flew in both directions. His continued to be filled with exotic and strange places; however, the children in turn would squabble in unison, telling him of the insane and strange things that had happened to them! It was hard to tell which side told the most interesting, scary or amazing stories.

His absence at times spanned over nine long months and the children were growing up without him. Upon his arrival he would notice that they were each a little taller. After one long absence he returned to notice that his little girls had grown out of childhood and had become adolescents. Then he heard about Sophia becoming princess of the Verbena and the attentions she received from César. It probably was the story about César that got the wheels of his mind turning. He was concerned that without a mother, to teach them so many things, they could fall into trouble. He decided to search for a reliable source; a role model of sorts and in his quest came up with the idea of Girl Scouting. With great purpose, convinced that he was on the right path, he went into Arecibo and started asking around. Sure enough there was a Girl Scout troop!

The James girls knew nothing about girl scouting and soon were being introduced to Miss Adela Parras who welcomed them into her troop. Scouting was a safe haven however, it only existed for them while there father was around. Once he was off to sea, there were no possibilities of attending meetings and no time for the luxury of being just a girl. Scouting during the short time it was in their lives, provided a true highlight in Sophia's life and one that would make her forever beholden to Girl Scouts.

One Saturday morning as Sophia and Karen tried to catch up on laundry they noticed a public car drive up to their front gate. They had been busy hanging out to dry a huge load of wash on a very long and cluttered clothes line. From the corner of her eye Sophia saw Miss Parras, her scout leader, emerge from the vehicle. Suddenly aware that her hair was a mess and her dress wet from washing clothes, she was embarrassed to see the woman arrive. Nevertheless, she put down what she was hanging up and walked over to welcome her leader.

"Señorita Parra, hello, how are you?" said Sophia visibly flustered and trying to pull back her hair while being aware that bicycles were out, the hose wasn't rolled up and Casiano's damn bar had its music blaring with patrons hanging out the window watching.

"Hola Sophia, I'm glad you were home. I need to talk to you; it's important and I didn't know if you were coming back to Scouts or not."

"Oh Miss Parra, please come in. You are very welcome here." Sophia was opening the gate and immediately gave the woman the customary kiss on the cheek as she invited her in. "Karen and I like scouting so much, and wish we never had to miss but our situation…well it's hard to be away with the kids being so little. When my Dad is here it's easy to go but once he leaves, it's just not so easy." Stumbled Sophia apologetically.

"Oh! Sophia, no, no, no, it doesn't matter about the meetings. I'm sorry I can't help you more. I have heard a lot about your situation and I think it's amazing what you girls are doing here. I came for a different matter. Let's sit down!"

A SPARKLE IN THE ROUGH

"Oh, yes! I'm so sorry. Please let's sit down here on the porch. The kids are watching the cartoons so it's too loud in there, besides the house is messy right now and we've just started straightening up. Could I offer you a glass of water?"

"No, no, thank you dear, but just sit down a moment with me and let me tell you why I'm here."

The scout leader in her forties was a good woman. She was a black lady that had never been married and was devoted to the Scout movement. She was known for going out of her way to offer opportunities to girls that needed guidance of any kind. She had proved that, by welcoming Sophia, as a senior scout into her troop. She could have denied her the opportunity.

"Sophia, I have just found out about a great opportunity for some lucky girl and I thought of you. There is going to be a trip offered, that will last seven weeks, with all expenses paid, plus $1,500.00 for personal expenses. The search is on for a scout that will represent Puerto Rico at an international scouting event in Lafayette, Indiana."

Sophia's face was blank; her eyes wide open but not quite understanding what this had to do with her.

"Sophia, I'm telling you this because I could nominate you from our troop and you could compete for this trip. I have come here because I believe that you could win it."

Sophia's head was spinning, and still unable to speak; her mind was racing with the thought of *'seven weeks in Indiana!'* It was like offering her the moon. The leader could see her shock and quickly continued on.

"The trip is this summer, five months from now, but any girl that would like to compete for the spot has got to get moving now. I would do my part in nominating you and getting the ball rolling. You on the other hand have to write the best essay you can. The topic is "Why are you the best Girl Scout to represent Puerto Rico."

"Oh!... I could do that!" said Sophia in a quiet voice as if afraid to have the wind hear her.

"Yes, you could." said the leader as she raised her eyebrows and continued with a smile. "The selection of the winner will happen by rounds. A lot of girls will write an essay, but only ten will survive to be considered for the next stage. Those ten girls will then spend a weekend in San Juan at the San Juan Hotel."

Sophia, inhaled, and with realistic eyes shook 'no' with her head.

"Oh, don't worry," jumped in the scout leader, "all expenses will be covered by the San Juan council and if there is anything additional our troop could help." She smiled and continued. "If you make the cut Sophia and write one of the ten chosen essays and have to go to San Juan then you will compete in the presentation phase. That means you will present yourself in full uniform to the council there and read your essay in person. They will be looking for a girl that shows confidence and good posture." The leader slowed down and looking at Sophia with a gaze of self-assurance, she said, "You could win this thing Sophia and it would be good for you and all of us! You'd put Arecibo on the scouting map!" The leader who had been speaking in a steady stream now sat and chuckled while watching Sophia's reaction.

"Miss Parra, when is this happening?"

"July, this summer.

"My gosh, my Dad would have to be here. You know he is a seaman and works away. Besides working on that essay I would have to start working on him to make sure that he is here." Sophia was speaking wistfully as if to herself.

"You do that Sophia, and let's proceed as if we know that he will be here. I really want to encourage you to do your best at writing that essay. Here." and she reached into her purse for a folded sheet of paper. She opened it and handed it to Sophia. "There you can see the due date, and the address you must mail it to. See the topic there? Your essay needs to be neatly typed Sophia. Will that be a problem?"

"Oh! I know how to type and I have an old typewriter here. I can do this Miss Parra, I can write a good essay. I don't know if I'll win, but I can promise you I'll give it my best shot." Sophia dared to smile timidly and her eyes though directed at her leader showed that she was already off in some distant place thinking…thinking, putting the puzzle together. As if coming back to earth she said, "I won't get my hopes up too high…but I will try my best."

The kind woman left and Johnny volunteered to accompany her down the road to the public car stop. There he waited with her until she was on her way back to town. By the time the perspicacious Johnny was back, he was excited.

"Sophia, you're gonna do it aren't you? You can win it! You know you can win it!"

The unexpected visit of Miss Parra that day resulted in a lifelong commitment by Sophia for Scouting. She would write her essay with all her heart and she would appreciate forever the opportunity her Girl Scout leader had given her.

A couple months later a trip to the post office yielded a letter from San Juan addressed to Sophia James. She had been wondering when she would know the result of her efforts of writing what she hoped was a winning essay. Now, upon seeing the letter anxiety gripped her. Yes! She was among the ten selected essays to compete at the San Juan Hotel. She was excited beyond measure and after sharing the news with the children they each gave her advice as to how to assure a win. Sophia began strategizing. She knew that a win was in reach and she knew that she wanted to win. She would not leave it to chance; she would be well prepared and excellent. The first thing she did was commit her entire essay to memory. She would not stand there holding a paper like everyone else. She would act it out, show passion and resolve.

At the beginning all the children would gather to hear her recite it from top to bottom. They would applaud and whoop it up, every time she finished. However, after a couple of weeks of hearing Sophia say, "Anybody want to hear the essay?" her audience severely dwindled. The week before the event her sole spectator was little Evy, who sat with wide eyes, a big smile and clapped every time Sophia finished with a deep bow.

The San Juan Hotel was the most luxurious hotel Sophia had ever entered. It was in El Condado and oceanfront. She arrived on a Friday, would compete on Saturday and would leave on Sunday.

Sophia won. She won it all. She had rehearsed her essay so many times that she pulled it off without a hitch in front of a room full of people and a line of judges. She recited while inviting them to be a part of her story and willingly they had joined in. She turned her essay into a play full of drama and she played to it making sure that her audience remained captive and amused. She ended with a well rehearsed deep bow and the room went up in applause. No one clapped harder than the Girl Scout leader from Arecibo, Miss Parra.

When Sophia's Dad arrived he couldn't hide his pride on hearing the details of how Sophia had won the competition. He and Miss Parra worked together in getting Sophia ready to know all about the details of scouting, so she could represent the island well. Camping out became an integral part of the plan and Sophia and Karen soon were on their way to Campamento Elisa Colberg on the opposite side of the island. Preparing caper-charts, learning how to set up a tent and build a campfire were crucial. Cooking in the outdoors, learning about first aid, on and on; Sophia was learning about many new things and her time was being well invested. Oh! The fun she had been missing. Scouting was full of novel ideals that were filled with fun.

One evening there was to be a party. It was a formal, like a ball, and its great purpose was to teach etiquette. The most memorable aspect of the evening was the fact that some girls had to play the male role, as there are no boys in Girl Scouts. They formed couples among themselves with a brave and wonderful girl accepting the role of gentleman. Between Karen and Sophia there was no doubt who the guy would be, as Karen was much taller than Sophia. With a smile and a huff she put on the pants and promenaded with Sophia who wore the sparkling, Milky Way dress she had sewn for the Verbena. With Karen in coattails and Sophia in her shimmering blue gown, the girls showed off their red painted lips, while the "boys" showed off their newly painted sideburns.

By the time it was time to leave for Indiana, Sophia could recite her Girl Scout promise in Spanish and the Girl Scout laws. She knew all about Elisa Colberg, who had brought scouting to Puerto Rico in the twenties, and had in her bags a load of swaps made by different troops so she could hand them out.

Sophia agreed with everything the Girl Scouts were teaching. She believed in the words voiced in the pledge and though she had previously promised to live her life abiding by those same rules, repeating them was comforting.

LA PROMESA DE GIRL SCOUTS ~ THE GIRL SCOUT PROMISE
Por mi honor, yo trataré: ~ On my honor I will try
De servir a Dios y a mi patria, ~ To serve God and my country,
Ayudar a las personas en todo momento, ~ To help people at all times,
Y vivir conforme a la Ley de Girl Scouts. ~ And to live by the Girl Scout Law.

Walking out onto the tarmac to fly away to Indiana was dreamlike. Not far away a crowd of well wishers waved to those walking towards the jet and Sophia could spy her father, who was the tallest in the crowd.

Climbing the steps to the aircraft she turned around, as Presidents do just before entering, and waved one last time.

Indiana was an opportunity to walk back in time and reacquaint herself with that which she loved and remembered. However, there was a bitter sweetness to this experience as she was returning to her homeland while representing another. The irony of it was monumental. There she was representing the island of her fear and hurt, representing the island she longed to escape. Yet, out of loyalty she would only present its gentle side. Girl scouting had broaden her perspective enormously. It had shown her a unity and caring from strangers all revolving around the same ideas; growth, correctness, the promotion of young girls to be dedicated and honest. "To be prepared" and "Be Your Best," were mottos Sophia had been surviving on and intensely believed in. She was proud to be associated with scouting and knew that she would be forever.

Lafayette, Indiana was a wonderful experience that passed by too quickly. Sophia arrived at Camp Sycamore Valley and was one of three international girls sharing experiences with the American girls. There was a scout from Germany, one from Mexico and Sophia from Puerto Rico. After a few days everyone was given a nickname and Sophia became, "Sparkle."

The camp was beautiful with horses and a couple hundred acres with a nearby river. Sophia learned how to canoe there and preferred the stern where she would take over steering, and make sure they'd make the landing spot when the river was high and water ran fast. Fun filled weekdays around camp were only topped off by adventurous weekends when host families would kindly show her around. The University of Purdue was a highlight until a lovely family took her south to the Indianapolis Racetrack. Sophia was in awe, she knew nothing about car racing but she had heard about the Indy-500. Rides were available and after a little coaxing she was in a sports car going around the historical racetrack. The same family picked her up on another weekend and whisked her north, to Chicago. There she saw the John Hancock Center which had just been built and its height and might reminded her for years of the lovely family that had been so kind to her.

Indiana was like a flash in time; first unimaginable, then present, and then gone forever. As she returned to Puerto Rico, it felt right to her. She had loved the experience but she knew that her time had not yet arrived. The time when she would fly independently was in the future and it yet depended exclusively on her resolve. The Indiana experience had been a timely gift. It helped her stay focused and on track. Sophia knew she was going places; she just had to be patient.

16

MARYLAND

"TU TIERRA ES MI TIERRA" ~ *"YOUR LAND IS MY LAND"*
Vea como los rayos del sol, ~ *See how rays from the sun,*
Se filtran de entre las nubes, ~ *Filter through amongst the clouds,*
Parece extenderse los cielos, ~ *It looks as if the sky is extending,*
Acariciar la tierra. ~ *To caress the earth.*
Y vea la tierra color marrón, ~ *And see the color of the land, brown,*
O vea la tierra verde, ~ *Or see the land be green,*
Quita zapatos, sienta brisa, ~ *Take off your shoes, feel the breeze,*
Pon tus dedos en tierra firme, ~ *Put your toes on firm land,*
Y brota la risa de entre tus labios, ~ *Allow a smile to creep onto your lips,*
Y ría, porque es tu tierra. ~ *And laugh, because this is your land.*
Tu tierra, es mi tierra, ~ *Your land, is my land,*
Mi tierra, es tu tierra. ~ *My land, is your land,*
Quiérala, que hay que quererla, ~ *Love it, we must love it,*
Cuidala, que hay que cuidarla. ~ *Care for it, we must care for it.*

The first layers of oils needed to set, so for several days Sophia stepped away from the painting. Painting is a process and, like most things in life, needs confidence, moments of boldness, moments of caution and moments when the creator must simply step away. The painting that Sophia was creating was far from finished. It still called for many moments where her hand needed to be guided by a steady pulse. For instance, the lines for the horses' reins were made by one confident stroke of shadow and one of light. Painting was a miracle in Sophia's eyes, and no matter what she was able to create she considered it a stroke of luck to have a little ability. She smiled when others called her an artist and in her mind she'd say *No, not really, I have seen Mona Lisa.* She believed that her painting ability was just strong enough for someone to pause and take notice. Sometimes even the ultimate prize, a moment of contemplation. That was sufficient.

Standing on her small balcony, Sophia looked out at the ocean. She unconsciously began picking off dried leaves from a bright fuchsia-pink bougainvillea bush in her planter. It was growing nicely and people had said that it would never prosper so close to the water. *They were wrong,* said the bright colors of the beautiful plant that looked happy as the sun beat down on it. The heat was stifling, it was close to that noon hour and the world was still, not a leaf moving. Sophia began to perspire and as she turned away to go back inside, she decided to put on the air conditioner. She placed herself directly under a vent and immediately felt the relief of rushing air. It was a sensation similar to walking in from the sweltering car in the hot Georgian summer, and entering the cool and refreshing rink. The ice skating world jumped back into her mind and she thought of how Maryland had proved to be a good place for everyone.

Upon arriving in Maryland, Sophia's husband rented a small house on a lot that abutted the Middle Patuxent Environmental Area. The property was not fenced in and wildlife roamed freely into their yard. They were surrounded by entire herds of whitetail deer, which lent a sense of magic to the place. To see the sleek, nimble and graceful animals up close was a gift, and to encourage their proximity, they placed a saltlick nearby. Through the windows of the small house that soon was nicknamed "Snow White's Cottage" the children watched deer venture up close and take turns licking the salt block. Maryland was beautiful. Its temperate summers were a cool breeze compared to stifling Georgia, and its winters were just as cold, but accompanied by beautiful, cleansing snow. To have great amounts of snow fall at one time was new to all of them. Other than on ski trips, the family had not been around snow and, for a long time, the chore of shoveling seemed more fun than a task.

Moving into Snow White's cottage had been done with a mindset of it being temporary, which never allowed the family to fully settle. The search for the permanent home proved unproductive and after scouring the area, it was clear that they would have to build. With that monumental decision in place, plans for what would become their home were drawn up. It became an exciting time, with each of them throwing in ideas and desires for the wonderful home that would belong to everyone. Sophia had learned long ago that success derived from the participation of all members of a team. She understood that participation begot ownership, which in turn nurtured a soul with resolution and confidence. To impart confidence was important, as a healthy dose of it could build a strong life but the absence of it, could snuff one out.

It was Sophia's forty-eighth birthday and she was determined to go out and find the land on which they would build their house. "Who wants to go with me?" called out Sophia. "Today is the day I am going to find the land on which we are going to build our house. Today is the day, I just know it!"

"I'll come," volunteered Colleen.

"Great! Thank you, Sweetheart, I didn't want to go alone. Let's grab our boots though; we might end up traipsing around in the woods."

The two hopped into the oversized conversion van and headed down Trotter Road. It wasn't much more than a mile away, when suddenly Sophia saw a little road that she had never noticed before. On a whim she turned toward the lane. The narrow lane was a mystery.

"Well, how about this? I never guessed I'd find around here a road I hadn't gone down already," she commented to Colleen who sat in the seat next to her, equally bewildered.

"Have you ever seen this road with Daddy?"

"No, Mommy, I never have."

The road was short; with two left hand turns and they could see that it dead ended. They continued past the first entrance and took the second one at the end of the road. Small houses were visible on large parcels of beautiful land. The terrain was hilly, and then they could see a meadow, and then hilly again. It was plush with growth and the cool, shady lane was inviting. The turning leaves of October appeared in startling red branches here and orange ones there. Then, as if in a fairy tale, a man six feet tall stood before them. Sophia slowed down her vehicle as she and her daughter took in the vision before them. The man with a kind face was wearing a tall hat, carrying a long staff and had on knee-high boots. He looked just like a character out of a Norman

Rockwell painting. Sophia, with an engaging smile, looked directly into the man's eyes and said, "Hi there, nice day isn't it?" and before he could answer she continued, "I'm looking to buy some land, do you have some?"

"Well now," said the man with a chuckle, "As a matter of fact, I do. How much are you looking for?"

"Oh, about ten acres." Said Sophia with a bright smile.

"I've got eleven."

"No kidding," said Sophia, almost laughing.

"Is the property around here?"

"Yep, I can show it to you right now."

One minute later, Colleen was in the back seat and a man they had never seen before in their lives was sitting up front directing them back to that first entrance on the left.

It turned out that the land Walt Rydzewski showed her that day was the land they bought, and with the land came the friendship of Walt, his Ella, and her sister, Vera Savory—the dearest people in the world.

The project took nearly two years and during that time life in the little house was well invested. It was a time when Sophia taught her children how to live and share in a way they never had before. Snow White's cottage was an old quaint house. Its brick façade was painted white, but over time the peeling and lack of maintenance helped give it an ancient look. The look was not one of neglect but more vintage-like. Inside, its old, oak wooden floors were worn, but the honey-colored stain kept them beautiful. At the stairwell's landing, the knob on the newel post shined—smooth as could be from the many hands that had grabbed onto it in the past. Now, that newel post invited their hands to seek support, luck, or fun, as the new set of children ran up and down the staircase. The old house was warm and welcoming with its old-fashioned sunroom, and its cozy fireplace in the small living room. The kitchen was off to one side, outdated by its linoleum floors, and a cheesy floating ceiling with fluorescent lights. Though spaces were small, each child had a bedroom. However, they all shared the single bathroom. The little house was a throwback to "Leave it to Beaver," and reminiscent of yesteryear in so many details.

On one cold day, the family gathered around the table for six, to have dinner. The table fit snug in a corner of the kitchen allowing the dining room to be converted into an office for Sophia's husband. Suddenly, small talk around the table was interrupted when a long, black, rat snake slithered into view, making its way to the warm space around the light in the ceiling. After the initial shock and screams, it was decided that getting it down would be harder than it appeared. So the harmless snake was nicknamed "Reggie," and every now and then it'd make an appearance, until one day Sophia put her foot down. That was it! It was the snake or her!

"I'm going to the store. When I get back, Reggie had better be gone!"

He was gone all right, by the time she got back, but the stories of how, when falling from the ceiling, he almost fell on one of the kids and then slithered behind the refrigerator went on and on. It was the brave Alison, the youngest, who finally caught him, much to the chagrin of the older ones.

Her children were prospering in Maryland. Alison, took up archery and was a great shot from the beginning, something that never changed and was later proven again when she learned how to shoot a gun. Chip, the eldest, who was away at school in Connecticut most of the time, was amused by the new setting and quick to declare that the empty open space of the attic was his. Seeing the potential, it was turned into a neat bedroom with a bonus TV area that everyone invaded as soon as dinner was over. Colleen's skating rink was twenty minutes away and Tommy's special school was wonderful. Everyone was moving forward and it was during this time that Sophia's husband concentrated his efforts on the home being built. Under his watchful eye, a great structure of glass, cedar and stone arose.

However, for Sophia, the experience of moving to Maryland was like reentering a zone she recognized. Again, she faced a great void in her life. The hole left behind when she stepped away from music. Her music, the melodious sounds that had been allowed to invade her every moment were now shut out, and they nagged at her, begging to be let in. She missed her music so much, but understood that this was no longer the time destined for it. Flying back and forth to Georgia and on to Miami for her music was impractical and this was a time when her family needed her most. Life was about making wise choices and embracing opportunities, and those concepts were clear to Sophia. She smiled knowing that when the opportunity to create music came, she had embraced it to its fullest and thus had no regrets. That knowledge gave her solace, and she forcefully shut her musically creative mind down. She often found herself looking around and wondering what the next gig in life would be.

Chit-chatting at night with everyone, sharing hopes and dreams while working on projects that Sophia laid out, made time pass quickly. For Sophia, the secret was to always stay busy. With this in mind, the living room became an active workshop where she placed several tables, each with a project inviting someone to "pick" at it. With a 'pick' here and a 'pick' there, all the projects were completed before it was time to move. On one table there was a huge rotating doll house with hundreds of details. It had railings, shingled roofs and stone walls, all tiny pieces that needed to be smoothed down, glued on and painted. Then the inside of the little house with its swooping staircase, fully furnished and electrical lighting, showing off freshly papered walls. On another table there was a large-size Christmas skirt beckoning to be adorned with the glue gun, beads and crystals that lay waiting. Finally, the largest undertaking was a massive five-by-five-foot, intricate, leaded-glass window that Sophia and the two girls had designed and were making for the window in the main bathroom of the new home. By the time it was complete, their stained-glass window-building skills were well honed. "Snow White's cottage," had become a true bonding place, with everyone sharing and helping without even realizing it.

It was within the walls of that small house backing up to the Middle Patuxent, where Sophia, once again, decided to pick up a palette and paint. Painting was a patient friend. It never took her away from her family, but sat, waiting for a convenient time. Picking up the palette was sparked by the need for a large painting that was to hang in the library of the new house. It needed to be a portrait, something with rich, warm colors—burgundies and dark hues. The large canvas became a portrait of her youngest daughter, Alison, sitting in front of the lake in Georgia. As Sophia critically surveyed her efforts, she smiled with the smile on the canvas, and wondered if painting were destined to fill the void left by music.

Sophia was at ease with the direction of their lives and felt that Maryland was a joyful and safe haven for all. It felt good and predictable, until one morning while she was brewing coffee in the kitchen. It was September 11, 2001 and then all time stopped. On that day, like for so many other Americans, a sense of fear took over Sophia at the recognition that life, as it had been, on a large scale would never be again.

It was shortly after that tragic day that the home being built was completed and the family, filled with excitement, moved in. The spacious home, nestled in the woods, surpassed their expectations. It was there where Sophia would become inspired, and painting would become a vital part of her. Large colorful canvasses began to dress the many walls and portraits of loved ones manipulated time. Inspired by the flurry of creativity and art, Sophia's youngest daughter Alison, picked up a brush and on a large canvas with oils, began her career as an artist.

For the twentieth time Sophia volunteered to be a Girl Scout leader, and for the next two years she guided big girls, senior scouts on high adventures. She had done everything with scouts over the years, from spelunking, to sleeping on an aircraft carrier, and on a submarine, to visiting the office of several congresswomen. She would stop at nothing to widen the eyes of those in her troop and broaden their perspectives. Scouting years with her daughters were years of learning and fun. Her last big hurrah with scouting involved the Gold Award. For two years her troop worked hard to raise funds and when they had the amount needed, they flew off to Venezuela. They worked for two weeks at an orphanage, each girl working hard to earn her Gold award. Alison built a sewing workshop from the foundation up. She donated six sewing machines and absolutely everything needed to produce a sewed garment. She taught the children how to sew and knew that she was teaching them a life saving skill. Each girl that traveled had an objective and each fulfilled it and earned the award. Sophia never was an easy leader. Everything was ensconced in fun and learning but each scout had to be her best. There was no way out. Sophia had always felt indebted to scouting.

The property found on that magical birthday was named "Deer Hollow." On a piece of land shaped like a bowl, a natural spring fed a meandering brook which nature outlined with tall, dark green grass edges. Onward it traveled, through the forest of Deer Hollow, making its way through a world of tall, old poplars. There, whitetail deer hid and played and then sauntered over to the salt lick.

17

THE CROSSROADS

"TREPA Y TREPA" ~ "CLIMB AND CLIMB"
Jazmín trepadora tu eres, ~ You're a climbing Jasmine,
Como provocas, ~ So provoking,
Reina de lo sofisticado, ~ Queen of sophistication,
Eres sencilla. ~ Yet simple.
Hoja por hoja, fachada cambias, ~ Leaf by leaf you change a façade,
Trazas el rumbo y te envuelves, ~ You trace a course and begin to wrap,
Tu perfume fragante, es camuflaje ~ Your fragrant perfume is a camouflage,
Para tu red. ~ For your net.
Trepa y trepa cada día, Ay! ~ Climb and climb each day, Ay!
Sabroso, si puedes hacerlo sí, ~ Sweet, you can do it, yes!
Tu llegarás hasta la cima, ¿Cuándo? ~ You'll make it to the top, when?
Cuando tú quieras. ~ Whenever you want.

High school years were finally coming to an end for Sophia. They were tough years, years that felt eternal and never-ending. Somehow along the way there was laughter, and friends were made. Somewhere along the way Sophia grew into a young woman. She had few joys throughout those struggling years and had her expectations not been so grand, she might have never finished high school. Her most joyous memories of those high school years revolved around the *Tuna*. The wonderful *Tuna* was a group of strolling troubadours, accompanied by musicians, that transported Sophia to a different place once a week every time they rehearsed. The enchanting *Tuna* wrapped her up in music and made life exciting and pure. How she loved it!

Karen also joined the musical group that differentiated itself from a chorus, by including musical instruments. The *Tuna* was made up with about twenty high school students. They rehearsed after school on a property nearby that housed Catholic ecclesiastical students. Several of these very devout young men wanted to sing with the *Tuna*, and were invited to join. It was Sophia's greatest fun and it was when she allowed herself to relax a little and escape into her own age group. Everyone who belonged to the *Tuna* had to wear a designated uniform when they performed. Girls wore a white blouse and a black skirt, while the boys wore a white shirt and black slacks. However, it was the cape everyone wore that made it magical. The cape was made out of shiny satin. It boasted the high school colors, navy blue on the outside and bright yellow on the inside. It was very full, tied around the neck with a small bow, and extending to mid thigh. At every performance the members of the *Tuna* received a colorful, long ribbon, with the name of the place where they performed written in glitter. The ribbon was pinned to the shoulder of the cape. After several performances, the cape became colorful and when the members of the *Tuna* swirled around, they looked vibrant and alive. The music they sang was festive, and after much work and practice it was beautifully harmonized. The *Tuna* was a safe haven, a place for Sophia and Karen to truly share as sisters, and not as coworkers. They made the same friends, wore the same clothing and held a common interest. Karen became alive on *Tuna* days. She was always of a quiet nature, but with the *Tuna* she found her voice. It was a clear, strong, and beautiful voice, and she excelled among the singers. Sophia was very proud of Karen. Sophia, on the other hand, found her strength and greatest joy in the instrumental section. She wanted to play an instrument and didn't want it to be the heavy accordion. Instead, guitars or the percussive instruments—drums, cymbals, tambourines and maracas—were options. Therefore, during freshmen year in high school, Sophia began learning how to play the guitar. It was always the most popular instrument and sought after by the *Tuna*. With the star guitar player graduating, she knew they would need another one. Sophia's dad bought her a guitar and Sophia spoke with a neighbor who she knew could play the instrument. He agreed, for little money, to give her a few lessons. Once she had the chords down, she started carrying her guitar to rehearsals and picking out the chords for the *Tuna's* repertoire of songs. It was a wonderful time, a little reprieve of normalcy in a world that, for them, had so little of it. On stage, singing their hearts away, the members of the *Tuna* twirled and moved to the music, bringing joy to every event. Sophia's love for music was being nurtured and when music engulfed Sophia's spirit, she was happy.

However, music, like everything else, could not appease the unwavering goal of getting out of the bleak, lonely place where she had been deposited, abandoned and used. That goal absorbed Sophia's every waking moment. She constantly spoke to her siblings about the value of improving themselves, so that they could earn scholarships and compete for spots at a university. To be hired by a serious company would only happen if they studied hard, were attractive, and interesting enough. These lectures were a constant and she tried so often to fuel their imagination so that they too would pursue what she wanted most. However, these lectures were often unnoticed and fell upon deaf ears. This frustrated Sophia and filled her with worry and sadness. She did not see the necessary fight in them and without it they could not succeed in getting scholarships. Still, the time was nearing when she would be reaching for one and once a scholarship was granted, she would be going off to study—going off to make her dreams come true. What would she do? Leave her brothers and sisters, like she was left? The question was more and more present as time passed and it bothered Sophia all the time because she sadly knew that she would.

For years they were alone. Their father faithfully sent checks that sustained them and visited every six months or so. But the truth is that they grew up alone, together learning about life and survival. Bumping their heads along the way but always picking each other up and dusting each other off. They loved each other and the small ones loved Sophia like a mother. Though, there were times when they, who had been so young when abandoned, blamed Sophia for not having this or that. They would forget that it was not her fault, and not realize that she too hungered for so many things lost.

Sophia had always been the head of the house, managing the money and deciding "what, when and how" about everything. The children's struggle had only been made more difficult because of the relatives that surrounded them. Trying to take from them what little they had, they made life for the six abandoned children even more difficult. It was like living amongst wolves, where one could never completely rest or fall asleep for fear of being eaten. From the age of nearly twelve, Sophia, the oldest of six, taught her family how, by sticking together, they could stay alive and keep danger at bay. Now as a young woman she intended to teach them how to beat the odds. She would become educated, excel, and fulfill her greatest dreams.

"I'm very sorry, Sophia, but you are not eligible for a scholarship." The principal of her high school said as she read the letter from the mayors' office.

Her head was swimming and her stomach felt sick and she asked, "May I sit down, please?"

"Yes, of course, Sophia. So tell me, can't your father pay for your university tuition?"

"No, my father can pay for nothing. I have no one in the world that can pay for me to go to school. I have no one." And with those words Sophia began to sob out loud, with pain showing, not caring who was present. Completely and shamelessly, she cried for her dreams, her hopes, her hard work, her never giving up. She wasn't eligible? Why not? How could it be? Who could be more eligible for a scholarship? She had nothing, nothing, and yet she had so much—so much weighing her down and trying to sink her. There had been too many years of hope and sacrifice; no one was going to deny her what she had rightfully earned. Her grades, a reflection of sheer determination, were excellent, her college entrance examination was powerfully strong compared to most, and the interview on the main campus of the University of Puerto Rico in Rio Piedras had been a success.

Sophia's gaze settled on the stack of papers on the principal's desk. "Accepted," "Accepted," read the blue stamp blazed across them. "Denied," in red ink said the sheet with Sophia's name on it, nothing more. One stamp was all, with no reason, no justification just one word that was supposed to end her dreams. It was all about prejudice and she knew it. It was her name, she was *La Americanita*, and a name like hers had to have money. The city would not hand over a scholarship to an American that must be rich. No one could persuade Sophia to stop crying. She was crying like she never had. She let herself go completely, and at that moment, cried for all of her years of sorrow. She cried for the mother that had left her; she cried for the father she hardly ever saw; she cried for the dances she missed; she cried for dashed hopes and dreams. The loud mournful wail echoed through the corridors and her sorrow was heard throughout the school, penetrating the soul of those that heard it. On that day everyone heard the strong girl—often sought by peers for advice and who had lovingly been nicknamed *La Abuela*, Grandma—cry a cry they'd never heard before—a cry that made them stand and take her side. At that moment the school silently committed to help Sophia get a scholarship, even if the whole school had to go to City Hall to get it.

Sophia's plight was not an unknown one. Every person in Factor knew the story of the abandoned American children. In the municipality of Arecibo, where the James children traveled daily to attend school, many were aware of the children that lived alone. Law enforcement, Judge Fuentes, who over the years became a friend and guide, teachers from high school and middle school, all helped at one time or another. Sophia would again seek their help and she knew that they would give it. One thing that Sophia had learned over the years was that Puerto Rican people were a giving people. They believed in traditions and loving families—families that struggled together and, no matter what, had fun together. Often Sophia had been guided by taking the lead from those families. The truth was that the fight for their lives and rights that Sophia had been forced into, was because they had been surrounded by the venom of the Risorios. Nevertheless, all those years of ugliness from the Risorios could not take away the beauty of so many other kind families on the island. Sophia believed that the island of Puerto Rico could have been for her and her siblings, as it was for so many, a true paradise.

Preparing to face yet another struggle, Sophia confidently sought out those people of Puerto Rico who had protected and helped them stay alive all those years. She asked for help and they came through, in a way she could have never imagined. At school, groups were organizing; students, teachers, and even the principal, were out to help the girl. Sophia visited friend after friend telling them of her situation. She visited her bank, *Banco Popular*, and spoke to the manager, who had known her for years, telling him of the rally that was being organized. It would be held a week later at midday to enable as many people to come during their lunch break. It would be staged in front of City Hall where the mayor would be engaged and the petition formally presented for a scholarship to be granted to her.

She spoke to the pharmacist, to her Girl Scout leader Miss Parras, to the Cabans who owned the clothing store *El Cielo*, to the owner of the shoe store *La Gloria*, where for years they had seen her file in with all her siblings lined up, looking nice and clean to buy what they needed.

Everyone knew her, and with the plea of support in her smile, Sophia repeated over and over again, "Will you come and support me?"

"I will be there."

"We will all be there."

"Wouldn't miss it for anything," were the replies.

Over the loud speakers at the high school and the middle school, students were told of the plan and encouraged to go to the rally. A week later, on a Thursday at midday, people gathered around City Hall. Sophia wanted to cry with gratitude as people she had known for so many years arrived and stood out front, smiling and shaking their heads in approval. A sea of students, the principals, teachers, store vendors, the pharmacists, bank employees, and so many silent heroes from Factor went to City Hall. The group at one point began to chant *"Una beca pa' Sofia,"* a scholarship for Sophia, was repeated over and over again. It became a noisy crowd filled with cheers, laughter and hope. Inside the building the principals of both the middle and high schools, and a few teachers along with the mayor went over Sophia's grades, goals and financial situation. It didn't take long, as the mayor could hear the chants and after peeking through his window saw a sea of faces looking up at him. Fifteen minutes passed and the mayor came out and stood with a big smile on his face and addressed the crowd.

"As I stand before you today, I am most happy to announce that after considering the academic merits that this young student has and taking into consideration the immense showing of support, I believe that Sophia James is deserving of a full and complete scholarship, that will be granted to her for this coming Fall." At this the crowd cheered calling out, *"Bien Sofia."*

"Good for Sophia," "Good for the mayor," and the boys, Karen and Evy all ran to hug Sophia. People started to leave and head back to their places of work and schools, giving Sophia pats on the shoulder, showing the "V" sign of victory. Everyone was happy, but no one as much as Sophia who, humbled by the showing of support, smiled wide with tears streaming down her face. However, this time there was no wail, only silent tears of joy.

The scholarship came through and indeed it was complete. Tuition, books, room and board were hers for the coming fall semester on the main campus of the University of Puerto Rico. Her dreams were within reach now and the excitement of all the possibilities filled her with a sense of optimism and joy. A wonderful future awaited her; she knew it. She would stretch as far as possible, grab it, and then hold on to it with all her might. The day of the rally would live among her most treasured memories. She, who wanted so many times to run away from the island, had been confronted with a scene of support that would forever wash away so many sorrows of the past.

Sophia was at the first major crossroad of her life: the goals that she worked for versus the children that she cared for. How does one choose one and let go of the other? Sophia was in turmoil and the joy of her triumph was difficult to savor.

The children were happy for her because they knew what it meant to her. They had always heard her tirelessly tell them to dream and work to make their dreams come true. They knew that her scholarship was her dream coming true and they couldn't begrudge her. However, they didn't want her to leave them but as the summer passed and she began to pack her few things, they became angry with her.

"So you're going to leave us, too!" Bobby yelled at her. Johnny sat quietly looking at her and waiting for her reply.

Karen was throwing things around and grumbling about, "Yeah, she's outta here and I'm stuck with all this mess." Frankie and Evy didn't say much, just listened. The comments came and went, and though they were meant to hurt her, they didn't. Sophia understood and stopped her packing and sat down with all the children that were not so little anymore.

"To leave is what I want most in the world and yet it isn't an easy thing for me to do. You all know how I feel about moving forward and going after one's dreams. Do you really want me to throw my dream away and stay here?"

"Not me," said Frankie.

"You go, Sophia, it's your time now. I'm happy for you." said Johnny.

Sophia touched his chin and said, "Listen, kids, you will get out or not; it will be up to you. I'm leaving you now a lot older than when we were left alone. Remember? Besides, I will be here on weekends and Daddy is about to quit going to sea and get his pension. He'll be here fulltime, so it won't just be you alone. In the meantime, you all know the routine and you must help Karen. You must all do your part. At the same time you have got to work on doing well in school." Sophia paused as if searching for an argument, "Look, kids, we have been beating the odds all along here. We were left all alone and no one has gone bad. When Casiano put the damn bar in front of us, he hoped that one of us girls would run away with someone, or one of you boys would start drinking, or worse, but we didn't. Now as I leave, I'm showing you the way it can be done. You must remember that if I can do it, you can do it too. But you have to really want it." Sophia's eyes started to fill up with tears as she spoke to the children from her heart. Looking at each one in the eyes she said, "Follow me, Karen, Bobby, Johnny, Frankie and you, little Evy. Decide what you want to do with your life and then fight for it. Never give up, you hear me?" With those words Sophia finished her packing. She hugged and kissed her siblings that were more to her than sisters and brothers and left the home that smothered her for so many years.

18

THE DREAM: UNIVERSITY

"QUIERO VOLAR COMO UNA MARIPOSA" ~ "I WANT TO FLY LIKE A BUTTERFLY"
Dando alas a mi mente, ~ Giving wings to my mind,
Busco la libertad, ~ I seek freedom,
Soñando despierta, ~ Daydreaming,
Hay sueños que buscar. ~ There are dreams to be pursued.
Quiero volar como una mariposa, ~ I want to fly like a butterfly,
Sentir mis alas en el viento, ~ Feel my wings free in the wind,
Tomar la brisa como una ola, ~ To ride the breeze like a wave,
Aleteando. ~ Fluttering.
Quiero volar como una mariposa, ~ I want to fly like a butterfly,
Buscando cimas cada vez más altas, ~ Seeking ever-higher peaks,
No importa si llego despeinada, ~ It doesn't matter if I arrive disheveled,
Aleteando. ~ Fluttering.

Sophia was about to finish her painting, "The Ladies in White." She was excited to get with it, so she got up early, took her brisk walk, and returned to it. The white, pleated and billowing dresses had yet to stand out in the bright sunlight. There is where she would pick it up. The contrasting shadows made by the horses on the sunbaked asphalt needed sharp edges. Shadows needed to lie flat and long, revealing the sizzling late morning sun. The bright greens would make the hot tropics simmer and she hoped to have the viewer share the stickiness and moisture in the air. Amidst it all, they will see unique beauty and the preservation of smiling generations, proud to be privileged, proud to show off their Paso Fino horses, proud to be Puerto Ricans.

Why had this image invaded her sleep compelling her to find the large canvas and spend hours searing every detail of it into her brain? Was it saying, admit it, *You always loved this island*?

She felt confused and spoke out loud to no one, as she was alone, "*Tomorrow* I'll be wiser," as if she were Scarlett O'Hara from *Gone with the Wind*. "Maybe I'll know the answer then," she added, tossing her head and smiling,

The making of the painting became synonymous with introspection. She couldn't help herself. It was as if, in the swift motion of picking up the palette, she picked up her past, leaving only her hands to work the present. Aware of that, she realized that she wasn't ready to go there and for a few moments avoided sitting in front of the canvas. Mindlessly, Sophia reached for the glass of passion fruit juice that she had placed earlier on a table nearby. Resting on that same table was a book titled, *Don Laws*. Sophia glanced at it fondly. That book had made her a published author. The writing she had taken up when she was a young girl, writing love letters for Rosa, marked a beginning for the love of writing. The play on words, the creativity, the sound of a sentence well structured, or the sound of an inventive sentence, was like a loving touch on the face by a soft hand. Writing was perhaps her truest love within the world of art, and being a published author, was a genuine source of pride. It validated all the beliefs she hung onto while fighting to survive. It proved that if one was widely read, believed in oneself and wanted to be good at something, in spite of it all, it could be done. She was almost sixty, but didn't feel that old at all. It was that joke she and humanity had going with Old Man Time himself. He kept claiming her and she kept attempting to deny him. How could she not? She still held fast onto so many dreams, yet to be completed.

Her attention went back to the painting and she squinted her eyes, checking the values of her chosen colors. The lights were getting there. She took a sip of the sweet, yet acidic drink, and put down the glass. She looked at the large palette knowingly and smiled the smile of submission. She picked it up, straightened her back, and settled in for another long stretch.

Sophia had entered a whole new world and with each step she was emboldened. The Río Piedras campus of the University of Puerto Rico was beautiful. Its wide front lawns at the main entrance were lined by Royal Palms. It was all majestic and now, it too, belonged to Sophia. Steps led to the campus tower, the school's main landmark, that was built in Spanish colonial architectural design. Its beige walls and roof, with Spanish terracotta tiles, made the main structure resemble a monastery. A tall tower arose from the center of its main building, a structure that boasted wide corridors and had a seemingly infinite number of arches. Its thoughtful design funneled a cool breeze through its corridors, which was felt immediately upon entry. Sophia enjoyed the transition from furnace to cool breeze and briefly touched her brow removing moisture. She was exploring. She took a small circular stairwell, climbed up and up as far as she could, and found a view. It was a wonderful view that allowed her to see the entire campus. The green lush and orange-flowered trees, the *flamboyans,* were everywhere, reminding her that she was still on the island. Yes, she was still on the island, but at the moment she was looking at it from a different perspective and she liked her new vantage point so much more.

Sophia was seventeen when she arrived at the university and was anxious to see it all, to figure it all out. She was introduced to its campus by a couple of her high school teachers. They had come back to their old stomping grounds and enjoyed seeing the wide eyed Sophia marvel at it all. They offered Sophia the option of boarding at their old boarding house. They recommended it with the key words "close, clean and safe." Sophia was glad to accept and to have yet another piece of the puzzle fall in place. It was all coming together and the week before school started Sophia explored the campus and delighted in her new environment. The new and more modern part of the campus was built at the north end and was home to freshmen. All core courses were taught in the spanking-new facility, painted a bright eggshell white, with the latest in modern equipment.

On the first day of school Sophia was thrilled to hurry about seeking out her classrooms and meeting her professors. She began the first semester by packing in the courses and giving herself the maximum twenty-one credits. The registrar teased, "What's the rush?" Sophia simply smiled and went off to buy a wheelbarrow full of books. Sophia knew that she had a full scholarship today, but life taught her that no one knew what might happen tomorrow. She was determined to work as hard and as fast as possible. She was aiming to get through pre-med and then apply to the medical school at the University of Navarra, in Pamplona, Spain. As time passed, the plan became more and more clear and she stayed focused.

The University of Navarra in Pamplona was a place that she had fantasized with for years. It was headed by the Opus Dei and introduced to her by Jorge, the older brother of a dear school friend, Rosita Caban. Jorge, also was to study medicine and knowing that Sophia harbored the same dream, spoke to her about the beauties of the northern parts of Spain. "Sophia, your Nirvana is in Navarra." Sophia listened and did not forget. Over the years she researched it and decided that it was there where she would study. Rosita's brother, an academic, never paid much attention to Sophia but one day he told her *"Valkiria llevame en tu carrosa hacia el Valhalla, Valyrie, take me in your carriage to Valhalla."* He laughed, and with time Sophia understood the subtleness of his silent affections.

Days were long, her books were heavy, and by days end she was always physically exhausted. *Three more flights, you can do it*, she said to herself as she opened the street door of Doña Paca's boarding house. The boarding house consisted of two apartments that took up the entire third floor. It was an inviting, light, and airy apartment and Sophia liked it the moment she entered.

However, she was not sure about the dorm mom, Doña Paca. The moment she met her, the old lady looked her up and down from head to toe and without a smile said, "I'll take her." Sophia remembered feeling as if she had just been bought. It hadn't mattered though. Over time, Sophia developed great affection for Doña Paca, who ran a tight ship. She was a stern woman who laid down strict rules for her boarders. Lights were turned out at eleven sharp and no arriving late was permitted. At that time the street doorway was locked and entry restricted. Breakfast and dinner were served punctually and tardiness at the table was not acceptable. Her orders were clear and precise and as time went by, Sophia appreciated her rigidness. There was order and all residents were considerate, responsible, and good company. Sophia was glad to be there.

THE DREAM: UNIVERSITY

School, library, and dorm became her universe, and she loved it. Though she had a heavy academic load, it was weightless compared to the one she had been lifting for so many years. She had no one to care for but herself and life became easy. For the first time in her life there was true order to her existence. She knew where she had to be, when she had to be there, and what needed to be accomplished before, in order to arrive successfully. Amidst her activities the children were always close in her mind, but she was at ease, knowing they were fine. Mr. James had returned home before she left for the university and was finally retiring. He received a pension, a small one, but no longer went away. The children were all older and would not be without a parent.

The semester began in full force and Sophia was finding out what it was to compete with students from private schools. Sophia found that catching up was tough and that the mountain she needed to climb was a very steep one. The fundamental learning skills she lacked needed to be acquired in a hurry. Without those tools, it was nearly impossible to succeed with high standards—standards required for students that had the ambitions of studying medicine and getting into a medical school.

The library was an ample building. It afforded anyone almost anything. Sophia began going there directly after classes. Her class schedule varied every day, with some days having classes continuously and other days having time off in between classes. Whatever the case was, she stayed on campus and in the library until a quarter to five, then quickly hustled over to Doña Paca's, where at five o'clock sharp, dinner was served. Everyone knew well that if they weren't at the table at five, they missed it. The seven boarders would come in from different directions and sit at a nicely set table. For Sophia, dinner was appreciated like no one knew. Often she was teased for involuntarily making a "hmmmmm," sound as she ate. Everyone laughed not understanding that those home cooked meals, made by Doña Paca, were the first in almost a decade for Sophia. The atmosphere was always friendly and harmonious with everyone sharing about their day. Sometimes, someone was absent because of parents visiting or off on a dinner date. However, Sophia never missed, she literally couldn't afford to. Her scholarship was complete and paid for everything but it did not leave her with pocket money, so going elsewhere for a meal was not an option.

After dinner, Sophia headed right back to the library where she remained till ten o'clock each evening. The main library room was huge and held many tables with chairs. Sophia had taken up a spot and always sat in a particular chair and after a while the chair became hers. As days went by, regulars began to know each other and when someone else sat in her chair another student would mention, "That's Sophia's spot and she'll be here any minute." She would arrive, spread out her things and try to concentrate.

There was always sound around her in that large wonderful space, but after a little time settling in, she would be fine. Sophia found during the first few days, while she was trying to establish a desirable routine, that returning to Doña Paca's to study after dinner was nonproductive. Carmen who was the only non-student of the seven, but instead employed, would come in and want to talk. For Sophia this spelled disaster, so her routine became the library. Everyone working at the library got to know her and Sophia's friendliness, honest and open joy and gratitude, made everyone like her. One day after a month of being at the university, the head librarian approached her as she was checking out a book, "Sophia, I see you here every single day."

"Yes, that's the truth. I'm taking twenty-one credits, Señora Díaz, and the only way to truly get everything done is almost living here." She said with a chuckle.

"Well, dear, when I see you, I'm reminded of something I've been meaning to ask you. I have a small office in the back, nice and quiet, with a desk and chair, which you could use, if you think it could be useful to you. The small office does have a door and a key, so you could leave your things there, and not have to haul them back and forth." She gave Sophia a wink and a smile.

"Really, Señora Díaz? My gosh, I don't know what to say. Wow!" said Sophia with excitement as both hands flew up covering her wide open mouth. "That would be terrific! I could never thank you enough for thinking of me. Sure, I want to take you up on that offer. When can I move in?"

"Right now, if you want to."

"My! It must be my lucky day! Thank you so much, Señora Diaz." Sophia stood up and gave her a hug. With a big smile on her face she went back to her table, quickly collected her things and after passing

THE DREAM: UNIVERSITY

the front desk, entered the office space that would be hers for all the years to come while she was at the university.

The year has no seasons on the island of Puerto Rico. It is like an eternal spring—always warm and with flowers in bloom. Time passes from one month to the next without great fanfare. For Sophia, that first year at the university was lived so intensely that as its end neared, the feeling for her was bitter sweet. It was a year of great contrasts, filled to the brim with novelty. It was consumed with constant learning and puzzling challenges which Sophia faced one at a time and resolved. The wonderful support system that surrounded Sophia provided an environment for success. Sophia was happy and anyone that knew her could see it. The library office proved to be a blessing. She could work and stay focused without interruption. She felt so lucky and loved her tiny office, living in it more than in any other space, anywhere. Her dorm house was solid and reliable. Doña Paca was as good as gold and though she never turned sweet, she never turned sour either and Sophia trusted her.

All year long she visited her family nearly every other weekend. On Fridays after class she left with dorm friends, Betsy and Belén, for Arecibo. A driver was contracted to drive the girls to their respective homes. Then the driver again picked them up on Sunday mornings and headed back to San Juan. Roads in Puerto Rico were improving and so what once was a five-, and then a four-hour drive, now was only three. Sophia loved her new University life but she missed the kids and so being around them was something she looked forward to. She also missed her dad and was happy he was not returning to his dangerous work. Too many Merchant Marines were lost while helping the homeland fight foreign wars and no one took notice of them. To be a seaman, transporting ordinance to our military was a mighty dangerous yet unappreciated job and the James family was ready to give their dad all the appreciation they could. He never forgot them and always came back.

However, with every visit Sophia could see that life was still bad for the James children. The dear dad who had always been their guiding light became lonely. After all, he had returned to an island where he hardly spoke the language and to a home full of children without a mother. It was hard for him and sometimes he would head over to Elias' bar and have a few beers too many. Gradually his drinking increased and, too often, he drank way too much. Sophia would come home to visit and see what was happening. While she was growing up, when her dad would return from the ocean, there were nights when he'd go out and stay out real late. On those nights, Sophia waited up until he returned, worried about him having an accident. But drinking was sporadic, not something he did constantly. Now, as he spent more time on the island the heavy drinking became more frequent. Sophia could understand that he was miserable. Nevertheless, his drinking took much needed money away from the family, and made the kids worry and suffer. With Sophia seeing the deteriorating situation at home, heading off to school was more and more difficult. Nevertheless, she would leave. She had to do it and each time she would repeat, to those that would listen, "Study hard, don't give up, you need a scholarship. You can do it!"

Sophia left her home with guilt. She felt that her life had become so much better than theirs that in many ways it wasn't fair. None of it was ever fair, it was all unjust and ugly. Her trips to Arecibo were painful and before the end of the year she applied for summer funds. With excellent grades she was granted scholarship coverage for eight credits, a humanities, an English course, and an elective: introduction to tennis. She was thrilled with her summer plans but she could never have guessed how thrilling indeed that summer would be for her.

As soon as she saw her humanities professor she was dazed. He was the most handsome man she ever saw in her life, tall and interesting. His perfect smile and dark eyes were mystifying. Sophia sat entranced, like most young ladies in the class. Yes, he was a real heart throb and she was sure he knew it. His class was fascinating and Sophia, who always studied hard, unwittingly made an impression on him. The quiet girl, with the long hair and direct eyes read her Marx, Lenin and Nietzsche's, "Thus Spake Zarathustra," and was not shy to voice her dissent, after all she had already given her mind to Ayn Rand. Discussions took place within the class and his well-thought-out dogma was often challenged by Sophia's undeniably well-formed opposite view. The handsome professor found himself throwing his head back in laughter, and saying, "Where did you come from?" *Ha!* Thought Sophia, *if you only knew!*

Tennis was another story. It was exhilarating for her, something she had only dreamt of doing. She had always been attracted to the sport and didn't know why. However, she figured that by being coordinated and having the desire to learn, she had the hardest part beat. Now, all she needed to do was practice. Every day, she went to her lessons and then on her own hit balls against a wall trying to improve. The exercise was wonderful and the sun on her helped take away her library pallor. Tennis was a splurge of true fun, a treat so seldom available. To be outside more often felt good and during that summer Sophia spent as much time out as possible. When not playing tennis she lay on a blanket out on the expansive open lawns of the front of the university . She would relax in the sun for a while and then take up her reading. Comfortable and happy, she had been studying for a couple of hours, when a voice brought her back to her blanket. Shading her eyes, she looked up into the sun and into the sunglasses of her humanities professor.

"Hey, Sophia, how's my favorite student?"

"Oh, hi, I'm fine, thank you. I didn't know I was your favorite student. I'm honored." said Sophia, looking him in the eye and smiling.

"Of course you do, Sophia. Aren't you having as much fun in my class with me, as I am with you?" He was outright directly flirting and she took it as a compliment.

"I am enjoying your class, professor. Would you care to sit down?"

"You can call me Alfonso, Sophia. So what are you studying?" he asked as he stretched out a little of her blanket and with crossed legs sat on it.

"Oh, I'm reading for my English class." She showed him *A Portrait of the Artist as a Young Man*, by James Joyce. "It's a wonderful classic that just hasn't gotten so wonderful for me yet. I've been laboring."

"You? Laboring? Why, Sophia I can't believe that." He was teasing her and she was a bit taken aback by it. This man was her professor and it was hard for her to all of a sudden be too chummy with him. She looked at him, said nothing and just smiled.

He sat on her blanket for about an hour. They philosophized, teased and laughed. Sophia had enjoyed the conversation and the attention given to her by the handsome man. She began to think of him more often and felt a little uncomfortable when it was time to see him in class. However, once class began she could not resist trying to shoot down, what she considered his illogical logic. He obviously looked forward to their matches, which more and more resembled a dueling of contrary ideas. It was in that manner that Sophia had caught his attention, marking the beginning of an adventure.

With the summer gone, Sophia again registered for a full academic load. Taking nothing for granted, she worked hard to keep her grades and her full scholarship. However, she did not want to let go of tennis which she enjoyed so much. Her only window of opportunity was early in the day, at five-thirty in the morning. For an hour, she would head over to the tennis courts to play with early rising tennis friends she met over the summer. The courts were only a ten-minute walk from her boarding house and she was often warned to be careful and keep her eyes wide open. She did that and still on one day she ran into a flasher. Like in a comic book, a man walking toward her, all of a sudden opened up a long raincoat. She jumped and was truly shocked as the disgusting naked man, who in a low voice said, "Look at what I've got here for you!"

However, Sophia immediately astonished herself with her reaction. She had no idea that the saving, instant reply she clearly voiced, was in her: "That? So *little*?" It must have been her psychology class talking. Her spontaneous attitude toward the flasher deflated his ego as fast as he had flashed her. He turned around and ran away from Sophia, almost as fast as she ran toward the tennis courts. The incident didn't stop her from playing tennis early in the mornings, but she did change her route after that.

By eight o'clock every morning she had played tennis, showered and was at her first class, wide-eyed and ready to go. Sophia never stopped being in awe of the fact that she was going to the university. There had been too many times in her life where the possibility of it looked so dim and impossible. Frequently she found herself staring at her surroundings in disbelief that she was really there.

Though Sophia had completed humanities, Alfonso kept showing up. He would "run into her" at the library and around campus.

"How about a cup of coffee?" and between one coffee and another and meeting each other for different shows on campus, Sophia was beginning to care for him. Alfonso was sweet, always showing up with a flower in hand, and complimenting her dress, her hair, or just anything. However, Sophia tread cautiously. turning down enticing invitations and refusing to play the love game her friends played: *Girl likes guy, girl does everything guy wants.* There was no denying that Sophia liked Alfonso but she wasn't "dying" for him. The fact that she wasn't surrendering to his charms, was precisely what kept him devoted to the con-

THE DREAM: UNIVERSITY

quest. He often surprised her by standing outside of her classroom with a rose in hand, waiting for her to come out. They would find a bench in the shade and fix the world. He was thirty years old, married once, and had a daughter. He was real smooth and Sophia knew that he was quite the playboy. However, when he told Sophia that he clearly knew what he wanted from life, she silently thought of his track record and remained skeptical. She enjoyed his company, felt flutters when he arrived, and thought that maybe she was falling in love. He was mature, not silly, interesting and intelligent, and though he was highly educated Sophia often found herself disagreeing with his points of view, and he couldn't convince her otherwise. Though only nineteen, Sophia had lived through so much in her young life that when she had a conviction, it became solid and it was not easy to dissuade her. Therefore, when the seasoned playboy expertly scooped her up in his arms and kissed her, there was a little voice cautioning her. There was some hidden reason that made her feel that she could not really trust him. That little voice always guided and guarded her so well that she couldn't help but listen. She would not let go of her heart, she would not deliver herself to Alfonso, but instead enjoyed the moments as she got to know him better.

As time passed, Sophia realized that in many ways Alfonso was very much the Latin macho. Traits that Sophia commonly saw everywhere, as she grew up, she found in him. It surprised her that someone with such a bright mind and mature sophistication could be the petty, jealous type. It was a disappointment, as she had thought he should be above that behavior. However, she could not deny acknowledging what she saw. If Alfonso found Sophia happily conversing with a guy friend, his true colors came out flying.

"Why are you talking to him? You like him, don't you?" he anxiously would ask, with his demeanor demanding an answer.

"Yes, I like him very much, he's a tennis friend."

After that he showed up randomly at the tennis courts to watch her. He didn't realize that jealous tantrums only belittled him in her eyes, and would do nothing to help him get Sophia. Nevertheless, Sophia wanted to be loved, and be in love. She thought that maybe wanting to be in Alfonso's arms was an indication of falling into true love. Still the little guardian within her was standing very much on alert, not resting for a moment.

As time passed, more and more frequently, Alfonso stood outside of her classrooms waiting for her to come out and then walked her to her next class. Sophia was always happy to see him and appreciated the envious glances from other girls her age. He was, after all, killer gorgeous and obviously smitten. However, Sophia began to realize that constantly escorting her wasn't so much out of love for her, but a desire to control her and she was beginning to feel smothered. He was often acting jealous, as if afraid that someone would capture her attention and snap her away. His lack of security in himself seemed so immature that Sophia started to become weary of him, and her feelings toward him began to change.

On a day when Sophia abruptly had a class cancelled, she found herself with some free time on her hands. She decided to cross campus and for once, surprise Alfonso outside of one of *his* classes. She hurriedly headed toward his building but by happenstance saw him in the distance heading toward the parking lot. She started running, thinking that she was going to completely miss him. As she continued to run she realized that he was not going to his car but to the building beyond. Though he was far away Sophia still tried to catch up with him and continued running trying to not lose sight of him. As she approached the building and went around the corner where she last saw him turn, she almost ran into him. He was in the arms of a student, kissing her. Sophia stopped, and did nothing but stare at him. She was shocked and as Alfonso turned and saw her, he said the lame, "Sophia, wait, let me explain."

Sophia could hardly believe what she saw and again her reaction surprised her. She looked him in the eye, and, as he said his one liner, shook her head and chuckled. It hurt, but she certainly wasn't going to let him see it. As if time froze she stood for a few moments looking straight at Alfonso and he stood looking at her. Disappointment was plainly on her face and when she found her voice, it was clear, that she was dead serious.

"Alfonso, take a good look at me, because this is about as close as you will ever be to me again."

"Sophia, please, I love you."

"Alfonso!" said the girl he was just kissing.

THE DREAM: UNIVERSITY

Sophia turned away as the first tear fell. She walked away with her head high knowing that he was watching her, and never once looked back.

She went back to her dorm, threw herself on her bed and cried. Everyone knew about Alfonso. Everyone had met him and they knew that he was her "first love." So when her boarding pals got home and heard the news they began filing in.

"Oh! Sophia don't worry, it'll be OK."

"He'll come back soon and want to make up with you." Sophia didn't offer much and the following day, for the first time ever, she skipped school. She had a little money saved up, just coins in a piggy bank. Wrapping the bank in newspaper, she broke it and on her bed she counted out eighty dollars, in quarters, dimes and nickels. It would do. That was a tidy sum in the early seventies and it would surely cover a couple of nights in a small hotel, transportation money and a little food. She would take a public car to the town of Guánica, on the southern coast of the island, and spend the weekend there. She wasn't expected home in Arecibo and she wanted to be alone. She needed to think, regroup, understand what just happened, and her feelings about it all. She told Doña Paca what she was going to do and that she would be back on Sunday, as usual.

Sophia found a small, quaint hotel on the water. It was perfect for her. She checked in and went to explore its beaches. It was a rocky beach with little sand. With an old pair of tennis shoes she made her way over boulders and rocks. The smell of salt in the air and the sight of the calm ocean were healing. Quickly she knew that she had done the right thing and arrived at the right place. A little ways down the stretch of beach, not far from the hotel, she found a tree of beach grapes. It was fairly large and its weathered old trunk was bent toward the water. Sophia easily climbed it and moved onto an outer limb. She sat directly over the water and her legs dangled in. She was comfortable and happy to have found such a quiet and pretty place. There on that limb, she looked into her soul and confronted many things, but found no real surprises. She admitted to herself that she was glad to have found Alfonso with another girl. Long ago she realized, but had not wanted to accept, that he was not the right person for her. His jealousies made her miserable and told her that there would never be trust. Sophia thought that if he couldn't trust her, then he must certainly be untrustworthy.

After all, she grew up witnessing the hurt caused by lies and deceit. For her, honesty was the most important virtue in the world. His constant criticizing of what she wore or didn't wear, "That skirt is too short, why would you want to show your legs off to everyone?" Sophia would then go off and change, but she hadn't really wanted to change, she was just pleasing him. It was that constant trying to 'change' her that she resented. She didn't want anyone to be changing her, trying to control her, to make her 'obey.' She was who she was and if that was too tough or not good enough for someone, well then that certainly wasn't the right person for her. However, the open deceit was the epitome of it all. While he professed his love for her, he was running around with someone else or others. She had no idea about the complexities of love but trust had to be the basis of it all. If that was shattered, how could a person get around it? Pretend? Forever? It was impossible. Sophia knew that getting away from Alfonso was the right thing and she dangled her legs carelessly in the water below.

In many ways Sophia understood that most anyone she met in Puerto Rico was going to have those *macho* traits. It was typical on the island. Alfonso proved that those traits infiltrated all levels. Independent of status, intellectual capacity or economic class, for a man to run around with several women at a time was—if not acceptable—understood, forgiven and endorsed. He was a man! Women didn't seem to aspire to be the only one, either, but just to be one of them, seemed enough. *He loves me more!* Often there were passionate murders because the woman was looking at another guy. Sophia believed that jealousy proved a lack of self-confidence, yet on the island, many girls believed that with jealousy men proved their love for them. When Sophia mentioned to her roommates that almost every day Alfonso was showing up to escort her from class to class, they thought he was so sweet for missing her. Sophia understood differently, more than *missing* her, he was deliberately telling others that he *owned* her, and you had better stay away. Sophia was glad to be rid of him. She didn't want love to be complex, she just wanted simple, natural, effortless true love someday. She was in no hurry. She was passionately enjoying her life as a student and for the first time felt that her life was hers. She was in no hurry to give it away to anyone.

As Sophia sat pensively watching the shimmering calm ocean, the sun lowered in the sky. Still she continued to ponder her life and her mind reached back to her beginnings. Her personality, her way of being and thinking all came from that strong core she developed as a child in California. Though destiny had taken her to Puerto Rico, and she lived, understood, and assimilated with the people around her, she never lost her core, her true essence. She never forgot where she came from, her original customs, and the ways of those she knew before coming to the island. The core she developed before the island sustained and protected her and her siblings, when important decisions needed to be made in a split second. The reality and undeniable truth was that Sophia remained at heart *the American girl from California.* Hence, many of her values and beliefs were different from those of her friends. She did not believe that hers were better or worse, they were just different. So—unlike her friends, who assured her to not worry because Alfonso would come back—in Sophia's mind, his coming back was the only thing that could worry her.

There on that healing limb that hung so gracefully over the water, Sophia reasoned with herself, and sadness gave way to a sense of well-being. She would remember Alfonso always. She would appreciate him for the valuable lessons he unknowingly taught her. He gave her tools that would someday help her recognize, why a special someone, would be the right one.

Upon returning to the boarding house around midday on that Sunday, Doña Paca, for the first time ever, grabbed Sophia and gave her a hug.

"*¿Cómo estás mija?* Are you all better?"

Sophia looked at her with a big smile, "All better, Doña Paca. Going away was just the right thing for me to do. *Muchas gracias.*"

"Well, wait for the girls to come home, they are going to have some stories for you about Alfonso."

"Really? Well then, I'll see them later on tonight, I'm heading to the library. I've got some good catching up to do."

The girls told Sophia about how poor Alfonso stood outside of their building all night Friday and Saturday. It was pouring rain and he got sopping wet but never moved. He was determined to speak with her and waited for her to return.

The girls explained to him that Sophia would not be back. That she had gone off somewhere because she wanted to be alone. He didn't believe it and stood around waiting. Sophia laughed and told the girls,

"*Que tonto.*" How silly of him. Did he think that such behavior was going to impress her? Anyway, she wasn't very interested and quickly moved away to organize her things for Monday's early morning class. Sophia was totally at peace with her decision and Alfonso would no longer play any role in her future.

The girls were mystified and asked her, "But Sophia, you are going to forgive him, aren't you? I mean you know that he loves you."

Sophia looked at her friends and smiled, "No, he doesn't love me, and if that is love, I don't want it. Thanks a lot to all of you for helping me out here, but the truth is I don't want to talk about him or hear about him anymore, OK?" Sophia went up to her boarding friends and gave each of them a hug while saying, "I'm fine now and this is one closed chapter."

Sophia was happy and was now a third year student completing her pre-med. She loved her university and strived devotedly to be the best student she could be. One day she noticed a sign. The registrar's office had an opening for a secretary. Sophia thought about it. She was sure that she could work for them, if they worked with her. With a flexible schedule she would do a fine job. Having work gave her a few extra dollars, and she wanted to save money. Her greatest dream was to visit California and the sooner the better. She did get the job and had her first working experience. However, after six months, a better paying opportunity presented itself and she went for it. One of her boarding pals, Carmen, saw in the building where she worked in Hato Rey, a short bus ride from the university, a notice soliciting a receptionist. She told Sophia about it and Sophia jumped for it. She interviewed and was hired on the spot. She started a week later after resigning at the registrar's office. Her new job was a half-day position as receptionist for an insurance company, Caribbean Industrial. Her morning classes were spread out among evenings and Saturdays. It worked. It was great and four hundred dollars every month for half days was wonderful!

Sophia felt that her life was coming together. She studied like crazy and with her job she was able to save a little money. That Christmas she was able to buy a gift for each of her siblings with her first earned money. She felt all grown up and productive. Her favorite gift turned out to be the one she found for Frankie. It was perfect. It was a first class unicycle. She knew that if there ever was someone that could learn how to ride that thing and laugh all the while, he would be the one. In

THE DREAM: UNIVERSITY 259

no time it was a reality. He was up and down the streets, riding through the pineapple fields and everyone that saw him stopped in their tracks and watched in amazement.

There was some stability in Sophia's life after so many years of chaos. She studied and worked and then one day God smiled on her.

19

THE FACE OF LOVE

"FANTASIA" ~ "FANTASY"
Bello y fuerte tan musculoso, ~ Beautiful, strong and so muscular,
Al mirarte como yo gozo, ~ How I enjoy seeing you,
Tu no sabes que te estoy viviendo, ~ You don't know how I'm living you,
Con tan solo verte un movimiento. ~ Just by seeing you simply move.
La risa brota de mi, ~ Laughter springs from me,
Si me miras me ves sonreir, ~ If you look at me you'll see me smile
Pasas muy cerca de mí, ~ You go right by me,
Pero para ti yo nunca existí. (No importa) ~ For you I have never existed. (It doesn't matter)
Sigo mirando y controlando, ~ I keep looking and controlling myself,
Cada dia más difícil es. ~ Every day it just gets harder.
Tu piel tan suave quiero tocarte, ~ Your skin so soft, I want to touch you,
Besar tu boca hasta pelarme. ~ Kiss your mouth until I blister.
Fantasía me haces vivir, ~ Fantasy, you make me live,
Fantasía no, no, no quiero de ti, ~ Fantasy, no, no I don't want from you.
Fantasía hacer realidad, ~ Fantasy, can become a reality,
Fantasía que me llegues amar. ~ Fantasy, that you come to love me.

A mini celebration was going on in Sophia's physics class because her professor announced that on the following Saturday there would be no lecture. The day was off and there was no assigned homework. Immediately, overloaded and overworked students began making plans for a day of fun, a concept that had almost become alien. Sophia was in. She would go anywhere to celebrate the rare day off. A girlfriend suggested they go to a beach. It was a beach Sophia had never been to and it was smack in the middle of the plush Condado area of San Juan. The Condado, was famous for its beach strip, lined by first-rate hotels. It was mostly where tourists were, as well as the rich and famous of the island. Sophia took two buses to reach the designated spot, near the five-star Sheraton Hotel, where she was to meet her friend. She packed a basket for the trip. It contained a novel for pleasure reading, a towel, and her very important paddles and ball. Sophia was a good player after playing for years against Bobby and Johnny. She looked forward to giving her friend Pat a good whipping.

Looking around and feeling conspicuous, Sophia felt that her tan-lacking, locked-indoors-white-student look was unattractive compared to the lustrous, richly tanned figures lying everywhere. Averting eye contact, she headed toward a deserted spot on the sand and stretched out on her towel. She pulled a book out of her basket and dived into it. No matter how she felt, Sophia looked good in her two-piece. She made a point of ignoring the young men that walked by and winked or blew kisses her way. Every now and then she would look up to see if she saw her friend Patricia.

It was a perfect beach day. The sky was as blue as could be and there were no clouds in sight. The ocean was alive and the sound of the pounding surf felt good. A few steps away another sound began to interrupt her reading. It was the inviting sound of a good game of paddle ball. A couple of guys nearby were playing and every once in a while, Sophia glanced over at them. She really hadn't looked closely at the players, it was the game itself that she watched, while wondering, *Where are you, Pat?* Resolved to enjoy her day, Sophia dove back into James Michener's "Hawaii." About a half an hour went by, when suddenly one of the paddle ball players approached her.

He noticed her basket with the paddles sticking out and asked, "Would you like to play?"

Sophia looked up at him. "Sure," she said getting up with a happy smile.

"Great! Play with him; I'm too tired to go on."

Sophia looked at the other guy and realized that he was unaware that a switch was taking place. She smiled at him and waved. "It's OK?" she said.

"Sure!" he smiled back.

Sophia served up a hard ball. He wasn't expecting a hard serve and laughed when he missed it. After that the balls went back and forth at a good pace. Sophia was having fun and so was he.

"Hey, Steve, where did you find her?" called out a friend of his.

Steve was a nice looking guy with a tall athletic body, and blond hair that was as straight as could be. He had a warm smile and an honest face. As Sophia sat down, he too sat on the sand next to her. He had been living in Puerto Rico for a couple of years, was working and completing a masters. He spoke Spanish fluently and loved tennis. As their conversation continued, friends of his stopped by to find out who the girl was. His friends seemed like nice guys and Sophia knew that she was in good company. He lived in the oceanfront apartment building, right there where they were playing. They were having a nice conversation and an hour later Steve asked,

"Are you thirsty, would you like a coke?"

"No, no, I'm quite fine, thanks." A while later he asked her again. This time Sophia laughed and again said no. Steve looked very trustworthy, but still she didn't know him and wasn't about to go upstairs to his apartment all alone. So though the coke, as time went by, was sounding better and better, she still refused.

A group of Steve's friends began congregating around them and everyone was having a good time. The next time Steve offered her something to drink, he invited all of his buddies up and Sophia, who could tell that these were good guys, said, "Sure, I'll have a coke." Up to the third floor she went with Steve and six buddies, two from the US and four from Puerto Rico. Sitting around, they all wanted to know more about the girl their friend had spent the afternoon with.

Sophia was not going to share her life story but when someone mentioned a fruit, indigenous to the island and in the same breath said, "But what would you know about any tropical fruits from this island?" Sophia unbuttoned her lips and a competition of sorts began. It was silly but distracting and no one could mention more indigenous fruits than she could. She knew them all and then some. The Puerto Ricans kept shaking their heads, saying, "I have never heard of that one. Where are you from?" They all laughed and laughed and then it was time for Sophia to head home.

"Well, I've really enjoyed myself. What a nice time I've had," said Sophia sincerely,

"but I've got to leave. I have two busses to catch, before I'm back at my boarding house, and I don't want it to get dark."

"Well, let me give you a ride home."

"No, I don't want to destroy your evening."

"Not at all. I'd be glad to make sure you get home safely. Besides, Río Piedras is close by. It'll take me no time." On the ride home, Steve asked Sophia out for dinner the following evening.

Her boarding house friends teased her the next day as she got ready for her date. She was excited and after changing several times decided on an attractive black and red knit dress. With her long dark hair she wore long red earrings, and her friends told her that she looked beautiful. Doña Paca didn't say anything but gave her a cursory look of approval. At six sharp, Steve was there to pick her up. His wide smile made her feel happy and as she got into his car butterflies fluttered in her tummy. They went to an Italian restaurant and the evening flew by. He was a traveler and had spent some time as an exchange student in Spain, which gave him insight into the Latin culture. Working in Puerto Rico had not been a happenstance. On the contrary, he sought out the international work. Steve was twenty-seven and though fun and light, he was quite mature. He laughed with confidence and ease and Sophia couldn't help but laugh with him. On that evening she shared some of her dreams and he listened with great interest. They were both adventurous and after such of an enjoyable first date, they decided to meet again.

The rope attached to her harness was pulling her and she began running to keep up, lest she fall and be dragged on the sand toward the water. Suddenly the parachute she was attached to, lifted off the ground and up she went with it. She was skyward bound and screaming,

"This is wooondeeerfuuuuul!!!!" at the top of her lungs knowing no one could hear her. She was going up and up into the clear blue sky and the boat below pulling her was getting smaller and smaller. For a person that always suffered from vertigo, she suffered not a trace of it that day. The ride was thrilling and much too soon the boat turned away from the open ocean and once again pulled her toward the buildings on the beach.

Then it was Steve's time to go up, as Sophia remained on the beach watching and thinking, *What nice legs he has*. The day was perfect. She couldn't remember when she last had so much fun. Sophia continued to see Steve when he invited her and enjoyed their outings. However, she made him aware that she was on a mission. Playing too much could get her into trouble. She needed to stay focused and she understood that he too had many obligations. However, every time there was some free time, they would steal it to be in each other's company.

It happened on the night when they went to see "Jonathan Livingston Seagull." After the soul-searching film it was still early and they went back to Steve's apartment. His apartment had an open layout, which revolved around the ocean view. The mighty ocean, lit by the moon, was full in their faces and the pounding sound of the surf shook their beings and filled their ears. Steve had the ultimate bachelor's pad and was an experienced bachelor and Sophia understood that well. Upon arriving at his apartment, he turned on nice music and offered Sophia a little cordial. Sophia knew nothing about liqueurs or after dinner drinks; she had missed out on those life lessons, but didn't want to confess her ignorance.

He asked, "What would you like Sophia?"

Sophia answered with a, "Oh . . . Whatever you're having would be fine."

"How about Crème de Menthe?"

"OK."

Steve proceeded to pour two small glasses of the mint-green liqueur. Out on the balcony of his apartment overlooking the ocean, Sophia tasted the drink. She didn't like it, but she wouldn't tell. She pretended to enjoy it, lifting the small glass to her lips to "take" tiny sips. Actually, when Steve wasn't looking, she spilt a little over the balcony. Sophia thought this could be considered deception, but she preferred to think of it as being polite. Sophia and Steve had seen each other on several occasions before that evening. They liked each other, there was no denying that. It was obvious from the moment they met. Suddenly their conversation died down for a moment and then magic happened. Out on the balcony, with the thundering sound of waves and the cool salty ocean air making them warm, Steve ever so gently looked into Sophia's eyes. He came closer, carefully as if she were a dove he might scare away, and delicately he touched her face. Sophia felt excitement and then his warm breath close to her, as he placed his lips on hers. The warm kiss was one like she had never had before. She felt his kindness and his goodness seep through and she loved it. Finally, it happened: she was given the first kiss in her life worth remembering.

20

TRAVEL, SUITORS AND TRUE LOVE

"BESOS CON FUEGO" ~ "KISSES WITH FIRE"
¿Has probado alguna vez, ~ Have you ever tasted,
Una fruta tropical? ~ A tropical fruit?
Se te hace manantial la boca. ~ It makes your mouth well up,
Es lo que me pasa a mí, ~ That is what happens to me,
Cuando me miras así, ~ When you look at me like that,
Se me vuelve la boca toda loca. ~ My mouth just goes wild.
Besos de pasión, son besos con fuego, ~ Kisses with passion, are kisses with fire,
Esos son los que quiero yo, ~ Those are the ones I want.

Sophia's part time work gave her options she never had before. She was finally able to save up and afford the trip for which it seemed she had waited a lifetime. A return to her roots, a return to the place from where hope always emanated. She dreamt of California's back roads countless times, of childhood friends, the big old eucalyptus tree. She wanted to go back and see it, make sure that it had all been real.

In the summer of 1975 that dream came true. Sophia James, twenty-one, flew off the island of Puerto Rico, LAX bound. She finally made it back to California, her California, and it looked wonderful. It was fashionable and clean, its highways were modern and she took everything in slowly, afraid to wake up from a dream. She wanted to hold on to time, so that her first impressions would indelibly register in her brain. She was there and was so happy.

She felt no fear of traveling alone and had thoughtfully planned out her itinerary. Her money was allotted carefully to every need and it was just enough to get her everywhere she was going. The first visit would be to her grandmother Odelia, in Menlo Park. The kind and quiet old woman, born in Hawaii, as her parents, immigrants from Portugal, Joe and Maggie Nobriga, made their way to a new life in the United States. Throughout all those years Sophia had never heard from her grandmother, yet felt certain that the old woman loved her and Sophia loved her back.

Then San Francisco, the Golden Gate, which was carved into her memory because of Ghirardelli Square, where a world of fudge awaited.

Finally, there was Sacramento, the feather in the cap, cousins and locations that she had envisioned a thousand times. This was the place it was really all about. Would she find her old home? The house that traveled down the road as the entire school watched and cheered it on. Would Alpha School, the two-room school house still be standing? Would she find Colleen Gray, Ricky Robinson and Ronny? She remembered them so well, would they remember her?

Then, before taking her flight back to Puerto Rico, Sophia would fly to Mexico City. Mexico was the splurge. Mexico had always played a key role in her life as she had been invaded by it through her father's stories and television. Mexican TV had been a way of life in Puerto Rico and it brought Mexican music with it. Jorge Negrete, Pedro Vargas, Pedro Infante—famous Mexican singers—had helped her learn Spanish. Yes, Sophia would proudly walk the Zócalo, while applauding herself for getting there on her own efforts.

The James family in California proved to be a real mishmash of personalities. Some of them much more disorganized than the family Sophia singlehandedly raised back in Arecibo. Those that did well for themselves seemed glad to see her, but their eyes revealed surprise when they realized her ambition and drive. A sense of self-consciousness became visible as Sophia, after all, represented the children that badly needed help and no one had stepped forward. Her presence reminded them of their aloofness and as Sophia stood proudly introducing herself, the pre-med student with hopes of a bright future, her relatives shriveled with the guilt of neglect.

Though Sophia didn't foresee the reception she received, she understood it. The Menlo Park she encountered was a place filled with angry strangers, relatives incapable of setting aside their bitterness for a day. The experience could have been one of great disappointment, but instead Sophia hung on to her grandmother's smile. Her Grandmother stood apart from it all and held within her being the same kindness in her soft hazel eyes that Sophia clearly remembered. They hugged deeply and her grandmother told her how beautiful she thought she was.

"You have my large Portuguese eyes, of course, when I was a young girl." She smiled and hugged her again. The old lady spoke with the accent of a lifetime, the one created by her Portuguese roots. It was distinct and familiar to Sophia. It felt good, warm, and loving.

Sophia stayed one night and left the following morning. She understood that a true gulf lay between her and her relatives. Sophia was fine with it all, none of it mattered. Her journey was one of celebration and the past was not invited. She was reveling in the present and she would not be denied its magic.

She reached San Francisco by bus and seeing the Bay Bridge and the Golden Gate made her cry. Had she had a banner with the words *I love you*, she would have worn it across her chest. Instead she walked around as if floating on air, convinced that everyone was floating right along with her.

Chinatown, Fisherman's Wharf, and then BART's Transbay Tube, the underground and under-bay train system that had recently opened to the public, were all a part of the surreal experience. Still, nothing could surpass the excitement of first smelling and then placing in her mouth, fudge bought at the beloved Ghirardelli Square of her memories.

Sophia allotted herself one day for San Francisco. In the early afternoon she hopped onto a Greyhound and after a couple of hours arrived in Sacramento.

It was hard for her to sit still as she began the most meaningful part of her trip. Looking out the window she recognized the vegetation and overall landscape of her early childhood. Her mind captured it and preserved it well in her memories. California was beautiful, and Sophia felt proud, she was a Californian. Suddenly the weight of a bag in her lap brought her back to the bus. The bag sitting there contained a whole pound of walnut fudge and Sophia had every intention of eating every bite of it. Then the urge hit her. Surreptitiously Sophia stuck her hand into the bag, to break off a piece of the mouth-salivating chocolate. The bag was a noisy one and no matter how she tried to be silent, it rustled. The sound of sneaky motion, made a passenger from across the aisle, peek over at her. Sophia looked up at the same moment and their eyes met, she couldn't help but laugh and say, "You caught me."

He laughed back and said, "What do you have in there?"

"Hmmm, fudge, the best in the whole wide world." she said with an irresistible triumphant smile.

"Fudge? What is that?"

"You don't know what fudge is?" teased Sophia.

"I don't think so," all the while the young man was smiling.

"It's chocolate. Real American chocolate and it has walnuts in it." Sophia savored the words as she said them, but offered none of her chocolate to him. Then she laughed,

"Would you like to taste it?"

"Why yes, please." As Sophia reached into her bag to break off a piece, the young man asked, "May I sit next to you?"

"Sure, let me move these things." She stopped fetching the chocolate and moved her small backpack, placing it under the seat in front of her. In a moment the young man was sitting next to her, once again looking at her bag. With a smile, Sophia again reached for the chocolate and broke off a piece. The young man took the chocolate and savored it slowly, as if reaching inside and disembodying its flavors. He was enjoying the chocolate. Sophia could clearly see that it passed whatever test he was giving it. The expression on his face was of total complacency and Sophia, feigning horror, said, "Oh, no; now you're going to want more."

"No, no, but it is quite nice, thank you."

Fine, thought Sophia, *we'll leave it at that.*

The handsome young man turned out to be quite interesting. He was a multilingual Swiss lawyer who immediately started showing off his Spanish and speaking it rather fluently. They talked and laughed the whole time which helped the bus fly through Napa Valley's wine country and, before they knew it, Sophia saw a sign saying "Welcome to Sacramento." She couldn't help but squirm in her seat and confessed her excitement. She was finally arriving and butterflies hit her stomach, the palm of her hands became a little sweaty. She was trying to appear calm but inside she was bursting with emotion.

TRAVEL, SUITORS AND TRUE LOVE

Nicholas tried to secure another encounter with Sophia. "Could I see you again, while I'm here?"

"I don't know, Nicholas. I am staying with family I haven't seen for over ten years. If it is not too impolite for me to get away, then perhaps we can visit a site together. Here is their phone number. Let's play it by ear, OK?"

"Play it by ear?"

"Leave it up to chance." said Sophia smiling.

Up to chance, is where Sophia's life, in matters of the heart, remained. The fondness that had developed between Steve and Sophia was undeniable. However, words of love had not been exchanged. After five months they were not ready to declare undying love for one another and were happy and relaxed. This gave Sophia the freedom to continue meeting other young men that life placed in her path. She didn't know if Steve was to be the love of her life, and meeting others only helped her evaluate and understand further her feelings for him.

The bus came to a stop and, as walking in a dream, Sophia descended its steps into the arms of her cousins.

Irene and Kathy were the part of the family closest to Sophia's memories; as a child she saw them many times. Now, as she returned all grown up, they were friendly and Sophia felt welcomed.

Her cousin Irene had a nice home and a nicer husband. Bob was all laughter and kindness. They had no children and were free to explore and travel. They owned a beautiful sail boat and often sailed across the Pacific, making their way around the Hawaiian Islands. They were an interesting couple and Sophia was proud to see prosperity in her family. Kathy also had married a wonderful guy and had a bunch of sons.

Sure enough, the next morning the friendly Swiss lawyer called, inviting Sophia to join him for a tour at Sutter's Fort. Luckily, the evening before, Sophia had mentioned the young Swiss attorney she met on the bus. When he called, perceptive Irene offered her a ride. It was Sophia's chance to see him again and she wanted to.

It was a great meeting place, interesting and rich with history. Sutter's Fort, the oldest standing fort in the United States, was built in 1840 by a Swiss immigrant, John Sutter. Hence, her new Swiss friend was particularly keen on seeing it. It was almost completely destroyed during the gold rush, but later restored to reflect its original appearance. The fort was filled with California's history and wandering through it with Nicholas was enjoyable and time flew by. Nicholas was well-educated, interesting, and likable in many ways. Sophia enjoyed his company and regretted that she would not get to know him better. He was leaving the next morning, early, and that was that. However, there was an interesting and revealing moment during that day.

As they walked outside of the Fort toward a park across the street, Nicholas suddenly grabbed Sophia and tried to kiss her. Sophia was insulted and directly told him. "You can't do that; just kiss me, out here in the street!" Sophia was caught by surprise and the indignation she felt was in her voice.

"Well, when and where could I kiss you?" Nicholas had a fleeting smile on his lips.

"You don't get to. I don't know you well enough. How dare you? Who do you think I am?" Sophia was serious and Nicholas profusely apologized.

By the time her cousin Irene returned for her, she and Nicholas were over the episode. He secured her address and promised to write, and that he did, all the time.

Sophia corresponded regularly with Nicholas receiving a letter from him every week for an entire year. She believed that the moment of the kiss was the defining one. That spontaneous moment told Nicholas more about her, than all the words during the bus ride and the visit through the Fort.

The few days that Sophia set aside for Sacramento were going quickly. Her cousin Kathy was the one to take Sophia on the trip she most looked forward to and, in a way, most dreaded. With nervousness Sophia got into the car for the drive out into the country. Kathy had no idea, as she drove the vehicle, of how much the trip meant to her passenger. They were on their way to see what was left of the memories that Sophia held onto so dearly. Memories, that had kept her on the straight and narrow, had fed her dreams, and lifted her spirit in her darkest hours.

On that day with Kathy at the helm they saw remnants of her old home near Fruitvale School. The Air Force base never was expanded after all, and though the homes on it had been long ago knocked down, nothing was built in their place. In identifying where the house lay, Sophia found tiles of a bathroom and bricks from the outdoor patio beyond. It was hardly anything, but still enough to give Sophia the precise location of where the house stood. Standing there, she saw herself reaching up to kiss her mother and waving goodbye to her as she headed out for school. She saw her father coming home from work, and picking her up as she ran to him, through the beautifully groomed lawn. She saw herself picking grapes that hung from vines attached to the trestle on the back porch.

"Let's go, Kathy, before I start to cry. I sure can remember a lot of good times here," she said with her voice cracking.

Out they drove to look for Alpha School and the possibility of an old friend. It wasn't to be; no one lived there anymore. They had all moved away over the twelve years Sophia had been gone. The little, two-room school house was still there, but it now was home to a family. Sophia timidly walked up toward its steps and spoke with a woman living there. She was a renter and had only been there for two years. She didn't know of the families that Sophia mentioned. So after looking around a little, Sophia then looked over at her old house. The house that on one bright day had come slowly down the road to the cheers and whistles of the entire school. She pointed it out and told Kathy the story. Then she asked Kathy to stop, because she wanted to see it again, the place that was her favorite spot in the whole wide world. Afraid to not see it, that it might not be there, she looked for the old eucalyptus tree. There it was, standing as proud and as glorious as before. However, it was not accessible now, as the large meadow had been parceled out and houses built. The tree now belonged to one family and not to everyone, as it had in Sophia's day.

As the jet smoothly returned her to the island three weeks later, Sophia lowered the back of her seat and pulled the blanket up around her. She cuddled up and closed her eyes and saw Steve's smiling face. No matter whom she had met along the way, she always ended up thinking of him. She had no idea where her budding love for him would go, but she had to admit it was there. Love, such a special word, such a special feeling, she would not easily surrender hers to anyone. The person needed to be very worthy, mature, honest, kind, intelligent, stable and so many other things. She couldn't help but smile knowing that Steve was all those things and much more. She had missed him, there was no denying it.

For several hours the long flight from Mexico made its way across the ocean and every now and then Sophia spoke with the elderly lady in the seat next to her. To a nameless stranger it was easy to open up and she freely told her about Steve. She surprised herself when confiding how much she liked him and how much she missed him.

"He promised to be at the airport to pick me up. Oh! I hope he's there and hasn't forgotten me."

With wise eyes the old lady looked at Sophia carefully and said, "He'll be there."

Steve was there. He was the first face that Sophia saw in a sea of people. He looked good. She could see his face tanned and his hair looked blonder. He was wearing a *guayabera*, an informal but elegant shirt typical of the tropics, and she couldn't help but let out a squeal of joy and ran to give him a hug.

"Oh, I'm so glad to see you. I had a wonderful time. Thank you for picking me up." Steve smiled happily back and said the noncommittal "I'm just a ride home." The remark sobered Sophia quickly and the romantic fantasizing that had begun on the flight, stopped dead in its tracks.

"No, Steve, you're much more than a ride home."

Sophia was living life one step at a time and life taught her to take each one with caution. With her pre-med completed within her bachelor's in science, she was now taking courses toward a master's. For once she could have a light study load and be able to hold on to more than a half-day job. Her goals were clear; she would interview and find a job that would pay well, while gaining entry into a medical school. Her first choice was in Pamplona, Spain, at the University of Navarra. It was the one her friend Jorge Caban had spoke of years before. The decision to go there had been compounded over time and by reading Federico García Lorca's love poems, Sophia was enraptured with Spain.

After conquering on her own the dream of returning to California, she was emboldened. She had no doubt that with dedication and a plan she could attain most any goal. She understood that she had to really want whatever it was, and if she did, who could stop her? Only she, herself; that was clear to her. She became focused on attaining entry into the medical school at the University of Navarra and throughout the year, took all the necessary steps toward that goal. Of course, she would apply to the medical school in San Juan, but it was so political, and entry greatly depended on who knew who.

On the morning Sophia James walked into the offices of Lady Dunhill, a hiring agency, she was well groomed, in mid-size heels, and confident. Her aim was to find an interesting position that would pay better than her current half-day receptionist job. Ana Kortright was the owner of the franchise, a very attractive, middle-aged woman. Her hair had an unusual deep red tint to it, almost a burgundy, which worked so well because of her large, light-green eyes. Her white teeth were perfectly straight and outlined by a smile that was infectious. When Sophia arrived, Anna Kortright had just come out of her office and was giving instructions to an employee. She looked at Sophia, flashed her gorgeous smile, and right then decided to personally interview her. After a typing test, for accuracy and speed, she invited Sophia into her office for the interview. What should have taken twenty minutes turned into an enjoyable hour. Sophia liked her very much and felt good about the interview and expected to soon have a favorable offer.

Three days later Anna called Sophia and wanted her to come by the office. "Sophia, I have checked your references and I have only heard the nicest things about you. It appears that you have made friends along the way. I have given this some thought and I am convinced that you are the person, that for some time now, I have been looking for. I want to retire Sophia and I need someone like you to take over my job here. I have been looking for someone with strong skills to manage these offices. Someone that can make decisions in unforeseen situations, someone responsible that I can count on." Sophia sat listening intently and without interrupting. Anna continued. "The job is interesting as you would interact with people all the time. I would want you to handle personally, all of our more important clients and the three employees that are currently here would be under your supervision. You would hold the keys to the office and open at nine each morning and close at four. You would have an hour off at lunch from twelve to one and I would pay you a thousand dollars a month, plus a Christmas bonus of no less than twenty percent." At those words Anna stopped and gave Sophia a warm smile.

Sophia was flattered and most graciously smiled back while saying, without hesitation, "Why yes, I accept. I'm excited. Would you be training me personally Mrs. Kortright?"

"Yes, I will. And you may call me *Anna*."

CHAPTER 20

The job at Lady Dunhill was a great thing for Sophia. She liked interviewing people and quickly deciphering their strengths. The relationships that she established with existing companies, clients of Lady Dunhill, quickly became solid ones. Those companies trusted that Sophia would find them someone wonderful, any time they called. The office employees got along well with Sophia, as she would praise their efforts, and they in turn gave her their best. With a good job and her light load at the university, life was better than ever.

To top it all, the tall building where Sophia worked was one block from Steve's office. It was in the center of San Juan's business Mecca, Hato Rey. Sophia had a wide range of interesting business men around her and she certainly was in the right place to meet them. Her building was occupied by foreign investment, so there were many young entrepreneurs and international companies there. Sophia's smile was fun and the excitement of living the life she was living was reflected there. It had garnered the attention of several young men and on many occasions, flowers in boxes were delivered to her office. Sophia enjoyed the attention and freely went on dates with them when she had the time; however, she would quickly cancel if Steve called. He was always her first choice. Also ever-present were the letters from the young Swiss lawyer, Nicholas, whom she met on the Greyhound bus to Sacramento. His frequent letters were friendly, filled with images of a beautiful land so far away. Switzerland was for all practical purposes as far away and foreign to her, as was the moon. Nicholas represented a life so completely different from hers, that at times she wondered what they could possibly have in common. Even though Sophia enjoyed receiving his letters and even looked forward to them, they reminded her of being insincere. As time passed, Nicholas's letters became more intense and his desire to come and visit her was apparent. Finally, Sophia decided to be completely honest with him and wrote Nicholas a letter telling him that she had fallen in love. As Sophia wrote this letter, she knew that she would be hurting his feelings. However, she didn't want to mislead him any further and she also needed to accept an unspoken truth; she was in love with Steve.

Sophia enjoyed him like no one else and one day she suggested that he go with her to Factor, and really meet the island of Puerto Rico. It was perhaps a test of sorts, one that needed to be seen through. Arecibo, was still the place where her Dad and her siblings were and she loved them.

It was a perfect day for such a trip. The sun was shining bright and, though it was hot, it was not too muggy. The drive west of San Juan always was a beautiful ride. The central mountain range of the island loomed to the south and the lowlands lying in between had sweet grass, nice and tall for cattle. Fields of bananas and, most of all, fields of sugarcane lined by palm trees, guided Sophia on her way back home to her family. Always green, the predominant color, in all of its variations made the land look fertile and healthy. As one neared the coastal areas the usual dry lands became visible and fields of pineapples could be seen. Sophia pointed out the different crops and told Steve everything she knew about them. Working in pineapple fields was even tougher than in the sugarcane. In the hot tropic sun, wearing thick clothing with long sleeves, workers fought heat exhaustion while ripping pineapples from the embrace of their thorny leaves. Those hard-working men spent hours hunched over mixing sweat and blood, as no clothing could protect them from being stuck by the fierce thorns.

When Steve drove down the road that led to the James's home, which in recent years had been asphalted, Sophia felt apprehension. She tried to imagine seeing her surroundings for the first time and couldn't deny that it all looked pretty shabby. As they approached the house and heard the blaring, hillbilly music coming from Casiano's bar, Sophia wanted to disappear under her seat. Instead she looked at Steve and laughed saying, "I warned you, it's pretty noisy country around here." As the blond, young man got out of his car, patrons of the bar hung out the window, with eyes popping, to see who the newcomer was.

Sophia quipped, "Look, Steve, smile; everyone wants to meet you." Sophia learned to laugh at circumstance. She could do it now for her mind had broadened and she no longer felt vulnerable. She knew that no one else but oneself could be in control of one's life. Staying put or venturing out, all depended on how much someone truly wanted whatever they sought. This was her family and she loved them. Among them is where she had grown strong and honest. On this day, it would be interesting for her to see how Steve would react to such different surroundings.

He took it all in good stride and laughed at all the many impossible situations that made Sophia turn pink. It was a good visit. Sophia's dad was friendly and Steve and he conversed all day long. Steve had already met Frankie who then was fifteen and Johnny sixteen, when he accompanied Sophia one day to pick them up at the airport. The boys were returning from an adventure in South America. They visited Colombia and spent a month traveling from city to city. Sophia's dad had given them an itinerary to follow and money to carry them through. Some of the stories they brought back were scary, but luckily they went and returned in one piece. Both the boys were happy to see Steve again and welcomed him. Bobby was the new face. He was friendly and stuck around for a while, but as soon as he could steal away, he was off to play basketball. Karen was not at the James's home that day and Evy took on the role of hostess. She fussed over Steve, offering drink and food, while they all stretched out around a table in the yard conversing and eating chilled papaya. With the air filled with sounds of a wailing guitar and the sad words of a love song, *El Coyote*, by Mexican José Alfredo Jiménez, Steve relaxed even as a strutting turkey began to hiss at him and a pheasant repeatedly jumped up on the table.

Ten months had passed since Sophia met Steve, and still no love words were spoken between them. Sophia had many moments to look at Steve and wonder what, if anything, did destiny have in mind for him and her. However, Sophia knew she loved him. She loved his kindness and his sincere easy-going personality. She trusted him and felt safe with him. She came to realize that he was the most genuinely good person she had ever met. Such goodness, however, gave him a sort of vulnerability and it made her think how someday he could be hurt if he chose the wrong person. She knew by experience how badly a woman could hurt a man, and the more she knew Steve, the more she hoped that in his life he would choose wisely. She loved being in his company and thought of him often when he wasn't around. When she went out with someone else, she found that she was pretending to enjoy herself and wishing she were with Steve. When she was with Steve, she could hardly wait for that moment when a kiss would occur, and when it did, it would touch the deepest fibers of her young soul. She wanted to stay there in his arms and have him hold her forever. However, she guarded her feelings. Steve would never know about those thoughts. Her pride would never allow her to say the words, "I love you," unless he said them first.

On occasion, Sophia hung out with her boarding-house buddies. On those evenings, anyone passing by could hear laughter floating down from a corner apartment on the third floor of a building that housed pretty, young students. The girls were all good friends and they all shared their happiness and travesties. Man talk was the most frequent topic and each of them had stories to tell. Sophia enjoyed listening more than telling. She had always been tight-lipped about herself. However, they all knew about Steve. He was without doubt the one she could not hide her feelings about.

They'd all gather around the balcony and watch for handsome guys to walk by and then, shamelessly, they'd begin whistling or howling. The more handsome the target, the more shameless they were. Doña Paca from inside would call out to them, scold them, and tell them to behave. But as the girls got louder and laughed harder, Doña Paca would end up in the middle of the group to see what the target looked like. Often during those interludes on the balcony, the old boarding mom would bring out oranges, as a treat for her young, fun boarders. "Now, don't forget to cut the peeling off carefully. You don't want to break the strand of peel. Remember if you make it all the way around and you don't break it, your dearest wish could come true." she would admonish.

There was a tradition on the island of Puerto Rico that was practiced by many. If a person succeeded at cutting away the peel without breaking it, then they could take the long strand of curled orange peel and approach a tree. At the tree they would make a wish. Then, with all the strength they could muster, they would throw the peel into the tree. If the peel on its descent caught a limb and stayed up in the tree, their wish would be granted. If the peel slipped all the way back down to the ground, then the wish would not be fulfilled. It was tricky to accomplish and many wishes were lost among the limbs of trees, but many wishes were not.

Sophia cautiously cut away at her peel making sure that she didn't break it and then in a slight cheat, she would throw the peel down from the third floor into a tree, rather than throwing it up into it. The girls cried, "It's not fair, it won't work," however, the odds were increased many times over by doing it that way and so she was confident that her breathless wish would be granted.

Gradually Sophia and Steve, began seeing each other more. Some days they grabbed a bite for lunch or he dropped her off at school after work. One Sunday Sophia rode her bike all the way over to Steve's apartment, which was about eight miles away, and surprised him announcing that she had the day off and knew just what they could do with it. The challenge was to go on bicycle all the way into Old San Juan, riding over tough cobblestones and making it to the *El Morro* fort. The ride was ten miles long and portions of the trip were without sidewalks. The trip could also prove to be a tough to ride, because of the cobblestones. If a tire found a deep rut, it could mean trouble.

The old walled city of San Juan was beautiful and filled with a wealth of Spanish history, dating back to the mid-sixteenth century. It was built on a narrow island connected to the mainland by three bridges, converting it into a peninsula. To the south it protected the San Juan Bay from the expansive Atlantic Ocean which lapped its northern shores. It was filled with tight, blue cobblestone streets and protruding balconies with elaborate wrought iron railings. Sophia loved to wander there. She could wander for hours dreaming of Florence or the backstreets of Paris. She had yet to see the old world, but until then, she had old San Juan and her imagination.

The large fortress, formally named *Castillo San Felipe de Morro* and simply known as *El Morro*, stood as a protector at the tip of the peninsula guarding its entrance and vulnerable low lands within. In the bright sunlight it was a sight to behold with its high, thick walls, ramparts and ancient lookout posts.

But it was at night, when the moon was full and bright that Old San Juan was at its best. There was a magical glow to the place and it was afforded by the moon's reflection on the blue cobblestones, which had paved its streets for centuries.

The Spaniards were very ingenious in building their main strategic holding in the Caribbean. To pave the streets of Old San Juan they brought stones across the Atlantic from Spain. Transporting them as ballast, they added stability by weighing down the bilges of a ship's hull. The fact that the stones were bluish was because they had been made from slag. Slag was a remnant of the process of smelting ore, for its metal components. In a recycling process of sorts, iron foundries in

TRAVEL, SUITORS AND TRUE LOVE

Spain centuries ago, took the slag, which was usually a discarded and wasted by-product of iron and steel, and made cobblestones by casting it into blocks. Centuries later, Old San Juan still enjoys the fruits of their labor.

Sophia and Steve easily cycled down those ancient streets on that Sunday. From his backpack, Steve retrieved a blanket and spread it out on the lawns of *El Morro* and with mischief in his eyes patted the spot next to him, inviting her to join him. They were lying on the blanket, enjoying the warmth, when suddenly Steve told her that his parents were coming for a visit and that they would like to meet her.

"Oh! Steve I'd love to meet them too." Yes, and by the way, his sister and brother-in-law were also coming. Sophia suddenly felt her stomach flutter and her expression must have reflected it, as the two burst out laughing, as their eyes met.

Sophia put on her best dress, made her hair lovely and hoped that Steve would think she was beautiful when he picked her up at her dorm with his parents. They were going to have lunch together and Sophia on that day didn't feel very confident. She was actually nervous. She tried to shrug it off, feeling completely silly about it all, but hadn't been able to. Perhaps it was because it meant so much to her. She cared about Steve, and having his parents like her was important.

His mother, Jane, was beautiful. Her blond hair and lovely blue eyes were only details on what was a happy and joyful-looking face. She had a wide smile and seemed to not fuss over details. She loved her son, it was very evident, and she often showed it by the many winks and expressions of camaraderie they shared. Sophia was in awe of her; she knew she was looking at a wonderful mother. Steve's father, Fred, was a confident man, both tall and handsome, with dark hair turning gray and light blue, friendly eyes. His parents had met at the University of Purdue and upon hearing that Sophia smiled. Steve's sister, Kathy, was tall and gorgeous. There was a resemblance to Steve. However, her auburn hair, with its lovely waves, was all her own. She laughed frequently and it was an infectious laughter. She got on well with her kid brother and teased him about everything. Tony, the brother-in-law, also was handsome and friendly. All in all, Sophia thought that they were wonderful people and clearly understood why Steve was the person he was. The day was over and Sophia enjoyed every moment of it. Steve was a wonderful host to his family, and on that day more than usual he gazed into Sophia's eyes.

He had introduced her by saying, "I want you to meet Sophia," and looking directly at her. With a playful smile on his lips he said, "This is the girl that I have told you about." Sophia felt her face go hot and was sure that she looked awkward. She didn't quite know how to place her legs or where to put her hands so she moved neither.

She smiled and softly said, "It's a pleasure to meet you," as her heart skipped a few beats.

Time went on and after a year, Sophia thought that maybe Steve would never speak to her of love. She stoically consoled herself by staying focused on her pursuit of entry into the Medical School in Pamplona. She knew that she was going to be accepted and expected the reply to be in her hands soon. She worked hard at getting a scholarship and received word from the school itself that if they gave her admission, she would qualify for one. She knew that in just a short time, she would head to Spain, far away, to accomplish a dream that would now be bittersweet. As in the past, she prepared herself to break away from her siblings, now she was mentally preparing herself to break away from Steve. Sophia couldn't help but feel sadness at imagining not seeing him again. However, if Steve felt for her the way she felt for him and spoke to her about it, Sophia would drop her plans for Spain in a heartbeat. Nothing was more valuable in life than the gift of finding true love. If she were lucky enough to have found it, she would embrace it for the rest of her life, and be thankful.

Sophia understood that marriage was the most important event of her life. She knew firsthand what the error of incompatibility looked like, and how it could cause the sad loneliness of a betrayed heart. She had suffered in the flesh the hurtful pain inflicted on innocent children, when adults are neither honest nor responsible. Education and careers were secondary in her mind, as she could eventually have several titles and still not be a happy person. To find true love was a blessing she would thank God for every day.

One night, while on a dinner date with Steve, Sophia shared that she had submitted her applications to the University of Pamplona in Navarra, Spain, and that they had offered her a scholarship. He seemed distracted, not completely paying attention, as if his mind were elsewhere. She nonetheless continued, "You know that I have always hoped to go there and now it seems that it's going to happen. I guess it's high time I left this island, anyway," she said as she tilted her head, shrugging a bit and giving him a tight-lipped smile.

At that moment he seemed to focus again and, coming out of deep thought, he looked at Sophia with great love in his eyes and simply said, "Sophia, I love you. I want to marry you. Would you marry me?"

Sophia exhaled and stood up while grabbing a corner of her painting apron and dabbed at her eyes. The sixty-year-old Sophia remembered that moment as clearly as if it were yesterday and the emotion of it always overwhelmed her. Sophia forever thought that her finding true love was God nodding and smiling at her. She was sure that it was her reward for not giving up, for standing on principle, even when she was too young to know what the word *principle* meant. Learning right from wrong, as a young child, had been guide enough to overcome insurmountable odds and make good.

True, she had walked away from it all and become a successful woman, achieving many wonderful dreams and goals, but she could never say that she got away unscathed. Her sad childhood marked her entire life, but she had fed off of it in a positive way. She learned early what not to do. Where as a child, she was cast away and thrown aside, as a mother she embraced and thanked the heavens for each of her own children, always. Where she saw the adult face of ugliness try to demean and disarm her, as a grown woman she led Girl Scouts for twenty-two years, instilling confidence and dreams into younger generations. Yes, it was within one's own hands, and of one's own making, to choose "to be or not to be"—to not be pounded into the ground by those who would do that, or to realize one's dreams by challenging challenges along the way.

Endless years of struggle, intertwined with dreams that were never forgotten, had been the story of Sophia James's life. Just as sugarcane would burn fast and hot, keeping the sweetness inside, Sophia's dreams had caught fire and had become reality. However, no matter what she might have accomplished in life, her absolute greatest achievement was to give her children what she had not had, a good mother. For Sophia, a good mother was the greatest honor life bestowed upon a woman, and she embraced the honor zealously. By actions and not mere words, Sophia's children had grown up in the presence of love. Now, forty years later, she herself was as in love with Steve, and he with her, as on the day they lay in the sun on the lawn of *El Morro*, in Old San Juan.

Her body was stiff from sitting still and she stood up with a groan and felt ancient. Looking around to make sure no one was seeing her hunched over, she smiled at her reality. Though she was young at heart, sometimes she had to admit that the years were creeping up on her, a fact she would hide and deny with a wink and a smile always. From the farthest corner of the room she was able to see the painting. She stood there scanning it carefully searching to find a spot that might need attention. Could she call it quits? She observed the horses, their mounts and the vegetation. The big, black Paso Fino "Sambuca," stood out with his legs stark against the light. Sophia liked him a lot. Then her eyes jumped over to the blond Palomino, "King;" such a beautiful and kind-looking animal! The ladies sat proud with their backs straight and their white dresses flowing. The tropical vegetation was loud with its contrasting bright lights and dark shadows making it warm as she had wanted.

Yes, she found a spot where one more stroke was needed. Sophia James, the sixty-year-old woman who had made a wonderful life by believing, made the last stroke with her palette knife. Like a conductor raising his baton for that last crashing note, the curtain was dropping and the time to take a bow was near.

She wouldn't take it alone, "Blondie, Blondie," she called with great excitement, "Come see, come see, I've finished the painting!"

THE END

EPILOGUE

The James children all made good and all three boys served in the United States Army. Karen married a fine man, and has a daughter. Bobby served in the Iraqi war, made a successful career in welding and is the father of five. Johnny, now a father of three, became a physician practicing at the San Juan Medical Center in Puerto Rico. Frankie served in the Iraqi war, became an accountant with a CPA, and is the father of two. And Evy, "the baby," went up to Alaska, found a husband, and has three children.

Sophia's father lived until he was eighty-six. A year before his death he told Sophia that he wanted to pass away in Puerto Rico. Steve bought a home in Arecibo so that he could have his wish. As Sophia flew back to the island with her doomed father she knew that she'd probably "miss" the moment he actually departed. The last words they shared with love in their eyes and a knowing smile was the halting whisper, "See you later, alligator."

"After a while, crocodile…"

SUGARCANE MILLS OF PUERTO RICO'S PAST

There is a certain honor in the island's history encapsulated in the memory of its sugarcane mills. It had been an exceptionally productive time, when so many depended on the cane and the cane depended on so many, each giving the other life. All these mills and others are now gone and the never-ending sea of blue green sugarcane, bent in the wind like a ripple on a wave, is only a fading remembrance.

Name of mill, approximate opening - closing years and location on the island of Puerto Rico

Central Aguirre (1899-1990) Guayama
Central Bayaney (1917-1922) Hatillo
Central Boca Chica (1903-1946) Juana Diaz
Central Cambalache (1877-1981) Arecibo
Central Canóvanas (1905-1965) Loiza
Central Caribe (1930-1946) Salinas
Central Carmen (1895-1945) Vega Alta
Central Cayey, (1926-1967) Cayey
Central Coloso (1830-2002) Aguada
Central Columbia (1901-1928) Maunabo
Central Constancia (1882-1954) Ponce
Central Constancia (1891-1962) Toa Baja
Central Cortada (1901-1974) Santa Isabel

Central Defensa (1926-1940) Caguas
Central El Ejemplo (1896-1961) Humacao
Central Esperanza (1850-1927) Vieques
Central Eureka (1850-1977) Hormigueros
Central Fajardo (1905-1977) Fajardo
Central Guamaní (1930-1963) Guayama
Central Guánica (1901-1981) Ensenada
Central Herminia (1932-1947) Villalba
Central Igualdad (1925-1977) Añasco
Central Juanita (1895-1963) Bayamón
Central Juncos (1926-1973) Juncos
Central Lafayette (1849-1971) Arroyo
Central La Plata (1910-1996) San Sebastián
Central Los Caños (1870-1972) Arecibo
Central Mercedita (1961-1994) Ponce
Central Monserrate (1894-1972) Manatí
Central Pasto Viejo (1904-1958) Humacao
Central Pellejas (1911-1949) Adjuntas
Central Playa Grande (1874-1942) Vieques
Central Plazuela (1896-1963) Barceloneta
Central Rio Llano (1939-1970) Camuy
Central Rochelaise (1908-1957) Mayaguez
Central Roig (1877-2000) Yabucoa
Central Rufina (1901-1967) Guayanilla
Central San Cristóbal (1896-1910) Naguabo
Central San José (1905-1952) Río Piedras
Central San Miguel (1927-1932) Luquillo
Central San Vicente (1973-1967) Vega Baja
Central Santa Bárbara (1910-1948) Jayuya
Central Santa Juana (1926-1966) Caguas
Central Soler (1910-1968) Camuy
Central Victoria (1920-1957) Carolina

CPSIA information can be obtained at www.ICGtesting.com
Printed in the USA
BVOW02*2139071213

338435BV00003B/3/P